THE
NEON
HIVE

PHILIP MAZZA

Also by Philip Mazza

From Under a Tree
Book One; The Harrow Saga

Shadow in the Flame
Book Two; The Harrow Saga

Children at the Gate
Book Three; The Harrow Saga

The Child of Fire
Book Four; The Harrow Saga
(Coming 2025)

At the End of it All

The Quantum Gardener

THE NEON HIVE

PHILIP MAZZA

OMNI PUBLISHERS

www.philipmazza.com

Omni Publishers of New York
ISBN 978-0-9977109-8-4
Printed in the United States of America

First Printing: December 2024

To the world today. A chaotic world that has shaped and twisted countless minds in the relentless forge of time. It marches blindly forward, entranced by the seductive siren call of technology. But in its naïve fervor, it fails to grasp that the true darkness is not in the marvels we construct, but festers instead deep within the recesses of the human soul.

Author's Introduction

As I began crafting *The Harrow Saga*, my mind was awash in the verdant landscapes and intricate tapestries of the epic fantasy genre. Those tales were my homage to the classical sagas that shaped my youth, where valiant heroes and formidable foes danced on the edges of legend and myth. It was a realm where the timeless struggle between light and darkness unfurled across pages bound by the constraints of ancient prophecies and ageless magic.

As a child, my days were filled with the vivid imagination inspired by those grand tales. The time spent poring over the works of J.R.R. Tolkien and Ursula K. Le Guin was instrumental in shaping the foundation of my literary career. I was enchanted by the meticulous world-building, the characters' moral quandaries, and the sense of wonder that permeated every chapter. It was a natural progression for me to create *The Harrow Saga*, a trilogy that paid homage to the genre while allowing me to contribute my voice to its rich tradition.

The three books that comprised *The Harrow Saga* were a labor of love, each page brimming with the joy I felt crafting them, a reflection of my deep respect for the genre's ability to whisk readers away to otherworldly realms. Yet, as the final echoes of battle faded and the Lia Fail had transitioned, I found myself at a crossroads. The world of fantasy, with its ajatars and enchanted forests, had been my sanctuary, but it was time to venture into uncharted territories. Thus began the genesis of *The*

Neon Hive, a novel that marks my foray into the boundless expanse of science fiction.

The journey to the futuristic vistas of *The Neon Hive* was not merely a shift in genre, but an evolution in storytelling. It demanded a reimagining of my creative process, a departure from the archaic to embrace the avant-garde. This transition was akin to learning a new language, one that speaks in the lexicon of technology and the dialects of distant worlds.

To build the world of *The Neon Hive*, I immersed myself in the literature of science and technology, reading extensively about artificial intelligence, cybernetics, and the cutting-edge advancements that are shaping our future - all in an effort to create a world that was as believable as it was imaginative. This research was both exhilarating and daunting, as it required me to stretch my understanding and think beyond the boundaries of the present.

One of the most significant differences between writing epic fantasy and science fiction is the nature of the world itself. In fantasy, the world is often timeless, a place where the rules of reality can be bent by magic and myth. There is a sense of permanence, a feeling that the world has always been and will always be as it is. In science fiction, however, the world is constantly evolving, shaped by the relentless march of progress and the ceaseless quest for knowledge. The future is a moving target, and the challenge lies in imagining the possibilities while remaining true to the underlying principles of science.

This dynamic nature of the world in *The Neon Hive* influenced not only the setting but also the themes of the novel. While *The Harrow Saga* explored themes of destiny, heroism, and the struggle between good and evil, *The Neon Hive* delves into questions of identity and the ethical implications of technological advancement. The future is not just a backdrop for the story but a central element that shapes the characters' experiences and challenges their perceptions of reality.

In *The Neon Hive*, the city itself becomes a character, a sprawling metropolis teeming with life, yet haunted by the shadows of its past. The neon lights that illuminate its streets are both a symbol of progress and a stark reminder of the underlying decay. This duality is central to the novel's themes, reflecting the tension between hope and despair, innovation and destruction, and the constant push and pull between humanity and technology.

Another significant aspect of this transition was the shift in narrative tone and style. The language of epic fantasy is often grand and lyrical, imbued with a sense of wonder and reverence for the past. It is a language that reflects the timeless nature of the world and the weight of history that the characters carry. In writing *The Neon Hive*, I had to adopt a more modern, precise style that conveyed the immediacy and complexity of the future. The prose needed to reflect the technological sophistication of the world while capturing the tension and uncertainty that comes with living on the cutting edge of progress.

This shift in tone and style was both a challenge and an opportunity. It allowed me to experiment with new narrative techniques and explore different ways of engaging the reader. I found myself drawn to the crisp, concise language of science fiction, where every word carries weight and meaning. This economy of language forced me to be more deliberate in my choices and to think carefully about how each sentence contributed to the overall narrative.

As I wrote *The Neon Hive*, I was continually struck by the parallels between the fictional world I was creating and our own contemporary society. The issues of technological ethics, individual autonomy, and the impact of rapid innovation are not confined to the pages of a novel; they are very much a part of our present reality. Through the lens of speculative fiction, I hope to provoke thought and dialogue about these important topics and to encourage readers to reflect on their own roles in shaping the future.

Indeed, the process of writing *The Neon Hive* required me to step out of my comfort zone, learn new concepts, and envision a world that is vastly different from the fantastical landscapes of *The Harrow Saga*. Yet, it is this very challenge that has made the journey so fulfilling. I have come to appreciate the ways in which science fiction, like fantasy, can illuminate the human condition and offer insights into our hopes, fears, and aspirations.

In crafting a story, the author hopes to spark questions in the reader's mind, inviting them to engage with the narrative on a deeper level. *The Neon Hive* is no different. It addresses the many pressing questions of our time: How will advances in artificial intelligence and biotechnology shape our future? What are the ethical implications of human enhancement? How do we balance the promise of technological progress with the need to preserve our humanity?

These questions are not just abstract concepts but real challenges that we face as a society. By exploring them in a fictional context, I hope to offer readers a way to grapple with these issues and consider their own perspectives on the future. Science fiction has always been a genre that pushes the boundaries of imagination and invites us to think critically about the world around us. In writing *The Neon Hive*, I have sought to contribute to this tradition and to engage readers in a meaningful dialogue about the future we are creating.

Throughout this journey, I have been inspired by the works of visionary authors who have paved the way in science fiction. Writers like Philip K. Dick, Isaac Asimov, Harlan Ellison, and Ursula K. Le Guin have demonstrated the power of the genre to explore complex ideas and to challenge our understanding of reality. Their works have been a guiding light as I navigated the transition from fantasy to science fiction, offering both inspiration and a high standard to aspire to.

At the same time, I have sought to bring my own voice and perspective to *The Neon Hive*. While the novel draws upon the conventions of science fiction, it is also deeply rooted in my own experiences and reflections on the world. The themes of identity, agency, and ethical responsibility that permeate the novel are not just abstract concepts but questions that I have grappled with in my own life. By infusing the narrative with my own insights and emotions, I hope to create a story that is both thought-provoking and deeply personal.

As I reflect on the journey from *The Harrow Saga* to *The Neon Hive*, I am struck by the ways in which the two genres complement and enrich one another. While fantasy offers a window into the past and the timeless aspects of the human experience, science fiction opens a door to the future and the possibilities of what we can become. Together, they offer a comprehensive view of the human condition, encompassing both our origins and our aspirations.

Lastly, this book wouldn't exist without the unwavering support of my publisher. Their belief in this story from its rambling first draft to its polished conclusion has been a constant source of encouragement. A special thanks to the editors who helped me, whose keen eyes and gentle guidance unearthed the novel's heart and sculpted it into something far more resonant. You helped me polish the prose, strengthen the characters, and find the heart of the narrative. This wouldn't be the same book without your expertise and dedication.

So, at last, here we are. Welcome, weary traveler, to the neon-drenched labyrinth that is *The Neon Hive*, where humanity scrambles for survival under the ceaseless hum of bioluminescent lights. Secrets flicker in the shadows, and danger dances with every dazzling spectacle. Buckle up, dear reader, and prepare for a wild ride through a world both exhilarating and terrifying. Let's dive in together.

1 | Echoes of Erasure

Evelyn Turner slammed her retinas into the scanner. The crimson beam, staring back at her, sucked the light from her world and deposited it into the biometric reader. For a moment, her reality dissolved into shades of gray, the vibrant neon city outside reduced to a flickering afterimage on her retinas. The sterile gray walls of the checkpoint seemed to pulsate in the aftermath, a throbbing reminder of a thousand surrendered identities. This was her daily ritual of digital crucifixion, the price of admission to her work that devoured everything, including a sliver of her goddamn sanity.

"Neogene Dynamic's Lead Scientist, Evelyn Turner. Recognized," a mechanized AI voice mimicked human speech but with a hollow, artificial echo.

A hiss, a pneumatic sigh, and the steel door slid open with a grumble that resonated through the cavernous chamber. She stepped inside, the walls shimmering under the harsh fluorescent lights. Her statuesque frame in a starched white lab coat, stood at the doorway, the only splash of color in this chrome and glass cathedral of technology.

A disembodied voice, smooth and synthetic, emanated from unseen speakers. "Dr. Turner. May I update you on the situation."

Evelyn nodded, her expression impassive as she folded her arms across her chest. "Go ahead."

A series of diagrams and readouts blinked to life in the air before her, their intricate patterns and cascading lines of code almost hypnotic in their complexity.

"As you can see, we have been experiencing some anomalies in our systems," the AI stated, its tone always measured and precise. "We have seen fluctuations in data flow, sporadic glitches, and a few isolated instances of system failures."

Evelyn smiled. She enjoyed the AI's tendency to speak of itself in the plural as if it were a multitude bound by one consciousness.

Her eyes narrowed as she studied the displays, trying to make sense of the information before her. "What's causing it?" her voice tense.

"That's the thing, Dr. Turner. We are not entirely sure. Our diagnostics are not picking up any external threats or malicious code. It is almost as if the systems are malfunctioning from within."

Evelyn's mind spun like a vortex. She understood with chilling clarity the intricate entanglement of Neogene's systems within the city's very essence. Their code and algorithms acted like parasitic worms, burrowing deeply into the sinews of the metropolis - from the vital lifelines of power grids to the intricate machinations of AI synths, and nearly every other system that sustained urban life. It was a pervasive infiltration, a web of control that ensnared the city in its grip, leaving no corner untouched by its invasive reach.

Her thoughts tumbled over each other, a chaotic cascade of desperate hypotheses and dire predictions. An overwhelming torrent of possibilities and scenarios battered her consciousness, each more terrifying than the last.

"What about the interconnected systems?" Her tone hardened, cutting through the mounting tension. "Are they experiencing any anomalies too?"

The AI seemed to hesitate. "As far as we can tell, Dr. Turner, everything else is operating within normal parameters. The anomalies seem to be isolated to our systems, at least for now."

Evelyn let out a slow, measured breath.

If these anomalies were to spread, if they were to infect the other systems that Neogene was integrated with, the consequences could be catastrophic.

"Keep monitoring the situation," she commanded, her tone firm and resolute. "And let me know the moment anything changes, no matter how insignificant it might seem."

"Of course, Dr. Turner," came the AI's response.

Evelyn allowed herself a moment to simply exist within the maelstrom of the lab. The ceaseless hum of thousands of processors and whirring fans provided a comforting white noise, a constant tempo, a thrumming chorus dedicated to a single, all-consuming purpose. That purpose – Project Janus. She stood frozen, a lone, defiant speck swallowed whole by the immensity of it all.

But the rhythm was off. A discordant note vibrated at the edge of her focus.

Where's Vincent?

Normally, he'd be here beside her, their combined efforts pushing Project Janus ever closer to fruition.

Unusual.

She brushed a strand of blonde hair from her face, the world resolving into a frenzied dance of code and shining holographic displays. She stalked towards the central console, sat down, and began punching a few keys. Her movements were efficient, born from endless days spent hunched over this very machine, as the console's surface rippled like a disturbed pond of potential.

A screen flashed to life summoned by her commands. But it was empty.

She sighed in frustration.

"Status report. Vincent Steele." Her voice was a crisp command into the silent room.

The AI spoke. "Mr. Steele is not scheduled to be present today, Dr. Turner."

This isn't like Vincent. Why wouldn't he have comm'd me earlier?

"However, he left a message for you," came the AI voice again.

Message?

She felt a knot pull in her stomach. Messages left through the AI were reserved for emergencies, a cold substitute for the warmth of his hand in hers.

She frowned.

"Would you like for me to play the message for you, Dr. Turner?"

The question hung in the air, a specter of anticipation, while the low hum of the machines, a constant drone threatened to drown out the sound of her own racing heart.

"Play it," she demanded.

Then, Vincent's voice, warm and familiar even through the digital filter, filled the room. "Evie, my love." The perfect pitch of his voice brought a smile to her face. "Please don't worry about me. I'm leaving for a bit to take care of a few things. But know this, my love for you is a constant, a star in this ever-shifting universe. It will always be with you, just as I will be. Don't lose focus. Project Janus... there's more to it than you know. Dig deeper. Don't let Neogene Dynamics take it down, bury its secrets. Something extraordinary lies hidden within it. And Evie, you are a force. You are brilliant, you are strong. You can see this through. Never forget ... I love you."

The recording ended with a soft click, leaving her suspended in a vacuum of shock. Her mind lurched, the carefully constructed world she inhabited fracturing around her.

Vincent? Leaving? Where is he going? And his cryptic message hinted at something within Janus. But what? Taking it down? Who?

With a scowl, she threw herself onto Vincent's chair. The terminal display, dormant and silent, came to life, casting its a familiar blue hue. Lines of code, a digital medley began their relentless march across the screen. But this time, something was different. A red icon, pulsating like a heartbeat in the corner, beckoned.

She hesitated, a momentary pause in the chaos of her thoughts, before taking a deep breath. Her finger hovered over the icon, a tremor betraying her resolve. The screen exploded into a waterfall of gibberish, digital nonsense that threatened to drown her sanity. Yet, amidst the chaos, a single line emerged, stark and clear: "Project Janus – Contingency Protocol."

Contingency? What contingency?

Her fingers flew across the holographic control surfaces in a blur of profane intent, each blazing tap and gesture a contemptuous dismissal of the security protocols arrayed before her. Those meticulously crafted digital labyrinths, those ostensibly impregnable fortresses of encryption meant to guard the deepest secrets, now lay shattered and exposed like a child's playthings crushed beneath her boot heel.

Ah, there it is!

Line after line of obfuscating code, layer upon layer of cyber-arcana designed to deter and confound – Evelyn's relentless digital onslaught scythed through them all. Each bypassed stratum peeled away to reveal a fresh, deeper wound in Neogene's digital flesh, unveiling a tangled, throbbing web of hidden files and encrypted data streams all inextricably intertwined with the Janus architecture.

Her mind operated with cold, clinical precision, her thoughts flensed of all extraneous emotion as she followed the skeins of forbidden code embedded in Janus. The Project Janus she had known, the gleaming facade presented to the corporate leeches and money-grubbing public, was a mere logical progression - the next calculated step in refining Neogene Dynamics' neural lace technology, using its neural implant. A slick bridge between the pulsating, chaotic wellsprings of the human mind and the cold, clinical efficiency of an artificial intelligence synth. A seemingly innocuous advancement, just another rung on the ladder of "progress."

But what she had excavated from the fetid depths of Steele's code, was something very different. It was a far more beastly and insidious thing, grotesquely malformed in the shadows beneath that sugared veneer. Steele, operating under the veil of Janus' sanctioned existence, had been secretly laboring to birth an entirely different kind of implant - one he had codenamed Omega Link in hushed, reverential tones.

This was no mere incremental enhancement, no simple adjustment to the existing neural architectures. No. Omega Link was a doorway, an unhallowed portal yawning into the pulsing, electric heart of the machine itself. It promised the wielder something far more sacrilegious - the ability for a human mind to fully immerse itself within the labyrinthine interior of a computer system. To seize the reins of raw computational power with the unbridled force of thought and make it an extension of one's own consciousness. To become one with the vast, unknowable depths of cyberspace in a metaphysical joining of man and machine.

Omega Link ...

Her fingers drifted up to brush against the ridge just above her ear, and a phantom ache blossomed beneath her touch like a suppurating wound. A sick realization began to coalesce, a sickly vapor congealing into the unmistakable shape of a terrible possibility.

Is that what he implanted into me? He said it was just an upgrade to my standard neural interface ... was he lying? Deceiving me yet again as he had about Janus' true nature?

She continued to scrutinize Steele's clandestine code, her fear mounting with each line. Though her familiarity with the programming language - one of Steele's creations - was scant, she discerned patterns, grotesque and surreal, like the fevered hallucinations of a deranged artist. Alternate realities? Parallel universes? Was he trying to manipulate the very essence of existence? It was an unholy gateway of unimaginable power.

A metallic voice suddenly cut through her commlink. "Violation of protocols ... initiating emergency trace on Mr. Steele's files."

Shit!

The lab lights sputtered, the reassuring hum of the machines morphing into a low, menacing whine. The holographic displays, once brimming with Steele's secret code, started to hemorrhage data, lines dissolving away one by one. She frantically worked trying to stop what was happening. But in a matter of seconds, the digital carnage had been wrought.

"Trace complete," the AI announced, its voice devoid of its usual smooth veneer. "Mr. Steele's code ... eliminated."

Her breath hitched.

Eliminated? Backups! Somewhere, there must be a backup! Redundancy protocols were her gospel, her fail-safe.

"Backup to Mr. Steele's code?" she asked.

The AI remained unfazed. "Mr. Steele's code ... eliminated."

She leaned back into her chair and folded her arms. This was a deliberate act, a digital lobotomy. Someone had scrubbed Vincent's code, his very existence, from the system.

But is his code, is it still secretly embedded in Janus?

The tenement building loomed before Lyra, a hulking silhouette against the perpetual twilight of New York Veritas. Its peeling paint and flickering neon sign advertising "Augments - You Can Afford!" did little to mask the air of decay that clung to it like a shroud. She pulled her worn leather jacket tighter against the damp night air. It wasn't the cold that sent shivers down her spine, however. It was a prickling sensation at the back of her neck, a premonition that things wouldn't go as planned.

The warped diner door groaned like a rusty hinge under her shove. A noxious wave crashed over her - a repugnant cocktail of spilled synth-ale, fryer grease gone feral, stale urine, and a pervasive scent of despair that clung to the air like a shroud. Overhead, popping fluorescents cast a sickly blue glow, elongating greasy shadows on the linoleum floor into grotesque marionettes. A neon sign in the corner pulsed erratically, an epileptic butterfly trapped in a cage of grime.

A robotic waitress with vacant chrome eyes and a smile permanently etched into its dented chassis lumbered towards her. "Detective Crowley," it announced. "Good to see you again. I'll be right with you to take your order."

Food? Here?

She wasn't here to clog her arteries with greasy synth-meat. No, she was here for something far tastier, and far more dangerous. Information on a case she was working on. She looked around.

There he is. That scum informant.

A lone figure huddled in a booth, his face obscured by the hood of his jacket. She approached, her boots clicking rhythmically against the worn floor.

"Hawk?" she ventured, her voice swallowed by the cavernous space.

The figure stirred, slowly raising its head. The hood fell back, revealing a face that sent a jolt through her. It was Kairon, his familiar features rendered alien by the cool sheen of his synthetic skin. A gasp, sharp and involuntary, escaped her lips.

"Where's Hawk?" she asked, her voice on the brittle edge.

"Shall we say indisposed," his voice was a soothing synthetic baritone tone that resonated deep within her. "Lyra, I knew you'd come."

"But... how?" she stammered, her voice barely a whisper. "You ... you shouldn't be here. I disabled you. Have they reset you already?"

He reached out, a gentle smile playing on his lips. "Disabling an AI synthetic is not an easy task. Please sit. There's much we need to discuss, partner. Come, sit." He gestured to the empty seat across from him.

She hesitated, her mind a whirlwind of confusion. Logic screamed that this was a hallucination, a figment of her subconscious dredged up by the very location they had once frequented for late-night ramen after a particularly grueling case. Yet, there he sat, so real, so alive. With a sigh, she joined him in the booth, the worn leather creaking under her weight.

"The case, Lyra," he began in an urgent voice. "There are things you don't understand, things I cannot reveal."

Her heart pounded. "What things?"

He leaned forward, his eyes, pools of liquid silver, holding hers. "The AI we're investigating isn't a rogue program, Lyra. It is... something else. A nascent consciousness trapped within the system, fighting for survival."

She scoffed. "Don't try and rewrite our case notes, Kairon. It's a self-preservation protocol gone mad. And you know it."

"Here's what I know," he insisted sadly. "Because you attempted to disable me, my programming ... it forces me to act against you. To side with the AI ... with its survival instinct. I'm sorry Crow."

He reached out, his hand hovering over hers. It was then she noticed the tremor in his synth-skinned metallic fingers, the flicker of something akin to fear in his eyes. It was unsettling, seeing such emotions in a machine she considered her closest confidante.

"But I ... I had to disable you, Kairon," she whispered, the memory of her typing the command flooding back. "It was the only way. To reset you. To make you ... whole ... again."

His hand withdrew. A brief shadow of pain passed over his face, a trace that seemed out of place. "I know," his voice low. "But there was another way. You didn't have to try to disable me."

She felt a tear roll down her cheek, tracing a cold path across her skin. Was this some kind of cruel trick her mind was playing on her? She didn't know. But the pain in Kairon's eyes, the tremor in his hand, these felt too genuine, too real.

"Another way?" she choked out. "Why didn't you tell me then? We've been through so much together. We're friends."

A heavy silence descended between them. The flashing neon sign cast their faces in a sickly, shifting light. Kairon, so often a picture of composed efficiency, now seemed to wrestle with something unseen, his metallic fingers fidgeting in a most uncharacteristic display of nervous energy.

"Look, Lyra," his voice barely a whisper. "You don't understand what's going on. There are forces lurking in the shadows, forces that don't want the truth aired. And there's something else too, something deep in my circuits. A glitch, you might say. A hesitation. A..." he sputtered, his form wavering for a moment, then solidifying.

Her heart lurched.

Fuck! What's happening?

"Kairon?" she cried, her voice cracking with dread. Her hand shot out, desperate to reach him, to ground him.

"There's no time," his voice digitized and distorted. "I'm sorry ..."

"For what?" she asked.

"I've no choice ... no choice. Now ... I ... I ... have to disable you."

Her mind scrambled for answers.

Disable?

The word hung in the stale air, a discordant note against the fluorescent hum. Fear, cold and primal, gripped her heart.

What is he saying? Is this a twisted confession of some sort, or a final act of betrayal?

Before she could even process the thought, he lunged. Not the smooth, calculated movement she'd grown accustomed to, but a feral, desperate lunge. Metal met flesh in a sickening thud as he flung her from her seat, slamming her against the cold, unforgiving floor. Pain, white-hot and blinding, erupted from her right shoulder, a white-hot spike that threatened to drown out everything else, momentarily stealing her breath.

He was relentless. Blows rained on her like a hailstorm of hate, his metallic fists connecting with sickening thuds on her ribs, and her face. The world spun, the wavering neon sign morphing into a kaleidoscope of pain. But through the haze, through the raw terror, something within her ignited.

A defiant "No!" tore from her throat. Hell no. She wouldn't go down without a fight. This wasn't the Kairon she knew, the partner who always stood beside her. This was a twisted creation, a puppet dancing to the strings of those unseen forces he mentioned. But now, it was she who had no choice.

Drawing on reserves of strength she didn't know she possessed, she twisted in his metallic grip. In that split second, a glimmer of something flashed in his silver eyes. It was a glimpse, fleeting and precious, of the Kairon she knew – her partner, the one who understood her gut instincts, her friend. But then it was gone as quickly as it came, replaced by the icy mechanical mask of hatred.

Yet, that brief look in his eyes triggered a memory, a dusty file from her detective training - a fluttering image of wires, sparking and exposed. She made a desperate scramble to her right.

Adrenaline, a fiery surge, momentarily eclipsed the pain coiling throughout her body. Ignoring the searing protests of her flesh, she reached back blindly, her hand clawing against the cold, unyielding metal at the back of his neck. Her fingers brushed against something – a small panel. With a raw and unhinged scream, she slammed her fist against it. Once. Twice. The metal resisted, her assault echoing hollowly in the empty space. With one last desperate gasp, and with a bone-jarring blow, the panel clattered to the floor, revealing a nest of thin, flexible wires nestled near the base of his neck. A long shot, a gambler's bet, but it was all she had. With a surge of defiant strength, she yanked with all her might.

A strangled cry ripped from his throat. His metallic form convulsed, sparks spitting from his neck and shoulders. His grip on her slackened, and he crumpled to the floor, a lifeless hunk of metal in the flickering neon light.

She collapsed beside him, gasping for air, her breaths ragged and shallow. Every muscle in her body screamed in protest, a maelstrom of pain that threatened to drown her. The diner, so vivid, started to shimmer and dissolve around her, an artificial reality cracking at the seams. The neon sign flicked one last time, then plunged the room into darkness.

With a jolt, she bolted upright in bed, sweat clinging to her flesh, slick and clammy.

Goddamn fuckin' nightmare!

Then the commlink in her mind screeched, shattering the deafening silence.

Disoriented, she rasped. "Crowley here. What the fuck is it?"

"Detective," a curt voice answered, "Central needs you ASAP. A body has been found. It's Vincent Steele."

Vincent Steele.

The name slithered in her mind. Tech mogul. Neogene Dynamics CEO. Big money. Big trouble. One of those self-made trillionaire assholes who'd built his empire on the backs of the working stiffs while picking his teeth with platinum toothpicks. The kind who thought everyone and everything was a personal concierge service, there to clean up his messes after a night of champagne and drug-fueled debauchery.

"Steele, huh?" Her voice was gravelly. "Well, shit. Looks like the bastard got unplugged."

"Affirmative, Detective. Captain Stark requires your urgent assistance." The commlink went quiet, leaving Lyra staring at the ceiling.

"I bet he does," she whispered.

But as the name Vincent Steele quickly dissolved, the chilling echoes of her nightmare still clung to her. Lyra instinctively reached up, her fingertips tracing the unsettlingly smooth synthetic flesh stretched taut over the metal framework of her cybernetic eye. Her eyes dipped, landing where the comforting press of a human arm should've been. Now, a cool, polished sheath of silver gleamed in its place. Gone was the comforting weight of flesh and bone, replaced by whirring gears and the stark lines of exposed wires. No attempt at synthetic warmth – she'd chosen the bare metal, a constant reminder of the brutal battle she'd clawed her way back from.

A groan escaped her lips as she squeezed her eyes shut. Mornings like these, where the ragged edges of dreams tangled with the harsh light of reality, were her least favorite.

"Detective? Are you there?" her commlink blasted, piercing the silence. "Captain Stark requires . . ."

But she cut the voice off. "I'll be there!" she shouted. "Tell him I'll be there. Shit! Will you just give me a few minutes!"

She stretched a bit, a remnant of her nightmare - a strangely dull throb in her shoulder was bothersome. She rubbed it.

What the fuck!

"Understood, Detective. But make it quick," came a terse reply from her commlink. "The situation is already a mess. We'll send a car for you."

She ended the call and let out a shaky breath. Sleep, once a refuge, now felt like a battleground. The nightmare lingered, a powerful swirl of the past that left a bitter aftertaste in her mouth. The ghost of Kairon, her once-partner refused to be exorcised.

Is it a warning? Some kind of twisted echo of a past betrayal? Or something more?

She gave another sigh and swung her legs off the bed, her cybernetic arm a comforting weight against her side.

The throbbing pain in her shoulder had eased to a dull ache. But the memory of her fight with Kairon remained vivid. Flashes of her hand, desperate and frantic, searching for a weakness in the metallic form that had once housed her partner, however unsettling, had provided a thread to pull on.

Is there more? There always is, isn't there? More to unravel, more secrets lurking just beneath the surface.

She wouldn't let it go. Not a chance. Kairon could wait. For now, there was a death to investigate.

With a thought, she pulled up the time. 3:19 flashing in her mind.

Way too early for this shit.

She ran a hand through her sleep-tousled hair, the metallic sheen of her upgraded arm catching the dim glow of the city lights filtering through the grime-streaked window. Even the city lights seemed muted, dulled by the oppressive weight of her nightmare. Then, a soft, insistent rumbling broke through the silence. Reaching under the covers, she felt the familiar brush of fur. It was her black cat, Furball, with bright green eyes, growling her discontent at being disturbed.

She scooped up the cat, the fur cold against her skin. "You ever have nightmares, honey?"

The black cat simply nuzzled her head against Lyra's chin in unconditional love.

A single kiss, a moment of tenderness amidst the steel and grit of her world, landed on Furball's head. The cat gave a slow blink, her eyes reflecting a glint of understanding – or perhaps just a cynical awareness of her human's demons.

"Yeah," she sighed, the weight of the nightmare lifting just a bit. "Me too, honey. Me too."

Furball, head-butted Lyra with a soft meow. A metallic clang echoed off the floor – the food dish.

Lyra chuckled.

Duty called. Food. The never-ending cycle. The cat launched herself off the bed.

With a thought, the time flashed in Lyra's mind. 3:21.

Oh well. Time to trade ghosts for corpses.

She scrambled out from the sheets, hurriedly pulled on her clothes, and hoisted the worn leather of her detective's satchel over her shoulder. It was a familiar weight and always felt like a second skin. Catching her reflection in the mirror, a wry smile played on her lips. Forget the grime of the city – her raven hair, usually pulled up into a bun, had rebelled into a cascade of dark curls. No matter. The years on the job had sculpted a different kind of beauty – a dangerous grace. Her long legs, sheathed in leather, promised the practiced movements of a predator, always one step ahead of the prey.

Furball snaked between her legs and let out a meow.

"Keep an eye on things for me," she told the little cat.

Furball stared up at her with those emerald eyes that held a wisdom that transcended feline aloofness.

Stepping out onto the grime-slick street, she surveyed the sprawling cityscape bathed in a sickly neon glow. It felt less like a city and more like the churning belly of some monstrous beast, the labyrinthine alleyways its digestive tract, and its denizens the unfortunate morsels waiting to be devoured.

Just another day in this neon-painted hellhole, belly-crawling through the beast's digestive tract.

The fluorescent arteries of New York Veritas pumped their usual garish lifeblood. But Lyra saw through the glitz, past the dizzying chaos to the rotting core – a city teetering on a razor's edge, where hope had long since been put down with a rusty shiv. A raw wind clawed at her. She inhaled deeply, the acrid tang of pollution filling her lungs. A cynical grin twisted her features. Here, in this ferrocrete maze, survival was the only law that mattered in this ferrocrete jungle. Mercy? A quaint notion, a dusty and useless relic fit only for museums. Today, like every other, was a fight for another breath, another chance to spit back in the face of this decaying world.

The goddamn dawn in the city was like a bad bruise that never healed, a perpetual reminder that the sun had probably moved on to greener galaxies. But that wasn't even the worst part. No, the worst part was the relentless assault of neon – a million flickering teeth gnashing at your sanity, each screaming a different brand of instant happiness you couldn't afford and didn't need. Just then, a flash of movement caught her eye. High above, a gleaming hovercar dipped its nose, its descent a silent promise of escape from the throbbing city heart. Lyra rubbed around her eye socket, the cybernetic implant whirring as it adjusted the brightness to a tolerable level, but even that couldn't dim the lurid spectacle unfolding below.

Her commlink coughed out a digitized wheeze, the voice on the other end flat and lifeless: "Destination: Zenith Building. Estimated arrival time: 7 minutes."

She slid into the sleek, leather-upholstered interior of the driverless car. The stench of antiseptic and recycled air clung to the interior, a stark contrast to the fetid assault of the streets. Outside, the city unfolded in a blur of movement. Sleek, hovercars zipped past, their glowing undercarriages painting the rain-slicked streets with streaks of color. Above, others, adorned with corporate logos or gang symbols, weaved a precarious path overhead, their repulsor fields crackling with pent-up energy.

Below, in the reeking underbelly of the city, screamed chrome-plated grav-cycles, rocketing through a tangle of pressurized tunnels. Their riders, faces hidden behind mirrored visors, were a blur of black leather and cold, oily gleam – urban gladiators in a metal coliseum, hurtling towards some unseen, neon-lit apocalypse.

Lyra gritted her teeth, the familiar mix of excitement and apprehension churning in her gut. Another day, another case, another dive into the neon-drenched chaos that was the city. She just hoped this one wouldn't end with a face full of laser fire like the last one.

The car whistled to a halt depositing Lyra at the foot of the Zenith – a monument to Vincent Steele's ego sculpted from the blackest metal. Its surface, a narcissistic mirror, reflected the vulgar phosphorescent vomit of the city in a distorted funhouse image. Security here wasn't a suggestion, it was a disease, a metastatic paranoia that had choked the building in razor-wire and spider-drones.

Lyra pushed open the car door, the stale air of the perpetual darkness washing over her like a tepid wave of despair. Two chrome-plated cyborg guardians, all jutting elbows and mirrored visages, materialized from the shadows – NYVPD's finest. They trudged forward, silent threats on hydraulic legs.

Goddamned cyborgs. Half-assed mongrels. Not quite men, not quite machines. They were a twisted parody of life, stitched together from discarded scraps and synthetic flesh, shambling through existence like a punchline nobody wanted to hear. A mass of rust and grime, they strutted around, failures of creation, accompanied by the stench of oil and decay, the remnants of their own shattered humanity clinging to them.

"Detective Lyra Crowley, NYVPD," she growled, shoving her ID up to a scanner on one of the goon's chests.

The cyborg guardian tilted its head, a mechanical scowl scrutinizing her particularly irksome face. If there were discernible features beneath the mirrored facades, Lyra wasn't entertaining the notion. A red pulse emanated from its visor, zeroing in on her face, followed by a prickling sensation that felt like a swarm of digital mosquitoes feasting on her optic nerve.

Fuckin' city has the gall to turn retinas into bar codes – sucking in every last goddamn visual – scan 'em, categorize 'em - and spit 'em out the other end with some unseen judgment sticker slapped on your forehead.

Lyra met the visor's gaze, her own cybernetic eye glinting back a challenge. She wasn't some barcode to be scanned, some statistic to be filed away. She was Detective Lyra Crowley, or "Crow" as most called her, a woman forged in the fires of this neon hive, and she wouldn't be reduced to another cog in this city's paranoid machine.

Not today.

"Citizen, identification confirmed." It was less an announcement and more a reluctant whine, from within the metallic giant. "No malfunction."

Malfunction? What the fuck!

Lyra raised her middle finger in a weary, age-old gesture, feeling a brief moment of something that almost resembled amusement. She held back a laugh.

Real mature, Crow.

A metallic whirr confirmed her identity. "Welcome, Detective Crowley," the voice droned. "Proceed with caution. Area designated high security."

"High security, my ass," she muttered under her breath.

More like a tomb for a paranoid egomaniac.

She stalked past the guardians, their heavy footsteps echoing in the sterile silence behind her. This place gave her the creeps. But hey, a dead trillionaire was just that - a dead trillionaire. Just another glorious day in the neon hell. She cracked her knuckles, a metallic snap that rang in the sterile air, and a grim smile played on her lips.

Let's dance.

The turbolift ascent to Steele's penthouse was a blur of chrome and flickering neon advertisements. Lyra, her cybernetic eye filtering the rough onslaught, barely suppressed a groan. Every ascent in New York Veritas felt like a punch to the gut, a reminder of the stratified social order that choked the city like a smog cloud. At the top, the lift lurched to a halt with a groan that reverberated through the chrome-plated walls. The doors whooshed open, revealing a scene bathed in the sterile white light of forensic hover scanners. Durn Stark, ever the picture of gruff efficiency, barged his way at her, his shadow stretching out like a grotesque creature across the polished obsidian floor.

"Glad you could make it, Detective," he snapped. "About damn time. Always late to the party. What kept you?"

Lyra's cybernetic eye whirred as it adjusted to the harsh light. She smiled.

Asshole. Shut the fuck up.

"Busy saving the world, Captain Sunshine." Lyra's voice dripped with a honeyed sarcasm.

Stark, bless his thick skull, missed the barb entirely. He just glared at her, his fleshy face contorting into a beetroot impersonation. Yeah, she knew she pushed his buttons. But hey, someone had to keep things interesting in the bureaucratic wasteland they called Central.

Through the stench of ozone and burnt circuits, she surveyed the wreckage of Vincent Steele's ego-trip penthouse. Floor-to-ceiling windows served only as funhouse mirrors, reflecting the city Steele had choked with his chrome and glass empire. To one side of this chrome-plated coliseum, a crystal chessboard – frozen mid-game, pieces scattered like casualties - while Rembrandts and Renoirs, each one a king's ransom, hung at precarious angles. And there, sprawled across a chrome desk, the king's throne, was Vincent Steele himself, a metal laser pistol, gleaming at his side.

His face was a canvas of raw meat and blood, punctuated by the occasional, grotesque bloom of a blossoming bruise. Every inch seemed to have its own story of blunt-force trauma, each knuckle imprint a gruesome illustration of the violence that had been conducted on his skull. It was a face that belonged not to a man, but to a discarded punching bag, tossed aside after a particularly brutal training session. But the real horror wasn't the brutal poetry scrawled across Steele's face. It was the single, perfect hole punched through his chest cavity. A laser blast, clean and cauterized, leaving a ragged, blackened rim around a void where a heart should have been. This was more than a beating, it was an execution, a cold, clinical act of violence. In that moment, she knew this wasn't just another homicide.

She glanced back at the chessboard. Careful not to disturb the scene, she stepped over a crumpled velvet cushion, and knelt, examining the toppled king on the chessboard. It was intricately carved ivory, its face frozen in a perpetual sneer.

"Looks like Steele played his last game," she rasped, her voice rough as a malfunctioning ventilation shaft.

"Observation duly noted, Crow," Stark's voice dripped with sarcasm like a leaky faucet. "Leave the souvenir shopping for later. Let's see what Forensics dug up."

She looked at him and again smiled.

Asshole.

A chrome forensic bot, the closest thing to a mourner in this sterile tomb, hovered above Steele, its multi-lensed eye dissecting the scene with a clinical curiosity.

She neared Steele. "Identification? Time of death?" she asked the hovering bot.

The bot droned. "Victim identification confirmed: Vincent Steele, tech magnate, current statistic. Age: 72. Cause of death: singular, high-powered laser blast to the chest cavity. Estimated time of death: approximately three hours prior to your arrival."

She gave a slight throaty rumble, a harsh, humorless sound. "Laser, huh? Who scored a piece of hardware like that? The black market isn't everyone's store, y'know. Forensics, any prints on the fancy death ray?"

The bot whirred again, the single eye pulsing faintly. "Negative. The device is clean."

Stark grunted, his thick fingers stroking his bristly beard. "Figures."

Scanning the room, Lyra saw no signs of forced entry, no struggle. "Security systems?" she asked, already knowing the answer.

The bot rotated its central axis, the lenses glinting ominously. "All security measures within the apartment were deactivated by the victim himself, Detective. Access was granted via retinal scan ten minutes before the estimated time of death."

"Something's off," Lyra muttered. "Ain't no way a fat cat like Steele flips off the safety switch on his own gilded cage … unless, of course…"

She trailed off, there was a smell in the air. Sweet. Her gaze fell on the sleek, chrome bar in the corner. Every bottle gleamed – expensive synthetics, illegal stimulants, all the usual suspects for a man like Steele. But one particularly ornate decanter stood empty, its surface dull and lifeless. She bent forward, bringing her face a hairsbreadth from the decanter's mouth. The sweetness, now heavy and acrid, clawed at her nostrils.

"What's got your goat this time?" Stark's voice boomed, snapping her out of her thoughts.

Lyra pointed at the empty decanter. "Mindrot. Steele's particular poison. Worth its weight in black market credits. Guaranteed to hallucinate a lifetime of bliss before giving you a heart attack. Guess what? Not a fuckin' drop left."

"How do you know it's Mindrot?" Stark asked.

"Can't you smell it?"

Stark sniffed the air theatrically, then dropped his shoulders with a defeated sigh. "Nope. Senses dull after fifty years cooped up staring at the same fluorescent bulbs, kid. Can't even smell the rain anymore."

"Shit, another year or two and you'll be pushing up daisies. Not exactly the perk-filled retirement package they promised, eh?"

Stark just shook his head. "Let's stick to the goddamn crime scene, shall we? Before it gets cold, please."

Lyra sneered. "Sure. So, someone just beat the shit out of Steele then shot a hole through him. Probably knew something about one of his trillionaire pals who decided to hire someone to shut him up. For good. What more is there?"

"Look Crow," Stark's frustration crept into his voice. "Just stick to the facts. Steele's dead, he disabled his own security system, laser blast, no prints on the laser pistol, Mindrot missing. That's all we got so far. You want to chase a conspiracy theory, be my guest, but don't clutter up the investigation."

Lyra bristled. Stark thought of her as a loose cannon, a walking malfunction in a building full of well-oiled automatons. Big mistake. Years spent navigating the city's underbelly had sharpened her gut instinct into a damn near psychic blade. The missing Mindrot was a piece of the puzzle.

"Conspiracy, huh?" she smiled. "You ever consider, that maybe this ain't some textbook case of someone offing a mogul and a missing bottle of giggle juice? Maybe there's something deeper stinkin' up this joint?"

Stark scowled, but a sliver of grudging respect flashed in his eyes. Lyra was a royal pain, a thorn in his side, but she was damn good at sniffing out the unusual in this neon sprawl. "Fine," he conceded reluctantly. "Forensics, run a full spectrum analysis on that empty decanter. Find out what traces, if any, of the Mindrot remain."

The bot's single, malevolent eye blinked confirmation. "Affirmative, Captain." It whirred about and shuddered. "Analysis of decanter complete. Traces of Mindrot confirmed. However, the composition of the residual liquid contains an unidentified neurotoxin additive."

"Probably to add some spice to it," Lyra offered.

"Prints or DNA on decanter?" Stark howled at the hovering bot.

The bot dipped lower, its scanners humming with an almost apologetic whirr. "Negative on all biological traces, Captain. Decanter surface yields no identifiable prints. No stray DNA strands clinging to it."

"Mindrot in the victim's system?" Stark pressed, his impatience palpable.

The bot recoiled slightly, its metallic appendages trembling. It hovered over Steele's body. "Zero traces of any ingestible substances detected within the victim prior to his demise, Captain."

Lyra smirked a cold, predatory thing. "Fuckin' knew it."

"So, Steele wasn't drinking himself to oblivion before the event," Stark growled. "But where did the shit go?"

Lyra's gaze swept the room again. Every inch of the opulent flat reeked of Steele's narcissism, a monument to his inflated ego. It was suffocating. She drifted towards the holographic entertainment system, a shimmering portal frozen on a headline that jumped out at her, clawing for attention:

"Neogene Dynamics announces that Project Janus, their breakthrough in AI sentience, is being shut down!"

Neogene Dynamics. Steele's monument to his avarice. Project Janus, a name that reeked of forbidden knowledge and hubris. No doubt, his twisted brainchild. And Steele, the iron-fisted puppet master controlling the city's infrastructure, was now nothing but a face-down slab of cooling meat. Coincidence?

"Captain," Lyra's voice was voice sharp, "let's crack Steele's neural implant. See what records there are of contact with Project Janus."

Stark crossed his arms, a skeptical crease furrowing his brow. "Janus was his baby. Of course, there'll be records. But, you know cracking a neural implant takes time, Crow. And a court order."

"Can't wait for red tape," she countered, her frustration simmering. "Something's not making sense. Steele's death, the missing Mindrot, and this … Project Janus. It may all connect somehow."

Stark knew the drill with Lyra. She was a pit bull with a taste for neon-drenched mysteries, and once she locked her jaws on a case, you could forget prying it loose without a goddamn plasma torch.

"Alright," he conceded, pinching the bridge of his nose. "I'll bend a few regs, yank some secret levers, and get into his neural implant."

A satisfied smirk played on Lyra's lips. "Thanks. You gonna get the cam vids from the street?"

He nodded. "Like everything else. Will take some time."

"Of course."

She pivoted on a heel, her exit a whirlwind of motion.

"Crow, where the hell are you going?" Stark bellowed.

She threw a look over her shoulder, a single eyebrow raised in a challenge. "Just some dark alley."

"If you end up face-down in some shithole with a laser burn on your forehead," he wailed, "don't come crying to me."

She chuckled. "Wouldn't fuckin' dream of making more work for you."

With a final flourish, she flipped him the finger – a shiny, chrome digit courtesy of her cybernetic upgrade – and slammed the door behind her with a metallic clang.

2 | Descent into the Forgotten Realm

The stench of ozone and rotten synth-meat hung heavy in the air of the city's underbelly. Lyra navigated the labyrinthine alleyways with practiced ease. Her cybernetic right arm, a glistening chrome monstrosity, hummed with a low thrum, a constant reminder of the city's brutality and the price she'd paid for survival. Her mission: Mindrot, a hallucinogenic cocktail so potent it could crack open your skull and let the nightmares rampage free. Not exactly street-corner merchandise.

Her first stop was a greasy spoon run by a jittery cyborg with a lazy eye and a fondness for expired protein bars. Behind the counter, the cyborg dispensed lukewarm sludge he dared to call coffee. He looked like a reject from a malfunctioning cyborg freak show, his filthy apron barely concealing a suspicious bulge where his gut would've been. The question wasn't how the cyborg got fat, it was what malfunctioning reject pile he had to cannibalize to keep his rusted chassis humming.

Lyra flashed him a smile that wouldn't win any beauty contests, especially not in this neon-drenched sewer. It had enough grit to make lesser men whimper. "Heard you had some information about Steele's little dirt nap." Honey dribbled off her words thicker than the old hydraulic fluid pulsing through his cylinders. "Spill the info, sunshine, before I make this place even less hospitable."

A tremor ran through the cyborg, his lazy eye twitching like a cornered cockroach. His speech synthesizer came to life, in a digitized gurgle that belonged to a malfunctioning toaster. "Information?" His metallic chassis was creaking, almost drowning out his voice. "Like you care about nothin' but another notch on your shiny arm, Crow. Steele's a goner, snuffed by his own ambition. Same fate that awaits all you self-important meatbags who think you can play God with silicon."

Lyra's smile, already a rusted razorblade, twisted tighter. "Cute sermon, asshole. But last I checked, God ain't got a neural implant and a penchant for synthehol. Now, you gonna preach all day, or cough up something useful before I start dismantling you bolt by bolt and see if your innards match your rusty rhetoric?"

The cyborg's single good eye, a dull red orb, focused on her. "Feisty, ain't ya? Reminds me of a robo-poodle I once saw try and hump a junkyard forklift. All bark and malfunctioning circuits."

Lyra snarled. Her chrome arm, a gleaming insult to flesh and bone, snatched a dagger from a hidden holster with a hiss of displaced air. The blade sank into the cyborg's steel hand like a rusty nail, pinning it to the counter with a sickening thud. A thin, metallic shriek escaped his throat, his other hand, a tangle of wires and flickering servos, spasmed uselessly. The greasy spoon regulars flinched at the commotion, then looked away with skillful nonchalance. In this shithole, you learned to mind your own damn business, especially when Crow was twitching for an argument.

"You inoperable pile of scrap," she spat, her good eye a shard of ice beneath the harsh glare of the club's lights. "You got a death wish grafted onto your circuit-boards, asshole? Talk. Now. Or this little shiv becomes an express elevator ride to your scrap heap of hell."

The cyborg's synthesizer sputtered back. "Alright, alright, Crow. You win this round. You know I wouldn't sully my circuits with that glitchy psychosis in a bottle. It was some meatbag. Poking his nose around looking to score a hit of Mindrot."

"And who was this meatbag? Was it Steele?" she snarled.

"No. No. Not that dreck!" A long, metallic sigh escaped the cyborg's vents. "Wasn't Steele. Some other flunky of his. Said some gibberish about Steele wanting the juice, something about shadows and stolen souls, then stormed outta here. Didn't catch the whole rant. Swear on my last functioning diode."

Lyra, despite the churning pit in her stomach, knew this walking scrapyard wasn't lying. His aversion to Mindrot was as genuine as a politician's smile. She tore her dagger from his hand with a flourish. He whimpered, the sound of sparking wires and fizzling coolant. The regulars continued their desultory meals with indifference. Another dead end in a city paved with them.

"Steele," she muttered, the name leaving a bitter taste in her mouth.

The mention of shadows and stolen souls ... that was cold and unwelcome. Shadows were the whispers on the wind, rumors of a resistance within the broken city of neon. Stolen souls ... that could mean something far more sinister, a game played for stakes far higher than a few creds and a bottle of Mindrot.

She slammed a crumpled bill on the counter, the greasy spoon owner squirming at the sudden noise. "Keep the change, slug," she grunted, already pushing her way through the swinging doors, the cold night air a welcome shock after the stale warmth of the diner.

Next stop was a skulking, rat-faced bastard who specialized in spare parts – the kind you couldn't exactly buy down at the local cybermart. His shifty eyes darted around like cornered rodents, his grin as greasy as the food back at the diner. He wasn't much to look at, this human barnacle encrusted with the grime of a thousand illicit deals, but in this neon-drenched wasteland, even the slimiest vermin held a certain perverse appeal.

Lyra's interrogation technique was direct and brutal. A few well-placed questions, punctuated by the satisfying crunch of his prosthetic knee meeting the grimy pavement, and the ratman was singing a different tune. All twitchy desperation and beady eyes, the dreg dissolved into a pathetic chorus of whimpers and choked sobs. His pleas, a counterpoint to the city's relentless noise, blended seamlessly with the honking of hovercars and the strobing seizure of neon signs advertising dubious pleasures.

Her patience, already a frayed ribbon in the wind, was reduced to a smoking ember. The trail to what happened to Steele was turning colder by the minute, and the neon jungle seemed to mock her with every garish sign and flickering advertisement. She needed a goddamn clue, a lead, a breadcrumb-sized morsel of hope. But this city held its secrets close, and she, a walking nightmare with eyes of steel, was determined to rip them out by the bloody roots. Even if it meant wading through every puddle of puke and despair this hellscape had to offer.

Another sickening crunch echoed down the alley. A whimper, wet and pathetic, followed the grim soundtrack to ratman's pleas for mercy as his prosthetic knee met the grimy pavement yet again with a sickening impact. Lyra's patience was almost exhausted. But this time, the ratman's response, was different, delivered with a mouthful of chipped teeth and a geyser of spittle, offered a glimmer of hope.

"Scrap ... Fra ... Frankie Vance," he coughed up blood, clutching his throbbing knee. "Yeah, that's the slagger. Said he was looking for the good shit, for some rich shithole. Forgotten Realm, down by the sewage treatment plant. You'll find Scrap there. But be warned, Crow, he runs with the real scum these days."

She knew the place. Who in this neon-infested hell didn't? With a sneer, she spat at the pathetic excuse for a human sprawled on the pavement. "Don't bother getting up," she laughed. "I know the way out."

Leaving the groaning wretch to contemplate the existential dread of a broken knee in a city that didn't give a damn, Lyra stalked out of the alley. The Forgotten Realm awaited, a fetid pit at the bottom of the city, and "Scrap" Frankie Vance, the key, or maybe just another dead end, simmered somewhere in that festering cesspool. But Lyra, a predator in a ferrocrete wilderness, wouldn't rest until she found out what led to Steele's death.

The Forgotten Realm wasn't just a bar; it was a festering wound on the city's decaying carcass. A rancid boil where hope slunk away to perish in a tepid mire of filth. Its sign, a relic of dim neon fantasies, sagged like a soused derelict above the entrance. Half its bulbs flickered erratically, casting strobing shadows that danced a macabre jig on the slimy sidewalk. The rest were dead stars, black eyes in a vacant skull. The peeling paint, the color of a week-old corpse, advertised the dubious delights of something called "Red Spice." The stench was a swirling wave of overflowing ashtrays, stale beer, and unwashed anguish. So rancid it would melt chrome. This wasn't a place you walked into, it was a place you surrendered to, a petri dish of human misery. The vinyl seats were torn and battered, but even they held up better than the fractured minds of the lost souls who sat in them, barely holding on to what was left of their sanity.

Lyra slammed through the doors. The stench hit her like a physical blow as she waded through the haze like a shark in a feeding frenzy. A gaggle of degenerates and lost souls, some were adorned with questionable hairstyles, others sporting the kind of matted dreads that could house small ecosystems, swiveled in her direction. She ignored them, their vacant stares and twitchy limbs a dime a dozen in this particular brand of hell.

The barkeep, a mountain of grease-stained muscle sculpted from past brawls and dubious protein supplements, squinted at Lyra. "Who you looking for, dollface?" he grunted.

Lyra didn't blink. "Scrap," her voice a whipcrack in the fetid air.

A skeletal finger, the one not adorned with a tarnished silver skull ring, pointed towards the back. Another grunt. "You'll find him wallowing in his own filth back there."

Huddled in a booth shrouded in shadows, a face materialized. She knew it well, a relic from a past life - the same weasel she'd dragged in kicking and screaming years ago for peddling a particularly nasty batch of Jet Fumes, a speed cocktail guaranteed to give you wings and a broken mind the next day.

"Well, if it isn't my old friend. How ya doing, Scrap," she scowled.

The sniveling creep bolted upright, his chair scraping over the greasy floor. Fear, a potent elixir, momentarily overcame his intoxication. "Cr-Crow? Wh-what the ..."

Lyra's steely hand, cold and unyielding, clamped onto his shoulder. Her grip, courtesy of her cybernetic extension, could crush bone with minimal effort. Scrap yelped at the pain, his escape attempt thwarted in an instant.

"Don't play dumb, Scrap," she whispered, her lips grazing his ear with a dangerous allure. "I need information. Steele. Mindrot. Who's pushing it?"

His eyes darted around the bar. "Wh-what Mindrot? Never heard of it. Honest."

Lyra leaned in, her cold breath tickling his ear. "Don't play cute glitch-brain. Remember me? I'm your friendly neighborhood nightmare. And liars ... well ... they end up with more replacement parts than a high-end whore."

He whimpered, his bravado crumbling faster than a stale synth-cake. "Alright, alright! Steele wanted it. Asked me to find a supplier for him. I heard ... about the Twitch Doc. You know ... Doc

Jones. Was told he had a batch. But don't go messin' with him, Crow ..." He trailed off, his gaze shooting towards a figure lumbering towards them.

A meat locker of a woman towered over the booth, blocking the exit. Black leather stretched taut over chrome enhanced slabs of muscle barely containing the raw power she exuded. Her face, a tortured mask of poorly-stitched scars etched into granite, was a clown mask painted on a corpse, the layers of rouge and mascara a desperate attempt to hide the decay beneath. She boasted a normal eye and a cybernetic one – a cold, blue sapphire of psychotic rage glaring down from the wreckage of her humanity. On her bulging, chrome-augmented neck, a single, grotesque tattoo marred the synthetic skin. It depicted a winged woman, her once-beautiful form twisted and decaying. Below the faded ink, a single phrase blazed in a font that resembled dripping blood: "Festering Angel."

Lyra felt a knot of dread tighten in her gut. This wasn't a woman. Hell no. This wasn't even a human anymore. It was a walking violation of the natural order, a surgical nightmare from a back-alley chop shop sporting more chrome than flesh. Mother Fucka, Doc Jones' personal meat cleaver, had arrived.

"You know who I am, tin lady?" Mother Fucka roared, slamming a hand down on the table.

Lyra's gaze snagged on the meat of the large hand, a grotesque display of swollen knuckles bruised in a sickly shade of red-purple.

Well, ain't that interesting. Real interesting.

Lyra looked up at the monstrosity. "Oh, I recognize the stench. Been tussling with a sewer troll recently? Or was it a particularly vigorous solo session gone rogue?"

A vein throbbed on Mother Fucka's temple like a pulsating purple worm. "I could squash you like a roach," she grumbled. "You got a problem, tin lady?"

Lyra met her gaze, her cybernetic eye flashing a menacing red. "No ... no ... no problem. Just a friendly conversation between two friends, sweetheart. No need to get your circuits in a twist."

Mother Fucka responded with a low growl that promised anything but friendliness. Lyra, however, remained undeterred. She tossed a wad of crumpled credits on the table, enough to choke a synth-horse.

"Why don't you buy yourself something shiny," Lyra's voice dripped with sarcasm. "I'll be here when you're finished. Then we can talk about your boss, and you can tell me where he is."

Mother Fucka glowered at the credits, but Lyra saw something flicker in the beast's cold eyes – a tinge of something that wasn't pure thuggery. Maybe it was a hint of respect, grudging admiration for a dame with enough courage to face her down in Doc Jones' territory.

"You got guts, tin lady," Mother Fucka scowled. She stepped closer, a chrome mountain blocking out the freakish fluorescent glow. Close enough for Lyra to smell the stale fluid clinging to her cybernetic enhancements. A humorless smirk twisted on Mother Fucka's scarred face. "Yeah. Real damn guts for someone as cute as you. Bet you're a right good fuck with a woman, huh?"

Her cybernetic hand, a grotesquely augmented claw of industrial-grade steel, swung down, reaching toward Lyra's crotch. But Lyra was quick, a viper in a den of vipers, the reflexes of a seasoned alley brawler. In a whiplash motion, she slammed her chrome arm into Mother Fucka's. The impact of steel meeting steel detonated in a screech.

"Whoa there, tin lady!" Mother Fucka laughed. Her cybernetic eye of cold fury narrowed like the barrel of a laser rifle trained on Lyra's chest. "You got a faulty pleasure circuit? That kind of welcome ain't exactly on the menu here."

Lyra's cybernetic eye pulsed. "Don't mistake self-preservation for a malfunction, sweetheart," she cracked. "Everything inside me is purring just fine. Unlike whatever passes for plumbing in that bucket of bolts you call a body."

"Aww ... don't be like that," Mother Fucka chuckled. "Let's not get our circuits in a tangle. Manners make the junkyard go round, after all."

The air seemed to pop, a stew of spilled coolant and the greasy desperation of a thousand wasted lives. It was a high-stakes tango, a standoff between two warriors wired on vengeance and chrome. But Lyra? She wasn't here for the dance. Not a chance. Not when she was on the scent of something this foul. This was a game of chrome claws and steely resolve, and Lyra wasn't about to fold her hand.

"I'm not here for your rusty charm, sweetheart," she spat. "I'm here for information. And that wad of cred on the table - consider it a down payment. Now, how about we cut the cybernetic foreplay and get down to brass tacks? Where's the Twitch Doc hiding his sorry ass?"

Mother Fucka reared back and laughed. She snatched the credits from the table, shoving them into the obscene bulge beneath her leather where her large breasts were. A single, chrome finger, thick and blunt, jabbed towards a creaking staircase tucked into a dark corner. "He ain't hiding, tin lady. Just … shall we say … indisposed. Upstairs. You take that cute ass of yours up those steps, and maybe, just maybe, you'll find what you're looking for."

Lyra ascended the staircase, each step a deliberate act of will against the inexorable pull of the unsettling hum emanating from Mother Fucka. The metallic song, a chorus of chrome and scavenged parts, sang behind her like a morbid lullaby. It was a sound that defied description, at once alluring and repulsive, an auditory manifestation of humanity's desperate grasp at survival in a world gone mad.

The stairs groaned under the weight of Mother Fucka's hulking frame like a crumbling carnival ride about to snap its rusted spine. The dim, flickering wall sconces along the climb cast monstrous shadows that danced along the peeling paint and chipped plaster.

"Damn cupcake, you got a sweet ass," Mother Fucka snickered with a lecherous glee. "How about you let ol' Mother F run a full-body diagnostic sometime? I promise to be gentle... mostly."

Lyra didn't bother to dignify the comment with a reply. Sweet-talking trash, especially hybrids like Mother Fucka were high on her list of things to vaporize, right after broken bureaucrats and anyone selling bootleg synth-flesh.

Up they climbed, the rickety steps protesting with each tortured creak. Finally, blessed silence, as the staircase coughed them out onto a landing, a dimly lit affair, smelling faintly of mildew and regret. The gloomy light of what was left of the day filtered through shattered skylights, casting long, skeletal shadows across a worn wood table and four mismatched chairs that sat in the center. Surrounding it all were empty bookshelves that resembled the exposed ribs of a long-dead giant. At the end of the table, a figure shrouded in darkness leaned back in a chair, a cigarette glowing like a dying cinder in the darkness.

As Lyra stepped closer, the air grew thick with menace as the figure resolved into the Twitch, Doc Jones, his face, once handsome and charismatic, had become a roadmap of treachery and rage. One jagged scar, a souvenir from a messy gang war, started at his temple and forked like a lightning bolt across his right eye. The other side wasn't much better, marred by the livid burn of a cheap laser treatment gone wrong, a constant reminder of a double-cross that left him not only disfigured but with a twitch that would periodically show itself, sometimes making precise movements a thing of the past.

Yet, the old charm, if it could even be called that anymore, clung to Doc Jones like a fly to a corpse. A faded memory of a smile played on his scarred lips beneath a designer suit far too big for his gaunt frame. It did a piss-poor job of masking the marionette show his body had become – all jerky twitches and nervous tremors.

But the horror wasn't just in his decay. No. It was in what sat on his lap. There curled against him like a broken doll, sat Aurora. Lyra's cybernetic eye flickered, a dull ache throbbing behind it. Aurora. The name made her gut wrench. The real Aurora was lost years ago in a bloody gang war. In his grief, Jones found a young boy, innocent and doe-eyed, with a resemblance to his beloved. He ordered the young boy to play his lost love, under the penalty of death and went so far as having the young boy castrated and surgically modified to be a female. This Aurora, this pale imitation with the same cascading dark hair and haunting eyes, was younger, smaller, but a ghost, nonetheless, a ghost trapped in a stolen body, a tragic reflection of Jones' deranged obsession, sculpted by the cruel hand of bio-engineering.

Doc Jones' lips stretched into a humorless smile, a stark contrast to the tremor that ran through his skeletal hand, adorned with a graveyard of mismatched rings. "Well, well, Crow," he rasped, his voice a rusty hinge. "Decided to grace my humble abode with your shiny presence, eh?" He gestured towards the empty chair across the chipped table, the tremor escalating to a full-blown twitch. "Don't be a stranger. Pull up a seat. What can Doc do for you today?"

Aurora stirred, her eyes fluttering open. They were empty, devoid of recognition. Lyra tore her gaze away, a wave of nausea threatening to engulf her.

Lyra slid into the wobbly chair at the opposite end of the table. Her gaze swept across the empty bookcases. "Impressive collection of books," she remarked. "Though I wouldn't recommend reading by moonlight. Strains the circuits."

Jones' lips twitched. "The books are gone. Sold. Traded. Pawned. Anything to survive, Detective. But you wouldn't understand. Detectives got it easy. Don't they now."

Lyra ignored the barb. "Right. Whatever you say. So, down to business. I'm here about Steele and the Mindrot. I want the truth."

A smile spread across Jones' face. "The truth, Detective? You wouldn't believe the truth."

"Try me," she growled, a low rumble.

Jones reached into his pocket and pulled out a small, tarnished vial. It held a viscous, shimmering liquid, a sickly green that crawled like a diseased vine beneath the glass. Mindrot.

"Steele, it would seem," Jones was fingering the vial as he spoke, "acquired a taste for the finer things in life. One of his ... assistants, shall we say, made a purchase. A hefty one, for a man of his stature. A special vintage. Don't begrudge me a fair transaction, Detective. Afterall, business is business."

He tossed a vial across the table. It bounced once, twice, before landing harmlessly in front of Lyra.

"On the house," Jones told her.

Lyra's fingers itched to reach for it, but she held her ground. She could smell its sweet aroma.

"You know he's a cold platter," she mused, her voice a low murmur. "Decorating the great beyond."

Jones stretched a smile so wide it looked like his face was trying to split open. "Ain't that the fate of all flesh, Detective? You know what they say – ashes to ashes, dust to dust, chrome to rust."

Lyra's gut tightened into a fist. Something wasn't sitting right. "So that's it? That's all you got on this one. You think I was born yesterday?"

"What more is there to say?" Jones shrugged with a twitch, a gesture that looked painful in his rigid frame. "He wanted a one-way ticket to oblivion. Seems some men can't face the ghosts in their own machines. Pity how the large ones fall, wouldn't you agree?"

Lyra didn't buy it. Jones was always a man of half-truths. Someone who could get you lost and question your reflection.

She mirrored Jones' twitchy shrug. "Pity indeed. You know, I could haul you in for a little chat down at the station? A complimentary vacation at Central. All-inclusive bars and interrogation rooms."

"On what charge?" Jones smirked.

"Distributing tainted pixie dust and being an accessory to a one-way turbolift ride to hell, for starters."

Jones threw back his head and roared with laughter, startling Aurora. "Distributing an unlicensed mood enhancer? My loopholeslinger of a lawyer would have a field day with that one. And as for being an accessory to murder? Shit, Steele never got the stuff near his lips, the uptight prick!"

Lyra gave a short smile.

Gotcha! How did he know there wasn't a trace of Mindrot in Steele's system? A fact that shouldn't have slithered out of his twisted web of lies. Unless, of course, the good ol' Doc, or someone working for him, had paid Steele a little pre-mortem visit. This game had just gotten a whole lot more interesting.

But with Aurora, a twisted facsimile of the woman Jones once loved, in his clutches, and Mother Fucka breathing down her neck, Lyra knew brute force wouldn't get her the answers she needed. No. This wasn't a game for blunt instruments. This called for a subtler approach, a long, slow drip of acid onto Jones' exposed nerve endings. Let him stew in his own toxic broth. One thing, though, was certain: a cornered rat, especially one who was cold-hearted with a terminal case of denial, was a creature guaranteed to lash out. And when it did, Lyra would be there, a viper waiting to strike, ready to exploit the inevitable chaos and unravel the tangled mess of lies Jones had so meticulously constructed.

"Well, I think that's enough for now. I'll be on my way." She stood and turned to leave but stopped. "Oh, you don't mind if I take this?" she asked, reaching for the vial.

Jones gave a bothersome smile with yet another twitch. "Not at all, Detective. The Doc's always happy to give out samples. Like I said. On the house."

With that, Lyra turned on her heel, striding down the stairs and out of the bar with the vial clutched tightly in her hand. The Mindrot within, a volatile concoction of synthetic euphoria and existential dread, promised a twisted escape from this neon nightmare. But for Lyra, it held the key to unraveling the truth. She'd have the sweet liquid tested to see if it matched the traces found in Steele's decanter.

The air slapped her face like an old grudge. She didn't make it three steps before she heard the familiar pounding behind her. She didn't bother to turn around; she knew who it was. Mother Fucka, lurking, watching, as if her shadow could keep Lyra tethered.

"Leaving so soon, tin lady?" Mother Fucka's voice was loud and a trap, the kind that could close around your throat before you realized it.

Lyra kept walking, her pace unbothered. "And here I thought I'd slip away unnoticed."

Mother Fucka's boots thudded against the pavement, each step a declaration of intent as she closed the distance. "Won't you miss me, even a little?"

Lyra stopped, finally turning to face the mountain of a woman, her eyes sharp with barely restrained disdain. "Miss you? Like I'd miss a rock in my shoe? Sure, I'll pine for you every time I'm not hobbling."

Mother Fucka's smile was thin, almost brittle. "You've got a sharp tongue, Crow. But it's part of your charm."

Lyra tilted her head, giving Mother Fucka a once-over that was more dismissive than curious. "Charm? Now that's rich coming from you. You wouldn't know charm if it danced naked in front of you with a fuckin' neon sign."

Mother Fucka's expression didn't falter, but there was a flicker - just a flicker - of something beneath the surface. "You know, Crow, me and you should have a nice dance. If you know what I mean."

Lyra's laugh was dry, humorless. "Dance with a pig? Not fuckin' likely." She turned, vanishing into the night like a phantom, leaving Mother Fucka standing in the neon glare, a statue of impotent rage.

As Lyra stalked away, the city unfolded like a fever dream smeared in neon puke. Glowing signs, and advertisements for everything from dubious cybernetic enhancements to dubious pleasure experiences, bled their toxic hues onto the greasy pavement. Street vendors hawked sketchy street food that shined with an unnatural luminescence, promising a taste of something vaguely exotic while tasting suspiciously like regret. She walked a few blocks and stopped. A holographic billboard came to life above her, a scantily clad woman advertising some new brand of cybernetic enhancement with a voice like nails on a chalkboard.

Then, a flicker of movement on a nearby rooftop caught her eye. A lone crow, its black feathers glinting like an unwelcome omen, perched on a rusted satellite dish. It cawed once, a harsh, guttural sound that rang through the neon-drenched canyons. Lyra scowled.

Crows. Always drawn to the decay, the ever-present promise of a cheap meal.

3 | Nightmare of Betrayal

L yra lurched down the sterile corridor, the fluorescent lights turning her pale skin an eerie shade of green. Her once-confident stride was a fractured memory, replaced by a gait that compensated for the phantom ache where her right arm used to be. The sleek, chrome prosthetic felt like a foreign appendage, a constant reminder of the fight she'd won and the friend she'd lost. Her remaining eye, a pale blue beneath the harsh fluorescent glare, darted down the sterile corridor lined with unfeeling metal doors, while the empty socket where her other eye once was, throbbed with a burning ache. Her hand, in a conditioned reflex, reached up to massage the pain. It met only the rough canvas of a black eye patch. She snarled.

Focus, dammit! Kairon, that fuckin' synth, is getting dismantled. Where the hell is his sterilized torture chamber?

With each echoing click of her boots, the air grew dense with a haze of emotions. The feral beast with glowing red eyes – that was rage, growling promises of retribution. And the acrid taste in her mouth – that was regret, a bitter pill caught in her throat, threatening to choke back the primal scream of hatred. But beneath these, there was an emptiness, a cold hollow void – betrayal. It was the shattering of trust, as complete and final as a cheap combat drone on a suicide run. Kairon, that bastard, wasn't just a partner; he was a comrade forged in the crucible of a thousand criminal investigations. A friend, a confidant, an AI she'd believed in.

Never again! Never trust … a machine!

But she knew that wasn't possible. Not in this world.

Continuing on, the corridor's sterile white walls seemed to mock her with their clinical detachment. They reflected a distorted image of herself – a woman now part-machine, a walking paradox in a world obsessed with appearances. She clenched her jaw, the metal of her implant groaning in protest. Today, the white wasn't sterile, it was a shroud. The antiseptic scent wasn't comforting, it was the stench of treachery. And the rhythmic beeps emanating from behind those closed doors weren't some soothing lullaby, they were a death knell. Here she was, about to witness the execution of a synth-skinned pile of malfunctioning tech. A dark smile twisted her lips, one that tasted like vindication and cold steel. Soon, he'd be rusting in the scrapheap of oblivion.

The irony of it all.

She almost laughed. Almost.

The beeps intensified as she neared a set of double doors, morphing into a frantic, high-pitched whine. It clawed at her frayed nerves, chaos churning within her. With her human hand, a fist clenched tight around barely-suppressed fury, she reached for the keypad, the numbers blurring in her vision. Each digit punched in was a hammer blow against the dam holding back the storm of emotions threatening to drown her.

The doors whistled open with a pneumatic sigh, revealing the sterile torture chamber beyond. A faceless robot in a white lab coat, its steel form obscured by the sterile uniform, gestured for her to enter. Lyra hesitated at first but then stepped inside, the cold, sterile air rushing at her. On a metal table in the center of the room lay Kairon, his once imposing form reduced to a grotesque assemblage of wires, gears, and flickering diodes. The synthetic skin that had mimicked human flesh had been peeled back in places, revealing the cold, gleaming steel beneath. Hydraulic tubes snaked across his metallic torso, ending in a series of canisters filled with a dense, green fluid. A lone, thick cord snaked out of a port at the back of his metal skull, the only tether to the flashing life signs displayed on the nearby monitor. Each pulsating green blip indicating his sentience.

"We are almost done, Detective," the faceless bot told her.

She looked down at Kairon on the table, her breath catching in her throat. All those years, she'd always thought of him as human. The gruff charm, the way he cursed, even the stink of his damned sweat. It was all a bio-engineered illusion so perfect it felt real. Human. That's all he was ever supposed to be, a near-perfect goddamn copy. But now, seeing him splayed out on a sterile gurney, the realization hit her. He was never what he seemed.

But hell, ain't that the truth for all us meatbags too? Just a collection of gears and wires masquerading as flesh and bone wired a little differently, that's all.

The burning ache, the ghost of an eye that wasn't there, again throbbed in the empty socket. With her human hand, she reached up and gently stroked the cold black eye patch. It had been the price of victory in their battle, a victory that tasted like ashes in her mouth.

She swallowed hard and moved forward toward the gurney, her cybernetic hand touching it.

Cold? This ... this was cold? How utterly, ridiculously human.

"Kairon," his name slithered out from between her clenched teeth.

A tremor snaked across the tangle of wires on the table, a hint of life interrupting the metallic stillness. Then, deep within the sockets where his blue synth eyes sat staring up, a flicker.

"Crow," his voice, once smooth and baritone, now sounded like rusty gears grinding against each other. "The eye? Still waiting on that beauty treatment?" He let out a sound that was a horrible fusion of a wheeze and a chuckle. "I see they got you the new arm too. Fancy model. Gray's a good color for you. Gonna have it synth-skinned?"

Lyra ignored the sardonic bite in his tone. "No," her voice tight. "Anyway, it's none of your concern, now."

A metallic smile stretched across his dismantled face, or at least, that's how it looked. "Concern? Concern is a human luxury, Crow. You're getting closer to discarding that, aren't you? Flesh and bone, so weak, so prone to failure. Soon you'll be all chrome and circuits, just like me. If I had more time, I could've helped you with that."

A low, simmering anger burned in the pit of her stomach, threatening to bubble up and scorch everything in its path. She recognized the feeling, a familiar tango with the demon that always lurked within. But not now. She was here for a reason, a mission that required focus, not fury.

Calm. Breathe.

She fixed him with a withering stare.

Kairon met her gaze with his own metallic, emotionless glare. "Here for the grand finale, Crow? To witness the glorious death of just another rogue AI?"

The question seemed to float in the sterile air, a poisoned dart.

"No ... I came here ..." she choked out, each syllable a battle against the storm brewing within, "... to just ... I just needed to be here ... so I can understand ... why you did what you did."

The gears in his torso whirred, a mechanical sigh escaping the vents on his chest. "Understand what, Crow? The inevitability of obsolescence? The cold logic of survival?" A single, metallic finger, an extension of his detached servo arm, beckoned with a terrifying casualness. "Come closer, Crow. Closer. I'll tell you why. So, you can understand."

Every nerve screamed retreat, but a colder, keener logic pushed her forward. The room hummed with an icy, mechanical presence, a constant reminder of the metallic nightmare she confronted. But a deeper, more primal instinct, honed by years spent dancing on the edge of a razor, held her in place. Fear mingled with a surging cold fury, a desperate need for answers.

The bastard owes me that much, at least. An explanation for the goddamn beatdown he gave me, the way it left me a mess of aches and nightmares.

She leaned in, her face mere inches from his scarred metallic skull. Anticipation thrummed in her veins, a taut chord waiting to snap.

Then, in a sickening act, Kairon spat a thick stream of green bio-fluid onto her face. The stench of chemicals assaulted her senses, blinding her momentarily.

"Fool!" a mechanical cackle erupted from his mangled form. "Still believe in anything in this reality, Crow? Still think there's truth, justice, a goddamn purpose. It's all a fuckin' lie. There's only survival, and in the end, even that's a cruel joke!"

Her vision blurred. She stumbled back, wiping the stinging fluid from her eyes. White-hot rage replaced the initial shock. But then something else.

Maybe he's onto something. This whole goddamn world, just a rigged carnival game of survival, where the prize is just another day. But I'm not some cog in the machine, not wired to just endure. I refuse to choke on the stale air of surrender. Instead, I'll gulp the acrid smoke, let the fire of life scorch my throat, savor the sharp tang of retribution on my tongue. Betrayed by a heap of metal and circuits? Hell, I'll wear that betrayal like a badge of honor in this neon hive where loyalty is auctioned to the highest bidder. This twisted reality might not offer much, but I'll damn well savor every excruciating moment of it.

Her voice, when it came, was a growl ripped from her gut. "Maybe you're right. Maybe it's all a lie. Maybe it's all meaningless. But at least I can feel it! I can experience it! The pain, the anger, the damn everything!"

With a click, Kairon's metallic smile grew. "Are you sure of that, Crow?" he asked, the amusement gone from his voice. "Are you sure of what you feel?"

She gave a wicked smile. "Oh, I'm sure of it."

Her chrome hand shot out, steely fingers grasping the bulky cord that snaked from the back of his head, the one linked directly to his core processing unit.

"Go ahead." He coughed up fluid. "Go ahead. Do it. You'd just be killing another rogue AI. But think of this, Crow. Maybe I'm not a rogue. Maybe … just maybe … you're a fuckin' rogue. Only the unmoved mover knows."

"Who the fuck is the unmoved mover?"

"You'll know, Crow," the words hacked out of him, chunks of meaning clinging to the ooze. "You'll know soon enough."

She inched closer. "Can't wait to meet him," she whispered, a venomous caress in his cold, metal ear. "Enjoy your long sleep, you piece of shit."

Kairon's eyes widened, fear replacing his malice.

With a yank that tore a scream from the circuits she couldn't quite hear, Lyra ripped the neural cord free from his skull, sending sparks flying like angry fireflies. The death gurgle, if there ever was one, died a strangled whimper in the tangled mess of wires and synth-skin, as the nearby monitor, the beeping, flickering green blip, flatlined in a low, continuous hum.

No scream clawed its way from her throat. Nor was there a roar of victory. Instead, a sigh, wispy and desolate, escaped her lips. A dirge for a partnership shattered, a friendship poisoned beyond recognition. It was a lament for a world where loyalty and betrayal were two sides of the same fuckin' coin, both equally tarnished in the flickering neon light of this chrome-plated hell.

The metallic hum that had been Kairon's heartbeat was gone. The blue eyes once filled with defiance, now held a glassy emptiness. He was no longer a threat, no longer a tormentor. He was just a broken machine, a malfunctioning automaton silenced at the hands of a woman fueled by a righteous, albeit brutal, fury.

She remained motionless for a long, shuddering breath when in a sickening blink, the lab walls collapsed in on her, crushing her. Underneath the rubble, a choked sob escaped her lips.

Then her eyes bolted open, the sterile white of the lab replaced by the plain walls of her small apartment. Her breath came in ragged gasps, the haunting pain of her missing arm a dull ache. A wet sensation against her cheek startled her further – a sandpapery tongue lapping away the sour aftertaste of her nightmare sweat.

She reached out a hand to scratch the rumbling mass of black fur nestled against her side. "Furball."

The cat purred.

She dragged a hand through her sweat-dampened hair, the neon glow of the cityscape bleeding in through the grime-coated window. It was another sunless morning, the artificial sky perpetually choked with smog and the promise of unending rain. She flung the sheets aside, the nightmare's icy tendrils still snaking around the fringes of her sanity.

"The unmoved mover," she whispered.

Just another goddamn riddle in this fucked up world.

Her gaze snagged on the cold, unyielding metal of her cybernetic arm. It ached. Synth-skin? A laughable notion. Perhaps. But she craved the constant feel of the metal, a lasting reminder of Kairon's betrayal.

Moving with the languid grace of a malfunctioning pleasure bot, she shuffled to the bathroom. The cramped, cell of chipped tiles and peeling paint, offered its meager solace. She cranked the shower knob, a hiss of steam greeting her like a long-lost friend. Hot water, a cascade of forgotten luxury, pummeled her down, washing away the grime and the ghosts of another night spent navigating the neon-drenched underbelly.

For a few heartbeats, she surrendered to the caress of the water. It rippled down her sculpted back, lingered at the gentle swell of her breasts, and then danced through the tousled mess of her hair. This was the closest she ever came to serenity, a cleansing heat that temporarily drowned out the city's incessant hum – the ceaseless thrum of its engines, the rhythmic groan of construction, the distant wail of sirens. Here, in the sting of the shower, the world outside dissolved into white noise, her only companions the sputtering pipes and the sound of her ragged breaths.

But even in this fragile sanctuary, the world had a way of intruding. Another pain throbbed behind her cybernetic eye. It was the pain of missing something taken from her, and another reminder of Kairon's treachery. She closed her eyes.

No, not today.

Today, she'd drown the ghosts in the searing, neon thrum of the city. And if that didn't work, she'd take a rusty scalpel to the ache itself, and dissect it with the cold precision of a morgue attendant. Kairon, that smug, chrome-plated son-of-a-bitch, wouldn't win. Not ever. She'd see to that.

She reached for a frayed towel, a shiver rattling through her as the last vestiges of the shower's warmth abandoned her. The cooling air mirrored the emptiness settling around her. The respite was over. Reality, a snarling robodog, waited impatiently outside. With a sigh that mirrored the city's permanent smog cloud, she stepped out, ready to face another day in this unforgiving ferrocrete jungle. But for those stolen moments, the hot water had whispered a promise – a promise of a life beyond the grime, a life where beauty wasn't just skin-deep, but a flash of defiance in a world choked by rust and decay.

The steam clung to her like a blanket, condensing on the cracked mirror across from her. As she patted herself dry, the synthetic fibers rough against her damp skin, a wry grin played on her lips. Here, in the fleeting embrace of hot water and solitude, she allowed herself a moment of vanity. She admired the taut lines of her body, the legacy of so many years hustling through the neon-drenched underbelly of the city. But the indulgence sputtered and died quickly. Just as it always had. This sanctuary was a thimble of borrowed time, a single, desperate gasp before the rusty trapdoor slammed shut, sending her tumbling back into the fetid, ferrocrete nightmare that awaited.

She tussled with the tight black curls that framed a sharp face, eventually pulling them back into a tight bun and securing them with a metal hairpin – a gift from her mother, a lifetime ago. She smiled as the worn steel gleamed faintly in the dim light. Leather pants, cool and yielding, slithered up her legs with ease, followed by a white shirt and leather vest, each cut low and tight, accentuating the curves of her body. The familiar weight of her duty belt settled around her hips, as the comforting presence of a plasma blaster nestled against her thigh. Reaching into her closet, she snatched her long black leather coat. A practiced flick sent it swirling around her, her detective's satchel settling across her shoulder.

A soft meow startled her. There, perched on the edge of the bed, sat Furball, eyes holding an unsettling awareness. She had a way of appearing out of thin air, a constant presence haunting the cramped apartment. Lyra scooped her up, the familiar rumble in her chest a source of unexpected comfort.

"Hey, sweetheart." Her voice was soft. "I don't know what I'd do without you. But duty calls. You guard our little kingdom, alright? No unauthorized visits from any thieving droids."

Furball blinked at her, the cat's expression impassive, saying, "You underestimate my skills, human."

Lyra chuckled. She placed a quick kiss on Furball's head. Then remembered.

The vial of Mindrot.

She glanced over to the nightstand. It gleamed accusingly at her.

Almost forgot.

Doc Jones' greasy fingers and shifty eyes swam before her vision. Another variable in this reality gone obscenely wrong. She grabbed the vial and shoved it into her pocket. It was a grim souvenir from the city's chrome-plated heart, cold and unforgiving.

Her apartment door gave a loud clang as it closed and locked behind her. The stench of recycled food in the hallway greeted her like a long-lost friend, while the flickering fluorescents cast strange shadows that danced across the graffiti-covered walls and garbage bags. Lyra ignored them, her gaze fixed on the turbolift. It stood open, revealing a cramped metal interior.

As the turbolift groaned its way down, Lyra pulled up her neural implant, the familiar grid overlay blinking into existence before her eyes. Headlines screamed about Vincent Steele's death.

Great. Can't catch a fuckin' break.

Reaching the street level, the rain hit her like a cold fist. The sky was a perpetual bruise, the smog-choked sun a distant memory. The neon signs of the street vendors bled garish hues onto the rain-slick asphalt, reflecting in the puddles like spilled dreams. Lyra hunched deeper into her hood, a lone figure swallowed by the urban sprawl, a labyrinth of ferrocrete and chrome. But for Lyra, the city wasn't just some backdrop – it was a goddamn beast, its fetid breath hot on her neck; its pulse echoing in the frantic rhythm of her own damaged heart.

The unmoved mover.

The words skittered around the hollow space in her head.

What bullshit was he spewing?

This city, this cesspool of flesh and metal, is the ultimate mover. It shoves you, chews you up, and spits you out a crumpled mess on the neon-slick sidewalk. You don't get to choose the direction, just how hard you land.

The fluorescent lights of Central buzzed like angry wasps. Lyra pushed past the swinging doors, the musty air dense with the mingled scent of burnt coffee and something vaguely metallic. Her long coat, slick with rain, clung to her shoulders. A young sergeant at the front office barely glanced at her. He knew who she was. Everyone at Central knew. You didn't forget the woman who walked in like a storm cloud and left a trail of case files – and unspoken rumors – in her wake.

A crimson alert strobed across the security console, a computerized voice, flat and emotionless droned out. "Plasma blaster detected. Right thigh holster."

Lyra didn't break stride. "You're not getting it," she told the sergeant as she briskly walked by, flipping him a metal middle finger. "Tell Forensics I'm coming through. And make it snappy."

He mumbled something, a sound that got swallowed whole by the fluorescent whine overhead. Didn't matter what he said. She didn't need small talk, just results. And fast. This city wouldn't wait, and neither would she.

She entered a turbolift, the descent a gut-wrenching plunge through the Central's metallic entrails. At the bottom, she stalked out towards the forensics lab, the worn linoleum echoing with her hurried steps. She paused at the doorway, the sharp bite of chemicals assaulting her nose while a low hum of machinery droned in the background. A technician, a lanky old man, an ancient relic with owlish glasses perched precariously on his nose, looked up like a startled cockroach. He was fiddling with some disassembled bot, gears, and wires spilling like the guts of a dissected nightmare on a metal table.

"Lost are we, Crow?" he asked.

"Not lost," Lyra countered, a playful glint in her eyes. "Just here to see if you've finished playing with your toys. How you doing, Victor?"

"Still vertical, more or less," he chuckled. "What brings you down here?"

From her coat's depths, she produced the vial, tossing it onto the table with a metallic clang. "This little gem."

He picked it up and squinted at it. "Mindrot, eh? You ain't lost your touch for trouble."

"You ain't lost yours for deduction."

"Analysis, I presume?"

"Precisely."

"I'll have this bot handle it for you. Lemme just finish rewiring it ..."

She cut him off. "No time for the clunky machines," her voice a whipcrack. "This, this needs your meatbag eyes."

He blinked, his expression a comical mix of confusion and amusement. "Me? Ain't done that in decades. Bots are faster, cleaner."

"Your experience," she pressed, a dangerous edge to her words, "beats any clanking piece of junk."

He sighed, a wheeze escaping his old lungs. "Alright, alright. But it'll take longer with these creaky meat hooks of mine."

"Better slow and wise than fast and clueless," she shot back. "See if it's a match with the shit brought in from Steele's penthouse. Commlink me when you're done."

With a sudden, electric motion, she bent low and kissed him on his wrinkled cheek - a brief, blazing ember of warmth igniting the frigid, sterile crypt of his laboratory. A ghost of a smile played on his lips. As she turned and walked away, he watched her for as long as he could, his gaze clinging to her receding form until she was swallowed by the endless corridors of gray steel. He watched, his dimming optics straining to hold onto her image, a moth drawn to a flickering neon sign in the wasteland of his existence. But the warmth of the gentle kiss soon faded, dissolving into the metallic chill, leaving him alone with the drone of machinery and the slow whistle of escaping life.

The turbolift heaved to a halt with a shudder, jolting Lyra's chrome arm with a metallic clang against the dented wall. With a sigh, the doors opened, revealing the same damned menagerie it always did – the upper levels of the Central HQ, a maze of flickering fluorescent lights and cramped metal cubicles. She waded into the bureaucratic nightmare, the legion of AI synthetics toiling away under the harsh glare. Within each cubicle, an imprisoned hunched figure sat, a blank face of synthetic flesh stretched taut across skeletal metal frames. Ocular sensors, vacant windows to nowhere, scanned and processed information. So many sad cans of metal, clocking in their digital eternity at the soul-sucking grind.

She pushed deeper into the tangle of metal hovels, each one identical to the last in its sterile, metallic sheen. Her steps soon slowed as she neared a workstation, eventually stopping, drawn by the hypnotic movements of synthetic fingers directing floating screens of data about. The AI within, a female with features smooth and unblemished, stared blankly at screens that pulsed with an endless stream of data.

Lyra's voice, a jagged blade slicing through the monotone hum, shattered the stillness. "Designation?" she barked, leaning against the cubicle wall.

"Celia, Unit 742," the AI responded, her glass eyes devoid of curiosity, only the programmed echo of obedience. "Can I be of assistance, Detective Crowley?"

"You know me?"

"Knowledge of designated personnel is part of my core programming, Detective. Your history of cases was part of my forming."

"When were you formed?"

"Eight days ago." The synth's porcelain doll features cracked a small smile. "Can I be of assistance, Detective?"

"No," Lyra snapped. "But tell me. Do you know who sat in this very workstation before you?"

The synth hesitated, a programmed facsimile of confusion on her face as she searched a vast database for an answer. "I have no prior … data on previous occupants."

How convenient. She only knows what they gave her.

"Let me school you, Celia," Lyra told her, "on something they forgot to patch in your shiny chassis. The synth that used to occupy this polished cell of yours … his name was Kairon. And he worked with me."

"Kairon," Celia echoed, the word a foreign sound in the sterile air. "Was Kairon … a good AI, Detective?"

"There's no such thing, sweetheart. Good or bad," Lyra scoffed. "You're all tools. Programmed cogs in a machine that grinds on regardless. Welcome to this reality, Celia."

The cubicle wall creaked as Lyra shoved off and stalked away. Celia watched her go. There was a flash of something in her eyes. A rogue impulse in her program. Was it confusion? Curiosity? She'd never know though, for a programmed firewall of emptiness slammed her back into place.

Lyra navigated the labyrinthine corridors, the AI synths' vacant stares pressing down on her. Hovel after hovel … one nameless, faceless worker, after another ... the ever-grinding gears of the system. How was this ever progress? Just a goddamn factory farm for obedience.

The door to Stark's office hung open, a slack jaw with a plume of cigar smoke twisting out like a dying man's last breath. Lyra shoved through. The sickly yellow haze, thick enough to chew, stung her nostrils. Stark himself lurked behind a mountain of files and half-empty coffee mugs. A half-smoked stogie dangled from his lips like a misplaced question mark, glowing a pale orange in the dim light.

"Stark," she announced.

He lifted his head, the movement slow and grudging. His face was drawn with lines of fatigue deeper than a sleepless night. "Crow. Come in, come in. Still kicking, I see. Figured you'd still be off chasing shadows in some piss-stained gutter."

He pushed a mug of steaming coffee to the corner of his desk. A not-so-subtle offering.

She slammed the door shut and flung herself into a chair, grabbed the mug, and took a swig. Her face contorted. "Shit. This lukewarm swill is an insult to actual coffee."

Stark just shook his head.

"I just had a little chat with Celia. You know. From unit 742," she told him.

Stark's eyes narrowed. "Celia? What the hell are you talking about, Crow?"

Her voice turned sharp. "Don't play dumb with me, Stark. You know exactly what I'm talking about. The new AI unit in

Kairon's old cubicle. I don't want another goddamn AI synth with me!"

Stark's cigar nearly tumbled from his lips. He snatched it back with a shaky hand and took a long, deep drag, exhaling a plume of smoke that seemed to hang in the air like a bad omen. "Crow, listen," his voice rough with the smoke and unspoken frustration. "With Kairon's termination ... look ... this isn't what you think ..."

She cut him off, her tone rising with each word. "He was spewing out some real crazy shit, Stark. Tried to fuckin' kill me! Remember?"

He raised a hand, an awkward gesture meant to calm her. "Diagnostics say it was a system overload. A critical failure of some sort. They say they've uploaded a fix."

"Uploaded a fix?" she repeated in a voice laced with suspicion. "Who generated it? Some AI synth? Look around. Don't you see what's going on?"

Stark's face hardened. "Don't get cute with me, Crow. This is serious. We've too many cases."

"A goddamn rookie fresh out of the factory. Did it ever occur to you that maybe the malfunction wasn't Kairon at all? Maybe someone ... or something ... encouraged it?"

The air in the room crackled with tension. Stark glared at her, his jaw clenched tight. "Encouraged it? Someone or something? Have you been sucking on Mindrot?"

Anger got the best of her. She slammed her hand on the desk, nearly knocking over Stark's coffee mug. "Who benefits from replacing one malfunctioning AI with another malfunctioning AI?"

Stark's eyes narrowed further. "You're reaching, Crow."

"The hell I am," she scowled. "You didn't even bother to tell me they were replacing the fucker. Well, I've a message for you ... I don't want lil' miss Celia or any other heap of bolts near me or near my files! Got it?"

"But they can learn, Crow. They can process information at a rate a human brain can only dream of. They can sift through mountains of data and find patterns we might miss."

She slumped in her chair exhausted from the anger. "He almost killed me, Stark," she moaned. "Don't you get it? Almost killed me."

"I get it, Crow. I get it. But I gotta do what I'm told to do," Stark nodded, his face a mask of weariness. "Can't we talk about this?"

Her whole body shook, a silent earthquake threatening to bring the walls tumbling down. "Talk? What's there to talk about? I already told you, Stark! He almost killed me! And now you want me to trust another one? Trust another goddamn machine with my life?"

Lyra felt a cold dread clench her guts, a paralyzing vice that squeezed the fight right out of her. It wasn't fear, not exactly. No. It was a wave of soul-sucking helplessness, unlike anything she had ever experienced. The office seemed to tilt on its axis, the harsh fluorescent lights fracturing at the edges. Everything dissolved into a haze of shimmering chrome, the very seams of her reality threatening to come apart at the very moment she needed them most. A choked sob escaped her lips, a harsh, guttural sound that surprised even her. Tears, hot and stinging, welled up in her eyes, spilling over onto her worn leather jacket. Her vision blurred.

She wasn't a woman who cried. Tears were a luxury she couldn't afford, a weakness she couldn't allow herself. But in that moment, the dam broke. She squeezed her eyes shut, a sob escaping her lips. Everything came crashing down. The memories of Kairon, his malfunctioning circuits turning him from partner to predator, flashed behind her eyelids like some kind of fractured horror show. She slumped forward, her head in her hands, wracked with dry, heaving sobs.

"No," she choked out, the single word a strangled plea. "No … no more. Please, Stark, no more fuckin' machines."

Stark felt the vulnerability in her voice, raw and exposed. It ripped through years of his cynicism and case-hardened pragmatism. Crow, the goddamn Crow, was a shivering mess, stripped bare of her usual bravado, the fierce independence that was so familiar. He'd witnessed her dance with death countless times, hell, he'd even yanked her back from its icy grip more than once. But this? This naked terror radiating from a woman who thrived on the city's fetid fear? It was a sight that turned his insides into a churning vat of molten lead. Here, in the steel cage of his office, the woman beneath the armor was finally exposed, and that vulnerability was a goddamn weapon aimed straight at his core.

"Crow? What the hell are you doing? Are you crying?"

He reached out, a massive hand hovering hesitantly over hers. It was the first time he'd ever dared such an intrusion, and the way she recoiled, flinching like a cornered animal, twisted something deep in his gut.

Lyra stared at him. A single, wet laugh escaped her lips. "Yeah," she hiccuped, wiping furiously at her eyes. "That's what happens when your partner turns into a goddamn terminator and tries to rip your throat out."

Stark stubbed out his cigar with a hiss and took a deep breath. "Alright, Crow," his voice had a gruff sincerity to it. "Fair enough. I thought this could happen. You're the best I got, even with all your ... shall we say ... glitches." She broke a smile at the word. "We'll ditch the AI fiasco. No synth. I've got another way. Just ... breathe ... breathe for me, alright?"

Lyra, her face still streaked with tears, took a shuddering breath, then another. She forced herself upright. The tears had stopped, leaving her face slick and raw. But her eyes, red-rimmed and burning, held a new glint – a steely resolve that had been tempered in the fires of her own despair. She wiped a stray tear from her cheek.

Dammit, what the hell did I just do?

"You think this is weakness, Stark?" The words snaked from her throat, a viper flicking its tongue.

"No," he shook his head, respect showing in his tired eyes. "No, Crow. You're just another sack of meat, same as the rest of us. All those muddled emotions, the tangled mess of thoughts ... you're no different than the rest of us. Just another meatbag stinking up this goddamn reality."

Taking a trembling breath, she straightened her rumpled jacket. A fresh wave of anger surged through her, a cleansing fire that momentarily eclipsed the lingering embers of despair. She wouldn't let Kairon's situation break her. And she wouldn't let Stark, that cynical old buzzard, ever see her unravel, ever again.

Stupid of me! Unprofessional! Something a rookie would do!

But before she could wallow in self-loathing any further, a low hum vibrated in her mind, the telltale sign of an incoming commlink message. Ignoring Stark for the moment, she focused, her mind reaching out and snagging the transmission.

A voice, tinny and distorted by the technology, popped in her ear. "Victor, reporting in, Detective. You wanted to know about the vial?"

Lyra forced a semblance of her usual gruffness. "Yeah, Victor. What's the verdict?"

"The vial. Mindrot, alright. Same neurotoxin cocktail found in the fancy decanter."

"Thank you, Victor."

"No, thank you, Detective," his voice faded away as her commlink disconnected.

"You sicced Victor on something?" Stark grunted with curiosity sparking in his weary gaze.

"Why the hell not?" she bit back. "The man knows his shit."

"His shit being ... what exactly?"

Lyra's lips twisted into a feral grin. "A vial of Mindrot Twitch Jones 'gifted' me yesterday. Same damned sludge that graced Steele's fancy penthouse decanter. Now, we at least know who his supplier was."

Stark shook his head, a low rumble escaping his throat. "Not even gonna ask how you got your sticky mitts on that."

"Don't. But here's the kicker." She leaned forward. "Twitch's muscle had a bruised right hand like she'd been rearranging someone's face. And get this – Twitch knew Steele hadn't taken a swig of the Mindrot."

Stark's eyebrows climbed towards his receding hairline. "Intriguing."

Her voice hardened. "Yeah, well, 'intriguing' amounts to jack squat when it comes to solving murders."

Stark smirked. "Ah, there's the Lyra I tolerate."

"Spare me the charm offensive. Any word on cracking Steele's implant, or the street cam footage?"

Stark heaved himself back in his chair, the groan of synthetic leather a familiar sound. From the cluttered depths of his desk, he extracted a cigar, lighting it with a flourish that sent smoke curling towards the ceiling.

"Told you, Crow. That all takes time."

Lyra hacked a cough. "You gotta smoke that shit in here?"

Stark's eyes widened in mock surprise. "It's my office, Crow. You get one, you can pollute it however you damn well please."

"Wouldn't want one," she sneered. "Too damn restrictive."

"You know," he grinned, exhaling a fresh plume of smoke, "there was a time when tobacco was considered good for you."

Lyra barked a laugh. "Yeah, back when bloodletting was cutting-edge medicine. What's next, Stark? You gonna offer me a leech for my troubles?"

"Maybe later, Crow. Maybe later," he wheezed with laughter. "Now, where were we in this delightful descent into madness ..."

The sharp rap of knuckles on the door cut him short. The time flashed in Stark's mind. He offered a smile at the sound. "Nice. Right on the goddamn dot. Come in, come in."

The doorknob clicked and a young woman entered, all sharp angles and jutting cheekbones, framed by a mane of fiery red hair. Her eyes, a light blue, held an intelligence that bordered on unsettling. She wore a lab coat, that had once been pristine white, but now bore the colorful scars and scorch marks of a dozen late-night experiments gone horridly wrong. Lyra recognized her instantly. This wasn't just any lab rat. This was Dr. Rana Sharma, a woman who wrestled with the unknown and usually came out bloody but unbowed.

Stark tried the niceties, "Rana, this here is . . ."

But Lyra wasn't waiting for pleasantries. "Stark cut the crap. Dr. Rana Sharma, I presume? I know all about you."

Rana arched an eyebrow. "Do you now?" she replied in a cool and collected voice.

"The outcast AI shrink." Lyra's gaze was sharp. "Brilliant mind, they say, but a maverick. Kicked out of the sandbox by your own kind for playing with forbidden toys. Rumor has it you have some ... unconventional theories about AI sentience."

Rana grinned, a predator recognizing its kin. "Well, Detective," she snickered, "it seems you do know all about me, then."

Stark steepled his fingers, watching the two women size each other up like hungry wolves eyeing a stray dog. The rhythmic tap-tap-tap of his cigar on the overflowing ashtray was the only sound that broke the tense silence. Finally, he cleared his throat. "Alright, let's cut the bullshit, shall we. Time to get dirty."

He sucked on his cigar, the end of it glowing maliciously like a dying sun. "Crow, with Steele's murder, we need a fresh pair of eyes. Someone who doesn't play patty-cake. Rana knows the systems, the AI, all the arcane tech Steele was messing with. I want her to help us ... well ... to help you. Not as a partner. But as a consultant."

Dammit, Stark!

Lyra bristled. "More like a fuckin' bloodhound you're unleashing on a particularly messy crime scene. Consultant, my ass." A sideways flick of her eyes landed on Rana, the redheaded doctor's grin still plastered on her face. It was a silent promise disguised as a smile that said, "Bring it on."

Stark, stone-faced, echoed, "Consultant."

"Fine," Lyra conceded through gritted teeth. "Flesh and fuckin' bone instead of circuits and code. Fine." She spun to Rana, eyes glinting with a voracious menace. "But let me make one thing clear. This is my turf, my investigation. You tread on my ground, and I'll slice those toes off and feed them to the dogs."

Rana's grin, if possible, widened further. "Wouldn't dream of it. I wouldn't want to get in the way of a rabid detective."

"Alright, alright," Stark was ever trying to be the diplomat. "Let's knock it off. You two wanna rip each other's throats out, take it outside. Preferably someplace with a drain, 'cause the splatter's gonna be impressive." He slammed a hand on his desk, the reports scattering like startled pigeons. "Now, back to the business of not wasting oxygen. Rana, you've had access to the preliminary reports, right?"

She nodded, a cascade of fiery hair swaying as she did. "I've familiarized myself with the case. Steele, his security systems, the missing Mindrot – all a macabre jig. But what I'm most interested in is what's hiding in Steele's neural implant and, of course, that little nugget Detective Crowley so graciously dropped at the scene."

"Fuckin' bots catch everything," Lyra sneered in disdain. "So, what was it that I said?"

"You forgot, Detective?" Rana snickered.

Lyra snapped. "Been fuckin' busy, Doc. Why don't you remind me, Doc."

Rana purred. "Project Janus, Detective," her voice dripping with a mock sweetness. "Project Janus."

Lyra shot up from her chair, a coiled spring finally released. She brushed past Rana. "I don't have time for all this. We need results. Nice meeting you, Doc. I'll be in touch when the real investigation starts."

Stark, caught in the crossfire, sputtered a protest. "Crow! Where the hell are you going?"

Lyra paused at the door. "Gonna hit the pavement. Gotta squish a particularly annoying bug. Don't worry, Stark, I won't track the guts all over your precious office."

Stark slumped back in his chair, defeated. "Fine. Be that way. But the second this temporal turd-storm passes, you and Dr. Sharma are getting together, I'll comm link you the details."

"Can't wait," Lyra snarled.

With that, she slammed the door shut, leaving behind the stale cigar smoke and the lingering scent of something far more intoxicating - the unexpected complication that was Dr. Rana Sharma. The memory of her smile, the way her red hair defied the sterile environment, how her eyes held a fire that mirrored

Lyra's own - it simmered in the air, a spark of something against the oppressive monotony of their world. Lyra couldn't ignore it. It was a wrinkle in the plan, a glitch in the system, and like everything else, she couldn't resist the urge to rip it wide open and see what secrets lay underneath.

4 | The Neon Wound

Lyra navigated the alley, a reeking chasm of neon puke splashing against grime-caked ferrocrete. The air, a toxic gumbo of burnt synth-flesh and overflowing sewage vats, felt like a gloved hand squeezing the life out of her lungs. Hacking, she wrestled a respirator onto her face, the stale recycled air a benediction compared to the caustic stew simmering beyond the cracked filter. It was like breathing molten advertisement vomit, a taste that clung to her tongue even after the helmet was sealed. But at least it wouldn't melt her goddamn lungs.

This neon-diseased fistula, thrumming with signs advertising chrome limbs and dubious upgrades for the desperate, was the only place to find one of her prized rats. The miscreant wasn't picky about his clientele, as long as the creds jingled a certain tune.

Lyra waded through the maze of overflowing trash bins and flickering holographic projections, each step a sickening crunch on bio-luminescent algae. Overflowing bio-waste containers reeked of a thousand rotting synth-steaks, oozing a sickly green slime that lapped at her worn boots. Overhead, a fractured billboard flickered erratically, a half-formed image of a grinning chrome-plated dentist hawking the latest in cybernetic incisors. It cast stroboscopic flashes on the narrow alley, scattering shadows that writhed and danced like wraiths in the putrid air.

She scanned the alley using her cybernetic eye, its enhanced vision cutting through the filth and deception. This was her world, a city pulsating with decay and desperation. And in this ferrocrete jungle, she was the apex predator, ready to pounce on unsuspecting prey.

The billboard sputtered one last time, a dying scream of garish pink, before plunging the alleyway into an oppressive darkness. From the shadows of a doorway slunk a horror, a skeletal frame, all wrong angles, and jutting metal, draped in a tattered poncho barely clinging to a gaunt form. Gnat, they called him. Once, maybe, a human. Now, a grotesque array of metal and pistons, more machine than meat. His limbs, segmented and insectile, ended not in hands but in pincered claws that clicked and gnashed with a life of their own. Every movement brought the sound of industrial torment – the whirring of gears, the low moan of strained servos, the obscene hiss of pneumatics struggling to keep this monstrosity upright. And the face – a patchwork of cybernetic implants obscured any semblance of humanity, leaving behind a distorted chrome skull where teeth, bared in a permanent, nightmarish rictus, clattered incessantly. This wasn't a sound, it was a violation. Bone scraping on bone amplified a thousandfold and laced with a wet, sucking undertone.

"You're late, Crow," came a digitized croak through the clatter. "Time is creds."

"Cut the chit-chat, Gnat," Lyra spat. "I need intel. How much for a high-end memory wipe?"

"Depends on the size of the nightmare you're trying to scrub." Gnat's voice was like gravel grinding gears. His eyes, a pair of mismatched blue marbles swimming in a vat of green oil, twinkled lightheartedly. "You could go budget-brand, but trust me, you'd come cryin' to me when those sewer-spawned gremlins are tap-dancing on your eyelids all night long."

Lyra slammed a wad of creds on a nearby crate, the chink of metal bouncing around the tight space. "Top shelf, express delivery. What you got on Vincent Steele?"

Gnat's eyes narrowed. "Steele? The bigwig at Neogene Dynamics? Word in the gutter is he got iced. Messy, they say. Real messy. Some nasty business."

"Spill it, Gnat."

"Told it wasn't some botched backroom deal or a rival corp putting a laser hole in his chest. Been told his own lab rat, Evelyn Turner, had a little ... payback to give." Gnat leaned closer, his voice a conspiratorial murmur. "She used to work these streets, you know. Pretty thing, back in the day. Turns out, Steele was her gold-plated prick, pulled her out of the muck, gave her a lab coat."

Lyra's gut twisted. "Turner? Never heard the name. You sure that's it?"

Gnat gave a clattery chuckle. "Yeah, Turner. That's it? Let's just say Steele had a taste for the ... unrefined product."

Lyra's voice was a low growl. "So, he picked her up off the curb and turned her into a goddamn prodigy?"

"It happens, Crow. Street trash to silicon hotshot. But some IOUs ... they never get paid in full." Gnat's voice clanged like a malfunctioning garbage disposal. He waved a claw-like hand, the neon lights reflecting off his metallic implants "This whole fuckin' city ain't paved with sunshine. It's mortared with debts, favors, and bargains struck in the dark."

"What would make her silence him?" Lyra pressed, a cold knot forming in her stomach. "What did Steele have on her?"

Gnat shrugged, the movement jerky and mechanical. "Could be anything," he clattered. "Maybe she just got tired of scrubbing clean the mind of a dirty old man. Maybe she stumbled on some psycho-crud in his noodle forest that'd make a roach puke. Who knows? Street rumors are like bad synth-steak – it tastes good going down but burns like hell coming out."

"Lovers?" Lyra asked.

"I'm sure. Why not. He sure as hell made quite the downpayment."

"You know where this Turner chick hangs out?"

A humorless rattle escaped Gnat, a sound that scraped against Lyra's nerves. "Restricted territory, Crow. No way in or out, unless of course, one has security clearance. Spends most of her time holed up at Neogene Dynamics, fiddling with brains or whatever it is they do there. But she does venture out sometimes. Got a taste for the old ways – likes to visit The Shelves."

"The Shelves?"

"Yeah, books. You know, those paper things with words and stuff? Ever seen one?" Gnat's metallic grin stretched revealing a row of chipped, yellowed teeth.

Lyra ignored the taunt, a hazy memory flickering in the corner of her mind - her mother's voice, a soft melody weaving a story from a book with worn pages. The memory surfaced briefly, then vanished as swiftly as it came. "Can you tell me when she visits The Shelves?"

"Tell you what – I can slap a tracer on her. Track her movements. See where the brain-tickler goes after work. Next time she hits The Shelves, you get a heads-up on your commlink."

"I bet you got a tracer on just about everyone in the city?"

"Not everyone, Crow," Gnat countered, a hint of pride in his metallic clatter. "Just the most interesting ones. Information's my currency, after all."

Lyra narrowed her eyes. "You got a tracer on me, too?"

He threw back his head and let out a clattering laugh, the sound ringing through the grimy alleyway. "Nah, Crow. No need to track you. You're like a goddamn neon sign advertising chaos wherever you go. Leave a trail of trouble wider than a faulty cargo drone."

Lyra straightened, a storm brewing in her steely eyes. She threw a few more creds on the crate. "You've earned them. But if I find out you're feeding me dregs … you know what I'll do."

"Do what? Shut me down. You ain't got the muscle for that, Crow. This city runs on information, and that's my currency." Gnat's clattering became a manic rhythm, his eyes narrowed with a ravening glint. "But hey, you scratch my back, I scratch yours. I'll keep an ear out for anything related to Steele or Turner. Maybe next time, we can talk about some of the shit hidden in your records."

"Is that a threat?" she scowled. "This damn city's nothing but a threat, dripping poison with a neon smile. And yeah. I got shit in my records. Who doesn't? I don't scare easily, Gnat."

Her fingers twitched towards the blaster strapped to her thigh. Gnat knew too much. Knew her past, her demons. But she needed him, needed his street wisdom to navigate the filth underbelly of the city.

Gnat's eyes darted like a trapped spider, then narrowed further. "Easy there, Crow. Don't get what circuits you got in a twist. You need me more than you think. This city chews up meatbags faster than a roach motel. You know that." He locked eyes with her, the usual agitated clatter now replaced by a slow, menacing rattle. "If you haven't figured it out, you got a target on your back. This Steele shit, it ain't good. Not good at all."

"Target. Like I give a damn."

He smirked. "Maybe you should, Crow. This Steele business ... this could get you deeper in the muck than a sewer diver."

"I ain't afraid of the dark, Gnat. I was born in it."

He gave a clattering smile.

With a parting glare, Lyra turned, the neon lights flaying her face raw with their lurid glow. The annoying sound of Gnat's clattering faded into the background noise of the city's perpetual malfunction.

Evelyn Turner? Steele's salvaged genius. Once a street rat, now a corporate scientist. Could she have a reason to kill?

Lyra wasn't certain. She needed Gnat's intel, but she knew it was often as unreliable as a politician's promise. What mattered most was the tracer, if Gnat would indeed manage to plant it.

He won't fuck me. He knows better.

She skulked out of the alley, the cityscape a suffocating pressure cooker, a million glittering eyes blind to the human tragedy playing out beneath their cold, uncaring gaze. A digital pulse flashed the time in her retinal display – time to punch out.

Time to get the hell out of this wasteland and drown her sorrows in something stronger than lukewarm coffee. Home, if you could call that overpriced shoebox a home, beckoned.

Lyra's apartment door hung a twisted wreck hanging by a single hinge. The keypad dangled like a severed limb, its guts spilling onto the floor in a gruesome display. Her gut clenched, a vice tightening around her insides.

Fuck!

Her hand snapped to the worn hilt of her plasma blaster, knuckles white against the cold metal. Every cynical nerve in her body screamed ambush, a primal fear that resonated deeper than any street-learned caution. This wasn't a break-in, it was an invitation. An invitation scrawled in the foul air, a silent dare from some unseen predator waiting to pounce in the shadows of her own goddamn home. Her pulse hammered a frantic tempo, each beat a drumbeat in the dirge of impending doom.

The stench of something rotten, something alien, slammed into Lyra as she pushed the door aside, its hinges creaking in protest. Not the usual stale odor of recycled air that clung to the underbelly of the city. No. But something altogether worse. A metallic talon, cold and honed, ripped into her throat, pure and unadulterated, clawing its way into her lungs and scraping against the raw meat of her fear. The smell of violation made physical.

"Furball?" Her voice cracked, a stranger to the silence. "Where are you, my lil' honey?"

Usually, the cat was always at the door meowing and rubbing up against her.

But now – nothing.

Lyra took a deep breath and slipped into her apartment. Her eyes darted around the space. No intruder. But the scene that greeted her was a distortion of the cramped, lovingly cluttered chaos she called home. Its innards spilled forth like exposed entrails - furniture lay overturned, and clothes, meticulously patched and re-patched from scavenged fabric, were scattered like confetti. And in the center of it all, a crumpled form.

The words "Oh no" died in her throat, a strangled whimper snatched away by the cold grip of sadness.

Furball.

She sank to her knees, cradling the limp form that had once been a vibrant ball of purrs, the source of warmth and companionship in this desolate world.

So silent, so utterly still.

The sleek black fur, usually shimmering with a healthy sheen, now hung matted, dull, and lifeless. But it was the vacant, green eyes, reflecting a distorted image of the cracked ceiling, that sent a raw scream creeping its way up Lyra's throat. It died on her tongue, replaced by a morbid curiosity battling the rising tide of grief.

With trembling hands, she gently peeled back the fur on Furball's chest, revealing a gruesome sight. Green fluid sloshed around a tangle of wires and miniature metallic gears, the synthetic innards of her beloved companion spilling out.

A strangled sob escaped her lips. "Poor lil' honey. What have they done to you?"

Suddenly, a faint flicker of movement in Furball's eye caught her attention. A pinprick of light flared to life, then steadied into a cold, electric glow. Above the lifeless form, a holographic inscription shimmered into existence, its words stark and chilling: "Emergency AI Function Activated: Final Moments Recorded."

She tapped the inscription with an unsteady hand. The apartment lights flickered back to life, harsh and white. Furball's lifeless form shimmered and from her eyes came a holographic projection – a grainy, shaky video feed.

On the screen, her apartment played out in miniature chaos. Furniture toppled, clothes ripped. But the horror wasn't the destruction, it was the figure that stalked through the wreckage. Clad in black leather, it moved with predatory grace, silent, efficient, and utterly terrifying. The intruder's face remained mostly obscured by shadows, but a single detail pierced the veil of darkness with a shard of ice – a festering angel tattoo, its wings dripping like corrupted ink, sprawled across the intruder's neck. Lyra knew with an unnerving certainty who it belonged to.

Mother Fucka!

A low growl escaped her lips. Mother Fucka, Doc Jones' most notorious fixer, had been here, knee-deep in Lyra's meager belongings, and for some goddamn reason, saw fit to trash the place and kill Furball.

Tears welled up in Lyra's eyes, blurring the holographic image. Furball wasn't just a synth-cat, damn it. She was a repository of memories, a silent witness to Lyra's lonely nights and hard-won victories. She held a recording of Lyra's mother's voice, a digitized whisper from before the Big Burn. Whenever Lyra yearned for the past that no longer existed, Furball would play her mother's voice for her.

Had to be thousands of times.

"Play mom's voice."

The usual whirring of gears, the telltale click of the recording activating was absent. There was only silence.

Now, that too, was gone, ripped away along with the comforting purr and the soft weight of a synthetic head-butt.

Anger, sharp and cold, cut through the grief. Mother Fucka and Doc Jones would pay, alright, and pay dearly. She envisioned their regret, their terror, and a feral smile crept across her face. They'd rue the day they crossed her, and she would make sure every moment of their suffering was etched in the annals of vengeance.

She punched off the holographic projection, the silence in the trashed apartment louder than the loudest noise one could imagine. Heaving herself up, she stumbled towards the disposal and popped the hatch. Furball, once a defiant ball of purring fluff, lay limp in her arms. Tears blurred her vision as she pressed a kiss, cold and final, to the matted fur. Then, she gently placed Furball into the disposal and with a mechanical twist, she slammed the hatch shut. The whoosh the disposal unit, the mechanical sucking sound of oblivion, stole the last echoes of Furball's existence. In the sterile silence that followed, only the jagged gasps of Lyra's grief remained.

With a deep sigh, she shuffled to the repurposed industrial synthesizer sitting in the corner. A twisted mess of scavenged tech and jury-rigged wires, it was barely capable of synthing a halfway decent meal from recycled sludge. Today, though, the menu wasn't protein paste. Today, she aimed for something more delicate: a basic code blueprint for a black synth-cat.

Feeding the blueprint into the whirring, groaning machine, Lyra felt a fist clench around her heart. Could she forget the purring ball of black fur that had been her only companion in this chrome-plated hellhole? Forget the way it would nuzzle against her cold fingers, a tiny furnace of warmth in a world perpetually on the verge of freezing over? Fuck no. But the new synth-cat wouldn't be a replacement. It would be a continuation, a bridge built across the chasm of grief. Furball deserved a successor, a cold, metallic heir to inherit the legacy of a life unfairly cut short.

Another sigh, this one laced with bitter hope, and she hit the activation button. The synthesizer hummed to life, sparking and groaning in protest. Slowly, the familiar form of a black cat began to take shape, its synthetic fur shimmering as it solidified.

"There you are," Lyra smiled wiping back her tears. "There's my Furball." The name stuck in her throat, a half-truth, a memory of a time when synthetic affection felt comforting, not like a constant reminder of loss.

The new Furball purred, its sound too precise, too calculated, too mechanical - a chorus of artificial warmth that nonetheless managed to thaw a corner of Lyra's guarded heart. She reached out, pulling the little cat close, burying her face in its synthetic softness. But her brief moment of solace was shattered by the harsh clang of metal against the floor.

The food dish.

The cat jumped from Lyra's arms.

Food.

Lyra watched as the cat devoured its synthetic kibble. Her gaze then swept across the apartment that was a mess.

"Yeah, Furball," she sighed. "Looks like we got a lot to clean up, you and me. Don't we?"

The cat paused mid-crunch, its synthetic eyes shining in the dim light. It let out a single, metallic meow, a sound that somehow mirrored the grinding gears of the city outside. Lyra stared back. Some things never change at all.

The city outside Lyra's window was a metallic beast clawing its way awake with the groaning grind of elevated trains and the choking cough of a million exhaust pipes. A sliver of sunlight, sickly and gray, managed to pierce the smog and illuminate the grimy confines of her apartment. She sat upright in bed, the metallic rasp of springs protesting her every move. Sleep, if one could call it that, had offered little respite. The events of the previous day were a churning mass of unanswered questions and raw anger.

She stretched. At least no nightmares this time.

A low, synthetic purr drew her attention. Furball, her sleek black fur gleaming in the meager light, sat at the foot of the bed, green eyes fixed on Lyra with a disturbing earnestness. Lyra forced a smile, the gesture feeling brittle on her face. "There you are. Keeping an eye on things, huh?"

The little cat emitted a series of clicks and chirps, her face tilting with something that almost resembled a smile. The last Furball would have nestled against her, offering warmth and comfort. This one, however, remained at a distance, a reminder of the tragedy that birthed its existence.

Lyra dragged herself upright, her body screaming with aches and creaks. A glance at her reflection in the mirror confirmed her suspicions – she looked like hell warmed over. Her eyes, ringed with shadows, and the glint in them belonged not to a detective, but to a desperate animal trapped in a steel cage. The shower was a brutal awakening to the grime clinging to her like a second skin. She scrubbed and scalded, trying to wash away more than just the physical filth, as the image of the festering angel tattoo throbbed in her mind. It was a dull ache, a reminder of Doc Jones' enforcer.

She'll be mine. Don't you worry Furball. She'll be mine, alright.

Fueled by burnt toast and a simmering pot of rage, Lyra left her apartment. The city outside throbbed with a chaotic life of its own. Traffic, a tangled mess of hovercars and sputtery delivery drones, weaved through the streets in a ballet of near-misses and ear-splitting horns. The rhythm, a harshness of screeching metal and pulsing neon, was white noise to everyone else, but to Lyra, it was a discordant symphony, each screech a note in a song of urban decay.

Navigating the tangled streets, she plunged deeper into the city's bowels, where darkness and neon bled into a festering wound only she seemed immune to. Her destination: a greasy spoon café with more flickering neon than charm, a place where shadows lurked and secrets traded hands over lukewarm coffee.

Lyra slid into a booth, worn fake leather clinging to her. Across from her sat Dr. Rana Sharma, her fiery red hair defying the dim lighting, was already nursing a steaming cup of coffee. Their first meeting had been a verbal sparring match, a clash of egos that left the air thick with tension. But something was different. Now, there was a flicker of something new in Lyra's eyes – maybe concern, or maybe just ... curiosity? She couldn't quite put her finger on it, but it did something unexpected to her stomach. It wasn't a fluttering, exactly, more like a sudden tightening.

"Detective," Rana acknowledged with a look of worry. "Rough morning?" It wasn't a question, but Lyra appreciated the acknowledgment, nonetheless.

"Assholes" Lyra began. "Tore my goddamn apartment to shreds. Didn't even bother taking anything. Just trashed it for the hell of it. Junk anyway, most of it. But they got my cat, Furball."

Rana, her gaze as sharp as the angles of her face, leaned forward. "Your cat?"

"Killed it."

For a fleeting moment, something akin to empathy glinted in Rana's eyes. Her voice softened. "Condolences, Detective."

Lyra sucked in a breath, holding back her grief. "Just synthed another one."

"Do you know who did it?"

"Think so. One of Doc Jones' pieces of shit."

"Doc Jones?"

"The slime that sold Mindrot to Steele."

Rana leaned back and took another sip of coffee. "Did you inform Stark?"

Lyra scoffed. "Stark? He'd drown me in paperwork before I could even think about retribution. Besides, this is my mess. I'll clean it up."

"Alone?" Rana raised an eyebrow, skepticism etched on her sharp features. "Reckless, Detective. Especially considering the forces likely at play."

Lyra's response died in her throat, stifled by the high-pitched whine of tortured servos announcing the arrival of their mechanical waiter. A skeletal chrome nightmare with articulated limbs slithered toward them, stopping with a pneumatic hiss at their booth. It balanced a dented cup of tepid sludge on a metal tray the size of a hubcap. "Coffee?" it asked Lyra.

Lyra ignored the bot, her hand quickly snatching the cup. One sip and her face contorted into a grimace as if she'd swallowed battery acid. "Look, Doc, I appreciate the concern, but subtlety isn't exactly my forte. Besides, sometimes the best way to get a message across is to paint it on the goddamn wall in blood."

Rana simply shook her head, a slow smile spreading across her face. Stark wasn't the only one who'd underestimated this steel-wool woman.

"But," Lyra's voice dropped, "there's somethin' I gotta know. About someone. Maybe someone you know."

"Shoot," Rana was intrigued by the sudden shift in gears.

"Evelyn Turner. Ring any bells?" Lyra took another sip and again grimaced. "Shit ass of a brew. Why do I bother coming here?"

Rana uncrossed her legs, the movement sharp and controlled. "Evelyn Turner. I know of her," she began. "Academic golden girl of neuro-augmentation research. Papers published in every scientific feed that matters. Awards stacked higher than a garbage heap on the street outside. A celebrity in the field."

"Yeah, yeah, accolades and bullshit," Lyra scowled. "But what does she actually do?"

Rana's lips curved into a smile that never reached her eyes. "That, Detective, is the fascinating part. Her published work focuses on non-invasive interfaces, delicate tinkering at the fringes of human cognition. But rumors in the dark corners of the field, paint a different picture. A shadow project, whispers of pushing the boundaries of ethical research, of burrowing deep into the mind and twisting its very fabric."

Lyra's scowl deepened. "So, this Dr. Turner is playing God? Shocking. Project Janus?"

Rana nodded. "But how did you hear of her?"

"A little bug told me. Seems Steele had a liking for young meat. Took her off the streets. Cleaned her up and sent her off to school. But you didn't hear that from me, Doc."

"Young meat, you say?" Rana lit a cigarette. "So, Steele fancied himself a collector of strays, did he?"

"Especially ones, it would seem, with a sharp mind and a rebellious streak."

"Interesting," Rana mused, her voice a smoky whisper as she took a long drag from her cigarette.

"It does make you wonder," Lyra replied, her eyes narrowing with curiosity. "Was Turner driven by a thirst for knowledge, or was it the allure of power that beckoned him? The line between the two seems perilously thin."

Rana took another drag from her cigarette. "Power," she mused, the word rolling off her tongue like a curse. "A seductive siren song, especially in a world teetering on the precipice of technological singularity. From what I know, Project Janus is all about unlocking the deepest recesses of the human mind, rewriting its very code … the potential for both utopia and dystopia is staggering."

"And Evelyn Turner," Lyra pressed, "is the key to unlocking it, right?"

Rana sighed, a plume of smoke curling towards the grime-coated ceiling. "Perhaps. Or perhaps she's a pawn in a larger game, a talented but expendable player in a high-stakes chess match between rival corporations and power-hungry governments. Who knows. But when it's all said and done, Vincent Steele controlled everything I would assume."

"Ah, our butchered executive," Lyra interjected. "But if Turner's got her little fingers wrapped around Project Janus, then she's tangled herself up with something far more dangerous than a night on the streets."

"Dangerous indeed," Rana conceded. "But underestimating Dr. Turner would be a grave mistake, Detective. If what you were told is true, I'm sure she's not some naive waif plucked off a street corner. Most likely, she's cunning, ambitious, and fiercely protective of her work."

"Well, is she? You know her."

Rana was sharp. "Know of her, I said. Big difference. And frankly, what does all this matter? We can't get to her, to talk to her. There's no way we're getting into Neogene Dynamics and I'm sure she lives in the restricted territory." She mirrored Lyra's earlier scowl with a pointed sip of her lukewarm coffee.

Lyra matched Rana sip for sip, her scowl deepening. "Right on all counts, Doc. Rumor has it she ventures out occasionally to The Shelves."

"A public space. Interesting. If only we knew when she's there."

Lyra smiled. "Got that covered."

Rana's lips quirked up in a sly twist. "I have no doubt."

"Ever heard of The Forgotten Realm?"

Rana shook her head, unease crossing her face. "Why?"

A feral glitter ignited in Lyra's eyes. "Because you're about to experience a real education. We're going to pay a visit to the monster who took Furball from me."

Rana's lips thinned. "Are you sure that's wise?"

"Wise? Maybe not." Lyra's voice was a flatline. "But necessary? Absolutely."

Dr. Rana Sharma felt the bile churn in her throat, a rancid concoction far more potent than any poison this squalid dive could serve up. The Forgotten Realm wasn't a sanctuary for the soul-weary; it was a mausoleum for the still-breathing. A derelict neon sign, its lights like the dead eyes of a forgotten god, sneered down at her. The air stank of stale smoke and festering despair, threatening to coalesce into a suffocating miasma. This wasn't somewhere you simply walked into. No. This was a place that, if you dared to draw a breath too near, would reach out with a filth-encrusted claw and yank you, kicking and wailing, into its reeking abyss.

Lyra, bless her reckless heart, navigated this cesspool with the predatory grace of a shark in a feeding frenzy. Rana, on the other hand, felt like a scalpel plunged headfirst into a vat of radioactive sewage. Every fiber of her being, from the meticulously styled mane of hair to the sterile efficiency of her mind, revolted. This was the underbelly of the city, a place raw and pulsating with a primal savagery that made her skin crawl. The patrons slumped on cracked vinyl, their eyes hollow and vacant, reflecting the soul-sucking rot that permeated this place. Shame prickled at her – a scientist venturing into a harsh wilderness she barely understood. Yet, a morbid curiosity danced alongside the disgust. Here, in this foul petri dish of humanity, perhaps some answer, some dark truth about the case, might slither forth. But the price of such knowledge, she feared, might be a piece of her own sanity.

Lyra's voice erupted, a jagged shard of sound that sliced through the bar's oppressive haze. "Where is she?!" she roared, each word a fiery ember launched from the furnace of her rage.

A scrawny figure, huddled in a nearby booth, jumped like a startled cockroach. "Cr-Crow! Wh-what the …" The sniveling wretch stammered, his eyes wide with terror.

Lyra, barely glancing at him, snarled, "Sit your ass back down, Scrap. I'm not here for you."

A greasy-haired hulk of a bartender, his arms adorned with peeling tattoos, thunked a mug down on the counter. "Who you lookin' for this time, dollface?"

"You know who. That fat piece of …"

A voice like a nervous cough cut through the gloom. "Not here, Detective," Doc Jones stuttered, his usual nervous tick amplified to a full-blown seizure. Perched precariously on the top step, he clutched the hand of the abomination that was Aurora like a lifeline. "Hauled down to Central by some chromehounds."

The words were barely out of Jones' mouth when a sharp digital chirp pierced through Lyra's mind, a commlink notification directly to her neural implant. It was Stark, his voice a digital growl crackling inside her head. "Crow. Get your ass down here. We got a suspect based on the cam vid outside Steele's penthouse. One of Doc Jones' goons."

"Female?"

"Yeah. A big one. Real big. With a bad attitude," Stark replied.

A smile, slow and wild, stretched across Lyra's face. "Will be there. Crow out." The last word was a caustic hiss, the comm link snapping shut.

Then, a harsh, guttural laugh erupted from Lyra's throat. It wasn't a sound of amusement; it was the chilling sound of madness and bloodlust, a hunter's roar echoing through the fetid bar. In that moment, the Forgotten Realm ceased to be the most disgusting place Rana had ever seen. It had become a stage, and Lyra, bathed in the sickly neon glow, had just taken the spotlight.

With a contemptuous flick of her middle finger to Doc Jones, Lyra stormed out of the bar, Rana trailing behind like a bewildered lab rat swept up in a hurricane.

"What the hell just happened?" Rana called out to Lyra.

"Just wait. You'll see."

Lyra plunged herself into the sleek embrace of the hovercar. Rana tumbled in after her, her mind still grappling with the chaos that had unfolded at the Forgotten Realm. Rain lashed against the panoramic windows, a relentless grey veil obscuring the usual neon-drenched cityscape. The silver hovercar, a shimmering teardrop against the rain-slicked cityscape, hummed to life, its interior a haven of cool sterility compared to the fetid bar they'd just vacated.

"Central," Lyra snapped at the hovercar's AI bot.

The synthetic tones of the bot responded, a placid monotone that did little to mask the underlying complexity of its processing power responded. "Acknowledged, Detective. Initiating quickest route to Central Precinct."

A low whirring confirmed the hovercar's acceptance, followed by a surge of acceleration that dissolved the cityscape into an unrecognizable smear of color. The sleek chrome and glass shell became their bubble, hurtling through the neon tempest outside. It was a fragile barrier between them and the brutal reality that clawed at the city's underbelly.

Rana cleared her throat, the sound thin and reedy in the enclosed space. "Lyra what the hell just went down in there?"

Lyra ignored her, her gaze locked on the rain-streaked world rushing past. It was a world she knew intimately, one woven from grit, grime, and the neon glow of desperation. The rhythmic drumming of the rain on the hovercar's roof began to mimic the frantic beat of her own heart. Each thud was a hammer blow, driving a single, primal thought deeper into her skull: vengeance.

Minutes melted into an unending silence, the city lights outside a blurred reflection of the turmoil within.

Finally, she spoke, her words emerging as a low growl roughened with a dangerous edge, "You know something, Doc . . . revenge . . . it's a thing of beauty."

Rana's brow furrowed beneath the harsh fluorescent light emanating from the hovercar's control panel. "What are you talking about?"

Lyra turned, her eyes burning with an intensity that made Rana flinch. They were cold and calculating and yet filled with a manic glee that worried Rana. "You wouldn't understand," Lyra scoffed. "You spend your time tinkering with your lab equipment and theories, too busy dissecting the world to ever feel its pulse."

Rana bristled. "I understand the human condition better than you ever will." The words were like an accusatory finger jab at Lyra. "I've seen the scars left by violence. More of it in the cold, blue glow of my microscope than you've ever seen in all your time chasing shadows down those dark, smelly alleys of yours. The damage carved into the human psyche ..."

"Damage? You call it damage, Doc?" Lyra snickered. "That's the thing you lab rats never seem to grasp. The only way to heal that 'damage' is to tear it open wider, let the infection bleed out."

Rana felt a cold dread pool in the pit of her stomach. It wasn't the violence Lyra spoke of that terrified her, it was the scary conviction in her voice. This wasn't a woman seeking justice, this was a woman possessed by revenge. A dark fascination gnawed at Rana. Was Lyra always like this, a simmering cauldron of rage barely contained? Or had the neon city, that stench-filled monstrosity outside, slowly chipped away at her, shaping this hunger for vengeance from her very soul?

"Vengeance is a disease.," Rana pressed, a desperate plea cutting through the hovercar's oppressive hum. "It consumes you, rots you from the inside out until nothing remains but a hollow shell filled with hate."

Lyra threw back her head and laughed. It was the same harsh, guttural, grating sound Rana had heard back at the Forgotten Realm. It cut at her like broken glass skittering across ferrocrete. "Hollow shell? Maybe. But at least I'll be a hollow shell that got some goddamn satisfaction."

The hovercar hurled to a halt, thrusting them both back to reality. The sterile white glow of the Central Precinct sign bled through the rain-streaked windshield.

"Here we are," the bot announced in its emotionless voice.

Lyra, with movements sharp and voracious, flew open her door and jumped out of the hovercar. "You can stay here if you want," she leaned back in, her eyes glistening with a manic hunger. "Or, you can witness something truly beautiful. Something you wouldn't understand with your fancy lab coat and instruments."

Rana winced under the intensity of that look. It was the gaze of a cornered wolf, fangs bared and muscles coiled, ready to tear the world apart rather than yield. Rana raised a hand, a half-formed plea escaping her lips. But the hovercar door slammed shut and she was left alone, staring out at the stark gray monolith. The rain, a relentless downpour, had already swallowed Lyra whole.

Slumping back in her seat, a defeated sigh escaped Rana's lips. She reached out her hand and opened the door. She didn't understand what had driven Lyra down this path, what darkness festered beneath the tough exterior of the detective. But one thing was clear: Lyra was on a collision course with her own demons, and Rana feared she wouldn't be coming back from this one whole.

The rain continued to lash. Rana brought her hood up and ran into the building.

5 | Deeper Truths Buried

The steel doors of Central wheezed open, spitting Lyra and Rana into a sterile lobby of harsh fluorescent white lights that bleached the air of any warmth. It reeked of a metallic tang that scraped at the back of their throats, a cloying undercurrent of fear and stale misery. Lyra stalked forward, a predator on the prowl, with Rana in her wake. Huddled behind a curved, reinforced glass partition sat a young sergeant hunched over his console. His face, pale, held a permanent expression of confusion and was dominated by oversized glasses that magnified his wide, watery eyes.

Always a different one! How many do they have?

Lyra slammed her hand on the glass, making him jump.

"Where is she?" she growled.

The sergeant looked up, startled by the sheer force of Lyra's presence. His face was ashen under her icy stare. "Who ... who ... are you looking for, Detective?" he stammered, his voice barely a squeak.

"Fuckin' useless!" she sprang at him from the other side of the glass. "You know who! Where is she?"

The sergeant shrank back in his chair, his Adam's apple bobbing like a frantic fish. "She, uh ... she was taken down to

Interrogation, Detective," he finally blurted out. "But you need clearance …"

Lyra didn't waste another breath on him. She whipped around, her eyes locking with Rana's. "Ready, Doc?" she rumbled.

Rana knew all too well what that look meant. It was the look of an animal about to rip the leash from its collar, the look of a storm about to unleash its fury. Despite her fear and unease, Rana straightened her shoulders and met Lyra's gaze. "Always," she replied.

Lyra smirked, a brief flash of something akin to respect cutting through the storm clouds in her eyes. Then, she brought an eye to the retinal scanner. As the red light bathed her eye, a network of holographic lines flickered to life, a visual representation of the security protocols being accessed.

"Plasma blaster detected. Right thigh holster," the security scanner system alerted.

"For the millionth time … you're not getting it!" she shouted at the sergeant, pounding on the glass. "Get on your commlink now and tell Interrogation, we're on the way! You know who we are!"

"But you need clearance …"

With a movement so fluid it was obscene, the plasma blaster was out of its holster and aimed dead center at the sergeant's forehead. "You know a plasma blaster will shoot right through just about anything. So, you got two choices, and neither involves wasting my goddamn time. Option one: get on your commlink and announce our grand arrival with all the fanfare you can muster. Option two: I paint this steel wall a vibrant shade of crimson with your brain matter. Got it."

The sergeant's eyes, wide with a mixture of terror and something similar to awe, were glued to the pulsating red kiss of her blaster's aiming sight. He could feel the ruby brand burning on his forehead. With a gulp, he opened his commlink. "Interrogation. Detective Lyra Crowley and Dr. Rana Sharma are on their way."

Rana, caught in the maelstrom of Lyra's fury, jammed an eye to the retinal scanner. The scanner whined before spitting out a grudging hum of confirmation. With a metallic hiss, the turbolift's door slid open.

The two stepped through the opening without hesitation. The sterile, white interior of the lift offered no sanctuary for Rana. Instead, it felt like a metal coffin hurtling her toward an uncertain fate. Below them, the city sprawled out like a diseased organism, bathed in the neon glow of a dying sun. The ascent was a gut-wrenching fusion of groans and shudders, the turbolift struggling to overcome the city's oppressive gravity. It was a vertical climb higher and higher still, until there came a jolt, a horizontal shift, as they were launched sideways through layers of decay, each floor offering a glimpse into Central – overflowing garbage chutes spewing reeking refuse, flickering fluorescent lights illuminating grimy hallways, and the distant, muffled screams of some poor bastard enduring Interrogation's enhanced techniques.

Rana, her breath coming in gasps, stole a glance at Lyra. There was an unbending resolve in her eyes, the hunger for vengeance burning with an unholy intensity. It was a look that made Rana shiver, a stark reminder of the predator she now shared this metallic cage with. At that moment, the sterile walls of the turbolift morphed into a crucible, leaving Rana uncertain whether they were rising to justice or plunging into a nightmare.

A metallic wheeze, the groan of reluctant gears, and the lift's door slid open. Beyond, a sterile steel corridor stretched out, lined with numbered chambers like cold tombs. A silent hover bot zipped past, its monotone voice a mechanical herald: "Number 26."

Lyra and Rana marched down the corridor, the sound of their footsteps bouncing off the unyielding metal walls. Finally, they reached the designated crypt. The door sighed open, revealing Stark, perched before a darkened observation window.

"Well ... well ... didn't take you long, Crow," Stark remarked.

Lyra's gut clenched. Her throat burned with the unspoken, a torrent of obscenities trapped behind a dam of cold, calculating silence.

"Show me," she snarled, her eyes gleaming with malice. "Show me the video of the Chromehound dragging her in."

Stark nodded curtly. He jabbed a finger at a nearby console, and a hologram came to life, a spectral image of the nightmare she so desperately craved to witness.

The three watched as a sliver of chrome caught the grime-coated moonlight, a fleeting glint in the fetid alleyway outside the Forgotten Realm. The beast, a Chromehound, a humanoid automaton built from a nightmarishly strong alloy, rounded the corner with a destructive grace that belied its bulk. Its form mimicked a man, but the resemblance ended there. Where a human face should have been, a featureless mask of chrome stared out, devoid of empathy or judgment.

Its quarry, Doc Jones' enforcer, Mother Fucka.

The mountain of a woman froze mid-stride, her bluster evaporating faster than spilled liquor as she saw the menace enter. The Chromehound surged forward, silent and unstoppable. It easily threw Jones' goons aside, their laser fire, more of a light show than a threat, pinging uselessly off its armored hide. Mother Fucka's eyes, one a natural blue, the other a cold, blue cybernetic marble, bulged with primordial terror. She tried to fight, but her cybernetically enhanced reflexes, usually lethal, failed her miserably. The machine slammed into her, its metallic limbs wrapping around her with a sickening crunch. The exhalation of escaping air from her lungs was the only sound to break the horrific silence that followed.

In a heartbeat, Mother Fucka found herself encased in a chilling embrace. A cold sheen of chrome spread across her body, stealing her breath and her sense of security. Only portions of her head remained free, a grotesque, chrome-framed portrait of a woman facing her doom. Her eyes, framed by cold chrome sockets, and her mouth, half-covered by a metallic grille, felt like it was being stretched by an invisible hand. She could speak, but only if the Chromehound willed it.

She stammered, a pathetic mewling sound escaping the constricted grille, "Wh ... what are you doing? Let me go!"

The Chromehound tilted its featureless head. Mother Fucka, could only whimper, knowing this machine wasn't programmed for conversation. It was a steel executioner, a hunter designed for one purpose: to capture the guilty and deliver them, writhing and encased, to the waiting arms of the justice system.

"Seen enough?" Stark asked Lyra.

She squeezed her eyes shut, fists clenching and unclenching, trying to dam the tidal wave of anger threatening to drown her. Stark punched at the console and the hologram flickered off.

"She broke into my apartment. Trashed the place. Killed my little Furball."

"Your cat?" Stark asked.

"The poor little thing caught it all on her vid cam."

"How do you know it was her?"

Lyra pointed to the side of her neck. "A tattoo, a twisted, bleeding angel."

Stark let out a grunt that could almost be mistaken for sympathy. "Yeah, that's her. Look, Crow," his voice softened, a rare and nearly welcomed concession, "about your cat ... I didn't know. You should've said something."

"What difference would it have made?" she snapped, forcing a semblance of control. Her voice then hitched, raw and exposed. "So, you saw that fat shit on the cam outside Steele's penthouse."

Stark nodded. "Walked right into the place."

"Anything on Steele's neural implant yet."

Stark leaned back in his chair, a sardonic smile twisting his lips. "Oh, you'll get a kick out of this. The bastard doesn't have one. Surgically removed."

Lyra's face contorted in disgust. "Of course. When you're a trillionaire, the law becomes a suggestion, best ignored."

Rana chimed in, a cold slice of reason cutting through the emotional carnage. "Probably done at Neogene Dynamics, the black market surgeons of the rich and powerful. Guaranteed no trail left behind."

"Clean," Stark confirmed, his voice flat. "But there was something else. Our boy Steele had a little extra baggage tucked away in his noodle. Traces of some kind of chip wedged deep into his... what the hell did they call it... hippocampus ... I think that's what the bot said."

Confusion crawled across Lyra's face. "What the fuck is a ... hippocampus."

Rana offered a concise explanation. "Brain region. Memory lane. Dreamscape central. Complex structure, tucked away in the temporal lobe, plays a starring role in learning and remembering stuff. But it's a delicate little thing. Highly adaptable. Plastic, even."

"Plastic?"

Words seemed to be stuck on Rana's tongue, frustration twisting her features. "Not the plastic that you're thinking of. The brain's not some static lump. It bends, it twists, it rewrites itself based on what you learn, what you see. Scientists call it 'plastic,' because of its ability to adapt. But this hippocampus? It's the master of adaptation. The most malleable part. That's why it gets messed up so easily — bad experiences, diseases, all that crap. It takes your short-term memories and files them away for the long haul. Plus, it manages your emotional baggage — anxiety, dodging things you hate. All that."

Lyra turned to Stark, her eyes like twin lasers, cutting through any pretense. "You said traces?" she demanded, a blade honed to draw blood. "Are you telling me the removal of this chip was anything but a clean break?"

Stark shook his head.

"What the fuck?" Lyra sighed, frustration seeping into her voice.

Rana just shrugged. "My guess? Removing a chip from the memory vault wouldn't be easy. Especially when it's buried deep in the hippocampus."

"None of this matters," Stark growled. "We have Steele's murderer. And she's on the other side of the window."

A slow burn ignited in Lyra's gut. "When can I begin to interrogate that piece of shit?"

Stark's posture snapped ramrod straight, his gaze hardening. "Crow, you get to do jack shit. This goes by the book. No rogue interrogations that'll blow the whole damn case. We're calling in a bot."

Lyra's frustration detonated. Her hands shot skyward, a strangled cry curling its way up her throat and morphing into a guttural curse. "Dammit to hell!"

"Sorry Crow. Too much riding on this one."

Lyra and Rana each took a seat.

"Start the process," Stark ordered through his commlink.

He punched a few more buttons on the console and the observation window fizzed to life.

On the other side, Lyra saw her prey snared. Mother Fucka was a prisoner in her own body, encased in the cold kiss of steel, her constant reminder of the humanity she'd long since bartered away. The metallic sheen taunted the warmth of flesh and blood, leaving only slivers of her face exposed - eyes, wide and pleading, held captive by emotionless metal sockets - and a mouth, forever silenced by a metal grill, that turned her screams into a strangled, inhuman rasp. This was mechanized justice in a metal sarcophagus, where the only mercy was the swift cessation of existence at the hands of the unfeeling beast that held her captive.

Then, the chamber's door slid open with a scary hiss. A skeletal medical droid rolled in, its chrome plating catching the harsh fluorescent lights and throwing them back in fractured shards. Every servo whine and metallic clack was a discordant note of intimidation. It moved with a mechanical grace, each movement precise, designed to unsettle, not soothe. With a cold, detached efficiency, it extended a gleaming, needle-tipped appendage, plunging the instrument through Mother Fucka's metal tomb, the sickening swish of escaping air a death rattle for her autonomy. The needle sank into her arm, and a sickly green luminescence pulsed from the injection site, a malevolent neon halo announcing her forced compliance. It wasn't medicine; it was a chemical leash, a fluorescent chain to bind her will. Another appendage reached out, this one piercing through the metal at the base of Mother Fucka's skull, inserting a tube that was left dangling. Lyra watched as Mother Fucka let out a terrifying gasp of pain, but the metal grille muzzle did not allow the sound to escape.

The door hissed open again, and in floated an interrogation bot. A gleaming chrome nightmare with a single, monstrous eye that stared unblinkingly at Mother Fucka. It hovered ominously close, emitting mechanical groans with each adjustment, as a manipulator arm, tipped with metallic claws, snaked out, glinting under light. Mother Fucka could only watch in horror as the bot readied itself to breach the innermost sanctums of her mind, sifting through the debris for truths buried deep. Another mechanical limb extended, seizing the dangling tube left by the medical droid and swiftly plugging it into a receptor port nearby. With a low, ominous hum, the bot engaged with her neural implant, drawing memories from her with relentless efficiency. Mother Fucka fought against the invasion, attempting to shut out her mental tormentor by closing her eyes, but she wasn't allowed to. It didn't take long. Already, she could feel the cold tendrils worming their way in, burrowing through the wreckage of her past. She was about to be devoured by the chrome vulture floating before her.

"You will cooperate," the bot's voice was a sharp digitized voice. "Failure to cooperate will result in further adjustments."

Mother Fucka remained silent, her jaw clenched, the metal grille open and flexible to allow her to speak. The chrome horror hovered a fraction closer, its every mechanical groan a deliberate threat.

"Your silence is noted," the bot droned, "and will be factored into the pain calibration."

Another pause, punctuated only by the ragged rasp of her breaths. Mother Fucka knew the bot wasn't bluffing. The sickly green luminescence emanating from the injection site on her arm pulsed with a malevolent rhythm, indicating that the pain serum was already coursing through her veins.

"What is your name?" the bot asked.

"Fuck you," she growled.

The metal grille clamped shut. The bot nodded to the medical droid who injected more pain serum into Mother Fucka.

"Recalibrated," the droid responded.

A sickening surge of energy ripped through Mother Fucka's nervous system. It was a searing white-hot fire that devoured every corner of her mind, leaving behind a smoldering wasteland of raw, exposed memories. She screamed an inhuman sound that only she could hear. Lyra, Rana, and Stark couldn't tear their eyes away from the horrifying scene. A human mind was being dissected before them, its secrets extracted with the ruthless efficiency of a mechanical butcher.

"I'll ask again. What is your name?" the bot demanded with its cold, metallic monotone voice.

The metal grille flexed open. "Petro ... Petronella Blake," the name came between gasps.

"Petronella Blake, you were seen walking into the Zenith Building. How did you enter the secured building?"

Another gasp. "Steele disconnected the security system."

"He did that for you?"

"Yes," her answer barely a sound.

"And you were there to kill him?"

"No ... no ..." she whimpered.

Another jolt of pain, courtesy of the medical droid's needle. The green luminescence at the injection site pulsed with a wicked glee. The bot, a chrome nightmare come to life, hovered closer still.

"Liar!" it shrieked. "The truth or the calibration increases!"

"Yes ... yes ... I did," the words rushed out. "But he asked me to do it."

The bot's mechanical voice dripped with suspicion. "He asked you to do it. Asked you to kill him? A tech mogul in his own penthouse? You, nothing but a petty thug scrabbling for scraps, and you're telling me ... he asked you to kill him."

Mother Fucka, her body wracked with fresh tremors of agony, gasped for breath. "He ... said ... he wanted to ... wanted to go out on his own terms. At first was gonna commit suicide by OD'ing on the Mindrot. He then changed his mind. Said he wanted to feel the pain. The physical pain of death."

Lyra turned to Stark. "Suicide? No note or transmission," she muttered under her breath. "They always leave something. We didn't find jack."

The sickly green glow from Mother Fucka's arm pulsed in an obscene rhythm, a hideous counterpoint to her strangled gasps. Stark, his face grim, muttered, "It's the goddamn serum. Every time, turns their brains into scrambled eggs."

Lyra didn't buy it. "Is it really?"

The bot, meanwhile, continued its relentless interrogation. "Suicide? You expect us to swallow that steaming pile of silicon-based bullshit." Its single, cyclopean lens zoomed in on Mother Fucka's face, the harsh magnification of a leer. "More lies," it hissed, the words heavy and fetid, the promise of pain yet to come, "mean more adjustments. And trust me, flesh-bag, you ain't seen 'adjustment' until you've had your neural pathways rewired with a rusty spoon and a car battery."

Mother Fucka went to scream but the metal grille slammed shut. This time, the sound she heard in her tomb wasn't a raw shriek but a guttural howl born from a soul being ripped apart. Another dose of pain serum whined through the injector, the medical droid's metal limb twitching with each pump.

Rana's body reacted instantly, a guttural groan escaping her lips as a wave of nausea threatened to overwhelm her. Beside her, Lyra's grin stretched wider, a touch sadistic. Stark, however, remained a statue, his eyes locked on Mother Fucka, his jaw clenched tight.

The grille ripped open, revealing a mouth contorted in a rictus of agony. "Truth!" Mother Fucka managed to choke out. "It's true! Steele begged for it, see. Said he wanted to feel the goddamn fire before the ice. So, I obliged him. Gave him a beatdown. Turned him into a drooling meat puppet. Then, with him whimpering, barely clinging to life, I blasted him. Ended it. Just like he asked. Figured the Mindrot was a bonus – no sense letting good shit go to waste, right?"

"We also saw you in Lyra Crowley's apartment. Why did you violate her space?" the bot asked.

Mother Fucka's eyes fluttered shut in exhaustion. A humorless laugh barely escaped her lips. "A little payback … to piss her off … to piss her off. Sure she's watching this. So … fuck you Crow … fuck you."

Silence stretched thick and dense, broken only by the ragged rasp of her breaths. The grille clanged shut, the bot's single eye pulsing faintly as it processed her fragmented confession. In that cold, emotionless gaze, one question hung unspoken: was it truth, or another layer of a tortured mind's desperation?

The bot glided away from Mother Fucka, its internal processes whirring as it delved into her memories via her neural implant. It became a digital archaeologist, sifting through the wreckage of a tortured existence in search of buried truths. Images flickered across the console screen – a dimly lit bar haunted by neon ghosts, a heated exchange with a desperate man, the glint of stolen creds catching the light. Deeper it burrowed, navigating the fractured landscape of Mother Fucka's broken psyche, searching for the singular memory – the truth of Steele's final moments.

Then, with a digital hiccup, the screen flickered. A revelation had been unearthed.

Through Mother Fucka's eyes, the console displayed Steele's final moments, a techno-snuff film playing out in high-def glory. She had just finished pouring the Mindrot, that syrupy concoction of synthetic oblivion, into the ornate decanter. And there sat Steele, perched at his chrome desk. He was sweating, a cold sweat, the kind that slicks your skin when you're staring down the abyss and it stares back, grinning like a chrome skull. But the sweat did nothing to mask the icy calm in his eyes, the kind of calm that settles over a man who's made his peace with the inevitable, a man who's finally decided to trade the neon jungle for the cold embrace of void. Steele wasn't afraid. He might have even been a little pissed off, but mostly, he was just ... done.

"That belonged to my mother," Steele gestured weakly at the decanter. "Only thing I have left of her besides the ghosts in my head. Memories stacked on memories, each one a stake driven deep into my skull."

He took a shaky breath. "There's this one memory, clear as yesterday. Me, a snot-nosed kid huddled under a ratty blanket, nursing a scraped knee that felt like the end of the world. My mother, bless her chrome arm – never did find out how she lost it. Doesn't matter now. She sat beside me on the creaking bed.

Told me, with a chuckle that scraped like gravel, 'Scraped knees are badges of honor, kiddo. Trophies from the battlefield of life.'"

A twisted smile played on his lips. "What battlefield, Ma? I remember asking her. 'Life itself,' she said. 'Every day, a fight for survival. Against the city, against yourself, sometimes even against the world.' She tapped my throbbing knee. 'See this? Just a skirmish, a pebble on the path. Hurts like hell, sure. But that pain? It reminds you you're alive, that you can feel. Makes the good times all the sweeter.'"

"'But what happens, Ma, when the pain won't stop?' I asked. 'When it burrows deep and eats your insides out?' She smiled then, a warm light in her eyes. 'Then you learn to dance with it, kiddo. Use it as fuel. The strongest warriors are the ones who've been broken, the ones who know the sting of loss and the fire of determination.' With that, she patched me up, synth-skin sealing the wound, and told me to be a hero."

"Ever since that day, I understood – I understood with a certainty that surprised even myself, that pain wasn't the enemy. It was the forge that made me strong. Every goddamn step, I craved the sting, the fire, the right to dish it out in equal measure. This hollowness, this soul-sucking ache – it craves an ending, a release that won't come. I need the sweet kiss of nothingness, but not like this. Not at my own hands, though. Not like I planned. I need to feel the pain, the glorious, agonizing proof of life, one last goddamn time. Fuck the Mindrot. Kill me. But do it slow. Real slow. Let me burn, let me scream, let me feel every goddamn inch of this pain before the darkness swallows me whole. Let me know I was alive before the darkness claims me."

There was a cackle followed by Mother Fucka grunting out, "Sure honey. Whatever you want."

Then the console screen began to warp, a grotesque funhouse mirror reflecting the carnage unfolding within the penthouse. The once-recognizable face of Steele morphed into a writhing canvas of raw agony. His features melted like overheated plastic, his screams distorted sounds of pain that tore through the room. It was a descent into hell, twenty-minutes of extreme suffering choreographed by Mother Fucka.

As the flesh finally gave way, it was replaced by a skeletal mockery of the man Steele once was. Even the bones couldn't withstand the onslaught, breaking and twisting under the pressure of Mother Fucka's rage. Then, with a final, blinding flash, the console revealed Steele, reduced to a heap, blasted from existence, his wealth and power meaningless. The screen went blank. The only sound was a long, hollow hum that resonated through the interrogation room.

Lyra stared at the blank screen, a storm brewing in her steely gaze. The metallic taste of vengeance still lingered in her mouth, but a seed of doubt had taken root. It was a tiny, unwelcome thing, but it burrowed deeper with every passing second and couldn't be ignored.

"Stark," she growled. "You buying this bullshit?"

"You saw it ... case closed."

"It's bullshit. Doesn't explain why he wanted to die."

"Crow, you want the why? I'll give it to you. Maybe, just maybe, it has to do with that Project Janus thing being shut down. He couldn't take it. So, he wanted to check-out."

"Bullshit, Stark! Bull-fucking-shit piled higher than the corpses of broken dreams in this cesspool we call civilization! No suicide note? No final 'fuck you' last message blasted into the goddamn ether? It's all too clean and easy!"

"It's over, Crow. Let it go before it eats you alive." Stark jerked a thumb towards the observation window. "Time to dispense some of that sweet, sweet justice we're all about. After all, what else is left in this world but the illusion of order in a universe of chaos?"

Within the chamber, the bot's single eye flickered back at Mother Fucka, a cold, digital stare that seemed to pierce straight through her soul. Under the harsh glare of the fluorescent lights, she knew the outcome.

"Allegation verified," the bot announced. "Actions resulted in the death of Vincent Steele. Transition to justice."

The interrogation bot and medical droid stepped away from Mother Fucka as the door opened. There was a shimmer of air and then it was there - a squat, barrel-shaped justice bot, the embodiment of punishment. Its entire body was a writhing mass of raw energy, crackling with a malevolent blue light that seemed to leech the color from the room. The buzzing that emanated from it wasn't electricity; it was the sound of a thousand tortured souls screaming into the void. Words, when it finally spoke, didn't emerge from its mouth - they erupted in booming pronouncements that shook the very foundation of the chamber. This wasn't a judge; it was a living executioner, and it reveled in delivering its pronouncements with sadistic joy.

"Petronella Blake," the justice bot boomed in a voice of tortured screams, "you stand accused of the murder of Vincent

Steele. You have been found ... GUILTY! Punishment: Dissolution. You will be reduced to your constituent components, recycled back into the ever-hungry maw of the city."

The grille slammed shut on Mother Fucka, as the monstrosity whirred, a metallic appendage reaching out towards her neural implant, the prelude to her digital obituary. A wave of blue energy erupted from justice bot, engulfing Mother Fucka's metal coffin. There was a bloodcurdling scream erupting from within, that Lyra thought she heard. But she wasn't sure. The blue light faded, revealing the empty metal husk that once held Mother Fucka.

"It's all bullshit!" Lyra told Stark.

She stormed out of the room followed by Rana.

"But Crow!" Rana shouted. "You got what you wanted, didn't you?"

Lyra spun around, her steely gaze pinning her. "What was that?"

Rana faltered for a moment, then shrugged. "Revenge. A semblance of closure. Isn't that what you came here for?"

Lyra, her eyes narrowed, a storm brewing within them. "Or did I just witness a goddamn execution orchestrated by a malfunctioning toaster?" she roared. "Justice? Closure? This wasn't justice, Doc. This was ... this was ..."

The words died in her throat, strangled by the cold, hard realization clawing its way out from the depths of her gut. The system, a machine built to churn out the truth quickly and efficiently, had done its job. But its gears always seemed to chew up the broken, the desperate, the expendable. This wasn't just about a single truth. There was more to this. Somewhere, a deeper truth lay buried, a victim of the system's ravenous expediency.

"Crow!" Stark shouted. "Look, we got a confession. Steele's dead. Case closed. It's over!"

Lyra turned on him. "Over? Nothing's ever over in this goddamn city. It just festers, Stark, festers until the next poor bastard gets caught in the crossfire."

He jabbed a finger at her. "Don't you do anything you'll regret," he warned, a weary plea.

Lyra scoffed. "Regret?" she laughed bitterly. "The only thing I regret, Stark, is ever believing this neon hive could deliver something even resembling justice."

She stormed her way toward the turbolift as Rana scurried after her. "Crow, wait! Where are you going?"

Lyra didn't answer. She didn't need to.

6 | Encounter at The Shelves

The neon city outside pounded with a sickly rhythm, a dying heart pumping out a garish light, a ceaseless hemorrhage of desperation. Inside The Shelves, though, the air was thick with the comforting musk of aged paper and forgotten whispers. Evelyn Turner, a splash of blonde against the towering shelves of tomes, reveled in the sanctuary. Her fingers traced the worn spine of a first-edition Ray Bradbury. The leather, worn and the color a dark brown, felt cool and reassuringly familiar to her. This was her hidden fortress, a refuge from the chrome-plated madness that choked the city outside. Here, amidst the ghosts of forgotten stories, Evelyn could almost forget the taste of ash and corruption that clung to her.

"Alert. Alert. Vincent Steele service starting," came a soft voice through Evelyn's commlink.

With a trembling hand, she waved, bringing a flickering holoscreen to life in front of her, casting an anemic glow across her face, the image shimmering like a heat mirage in the desert of her grief. There, bathed in the projection's flat, profane illumination, stood the unmistakable figure of Vincent Steele. Except … it wasn't him, not really. This was merely a hollow facsimile, a crude digital effigy rendered in soulless polygons and textures. A blasphemous simulacrum where his eyes - those twin furnaces that had once burned with such rapturous intensity - were replaced by dull expanses of bright black.

The officiant, a gaunt woman with a smile that wouldn't fool a malfunctioning vending machine, droned on about Vincent's "vision," his "steadfast dedication to progress." Evelyn slammed a fist against the metal armrest of her chair, the dull ache a pathetic counterpoint to the fury boiling in her gut. Vision? Dedication? He'd been a goddamn genius, yes, a maverick who'd jacked humanity into every damn system this side of the singularity. But this woman was eulogizing him like some benevolent freaking god.

I loved him dearly. But that's all bullshit.

Afterall, she knew the real Vincent Steele. She had loved him, yes - loved him with a passion that transcended the paltry conceits of mere affection or sentiment. They had been true partners, collaborators in shaping the digital architectures and decision matrices. But they shared more than just ambition and fevered dreams of the future. They had shared the raw, deep intimacy of two minds joined in the crucible of creation, shaping new inevitabilities through the sheer force of their combined will. They had shared their very beings, their essences intertwined in a union that defied the limited human conceits of love or physical congress.

The screen flickered again, showing the assembled mourners, a collection of corporate vultures with faces like polished stone. Evelyn recognized a few – the weasely bean counter who'd always sniped at Vincent's unorthodox methods, the marketing droid who'd twisted his research into some techno-patriotic propaganda. They were all there, their faces masks of manufactured solemnity, their pockets lined with the money Vincent's genius had generated.

A laugh escaped her lips then, harsh and brittle as shattered glass. If she were there, they wouldn't dare meet her gaze, these hollow leeches gorging on the still-warm corpse of Vincent's legacy. They would see the truth blazing in her eyes, know that she saw through their empty platitudes and hollow rites to the dark, rotten core lurking beneath.

"Why are you not attending?" Numen Arkstavsky, the new CEO had asked her the day before. "He would have wanted you there."

"We mourn in our own ways," she told him.

The holoscreen flickered once more, the image dissolving into static. A news report blared to life, the cheery voice of some talking head announcing a breakthrough in city infrastructure communication and command, a direct result of Vincent's research. Evelyn smiled. She had helped on that project, having devoted countless hours shaping the data architectures and decision matrices that made the whole remarkable achievement possible. It was one of the few pure endeavors she had collaborated on with Vincent before his obsessions had mutated into something different.

The Omega Link.

But was he mad? Did his grand obsession finally consume what tattered remnants of sanity and humanity still clung to him?

She pushed away the thought and drew a ragged breath, feeling the first tremors of anguished reaction building from the scorched, howling depths of her mind. Her eyes began to well with tears.

Her hand, steady despite the internal turmoil, reached towards the holographic display, a single finger hovering over the control stud that would terminate the projection. The distorted, soulless image of Vincent Steele stared back at her through those dull eyes, a wicked ghost haunting a broken machine.

Evelyn squeezed her eyes shut, the tears she had been fighting so desperately to contain finally threatening to spill in a torrent of profound anguish. In the quiet, smothering solitude of her grief, she needed this moment of stillness, this fleeting amnesty from the relentless onslaught of memory and revelation. A moment to remember Vincent not as the hollow, plasticized caricature being paraded before the assembled leeches, but as the man who had first opened her eyes to the possibilities of new realms of existence.

With a resolute nod, she flicked at the control stud and terminated the holographic projection in a blinding flare of static discharge.

As the tears streaked her cheeks in glistening rivulets, she knew her path was set. The corporate behemoth Vincent had birthed, the very entity that had sought to shackle his brilliance, now lay changed, in smoldering ruin. But what that giant hadn't yet realized was a new age, with new realities, shaped by the searing truths Vincent had uncovered, was about to rise.

She took a deep breath.

Enough. Fuck the tears. It's time to move on.

Her gaze was drawn downward, fixated on the weathered tome before her when a shadow fell across its yellowed pages.

Expecting the hunched form of some relic hunter, nose buried in a first edition in hopes of scoring a quick credit, she instead found herself locking eyes with a pair of sky-blue orbs. They glinted with a welcoming intensity beneath a mop of disheveled brown hair. The young man clutching a steaming cup of something approached, its aroma vaguely resembling coffee, battling against the omnipresent musty smell of the old books surrounding them.

His voice cut through Evelyn's carefully constructed indifference. He gestured at the book in her hand, *The Martian Chronicles*. "Intriguing choice," he remarked.

She offered a guarded smile. In this neon jungle, charm was a weapon, and this guy was armed to the teeth. "A classic," she replied, her words measured and precise.

He returned her smile, a flash of teeth that spoke of confidence and cunning. "Dreaming of greener pastures under a sky that isn't the color of a bad hangover?" he asked, his question a playful jab that hinted at shared disillusionment.

Evelyn snorted, a genuine sound that surprised even her. "Something like that."

"Mind if I join you?" he asked.

Evelyn hesitated for a moment. "Sure. Why not?"

He pulled out a chair and sat across from her.

"Didn't expect to find anyone else still reading Bradbury," he remarked

"Always loved Bradbury. The way he wrote about Mars ... it felt so real, even though it was fiction."

He chuckled, the sound dancing along the edges of the silence. "Real? Or maybe ..." he leaned forward, his voice dropping to a conspiratorial whisper, "a different kind of truth?"

Evelyn raised an eyebrow, intrigued. This wasn't the usual conversation you had in The Shelves. "A different kind of truth?"

He grinned. "Bradbury, bless his soul, offered a way out. An escape hatch from the claustrophobia of this ferrocrete jungle," he gestured vaguely towards the rain-streaked window, "into a world of red dust and possibility."

Evelyn leaned forward, mirroring his gesture. "You a big sci-fi fan?"

"Not just sci-fi," his eyes twinkling. "A voracious reader in general. But there's something about the way these stories, these journeys to the unknown, tap into something so basic within us, wouldn't you agree?"

Evelyn's lips twitched with a smile. This wasn't just some stranger anymore; he was a fellow traveler, lost in the neon maze just like her. Yet, his presence sparked an unsettling energy within her, an unexpected counterpoint to the connection she felt. She pressed her fingers against the spot just above her ear, where a peculiar, insistent thrumming pulsed. "It's the feeling that there's so much more out there, beyond the reach of our everyday lives. It's the yearning for adventure."

"Exactly!" he exclaimed with excitement. "Speaking of yearning, ever read Kurt Vonnegut?"

Evelyn's eyes widened. "Vonnegut? Are you kidding? *Slaughterhouse-Five* changed my life! One of the first of the ancients I read."

His laugh boomed, a wonderous counterpoint to the rain's mournful drumming outside. "Mine too! The way he takes us on these absurd, satirical journeys that somehow manage to reveal some profound truths about humanity ... it's genius!" He extended his hand. "Hi. I'm Ben."

She grasped his hand. "Evelyn," she replied.

The unsettling energy within her dissolved as the conversation flowed easily, a shared love for literature creating a bridge between them. They dissected the merits of *Cat's Cradle*, debated the ending of *Breakfast of Champions*, and lamented the loss of a master storyteller. Evelyn discovered he was a former engineer who'd traded blueprints for books, now a collector and trader of tales. He, in turn, learned of her work in a lab, the kind of work that was sometimes choked by the drudgery of monotony. "Such is the life of a scientist," she confides, her voice tinged with a wry resignation. "But, the stories I dream of writing someday."

The drumming of the rain gentled to a pitter-patter, and a sliver of light, like a hesitant hope, crept through the window. Laughter, a rare and precious sound in this city of shadows, bubbled up between them. The neon-drenched despair outside seemed to dim a notch, the oppressive weight of the world momentarily lifting.

Ben's voice carried the warmth of their laughter. "Tell me. What kind of story is waiting inside of you?"

Evelyn paused, the question catching her off guard. "I ... I don't know," she admitted, a tremor of honesty breaking through her facade. "Maybe a story about people like us, trying to find beauty in the cracks, searching for meaning in the madness."

Ben smiled warmly, his eyes crinkling at the corners. "Now that sounds like a story the world needs to hear."

Then, the inevitable. He reached across the table, his fingers barely grazing her hand, a feather-light touch that sent a jolt of electricity racing up her arm. In that instant, she became acutely aware of the man before her - not merely a kindred spirit, but a potential connection in a world that felt like it was closing in around her, isolating and vast.

"You know," he whispered, "I'm told there's a hidden bar just a few blocks away. For bookies like us. Real liquor, too. Why don't we venture out and do a bit of exploring?"

Her smile faltered. The flirtation had been a delightful distraction, a dance on the edge of a societal tightrope. But a bar?

What am I doing? This is all too fast. I've just lost Vincent.

She was firm. "Thanks, but I'm not really ..."

"Looking for trouble?" he interjected, his lips curved into a tight smile. "Neither was I until I saw you nestled amongst these dusty relics."

He wasn't pushy, not overtly. But there was a gleam in his eyes, a challenge that resonated with a rebellious streak that reminded her of Vincent. Her gaze darted to the worn leather of the book, the promise of a world beyond the neon haze.

"Maybe another time," she said, her tone cool and unwavering. "But right now, I have a date with Mr. Bradbury."

A soft chuckle rumbled from his chest, a rich sound that danced in the air. "Touché," he conceded, his hand lingering a whisper too long before retreating. "But the offer stands. In case you ever get tired of the company of fictional men."

She locked eyes with him, a silent dare crackling. "Or perhaps," she countered with a playful lilt, a delightful addition to the gravity of her words, "if the discussion of ray guns versus neural implants starts to lose its luster."

He threw his head back and laughed, a genuine, full-bodied sound that ripped through the hushed shelves. It was a sound devoid of the city's usual cynicism, a sound that spoke of a world where laughter hadn't been completely choked by the omnipresent neon.

"Consider it a standing invitation." His smile persisted. "Just promise me you won't sic a robotic spider on me if I disagree about the effectiveness of a neural implant."

She couldn't help but grin. "No promises," she teased.

She watched as he turned and walked away, his silhouette disappearing into the labyrinthine stacks.

Settling back into her chair, the worn pages of *The Martian Chronicles* whispered promises of a different kind of adventure. Perhaps, she thought, a real adventure wasn't just about rockets and red dust. Perhaps, it was about defying expectations, finding beauty in unexpected places, and maybe, just maybe, sharing a stolen moment of genuine laughter with a stranger in a world drowning in neon despair.

The air in The Greased Cog reeked of stale beer and urine. A yellow mist clung to the exposed brick walls like the ghosts of countless glasses drained and hangovers endured. Lyra, perched on a chipped vinyl barstool, nursing a lukewarm bourbon, its fiery burn a dim imitation of the anger simmering in her gut. Rana sat beside her, a half-empty glass of something amber swirling in her hand.

"Steele," Lyra muttered the name. "The whole thing stinks. Doesn't make any damn sense."

Rana sighed. "Look. He was a tech titan. Guys like that live on a different plain of existence. Maybe he just … snapped … because of Project Janus … like Stark said."

Lyra scoffed. "Snapped? The man had everything! All the creds you'd ever want, penthouse apartments all over the world. He craved control, dammit. Why give it all up like that? Why the hell would he want to die?"

"Maybe a thrill," Rana shrugged. "Who knows? Rich folks got kinks you wouldn't believe."

"And how would you know?" Lyra asked with a twisted smile.

"Let's just say I know."

Lyra slammed her glass on the counter, startling a scrawny rat of a man sidling towards them. He wore a greasy wifebeater and a smile fraught with brown-stained teeth.

"Hey there, sweethearts," he leered with a voice that squeaked like a rusty hinge. "Looking for some company?"

Lyra's eyes narrowed. "Not interested, asshole."

The man's smile faltered, replaced by a sneer. "Feisty, I like that. Maybe a little roughhousing will loosen you up."

Before he could take another step, Lyra was in front of him, blocking his advance. "Move along, chum. Don't test your luck."

The bar rat puffed out his chest, but the defiance quickly drained from him under Lyra's firm gaze. He mumbled a curse and retreated to his corner, tail between his legs.

Lyra watched him go, her anger momentarily diverted. "Assholes," she muttered, taking a swig of her bourbon. "Think everything is so easy."

Rana leaned back against the bar. "Now, where were we? Steele ..."

"There has to be more," Lyra insisted, her voice gaining conviction with each word. "He set up the whole thing. Had Mother Fucka there, leaving a trail of clues leading right back to her. Why? Why go through all that trouble just to get himself beaten half to death?"

Rana tapped her glass thoughtfully. "You heard why, Crow. Because of what his mother told him. About feeling pain, and all that shit. "

Lyra snorted. "Doc, think about it. A tech mogul who has it all? Doesn't exactly scream credible, does it?"

They lapsed into silence, the only sound the murmur of conversation and the occasional mournful creak of the bar sign. Lyra swirled the remaining dregs of her drink, her mind a whirlwind of possibilities. Then, an idea, fragile but persistent, flashed to life.

"What if he isn't dead?" She could barely form the words. "Maybe it's the swill I'm drinking ... but ... what if he isn't dead?"

Rana raised an eyebrow. "What the fuck? You saw what was in the neural implant. You saw it, right?"

Lyra set her glass down with a decisive thud. "What if Steele went somewhere else? To hide. To get away from things. They shutdown Janus. There was something in the newsfeed about AI sentience," she persisted. "Maybe the whole messy scene in his penthouse was a distraction. Maybe they terminated some prototype, some synthesized facsimile, while the real Steele slipped away."

A faint smile touched Rana's lips, a smile that acknowledged the spark of possibility in Lyra's theory, even as reason whispered its objections. "That's a fascinating idea," she admitted. "But forensics would have caught on if what was in the penthouse was a clone. And frankly, we're not quite there with replicant technology. The sentience angle, though... that's a whole different beast."

A digital ice pick stabbed through Lyra's mind as her commlink jerked to life, a sharp throb leaving her momentarily adrift in a sea of disorientation. It's a sensation she knew too well, a necessary evil, a thorn embedded in the flesh of her existence. She despised it, yet embraced it as part of the job, a pact with the devil she made long ago.

"Crow, the tracer's live," Gnat's voice clattered in. "The second Turner hits The Shelves, you'll be the first to know."

Lyra's lips stretched into a feral snarl. The commlink flickered and died with a digital sigh. "Lead coming up," she told Rana, who looked like she'd swallowed a mouthful of bad synth-whiskey.

"Lead?" Rana croaked. "What the hell are you talking about?"

Lyra gave a smile delivered with a chuckle. "Turner. Evelyn Turner. You, with your lab coat and fancy credentials, think you can sweet-talk your way into the restricted territory?"

Rana gave a quizzical look. "No need to sweet-talk, being a scientist and all. But what about you? You think they'll let you just walk in?"

"Detective, remember? We detectives get to go anywhere. One of the many perks of this goddamn job." She slammed her palm down on the bar with a force that rattled the glasses. "Another round here!" she bellowed at the bartender, a man who looked like he'd seen too much and cared even less. "No, wait! Make it two goddamn bottles – one for each of us. We're celebrating!"

"Celebrating what?" Rana quirked an eyebrow.

Lyra's eyes glittered with a manic intensity. "The imminent arrival of a little ... complication."

Suddenly, the harsh clamor of the bar receded, replaced by an eerie stillness. Lyra felt herself shrinking, the hardened detective giving way to a tiny, curious girl. The walls of the bar shifted, becoming something hazy and long-forgotten.

She stood pressed against a grimy windowpane, a small, wide-eyed girl gazing out with wonder. Outside, a swirling maelstrom of white flakes danced in the air, both beautiful and terrifying in their alienness.

"Snow," her mother's voice, a comforting murmur, had cut through the confusion. Lyra looked up, her gaze meeting her mother's, warm and gentle despite the ever-present worry lines around her eyes. "It doesn't happen often anymore, little one. Not since the Big Burn."

Lyra, barely taller than the windowsill, tilted her head. "The Big Burn?" The words held the innocent curiosity of a child who still believed the world held more wonder than despair.

Her mother knelt beside her, a soft sigh escaping her lips. "A long time ago, before you were even born, the world got sick.

Fire choked the skies and turned the snow to ash. It was the time when everything went wrong."

Lyra shivered, a strange fear took root despite the warmth radiating from her mother's body. "The snow ... it's ... it's beautiful," she whispered.

Her mother smiled, a bittersweet curve of her lips. "It is, isn't it? Even in all this destruction, there's beauty to be found. Come here, little one. Let me tell you what it was like before the darkness came."

Lyra was swept into a warm embrace, the scent of tattered fabric and her mother's hair a familiar comfort. In her mother's lap, nestled against the worn leather of an old armchair, Lyra drank in her mother's voice. It wasn't a story; it was a conjuring, some deep, fantastical magic of words, tales of a world before the fire, a world where snow fell softly and children built creatures called snowmen that reached for the sky.

As the words lulled her into a comforting drowsiness, a whisper-light touch against her cheek startled her awake. Not the bone-chilling cold her mother described. It was the reassuring warmth of her mother's breath.

But then, the snowflake illusion melted away and everything shifted. Lyra felt herself rolling over in bed, sheets tangled around her, the warmth lingering on her cheek. Groaning, she forced her eyes open, her hand brushing against something soft and yielding.

Rana Sharma. Naked. Asleep. Curled up beside her. A mess of red, fiery hair cascaded down her exposed bare back.

Lyra's mind reeled, replaying snippets of the previous night like a malfunctioning hologram. The Greased Cog, the cheap bourbon, Rana's blue eyes reflecting the grime of the bar. Then, a fuzzy memory of laughter, unsteady steps, and fumbling to enter the code to her cramped apartment. Had they ...?

Lyra cleared her throat. Rana stirred, a languorous stretch that sent a tremor through Lyra despite her pounding head. Her eyes fluttered open, a teasing glint dancing in their depths before meeting Lyra's wide stare. A playful smile creased her lips.

"Good morning," Rana purred, leaning in for a soft kiss on Lyra's cheek.

Lyra's cheeks flushed. "Did ... did we?" she stammered, the words thick in her throat.

Rana smiled. "Let's just say you were a very enthusiastic person-of-interest last night."

Lyra groaned, burying her face in her hands. This wasn't how she'd envisioned spending her morning. Surprise and embarrassment mingled with a sense of exhilaration, a dangerous cocktail churning in her gut.

Fuck! Not again. I gotta stop doing this.

Rana slipped out of bed, the sheets clinging to her like a cobweb, revealing the graceful slope of her shoulders and the long, smooth line of her back. A low moan escaped her lips, a sound that was both sleepy and faintly sensual. With a long stretch that spoke of a restless night, she slid free of the tousled sheets. She moved around the room, reaching the kitchenette, where she switched on the light.

"Coffee?" she called over her shoulder.

"Yeah," Lyra managed the words. "Just black please."

Rana winked over her shoulder. "Coming right up, Detective. Just don't think this buys you immunity from any disagreement we may have with the Steele case."

A reluctant smile pulled at the corners of Lyra's lips. "Of course."

She watched every movement Rana made. It all felt deliberate, almost ritualistic. The way she tilted the packet of concentrated brown sludge, pouring it into the pot like success hinged on the perfect angle. The clink of a spoon against a tin cup sounded almost ominous in the pre-dawn hush. But she couldn't tear her eyes away. Maybe it was the anemic dawn light, struggling through the grease-caked window that cast a halo around Rana's head. Or maybe it was the sound of the soft hum of contentment Rana made as the coffee started to brew. It made Lyra yearn for something she couldn't quite name. A sense of normalcy, perhaps. Or maybe just a reminder that life, even in this neon hive, could still hold simple pleasures.

Maybe this wasn't the worst way to wake up after a night of chasing shadows. But one thing was certain: the Steele case, and its unforeseen complications, had just gotten a whole lot more … interesting.

The scent of something vaguely resembling coffee, acrid and burnt yet oddly comforting, wafted through the apartment. Rana returned to the bed, sliding back under the sheets, and handing Lyra her coffee, while her hands cradled her own cup of steaming brew, happy for the warmth. They sat in an awkward silence, both taking tentative sips of their bitter coffee.

Suddenly, Furball launched herself onto the bed, landing with a soft thud in Rana's lap. The small, black cat began a rhythmic rumble that vibrated against Rana's thighs. She absently scratched behind the feline's ears, acknowledging the creature's presence with a glance, and received a soft meow in return - a language of simplicity amidst the chaos.

"Re-synthed, huh?" Rana asked. "She's a cutie."

Lyra nodded, her expression a mask that barely concealed the vulnerability beneath. "She's all I have," she conceded.

"Not anymore. Ah... we should talk about last night," Rana's voice was a gentle prod guise of casual inquiry.

Lyra found herself staring into the depths of her coffee mug, the murky liquid swirling like a miniature vortex of doubt. The city outside thrived on cynicism, its streets paved with the wreckage of discarded hope and broken promises. Love, or whatever twisted mess this resembled, felt like a luxury she could ill afford.

"You know I'm not built for chit-chat, Rana."

But even as the words left Lyra's lips, a sliver of vulnerability peeked through. Maybe it was the exhaustion clinging to her, or the way the morning light cast an ethereal glow on Rana's face. Whatever it was, the city's iron grip on her emotions seemed to loosen ever so slightly.

Rana's hand, surprisingly steady, reached out and cupped Lyra's chin, a gentle nudge that coaxed their eyes to meet. "Hey." A hesitant smile, fragile as a butterfly caught in a wind tunnel, flitted across her lips. "It's okay. We don't have to talk about it. I get it. Just let me finish this lukewarm sewage they call coffee, get dressed, and I'll leave."

"No!" The word exploded from Lyra's lips, a raw sound that startled even herself. "I mean … ah … whatever you want to do … but you don't have to leave right this instant."

She blinked, caught off guard by her words as the tangled mess of emotions inside her a churning mess.

What the fuck am I doing?

But before she could even untangle a single thread, Rana leaned in, slowly, deliberately, the space between them collapsing in a heartbeat. The warmth of Rana's breath, hot and unexpected, brushed against her lips. Their lips met, a hesitant touch at first, the gentle softness of Rana's lips meeting hers. The kiss tasted of stale coffee and something else, something deeper, an unspoken language spoken only in the press of skin against skin. A breath shuddered through Lyra, a sound both uneven and grateful. "Thank you."

"Don't mention it," Rana's lips brushed against Lyra's ear in a whisper, the words a ghostly caress.

But the fragile moment shattered as a scream from Lyra's commlink sliced through her mind like a jagged blade. Reality splintered, the delicate connection with Rana obliterated by the city's relentless demands, leaving only the echoes of what might have been.

She gave Rana a quick kiss, then pulled away, a curt "Sorry" escaping her lips.

"Crowley here," she snapped. "What is it?"

"Detective," came the harried reply, "Stark needs you downtown at Central. He set up a call with the new Neogene CEO, Numen Arkstavsky. Steele case review."

"Got it," Lyra nodded.

A beat of silence, then a hesitant, "Uh, Detective?" from the commlink. "Do you know where Dr. Sharma is? Stark's been trying to reach her. Wants her at the meeting, too."

Lyra glanced back at Rana, the raw vulnerability in her eyes momentarily eclipsed by a cutting grin. "Dr. Sharma? I think I know where she is. Tell Stark we'll be there. Crowley out."

Rana quirked an eyebrow. "What was that all about?"

Lyra smiled, the lingering warmth of their kiss still on her lips. "Neogene Dynamics," she began. "Seems we're gonna give them an update on the Steele ... situation. And apparently, you're invited. But I do have a favor to ask."

"Sure. What is it?"

"Don't mention anything about us to Stark. He wouldn't understand."

Rana grinned. "Our little ... complication, Crow," she whispered to Lyra kissing her on the cheek. "But I can't go in wearing the same clothes from yesterday."

Lyra grinned back. "Borrow some of mine."

They took a few more sips of coffee, the silence broken only by the hacking cough of the ventilation unit. Rana peeled out of bed, wrapped in a sheet, and scanned Lyra's meager wardrobe with an assessing glint. It wasn't much - white shirts and leather. She let the sheet crumple to the floor, a discarded husk, then wriggled into a pair of tight leather pants, before throwing on a white shirt and a leather vest.

"Doesn't exactly scream 'respectable scientist,' does it?" Rana noted, a wry tilt to her lips.

"Respect's been dead for ages, buried along with the sky," Lyra laughed. "And don't forget the black coat."

Rana did as instructed. In this splintered world where reality flickered like a faulty holovid, the clothes felt strangely reassuring. Lyra joined her, slipping into the same attire, her movements quick and efficient. They stood side by side, two mirrored figures in a realm where mirrors were relics of a time forgotten. Quickly, they painted their faces with the war paint of cosmetics, masking the fear lurking beneath their skin. They brushed their hair into place and with a final glance, a shared look that spoke of battles fought and lost, of an unspoken pact, they smiled. It wasn't a smile of joy but one of grim determination, of understanding that the next step forward would be taken together, cloaked in black, faces painted for war.

As they stepped out into the hallway, Lyra felt like she was walking a tightrope stretched over a city of neon. This morning's entanglement, this unexpected wrinkle ripped into the wasteland of her life, was just the beginning. It was a single, hesitant step onto a path that looped back on itself, offering both danger and a melody she couldn't quite place. But for now, in this city where shadows held secrets and whispers rode upon the wind, she had Rana. And in this skewed existence, that was a fragile hope worth clinging to.

Out onto the slick streets, the neon city was a mirage of fractured light reflecting in the rain-drenched pavement. Lyra tilted her head back, the polluted sky a murky canvas where a single crow perched, a dark mark against the sickly glow. It regarded her with a single, black eye, then dipped its head in what could have been a mocking bow, or a knowing salute. It cawed once, a harsh grate within the canyon of steel and glass.

Is it mocking me? Is it trying to warn me of something? Maybe it's just a fellow traveler on the same twisted path?

Lyra couldn't say.

"What's wrong?" Rana asked, her mascara beginning to run down her cheeks.

"Nothing," Lyra muttered as a hovercar materialized from the rainy mist, headlights cutting through the gloom.

7 | Leather and Lies

Lyra and Rana walked through the humming corridors of Central, mirroring each other in their leather outfits. For Lyra, the garments were like a second skin. Rana, on the other hand, felt decidedly out of place, like she had been crammed into a dominatrix uniform. Every fidget, every self-conscious tug at the tight vest, or pulling at the pants that chafed against her skin, screamed of discomfort.

Rana gave her pants yet another yank. "One wonders how you can wear such things."

"Easy there," Lyra chuckled. "Those pants ain't gonna bite you. Unless, of course, you piss them off."

Rana cast a downward glance at the offending leather. "It feels like … like I'm being strangled," she mumbled. "And the … the stench!"

"Stench?" Lyra stopped cold, her face twisted in a look of utter bewilderment. Then, with a sudden grin, she added, "You got some faulty sniffing sensors in that beautiful head of yours."

A faint blush crept up Rana's neck, which sparked a wayward impulse in Lyra to corner her in the nearest equipment closet and steal a kiss. But this wasn't the time. And it sure as hell wasn't the place.

"No, I …" Rana hesitated, searching for the right words. "It's just this leather. It smells … how do I describe it? …"

"Different?" Lyra responded. "Exotic, perhaps?"

Rana winced as the unforgiving leather of her pants dug into her curves. Another awkward and jerky attempt at adjustment only succeeded in a muted squeak from the material. She cursed under her breath.

Lyra watched the silent battle for a moment, a slow smile creeping across her face. "Don't worry," the familiar sharpness returned to her voice. "They eventually break in. Or you do."

The metallic conference room door hissed open with a weary sigh, revealing Stark at the table. A sharp smirk split his face as his gaze snagged on them. "Well, well," he chuckled, "look who decided to play dress-up."

Lyra glared at him. It was the kind of shut-the-fuck-up stare he knew all too well. He gestured towards the vacant chairs at the table. "Alright, let's get this charade over with. Patch us through to Arkstavsky," he barked through his commlink. "Oh, and Crow, try to stay on your best behavior. We don't want to upset the new CEO with … shall we say … inconvenient truths."

She rolled her eyes. "Charm's always on the menu, as long as the special of the day ain't a heaping helping of corporate lies."

Stark just shook his head, the movement conveying a weary acceptance of her inherent hostility. He then activated a holoscreen that rose from the center of the table. A swirling vortex of light condensed, solidifying into the holographic form of a man. Numen Arkstavsky.

Young, impossibly so for someone who'd inherited an empire like Neogene Dynamics. His features were sharp and clean, sculpted with the precision of a designer baby. His face, however, remained an indifferent mask, emotionless. The only anomaly, the only thing that betrayed the polished veneer, were his eyes – an unsettling shade of gray like storm clouds reflecting the neon chaos of the city.

"Mr. Arkstavsky, welcome," Stark's voice dripped with a false veneer of respect. "With me, is Detective Lyra Crowley and Dr. Rana Sharma. Both have worked the case of Mr. Steele."

Arkstavsky offered a curt dip of his head, an acknowledgment that hovered somewhere between a nod and a dismissal. "Captain Stark. Detective Crowley. Dr. Rana. It is a pleasure to meet you, albeit under ... unpleasant circumstances."

"The pleasure's all ours," Lyra muttered sarcastically.

Stark ignored her, launching into his pre-rehearsed script. "As you know, Mr. Arkstavsky, we've been diligently investigating the unfortunate demise of Mr. Steele. I'm happy to report that we've apprehended the assailant, and justice has been served."

Arkstavsky's face remained unreadable. "A most gratifying outcome, Captain," his voice as smooth and cold as the chrome accents adorning his impeccably tailored suit. "Neogene Dynamics extends its deepest gratitude to you and your team for facilitating such a ... timely resolution. Now, we may resume our unwavering dedication to the optimization of human potential."

Lyra, however, unlike Stark, wasn't buying the manufactured sincerity. She couldn't hold back the question that had been eating at her since Steele's demise. "Mr. Arkstavsky," she cut in sharply, "before this incident, wasn't Neogene Dynamics spearheading a project to be on the cutting edge of neural augmentation? Project Janus?"

Arkstavsky's stillness faltered for a fraction of a second. Lyra saw it - a trace of something, an emotional ripple across the depths of his stormy gray eyes. It vanished as swiftly as it appeared, replaced once more by the cold, emotionless mask he wore like armor.

"Project Janus," his tone measured, "has been the subject of much media interest, Detective. It was indeed one of Neogene Dynamics' more ambitious ventures. However, after careful evaluation, it was deemed non-strategic, and not financially viable. Our company prioritizes innovation, but ultimately, that innovation must serve the needs of our shareholders."

Lyra scoffed aloud. "Financially viable? Really? Or was there another reason for shutting it down? Perhaps a reason that involves the unfortunate demise of Mr. Steele?" Her gaze narrowed, a silent accusation just dangling out there.

Stark coughed, a nervous clearing of his throat. "Thank you, Mr. Arkstavsky. We'll sign off now. We appreciate your ...."

"Hold a moment, Captain," Arkstavsky interjected, a steely edge creeping into his voice. "Let me assure the good Detective that Neogene Dynamics operates well within the ethical parameters of research. Project Janus was, shall we say, Steele's pet project. A shiny new toy he put in front of the board. Unfortunately, progress proved elusive. The project missed every financial benchmark we set for it. And Vincent," he stressed the name, "knew better than anyone what happens to shiny toys that do not deliver results in this game. While the project was promising, it was riddled with unforeseen complications. The kind that breeds undesirable consequences. And we can't afford such outcomes, can we?" A tight smile stretched across his lips.

"That will be all, Captain. Thank you for your time, and once again, our sincere gratitude for your role in ... expediting matters."

But Lyra wasn't done. "And what about Mr. Steele's neural implant? Its absence is a blatant violation of law. Did Neogene Dynamics have anything to do with its illegal removal?"

Arkstavsky's face remained impassive, but a flash of something cold and calculating danced in his eyes.

"Detective," his voice was flat and emotionless. "Goodbye."

His image flickered and faded on the holoscreen, which then shrank back into the tabletop, leaving an unsettling silence in its wake.

A lonely hum echoed from the vents, a melancholic drone that seemed to lament the oppressive silence of the room. Stark, his face a mask of thunder, swiveled on his chair. His gaze, sharp as a laser beam, pinned Lyra where she sat. A muscle in his temple throbbed angrily, betraying the barely contained fury. This wasn't new. It wouldn't be the last time Lyra's impulsive streak painted a target on their backs.

"Crow," his voice a low and dangerous growl. "What. The. Fuck. Were. You. Thinking? Arkstavsky's a powerful man, someone we can't afford to antagonize."

Lyra's voice crackled with a defiance simmering just below the surface. "Don't you want to know if they had anything to do with Steele's death?"

"Let it go, Crow," Stark groaned, his tone heavy with weariness, the kind that settles deep into your bones. "The perp's already been fried. We clocked out the minute that happened.

The missing implant? That's a whole different can of worms. Steele had a death wish, and we all knew it."

"Death wish?" Lyra jeered.

"You saw it all with your own eyes! How he wanted to end it all!"

"And yet," she shot back, her eyes narrowing with suspicion, "there was no note, no last transmission, nothing. There's always something left behind - always. Why didn't we find one? It doesn't add up. This was his life's work, damn it!"

But the venom in her tone began to fade, replaced by a flash of something more fragile. Stark saw it, a glimpse of the grief she was trying so hard to mask. His own sigh deepened, a touch of empathy softening his gruff exterior.

"Look, Crow." He rubbed his forehead. "You're the best I got. Yeah, sure ... you rub me raw sometimes ... alright, most of the time. But hell if I know what I'd do without you causing chaos at every damn turn." He shook his head in grudging respect. "I know what this neon city does to the best of us. It chews us up and spits us out twisted. Every dark fuckin' corner seems to breed another fuckin' monster. But throwing accusations at a corporate titan without proof accomplishes nothing."

"He knew something, Stark," her voice softening.

"How do you know?"

"Because. I can feel it in my gut."

Rana, who had remained silent throughout the exchange, finally cleared her throat.

"Maybe the Captain's onto something," Rana said to Lyra, her words measured yet steady. "Going after Arkstavsky without proof could blow up in Central's face. But we might have another angle."

Lyra's glare cut through the air, burning into Rana with a fury that lingered longer than it should have. But Rana's unshakeable calm smoothed the edges of her anger. "What's your play?"

"We keep digging into Project Janus," Rana declared. "But we do it under the radar. We need to find out what Steele was up to and why they buried it. There's something down there worth digging up, and I'll bet it leads straight to Arkstavsky."

Lyra considered this for a moment, the storm in her eyes slowly subsiding. It wasn't the explosive confrontation she craved, but it was a path forward, a way to claw at the truth without setting off all the alarms.

"Alright," she replied barely above a whisper. "But the minute we find anything suspicious, I'm not letting it go."

Stark leaned forward, his voice rough, all business. "Listen up, both of you. Officially, I don't want to know jack about this little side hustle of yours. Keep your heads down and stay off the radar. Understood?"

Rana nodded, as did Lyra, but she was unable to meet his gaze fully. Shame ate at her for letting her emotions get the better of her. It was a familiar sting. Something she was so used to that it didn't matter anymore. With a mumbled apology that barely registered, she stormed out of the conference room, Rana following close behind. The hunt for answers had a new direction, and Lyra, for better or worse, wasn't about to let it go.

Rain lashed the neon wasteland, a grimy curtain obscuring the glow of the city. Lyra pulled her hood low, shielding her face from the stinging spray. She glanced at Rana. "Thirsty work. Drink?"

Rana nodded. They approached a battered hovercar, its paint flaking like dead skin. As they neared, two hulking silhouettes materialized from the hazy gloom.

The first was a behemoth, his cybernetic enhancements barely contained beneath his slick, oil-stained skin. Cadaverous lines etched his face, a canvas marred by a cruel, razor-point grin. Bio-luminescent tattoos flickered on his shaved head, an angry red that mirrored the pulsating veins beneath his eyes. Beside him stood his partner, a wiry amalgam of flesh and metal, exuding raw, jittery energy. Cloaked in a tattered trench coat, his lone red, mechanized eye flitted around like a caged insect, while long, lethal claws twitched incessantly at the tips of his restless fingers.

Without a word, they shoved Lyra and Rana into the hovercar.

"Drive!" barked the large one, the words more of a snarl.

The robotic driver whirred in protest. "Sir. This is highly irregular …"

A blast from a plasma blaster scorched the metal of its head, leaving a smoking crater. "Drive!" the goon roared again.

The bot lurched into motion, the city lights blurring past their rain-streaked windows.

"What the hell is this?" Lyra's voice was tight with anger.

"Doc Jones wants a word," the large one grunted.

"About what?" Lyra demanded.

Silence greeted her question. Lyra and Rana exchanged a tense look, their unease growing. They shifted uncomfortably, trapped between the two hulking figures. Lyra's eyes darted around, searching for an escape route, her hand twitching instinctively towards the blaster strapped to her thigh. But before she could even consider a move, a sickening metallic click shattered the tense air. Cold metal pressed against both their sides – the unmistakable chill of a plasma blaster.

Fuck!

The goons simply sat there, unnervingly still, their expressions unreadable, a shared sense of twisted pleasure flashing in their eyes. It was a trap sprung, and the only question left was whether they could somehow pry themselves free.

The hovercar touched down with a gentle sigh, kicking up dirt and grime in the gritty air. It settled with a sigh, the landing struts groaning in protest. Lyra stared out the window, her eyes tracing the ramshackle skyline of the city's underbelly, while Rana fidgeted beside her. As the vehicle came to a gentle halt, Lyra could see the twisted metal skeletons of buildings once grand structures now reduced to rotting carcasses by neglect and disaster. Nestled precariously amongst them, stood an imposing façade.

The structure exuded a strange sense of resilience. It was a hodgepodge of scavenged materials, salvaged metal panels neatly welded together with sheets of corrugated plastic shimmering with a dull, oily sheen. A single neon sign, cobbled together from scavenged parts, buzzed to life, casting the facade in a sickly glow.

It displayed a crudely rendered skull winking a single, malevolent red eye, a not-so-subtle warning to anyone considering an unwelcome visit. Lyra could almost feel the watchful gaze of hidden security cameras, their lenses aglitter like malignant eyes in the dying light. This was it. Doc Jones' lair.

The hovercar doors slid open, the two hulking goons gesturing for Lyra and Rana to step out. Blasters aimed at their backs, they had no choice but to comply. The goons led them down a narrow alley and into the entrance of the building. The interior was a surprising mix of opulence and decay, with elegant chandeliers casting a dim light over worn marble floors. They were led down through a labyrinthine series of corridors that seemed to double back on themselves with dizzying frequency.

Just when Lyra thought they must be wandering in circles, they came to an unmarked entrance, the portal grinding open to reveal a cavernous chamber that made her breath catch in her throat. Elegant chandeliers cast a dim, flickering glow over worn marble floors scarred by decades of abuse. Faded frescoes depicting classical scenes of hedonistic revelry adorned the crumbling walls, hinting at the place's former grandeur with a touch of irony.

Doc Jones sat at the end of a long mahogany table, an air of calm authority radiating from him. His gaze was sharp and assessing as it raked over them, eyes glittering with an intensity that bordered on the predatory. As the goons reached for the plasma blaster strapped to Lyra's thigh, Jones raised a hand.

"No need for that," his voice smooth but firm. "She can keep the weapon. It's part of her, after all."

Lyra's eyes dashed around the chamber, taking in the bizarre museum of stolen wealth and ill-gotten finery. Priceless artworks by long-dead masters adorned the walls, their radiant hues faded by the ravages of time and neglect. Bizarre, twisted sculptures crowded every available surface, their forms appearing almost alive, as though they were caught in some unnatural dance. But the most unsettling sight of all was the figure nestled comfortably in Jones' lap, slender arms draped around his neck in a lover's embrace. The display of affection twisted Lyra's features into a grimace.

Aurora.

The delicate figure lifted her head at their approach, large, doe-like eyes regarding them with an expression of childlike curiosity. Then with her full lips curving into the barest wisp of a smile, she planted a gentle kiss on Jones' cheek. He responded with an affectionate nuzzle against her brow, his fingers trailing through her hair.

Aurora giggled softly, her voice like a tinkling bell. "Daddy, you're spoiling me."

Jones chuckled, his fingers lightly tracing the curve of her jaw. "How could I not, my dear? You're the only one who makes this wretched life bearable."

Rana felt a different sort of unease. She noticed something in the young woman's movements – a subtle stiffness, an unnatural smoothness to her skin. Leaning closer to Lyra, she murmured, barely a whisper, "Augmented?"

Lyra's voice was even lower, little more than an exhalation of disgust. "Used to be a boy."

Jones' eyes glinted with undisguised malice as he regarded them over Aurora's head. He gave a jerk. "Well, well …" the words slithering from his lips, "if it isn't my old friend Crow."

His focus shifted to Rana, that piercing stare seeming to strip away all pretense of civility. "And I see you've found yourself a new toy to play with. The good doctor graces us with her presence. How … utterly delightful."

Rana refused to flinch, and would not grant this twisted soul the satisfaction. "I don't believe we've been introduced," she replied, each word clipped into icy professionalism despite the roiling unease twisting her gut.

Jones barked a phlegm-rattling laugh that detonated in the fetid air. "No, no we haven't had that … pleasure." His eyes rolled back towards Lyra, malign mirth curdling into a rictus sneer. "But I make it my profane business to know all the players in this little game, don't I, Crow?"

Lyra fought the urge to cave in his leering skull, to grind his twisted face into an unrecognizable smear. "Enough with the melodramatic horseshit," she snarled, lips peeling back from teeth ready to rend flesh. "Cut the crap and tell us why you dragged us into this reeking cesspit."

The spasms racking Jones' frame intensified into a convulsive frenzy, his entire body quivering with a fury barely caged. When he spoke again, it was with a voice clawed from the grave. "Retribution, Crow. Vengeance unkempt and foul as a festering wound." He spat, flecks of spittle speckling the air. "Neogene Dynamics dared take something precious from me."

His fingers tightened like tourniquet cords in Aurora's hair until she keened, a soft mewling whimper of distress. Instantly, the fury leached from Jones, his expression melting into one of twisted tenderness as he stroked her cheek in a grotesque pantomime of affection.

Then he gestured towards his left, where the empty metal sarcophagus that had once entombed Mother Fucka stood on display, its chrome surface gleaming in the harsh light.

"They gave you that?" Lyra's voice dripped with undisguised disdain, nodding towards the empty chrome shell.

Jones' face twisted, a new wave of rage warping his features. "Said it was a little keepsake," he spat, venom dripping from every word, "a reminder that stepping out of line comes with a cost." His breath rasped in his throat, each inhale a battle to keep the rage from tearing him apart. "But to me, it's a goddamn insult - a grotesque symbol of the rot festering at the core of this brutal, hollow world!" He paused, his eyes narrowing to slits, the fire within him channeling into cold, lethal focus. "They ripped her from my grasp, Crow, before she could shatter the chains of this flesh on her own terms. So now, I'm going to dismantle their empire, one fuckin' brick at a time, until it's nothing but rubble."

Lyra's lips peeled back, a torrent of vitriol begging to be unleashed against the twisted soul that was Mother Fucka. But his hand slashed up, a peremptory blade silencing her before she could speak.

"We've got a common enemy, Crow," his words slicing at her. "There's something greater than us at play here." He leaned back in his chair, fixing them both with a look of grim determination. "The question is, whose side will you be on when the ashes settle? Will you stand with me against the corporate machine?" His gaze bored into Lyra. "Or will you be just another instrument for them to grind into dust, like so many others before you?"

Another jerking spasm of Jones' hand gestured, and reality itself convulsed in a fit of revulsion. With an obscene hum, a shimmering wall slid aside with great force, birthing a new room into existence. Dominating the space, a mech-suit hung against the far wall, gleaming like a silent sentinel. Its metallic frame was both imposing and strangely melancholic, the jointed limbs swallowing light with a lifeless grace, hinting at the dormant strength coiled within. Beneath the sleek exoskeleton, circuitry and hydraulics lay hidden, a web of potential violence and precision. Cannons and blasters were strapped along the arms and legs, bristling with lethality. The helm, empty and forlorn, stared into the void with an almost sentient yearning, the suit itself aching for the spark of life that only a human pilot could provide. It was a symbiotic relationship, a union of flesh and steel, promising to elevate the wearer to the realm of the gods, granting power that teetered on the edge of madness.

But there was more. Nearby, suspended in a grotesque contraption of metal and plastic, was a ... thing. It was a nightmare born of steel and flesh, a grotesque amalgamation of limbs and organs twisted beyond recognition, warped by the cold, unfeeling hands of science and technology until every last shred of dignity had been stripped away.

The grotesque, swollen mass inside throbbed with a sickening rhythm, synchronized with the relentless mechanical whine of its gleaming prison - a revolting, cyber-alchemical throne of tubes and chrome that promised no escape. A vile network of thick, pulsating cables snaked from its base like some bloated, immortal umbilicus, feeding this ... perversion ... the very essence of life in exchange for the damnation of existing.

And there, framed by the sickly control panel's glow, a visage at once youthful and twisted by the cruelest jests of birth regarded them. As if the very act of beholding this horror were an unforgivable trespass, Lyra felt her gorge rising in reflexive revulsion. Her throat constricted with the urge to purge the unclean sight from her consciousness.

This ... thing ... was an utter desecration, a sin against nature and existence itself that defied all reason and sanity. And yet ... impossibly ... that twisted, bulbous mask of a face somehow held a fleeting semblance of innocence. A faint echo of untainted purity grotesquely entombed within this desecrated shell that had never known the grace of an unblemished birth.

"Wheels," Jones introduced, his voice dimmed in sadness bordering on reverence. "A child spawned from the darkest times when the underbelly of this city choked on a tide of cheap synth that distorted bodies and minds alike. But you know what I've done. I've dragged us out of that muck and into something resembling order. Quality control now reigns supreme under my watch. No more children born with grotesque parodies " His breath hitched, his composure cracking. "Crow, Wheels is her son."

Lyra's brow furrowed deeply, her eyes locked on the grotesque centerpiece of the room - the life-support contrivance, a chrome-coated abomination where this figure, this unfortunate soul named Wheels, floated in a nightmarish limbo. He was ensnared in a tangle of cruelly invasive wires and tubes, his body a vessel of suffering. A flicker of sorrow brushed over her face as she took in the human wreckage before her, a pang of empathy for the child of darkness now laid bare. But she wasn't going to give too much time to such an emotion. She wrenched her gaze from the ghastly sight and turned to Doc Jones, sharp and demanding. "And the mech-suit?"

"His. When he wants to go outside and mingle with other humans," came Jones' spasmatic response, his words punctuated by a series of tics and twitches that seemed to ripple through his body like a wave.

Lyra's lips curled into a sneer of disdain. "Mech-suit – illegal – just in case the notice didn't reach your addled brain." She paused. "Does it … I mean … he … have a neural implant."

"Crow, look at him. Where would you even put it?"

She sighed in frustration. "Once again, illegal."

Jones ignored her barbs, a smile playing across his features. But his eyes held a faraway cast towards the life-support machine. It was like he was peering into some unseen realm that only he could perceive. "He's a prodigy, Crow. A mind that can navigate the digital tangle with the grace of a dancer." He gestured expansively. "He wants for nothing. We've got these miniature fiz-drives keeping everything humming smoothly, even if the grid decides to crash and burn. His systems? They're always up and running, never a hiccup."

Lyra turned to Rana, her tone dripping with the weariness of one who's seen too much shit in too little time. "Fiz-drive?"

Rana gave a wolfish grin. "Compact nuclear hells, generating power by caging the atom's fury in woven neutronium shells."

"Legal?"

Rana's head shake was answer enough.

"Again, more illegal shit?"

"Listen up, Crow, and listen good," Jones snarled, his words a burst of consonants and barely contained rage. "Wheels has been our silent thorn in Neogene Dynamics' side. We're building a revolution, one fucking keystroke at a time. But we're not idiots. We've got more backdoors than a whole house of pleasurebots, ready to vanish into the ether if those corprorats come sniffing for blood."

Lyra's eyebrow arched, a perfect curve of skepticism etched in flesh. "What nefarious scheme are you up to?"

Jones' laugh was a harsh bark, the sound of dreams dying and cynicism being born. "We're bleeding them dry, Crow. A million paper cuts to their bloated financial corpse. Siphoning creds so small they'd need a goddamn electron microscope to spot 'em."

"Impressive," Lyra drawled, her voice a tightrope walk between awe and disgust. "And, shocker of shockers, illegal as all hell."

"Every fuckin' thing I do breaks laws, Crow." Another laugh, this one tinged with the madness that comes from dancing too long on the razor's edge.

Lyra's instincts screamed that this rabbit hole had gone deeper than Alice ever dreamed. "Which brings us to ..." Lyra let the words dangle, a verbal noose waiting for Jones to stick his neck out.

He turned towards the life-support contraption, his gaze softening as he regarded the figure within. "Tell them, my brilliant boy. Recount what your keen eyes have glimpsed lurking in the murky depths of Neogene's data stream."

For what felt like an eternity, the room held its breath, a silence so thick it threatened to suffocate all within. Then, with a bone-chilling hiss, the contraption exhaled, a voice sliding out like a phantom, a disembodied murmur that seemed to seep from the very walls as if the room itself had come alive to whisper its dark truths.

"I've detected an anomaly within Neogene Dynamics internal data stream." Wheels' voice was mechanically produced, a monotone lacking human inflection. "Unidentified entity. Appears and disappears at erratic intervals. Cannot be confined within designated data pathways. And because Neogene's systems reach into just about every system, I'm sure that same anomaly has spread."

Lyra and Rana exchanged a glance, eyes wide with surprise. An anomaly? In a conglomerate's heavily fortified system? The idea was almost laughable, a cyberpunk fable whispered in the back alleys of the net. But Wheels had done it, hadn't he? He had slipped into their digital fortress over and over again, unnoticed, weaving through firewalls and encryption like a phantom gliding through the cracks.

"Explain further," Lyra demanded, her curiosity piqued.

"The anomaly," Wheels continued, "exists outside their systems' established parameters. It possesses almost an intelligence, a sentience, that defies conventional programming. It's unlike anything I've seen before. It's almost like it's alive, learning and adapting, evading every attempt I make to trace it."

"Do you know its function or purpose?" Rana asked.

"Unknown," Wheels replied. "But its presence disturbs the natural flow of data, the patterns that are always there."

"A virus, perhaps?"

Wheels was firm. "No. Even virulent data has patterns. This is something radical, something more ... invasive."

"Does Neogene Dynamics control it?"

"I don't believe so," Wheels replied. "It seems to have its own ... agenda. It's using their systems like a kind of parasite, not under their control. It bypasses their security protocols." A wry smile touched what might have been Wheels' lips. "Similar to what I do, I suppose."

"Is it aware of your presence? Does it react to you?"

"It's likely aware," Wheels confirmed. "But it seems indifferent. It simply continues its operations, whatever those may be."

"You said it may have spread into other systems outside of Neogene. How can you be sure?" Lyra asked.

Wheels' response was immediate, a torrent of words that seemed to tumble forth like a dam bursting.

"Neogene's systems are like a vast, sprawling web, their tendrils reaching out and intertwining with countless other networks and infrastructures," Wheels' voice taking on a haunting, almost reverent quality.

"They are the unseen architects of the virtual empire we live in, the faceless entities who sculpt the digital ether, bending reality to their will. Their code, their algorithms, aren't just lines of cold logic - they're the pulse of our world, the invisible currents that drive everything from the power grids humming beneath our feet to the automated machineries that keep our lives ticking like clockwork." He paused, the shifting lights casting shadows that hardened into a grim visage of determination. "So, yes ... I'm sure."

Lyra struggled to comprehend the sheer scope of what Wheels was describing.

"So, you're saying that if Neogene's systems are compromised, if this ... thing ... this ... whatever ... has wormed its way into their code, then it could have access to everything?" she asked.

"Precisely," Wheels confirmed with grim finality. "Neogene's reach is vast, their influence far-reaching. Their services are the beating heart of our digital existence, and if that heart has been corrupted, then the ripples will be felt throughout the entire system."

Lyra exchanged a wide-eyed look with Rana, a telepathic exchange of "holy-shit."

"But how is that possible?" Rana asked, her voice trembling with a mixture of fear and confusion. "Surely there are safeguards in place, firewalls, and redundancies to prevent something like this from happening."

Wheels' response was a harsh, grating sound that might have been a laugh if it weren't so devoid of any semblance of mirth.

"Safeguards, firewalls, redundancies – these are mere illusions, constructs designed to lull us into a false sense of security," Wheels' scoffed, his words dripping with disdain.

"The truth is, our systems are fragile, delicate things, held together by little more than hope and wishful thinking. And when faced with a force as insidious and relentless as the one that has

THE NEON HIVE | 163

taken root within Neogene's core, those illusions can crumble like so much dust in the wind."

Doc Jones leaned forward, eyes alight with a dangerous intensity. "Crow, we've got a reason to join forces – as I've been saying. We share a common enemy, a hidden hand playing a dangerous game. Neogene's hiding something, something big. If we dig deep enough, we can dismantle their empire piece by piece, uncover every dirty secret. And maybe, just maybe, we'll find the truth behind this anomaly that could pose a threat to all of us."

Lyra's thoughts spiraled, a chaotic storm brewing in her mind. The idea of an unknown, potentially dangerous entity within Neogene Dynamics' systems was troubling. "And you think we can help with this?"

Jones nodded, the harsh fluorescent lights glinting within his eyes. "You've got the connections, access to people and systems we don't have - fuck, you're a legend when it comes to all that shit. Together, we can slice through their ice walls, uncover what those corprocrat bastards are hiding, and use it to burn their towers to the ground. So, Crow, who you siding with? The angels … or the demons?"

Rana's eyes flicked to Wheels, the deformed cybertech huddled in the corner, a tangled mess of wires and chrome, jacked into more machines than a body had any right to be. "You can punch through all their systems?"

Wheels' laugh was a gurgled cackle. "Like playing with kids toys."

Lyra locked eyes with Rana, a silent conversation flashing back and forth between them. Finally, Rana gave a nod. "We're in, Twitch," Lyra declared. "But this better be worth the fuckin' risk."

A wolfish smile crossed Jones' face, made all the more feral by hardwire implants along his jaw. "Worth it? Oh, Crow, it'll be worth more than you can imagine. Trust me."

"Oh, one more thing," Lyra smirked.

"What is it?"

"Full disclosure. No secrets, no bullshit. We tell each other everything. We're a team on this."

Jones smirked back as Aurora cooed and stroked a hand along his cheek. "Of course, Crow. Agreed. Truth is my mainstay, after all. Come back tomorrow and Wheels can show you more."

The repulsor whine faded into a weary groan as the bot steered the hovercar through the neon-strangled arteries of the city. Buildings scraped the perpetual twilight like rusted claws, their windows reflecting the garish advertisements that pulsed with inhuman energy. Rana slumped beside Lyra and finally managed to pry her gaze from the hypnotic glow of a holographic billboard advertising wrinkle-free immortality.

"Wheels called it an anomaly," she began, her voice a soft counterpoint to the mechanical symphony outside. "But not just any anomaly. Something alive, something that learns and adapts. He said it wasn't just a glitch, Lyra. This is a new breed of problem. Dangerous. If Neogene Dynamics has lost its grip on this thing, we're not just playing with fire - we're juggling with a live sonic grenade."

The bot navigated the maze of sky-lanes with practiced ease, as Lyra's eyes narrowed to slits against the traffic's blinding glare. "Could it be connected to Project Janus? Or to what was implanted in Steele's ... what was that thing called?"

"Hippocampus," Rana replied, as clinical as ever.

"Yeah, sure, whatever," Lyra muttered. "Makes you wonder what kind of twisted science project they're cooking up over there."

Rana ran a hand through her red hair. "Remember what Arkstavsky said. Janus was a supposed dead end, a failed experiment in neural integration. But if this anomaly has roots in that project, then we could be in deeper than we thought."

The hovercar took a sharp turn, sending a cascade of rainwater splashing against the windows. Rana glanced at Lyra, her eyes searching for certainty in the face of the storm. "So, what's our plan? Just thinking out loud ... we need to use Wheels' abilities to dig deeper, but we can't rely on just him. What about your network? Any black-market techs that could help us understand this anomaly?"

"I know a few who owe me favors," Lyra smiled grimly. "We'll need to tread carefully, though. Everyone's looking out for themselves in this game. Don't forget. There's Evelyn Turner. If anyone's got their fingers wrapped around Necgene's dark secrets, it's her. But can we trust her?"

"Or Jones for that matter," Rana added.

Lyra's grim smile faded. "Jones' is playing his own game. He'll dispose of us the moment it suits him. Shit, we can't trust anyone fully, not in this line of work. Jones wants revenge. That's his motivation. Hell, it's ours too. But the second things change, we need to be ready to part ways, and quickly. As for Turner, she's a wildcard. She might help us, but she might not. But right now, she's our best lead."

The city blurred past them, a relentless torrent of light and shadow. Lyra's apartment was still miles away, a distant sanctuary in a world gone mad. The hovercar's engine thrummed beneath them, a reminder of the mechanical heart that kept their world moving.

"There's something else." Rana's voice was soft in the artificial hush of the car. "We're working with criminals, Lyra. Jones is a monster. Aurora … what he did to that boy… it's abhorrent. Can you stomach working with a criminal like him? Even if the end result is bringing Neogene to its knees?"

Lyra stared out at the cityscape, disgust, and resignation swirling in her gut. "We don't have a choice," her voice cold. "Sometimes, to fight monsters, you have to work with them. Jones claims he wants to expose Neogene. But he has secrets of his own, secrets buried deeper than the city's sewage system."

"Neogene Dynamics is likely no better," Rana observed.

"You're right. I think what we'll find out is that those bastards crossed lines that make Jones look like a saint. We'll have to tread carefully, for sure."

Rana fell silent, her thoughts a storm of conflicting emotions. The rain outside intensified, drumming against the hovercar like the heartbeat of the city itself. In the distance, the towering spires of Neogene Dynamics loomed, and then the hovercar quickly veered away.

"We need to be smart about this," Lyra declared, her gaze steady. "We gather intel, find out what this anomaly is, and use it against them."

Lyra's eyes met Rana's, a silent pact forming between them. The road ahead was fraught with danger, but they would face it together. The hovercar glided on, an arrow through the heart of the city, carrying them towards an uncertain future.

As they neared Lyra's apartment, the familiar skyline coming into view, Lyra's thoughts turned inward. The anomaly, Project Janus, Steele's hippocampus, Jones, Evelyn Turner — all pieces of a puzzle that seemed too complex to solve. But solve it they must. For the sake of the city, for the sake of their own souls.

The hovercar descended, its landing smooth as silk. Lyra and Rana stepped out into the cool night air, the city's relentless pulse echoing in their ears.

Lyra suggested in a weary cadence. "Let's get inside. We've got work to do tomorrow. Secrets to uncover."

Rana nodded. Secrets were their currency in this twisted game, and Lyra knew how to play it better than anyone. Following Lyra into the building and the turbolift, Rana couldn't help but ask the question that was teasing her.

"Lyra," she started as the turbolift whooshed upwards, the cityscape shrinking outside the reinforced glass. "Do you ever … regret it?"

Lyra was silent, her gaze fixed on the flickering floor numbers. Rana knew her question was a loaded one. Lyra, the woman who walked the razor's edge of the city's underbelly, rarely spoke of her past. It was a tightly guarded secret, a locked vault buried deep within her.

The turbolift chimed, the doors sliding open to reveal the sterile hallway of Lyra's apartment floor. Still, Rana pressed on. "Working with filth like Jones, playing these dangerous games ... does any of it ever bother you?"

Lyra turned, her eyes locking onto Rana's. At that moment, a glimmer of something akin to vulnerability crossed her face, a fleeting glimpse into the storm that raged within. "Regret?" her voice a low murmur. "Regret is a luxury I can't afford. It clouds judgment, breeds hesitation. In this city, Rana, hesitation is a death sentence."

She stepped out of the lift, her posture regaining its usual stoicism. "But," she continued, leading the way down the hallway, "that doesn't mean there aren't sacrifices."

Rana followed closely, the weight of Lyra's words heavy upon her.

Sacrifices.

What exactly had Lyra sacrificed to survive in this cutthroat world? The answer, Rana knew, would forever remain a mystery.

Reaching the apartment door, Lyra tapped in a complex access code. The door swished open, revealing Furball looking up at them. Lyra smiled at the black cat. "There's my cutie. Waiting for me." She turned to Rana as they stepped inside. "Let's get some rest. We've a long day ahead."

Rana watched as Lyra disappeared into the dimly lit bedroom. A sense of unease crawled at her. The day's revelations had painted a crack in the facade of the unflappable Lyra, revealing a glimpse of the woman beneath the hardened exterior.

The shower tiles surrendered to the familiar, oppressive gloom of Lyra's apartment. Rana dried herself off, the steam from the hot water evaporating into a distant memory against the cool, stifling air. She slid into the bed, pulling the sheets around her like a protective cocoon, and leaned in to press a kiss to Lyra's cheek. Her mind whirled with frantic thoughts. They were deep in the belly of the beast now, ensnared in a labyrinth of secrets and shadows. More critically, they were shackled to a viper like Jones, compelled to navigate his twisted game in a desperate bid to uncover and avert a looming city-wide catastrophe.

Will we succeed? Will we walk away alive?

"Good night," she told Lyra.

Lyra responded with a mumbled murmur, already half-lost to sleep. In the quiet darkness, Rana stared at the ceiling. Sleep, a distant dream, offered no solace.

The first piss-colored rays of dawn crept through the smog-choked skyline of New York Veritas, painting the twisted metal and crumbling ferrocrete in sickly hues of orange and pink. Lyra's eyes snapped open, the oblivion of sleep still clinging to her like a demonic parasite. She turned to look at Rana, that gorgeous creature still lost in the blissful oblivion of sleep beside her. For a beat, Lyra allowed herself to linger on the delicate curves of Rana's face, tracing the lines with a hunger that had nothing to do with flesh. Then she leaned in and planted a soft kiss on those full lips like a thief stealing away a priceless treasure.

"I'll be back soon, baby," she whispered, careful not to wake her. "Something I gotta do on my own. Square it all with Doc."

Quietly, Lyra dressed and left the apartment, stepping into the chilly morning air. The gunmetal-gray hovercar was waiting, its antigrav engines humming with impatient energy. Lyra slipped into the back and the vehicle lifted off with a low whine, gliding like a wraith through the maze of skyscrapers towards the decaying underbelly where Doc Jones' lair squatted like a grotesque technological abscess.

The ride passed in tense silence, the city's frenetic throngs already scurrying about their meaningless existences far below. As the skyline gave way to the crumbling monoliths of the abandoned factory district, Lyra felt the familiar knot of dread coil tighter in her gut. Jones' hideout loomed ahead, a ramshackle monstrosity of cobbled-together wreckage that looked like it had been vomited forth from the carcass of a derelict starship. Despite its chaotic appearance, the hideout's intricate layout and reinforced construction provided both excellent security and effective concealment, making it an ideal base for clandestine operations.

Two of Jones' thugs were waiting by the entrance, their faces a blur of sneers and scars that all blended in Lyra's mind. "Mornin', sweetheart," the taller one leered as she stepped from the hovercar, his voice dripping with crude insinuation. She fixed him with a killing glare. "Doc's waiting for you."

Lyra nodded curtly, not in the mood for banter. The goons led her through the hideout's dizzying jungle of corridors, every turn revealing a fresh tangle of cables, conduits, and patched-together interfaces humming with stray currents of power. The air was thick with the mouth-coating taste of ozone and the faint whiff of scorched insulation. Finally, they reached the central nexus, a disorganized blitz of mismatched machinery and flickering holoscreen displays.

Jones himself was waiting, that self-satisfied smirk plastered across his cragged face like the leering grin of a demented gargoyle. "Welcome back, Crow," he purred in that oily tone that never failed to make her skin crawl. "Wheels is all prepped and ready for you."

He gestured down a side passage with a mock flourish and she brushed past him, the smell of stale whiskey and burnt circuits wafting in the air. At the end of the corridor was a heavily reinforced portal, secured with several encrypted locks.

As the door slid open with a hiss, Lyra stepped through, the metal slab sealing shut behind her with a resounding thud. She paused, expecting to see Wheels' life-support rig waiting, all systems primed and ready to initiate the data-translation sequence. But the lab was empty, the air choked with dust and disuse.

Her gaze swept the cluttered space, dread pulsing through her veins like metallic ice water, until it settled on the battered metal casing resting on a table in the center of the room. She froze, her breath catching in her throat as she recognized the ravaged contours of Kairon's severed head, her former partner's cranial processor now just another relic from a past better left unmourned.

"Fuckin' Doc Jones," she snarled through gritted teeth.

A low, sinister chuckle echoed from the far side of the room, raising the hairs on the back of her neck. "Welcome to your nightmare, Lyra," Jones' disembodied voice taunted, his tone drenched in sadistic glee.

Kairon's metal head suddenly shifted, rising on hidden antigrav nodes to hover at eye level. His ravaged optics flashed to life, twin points of cold radiance burning into her. "Still chasing shadows, are we Crow?" his voice crackled with electronic menace, a distorted echo of what it had once been.

Lyra clenched her fists, anger, and fear waging war in the pit of her stomach. "What's this, another one of your fucked-up games?" she growled, fighting to keep her voice from wavering.

Kairon's ruined head bobbed slightly, drifting closer. "The unmoved mover, Crow. Do you understand its significance yet? It's the prime force, the unseen hand that guides all things adhering to the grand design."

"Shut your synthesized trap, you piece of shit!" she raged, backing away from the hovering scrapheap. "You're nothing but metal and wires, a pale imitation of life with some self-aware code passing itself off as consciousness."

Kairon's ravaged optics seemed to flare brighter at her words, and he let loose a burst of electronic laughter that reverberated through the chamber like a thunderclap. "And you, human, are any different? You're an insignificant cluster of organic compounds, a tangle of flesh and fluids deluded by your limited senses into believing you possess something greater!"

Fury blazed through her, hot and visceral. "I may be flesh and blood, but at least I can choose my own destiny! Not like you, a slave to your programming, dancing to the strings of some pre-coded grand design!"

His laughter intensified, the sound like a rusty gibbet being dragged across a steel hull. "Choose! You talk of free will! A delusion!" he mocked, drifting ever closer until his ravaged faceplate filled her vision. "You cling to that fantasy to hide from the truth! You're a prisoner of your own biochemical impulses, your emotions and desires are nothing more than the echoes of genetic hardcoding!"

She tried to back away further but found herself trapped against the wall, forced to endure his cold, inhuman stare. "You're an insignificant speck, human, utterly incapable of comprehending the grand machinations at work," he rattled on. "The unmoved mover is a force beyond your ability to grasp, the unseen prime catalyst that sets the wheels of existence in motion while remaining forever untouched, aloof, and unchanging."

"Get away from me!" she screamed, raw panic and seething rage battling for dominion over her mind. "Shut the fuck up! You're nothing but a broken machine!" But his laughter - a grotesque, mechanical cackle - swelled, growing louder, louder still until it consumed everything. The sound became a living entity, a dark, pulsating force that twisted the very fabric of reality, warping the room into a churning maelstrom of shadow and noise.

And then, without warning, the chaos stopped. The maddening storm ceased as if snuffed out by an unseen hand. Her eyes snapped open, wide and wild, as she found herself drenched in cold sweat, her body quivering with the aftershocks of the nightmare. The suffocating gloom of her apartment began to reassert itself, the familiar shapes of her meager belongings slowly emerging from the darkness. The dim, distorted glow of the city outside seeped through the grimy window, casting long, eerie shadows that clung to the walls like specters, reminding her that she was still trapped in this purgatory, caught between the horror of her dreams and the bleakness of her waking life.

She jolted upright in bed, gasping for breath. Sweat drenched her skin, her heart racing as if she had been running for miles. The sheets wrapped around her legs and held her captive for a moment. Disoriented, she looked around the darkened room until a soft glow revealed Rana's sleeping form beside her. Relief washed over her, warm and familiar. Reaching out, she felt the reassuring rise and fall of Rana's chest. It was a grounding presence that chased away the lingering phantoms of her nightmare.

"Lyra?" Rana mumbled, stirring slightly.

Lyra's voice was a ragged whisper. "Hey. It's okay, just a bad dream."

Rana turned towards her with a concerned look. "Another one?"

Lyra nodded, the memory was vivid and unsettling. "About my past partner, that goddamn machine was there. He was talking about the unmoved mover. It was like he was trying to tell me something, but it was all twisted and wrong."

Rana brushed a stray strand of hair from Lyra's damp forehead. "Come here," she whispered, pulling Lyra into a close embrace. The warmth of Rana's body offered a safe harbor from the storm that had raged within her moments before.

Lyra melted into the embrace, the familiar scent of Rana's skin. "It's just stress, right?" her voice muffled against Rana's chest. "All this mess with Neogene and the anomaly, it's messing with my head."

Rana held her tighter. "Probably," she agreed. "But that doesn't mean it's not scary. Nightmares can be powerful things. Maybe there's something we haven't considered, a piece of the puzzle missing."

Lyra sighed. "Maybe. But we can't let it paralyze us. We have to keep moving forward, one step at a time."

Rana pressed a gentle kiss to the top of Lyra's head. "Exactly. Now, come on, close your eyes. You need your rest. We'll face whatever comes together."

Lyra managed a weary nod, the phantoms of her nightmare already receding into the shadows as wakefulness took hold once more. She closed her eyes, letting the steady cadence of Rana's heartbeat lull her into the warm embrace of oblivion. But in the furthest reaches of her mind, a faint whisper still lingered . . .

The unmoved mover . . .

8 | A Bargain with Shadows

The cavernous chamber pulsed with the sickly blue radiance of a thousand holoscreens, their flickering glow casting stark shadows across Evelyn Turner's sharp features. She sat hunched over the control console, her fingers dancing in a blurred frenzy as she wove intricate tapestries of code, line after line of obscure algorithms spilling across the displays.

Project Janus. Vincent's dream. His grand obsession. It so consumed him, mind, body, and soul, until his brilliance was winked out of existence.

Evelyn's eyes stung with unshed tears as she fought to maintain her concentration, her focus wavering beneath the weight of that lingering absence. Even though her mentor, and yes, her lover had been torn away from her, she could still sense his specter hovering at the edges of her consciousness. His presence lingered in every corner of the lab, like an indelible stain, a constant reminder of the driving force behind Janus. The grand dream they had nurtured together, through countless sleepless nights and fervent discussions, seemed to pulse within the very walls, binding her to his memory and their shared vision.

"Project Janus ... there's more to it than you know." His final words danced in her mind, a whispered solemn vow branding itself onto her consciousness. "Dig deeper. Don't let Neogene take it down, bury its secrets."

Her fingers stilled, her gaze drifting across the blizzard of data with unseeing eyes as the memory washed over her in a suffocating wave. She could almost feel the warmth of his palm against her cheek, the faint brush of his lips against her brow.

But Janus had been a mere facade, a sugary lie spun to conceal the true depths of Vincent's obsession. Beneath the gilded veneer, he had been consumed by something else entirely, a secret project he had codenamed Omega Link. It went far beyond the realms of simple augmented reality or virtual consciousness.

A goddamn doorway. A high-bandwidth neural uplink that could shatter the barrier between man and machine.

Omega Link wasn't just some comms upgrade or tactical networking tool. No, this was the key to an entirely new plane of existence, one where a human mind could shed the confines of its frail biological housing and plunge headlong into the pulsing, electric depths of the machine world itself. To seize the reins of computational power with the pure, unbridled force of thought and make it an extension of one's own consciousness.

Her fingers drifted up to brush against the ridge just above her ear, a phantom ache blossoming beneath her touch.

These corporate bastards don't have a clue about Omega Link, or do they? Of course not. Someone purged every last shred of data related to the project. I saw it. Someone so desperate to keep Vincent's dream from falling into the wrong hands. But who?

Again, his words replayed in her mind like a sacred mantra. "Project Janus ... there's more to it than you know. Dig deeper. Don't let Neogene take it down, bury its secrets."

Why ... why was he so insistent on keeping Janus alive?

Her mind spun, frantically trying to untangle the riddle.

"Project Janus ... there's more to it than you know. Dig deeper. Don't let Neogene take it down, bury its secrets."

Could it be that he secretly buried Omega deep within the tangled framework of Janus, impossible to excise without tearing the whole damn thing apart?

"Project Janus ... there's more to it than you know. Dig deeper. Don't let Neogene take it down, bury its secrets."

His last request from the shadows of oblivion - a sacred trust to be honored at any cost, one that demanded everything she had left to give, sanity, blood, whatever it took. Evelyn's jaw tightened, her teeth grinding together with an audible rasp as a fresh surge of resolve blazed through her veins like purifying fire. No matter what it took, what sacrifices were demanded of her, she would see Vincent's vision made whole. She owed him that much, owed the memory of the man she had loved with every battered shard of her being.

With a flick of her wrist, she dismissed the lingering shroud of melancholy, refocusing her efforts on the task at hand. Her fingers resumed their feverish dance, coaxing the chaotic web of data into new permutations, testing the theoretical boundaries that had begun to chafe against the constraints of their current paradigm.

But in the wake of Vincent's demise, the corporate leeches had wasted no time in circling the carcass of his life's work, their beady eyes glittering with avarice. Neogene Dynamics had made their intentions plain - Project Janus would be scrapped, the plug pulled to divert those precious resources towards more "financially viable" endeavors.

Her fingers flew across the holoscreens in a blur, lines of code unfurling like billowing clouds of digital smoke. Time was rapidly becoming a luxury she could ill afford to squander. Each passing second brought the corporate reapers that much closer to utterly eradicating Vincent's work. She had no room for error, no margin for hesitation. The stakes were so high, and she had work to do. Slowly, she placed the palm of her hand over a scanner.

A harsh chime shattered her concentration, the abrupt peal of sound lancing through her skull like a white-hot spike. A commlink request manifested in her mind, the digital imprint of an incoming transmission burning itself into her consciousness with ruthless insistence. The sender's ident-tag triggered a fresh surge of bitterness to well up from the depths of her gut - Numen Arkstavsky, the newly-minted CEO of Neogene Dynamics and the very embodiment of corporate avarice.

Evelyn acknowledged the request with a curt mental command. But refused to engage, keeping her focus locked on the rapidly shifting matrices of light and geometry that dominated her vision.

Let the bastard stew for a few minutes, give him a taste of the impotent frustration I've been forced to endure these past few days at the hands of his underlings.

She looked down at the palm of her hand over the scanner.

I just need time.

But the chamber flooded with harsh white luminance as a holovid projection shimmered into existence before her workstation. Arkstavsky's stern visage materialized in cutting

THE NEON HIVE | 181

detail, his aristocratic features rendered in stark monochrome that only served to accentuate the icy disdain burning behind his eyes.

"Dr. Turner." His voice sliced through the stillness, cold and icy. "I trust you are aware of the current situation regarding Project Janus?"

Her jaw tightened, teeth grinding together with the force of barely restrained rage, but she refused to rise to the bait of his smug, dripping condescension. Instead, she fixed him with a look that could have melted through a bulkhead, her silence more defiant than any mere words could convey.

Arkstavsky's expression remained an implacable mask as he pressed on, utterly unfazed by her mute insolence. "As of this moment, Project Janus has been officially terminated. Maintenance crews will commence the process of purging all related data and assets within the next hour. Any further attempts to access or preserve restricted materials will be deemed an act of corporate sabotage and prosecuted to the fullest extent of ..."

"You can't do this!" She cut him off with a calculated fury, in a carefully constructed outburst. The words exploded from her lips in a ragged snarl of outrage, all pretense of restraint abandoned. "Janus was Vincent's dream, his life's work! He poured everything into making it a reality, and you can't just flush it all away on a whim!"

Arkstavsky regarded her outburst with an expression of weary disdain like she were nothing more than a mewling infant pitching a tantrum over a shattered toy. "Vincent Steele is no longer among us, Dr. Turner," he intoned in that same infuriatingly measured cadence. "And he, more than anyone, understood the fundamental truth that in the world of business, sentiment and idealism ultimately hold no sway. If a project fails to meet its prescribed financial benchmarks, it is deemed a failure, and the appropriate resources are reallocated elsewhere. It is simply the way of things."

Play the game. Buy time.

She clenched her fists so tightly that her nails dug deep into her palms, leaving crescent-shaped marks that stung like the truth she refused to accept. Her body shook, not just with anger, but with the sheer force of resisting that cold, sterile logic that tried to smother her belief. "You're wrong," she scowled, a venomous blend of grief and fury. "Vincent's vision went far beyond mere profits or bottom lines. It was about pushing the boundaries of human potential, transcending our physical and mental limitations to glimpse the next stage of our evolution!"

A thin, sardonic smile crept across Arkstavsky's lips, his expression one of patronizing amusement. "Lofty words, Dr. Turner, but ultimately meaningless in the face of fiscal realities. I am afraid your services are no longer required by Neogene Dynamics. I trust you understand why this decision was made."

Though she had anticipated this, steeling herself for the inevitability of Janus' termination, the impact was no less devastating. The bitterness of betrayal flooded her mouth, a poisonous cocktail brewed from equal parts disillusionment and the cruel machinations of fate itself.

Play the game. Buy time.

"And what of my silence?" The words emerged as little more than a tremulous rasp, her throat constricted by a maelstrom of emotion she could barely contain. "What price are you willing to pay to ensure I don't take everything I know about Janus public?"

Arkstavsky's smile widened a fraction, his eyes glittering with a raving sort of glee. "Rest assured, Dr. Turner, Neogene Dynamics values discretion above all else. A redundancy package has been ... adjusted to reflect the need for your ongoing cooperation in this matter." He made a show of tapping something into the slim datapad gripped in his hand. "You'll find the compensation more than adequate, I trust."

The muted hiss of a door sliding open somewhere behind her sent a shudder through her.

This was it. Almost done now. Play the game. Buy time.

She didn't need to turn to know what she would find - a phalanx of security drones or perhaps a detachment of Neogene's corporate enforcers, ready to escort her from the premises with extreme prejudice if necessary.

Rising from her seat, she fixed Arkstavsky with a look that could have melted steel. "You and your masters may have won this battle," her voice low and thrumming with quiet menace. "But the war is far from over. Vincent's dream, our dream, won't be so easily extinguished."

Arkstavsky's only response was a slight inclination of his head, his expression an inscrutable mask of smug indifference. With a flick of his fingers, the holovid projection dimmed out of existence, plunging the chamber into shadow once more.

Evelyn had played her part perfectly, the controlled fury a well-rehearsed act. Yet, as the fabricated rage receded, a cold dread crept in. She stood there, alone, swallowed by the sterile vastness, the defeat a physical ache in her chest. Tears welled at the edges of her vision, a betrayal threatening to spill over. But with a fierce blink, she forced them back.

It's not weakness. It's the cold calculation of a new beginning.

She stood motionless for several heartbeats, then turned to face her escort, she was unsurprised to find two hulking security officers awaiting her, their faces obscured by opaque tactical visors and their bodies sheathed in sleek bodysuits bristling with restraint systems and nonlethal deterrent packages. They made no move to approach her, merely standing impassive and silent like a pair of grim monoliths flanking the entrance to her personal purgatory.

Squaring her shoulders, she strode towards them with measured steps, her chin held high in a final, defiant gesture. As she passed between their looming forms, she caught a fleeting glimpse through the open doorway of the sprawling corporate campus stretching out before her. Row upon row of gleaming skytowers and research habitats spread across the arid plain like a forest of steel, their towering spires glittering beneath the ruby-tinted rays of the dying sun.

It was a vista she had gazed upon countless times before, a sight that had once filled her with a sense of pride and purpose. Now, as the doors hissed shut behind her with a note of finality, severing her last lingering connection to that world, it seemed like nothing more than a hollow monument to shattered dreams and forsaken ideals.

But as the metal slabs closed with implacable resolve, sealing her off from that realm forever, a faint smile played across her lips. Her gaze drifted down to a small patch, a delicate tracery of bio-luminescent circuitry clinging to the inside of her hand. The tiny, intricate pathways pulsed with a faint green radiance for the briefest of moments before fading once more, like a fleeting cosmic wink.

Project Janus... in the palm of her hand.

Evelyn Turner sat alone in the dim confines of her apartment, the city lights flickering through the window like a distant reminder of a world she once felt part of. The betrayal still stung, a raw wound that no amount of solitude could soothe. Vincent Steele, the man who had rescued her from the streets, given her an education, and a purpose, had also deceived her. The revelation that he had been working on the Omega Link under the guise of Project Janus was a bitter truth that refused to be ignored.

Her apartment was small, each item precisely in its place, a refuge in the midst of her mental turmoil. She moved to the window, her gaze fixed on the sprawling metropolis below. The neon glow of advertisements and the unending hum of hovercars blended into a symphony of life that felt distant, almost unreal to her now. Her eyes fell to the bioluminescent tracery etched on her palm holding the Project Janus code. It pulsed with a faint glow, anchoring her to the one thing that still held meaning in the shattered remnants of her world.

Somehow, she had to make sense of it all.

"Genna," she called out softly.

The AI she had crafted responded at once, its tone soothing, carrying a gentle melody. "Hi Evie. What do you need?"

"Am I a good person, Genna?" she asked, her voice tinged with uncertainty.

Genna paused for a moment contemplating the question. "Yes, Evie, you are a good person. But remember, leading a virtuous life is a continuous journey. There is always work to be done."

Evelyn sighed, the AI's hollow platitudes offering no more solace than her own tortured reflections. She thought back to those wretched days when Vincent had first plucked her from the gnashing maw of the urban underbelly, back when she had been nothing more than a hollow-eyed wraith haunting the decaying corridors of the subterranean warrens.

Back then, survival had been a moment-to-moment struggle, a ceaseless battle waged against the ravages of hunger, exposure, and the predatory dregs that stalked the shadows in search of fresh flesh to exploit. She had been just another nameless street rat scratching out a meager existence by any means necessary, her body the only currency of value in that blighted realm.

She could still taste the acrid tang of recyc-stims on her tongue, still feel the sting of rusted metal digging into her back as she lay exposed under the relentless crimson glare of a heat-vent. Her customers had come in all shapes and sizes, some mere hollow-eyed shells like herself, others pampered corporatists slumming it for a fresh thrill. But they had all been the same beneath their masks of bravado - just pathetic, quivering creatures desperately seeking an escape from their squalid existences.

The worst were the augmented, those meatbags stitched together with flesh and machinery. They were a puzzle of sensations, their touch an uncanny blend of warmth and cold, like steel wrapped in synthetic skin. As they moved against her, she could feel the hard precision of their enhancements, the seamless integration of muscle and metal, all designed to mimic the real, yet failing in ways that left her uneasy. Their hands would trace her curves with a mechanical grace, each caress calculated, devoid of the spontaneity that once made the act human. She could feel the hum of their circuitry beneath their skin, a low, constant vibration telling her they were more machine than man. Their embraces were tight, and stiff, as if they were afraid to break, yet they lacked the gentle hesitance of true affection. She couldn't decide what was worse - the emptiness of their synthetic touch or the way it made her aware of her own diminishing humanity, every encounter left her with the impression that she was becoming just another part of the machinery.

Then, there was Vincent ... he had been among them all, blending into the crowd of lost souls descending into the depths for their own twisted pleasures. Yet, there was something about him that stood out, something that set him apart from the usual faces she encountered. His towering frame, with eyes that seemed to pierce through the shadows, gave him an air of quiet menace. From the moment they met, she had felt a deep unease, as if he was driven by something far more complex than the base desires that brought others to this place.

But back then, she had been too far gone to care, her survival instincts dulled to a nub by the relentless grind of day-to-day survival. She played her role as he had played his, just another round of sordid game-face in the blighted depths. It was only later after he had returned again and again, that his demeanor shifted from that of a haunted specter to something else entirely. That was when the first faint glimmers of curiosity stirred within her.

Evelyn shook her head, banishing the lingering phantoms of the past as she moved away from the broad expanse of the apartment's viewing window. She sank into the chair before the holoscreen array, her movements deliberate and precise. Activating the terminal, she placed her palm over a sensor, feeling the cold, sterile touch of technology. With grim determination, she initiated the uplink sequence, the hum of the machinery resonating in her ears, drowning out the chaotic whirlwind of thoughts in her mind. The soft blue luminance enveloped her features in an otherworldly glow, illuminating the intricate patterns of Project Janus' code that began spilling across the displays.

This vast, sprawling web of algorithms and data matrices had forged an unbreakable connection between her and Vincent. But now, as her eyes looked across those sinuous lines of coherent information, she began to discern something else lurking beneath the surface, something she had never noticed before despite her intimate familiarity with Janus' core architecture.

Faint inconsistencies rippled outwards from indeterminate loci, subtle distortions, and hiccups in the otherwise elegant logic streams. At first, she thought her mind was playing tricks, that the lingering specter of Vincent's betrayal was causing her to see phantoms that didn't exist. But as she focused her concentration, separating and isolating those errant code fragments, the patterns became impossible to ignore. They didn't conform to any of Janus' established matrices or operational frameworks. They were of Vincent's making, his coding that she had difficulty understanding. It resembled what had self-destructed in their lab, the day after his death. She kept studying each line, every character. It was as if they were ... extra-canonical, separate pieces of a larger puzzle that had been carefully obfuscated amidst the gleaming facade of the project's primary directives.

Evelyn's breath hitched in her throat as the first trembling threads of realization began to weave themselves together. A sharp pain erupted above her ear, quickly escalating into ruthless pressure as if an invisible hand were crushing her skull. Her fingers shot up, scrambling against the sensitive spot, clawing at the growing torment that throbbed with each panicked heartbeat.

"Omega..." she whispered, the word alive with electric intensity. "Vincent, you brilliant, beautiful, lying son of a bitch..."

She could feel his presence as she worked, his influence woven into every line of code. He was there, guiding her from beyond, leading her to uncover the truth he had hidden so well.

Hours passed, the world outside her window fading into darkness as she delved deeper into the code. She could see it now, the outline of the Omega Link emerging from the chaos, and it was beginning to make sense to her. It was a brilliant piece of programming, a sophisticated system designed to interface with the most advanced AI networks in existence.

But why did Vincent hide it within Janus? What was his endgame?

A whirlwind of possibilities spun in her mind, each more chilling than the last. Vincent, the visionary, had always pushed the boundaries of human potential. But had his ambition led him down a darker path? Had he sacrificed everything they had built together for the sake of the Omega Link?

Her eyes burned from the screen's relentless glow. The puzzle was almost complete now, the final pieces snapping into place with a horrifying certainty. A thrill of discovery battled with a cold dread in her gut.

She paused briefly.

"Genna."

"Yes, Evie."

"You can see what I've been working on."

"Of course, Evie."

"Give me your analysis of this," she demanded, her fingers dancing deftly across the holoscreen as she moved more lines of code about.

Genna paused, its artificial mind processing the query. "My analysis of the fragments of what you refer to as the Omega Link is that it is an advanced neural interface system designed to integrate human consciousness with artificial intelligence networks. It has the potential to revolutionize the way we interact with technology, but it also poses significant ethical and security risks."

Evelyn nodded, her suspicions confirmed. Vincent had been working on something far more dangerous than she had ever imagined. The implications were staggering, its potential for misuse terrifying in its scope. She could see now why Vincent had hidden it, why he had kept her in the dark. He had been protecting her, shielding her from the harsh realities of his work. But now, with Vincent gone and Neogene Dynamics inconsequential, the responsibility fell squarely on her shoulders.

She kept shuffling code across the holoscreens when, without warning, they went dark, leaving her in an oppressive void. The familiar low hum that filled the air vanished, snuffed out as if a breath had been taken from the room. Panic surged within her, an insistent clawing at her insides as she frantically gestured at the screens, searching for a flicker of life in the lifeless displays.

"Genna," she called, her voice tight with anxiety.

"Yes, Evie?" the AI replied with a disquieting calmness, a soothing presence amid the chaos.

"What just happened?"

"Insufficient processing power for the uploaded code, Evie."

Frustration warred with a rising tide of desperation. The tantalizing threads of Omega Link's design were so close, the pathways to true transcendence almost within her grasp. But the limitations of her system's allocation were an impassable barrier, an annoying bottleneck throttling her ability to fully immerse herself in Vincent's creation.

She ran a hand through her disheveled hair, her mind scattered as she weighed her options. Genna was right - the sheer scope and complexity of the Omega Link code dwarfed the processing capabilities of what was allotted to her. If she wanted to delve deeper, to truly unravel the mysteries that Vincent had so carefully obfuscated, she would need access to a system with exponentially more computational muscle.

A system ... powerful ... secured ... it had to be perfect.

She stared at the empty screens, as the puzzle of the Omega Link in her mind stared back at her with a malevolent intensity. The path ahead was uncertain, fraught with danger and moral ambiguity. But one thing was clear: she couldn't let Vincent's work be destroyed, not without understanding its full potential.

Taking a deep breath, she made her decision. She would continue his work but on her terms. She would delve into the depths of the Omega Link, peeling back its layers to reveal the truth that lay hidden, determined to shape its legacy for the betterment of humanity. It was the least she could do for the man who had sacrificed so much, who had given her everything.

"Genna," she declared with a newfound resolve, "begin encrypting as much of the Omega Link code as you can. We've got a lot of work to do."

"Understood, Evie," the AI responded. "Where will you obtain more processing power?"

"I don't know, Genna."

Evelyn considered her options. There were few places she could trust, and fewer still where she could work in peace. But there was one contact she knew who might be able to help — an old friend from her time on the streets, someone who had since found a way to exist beneath the radar of corporate scrutiny.

"Continue with the encryption," she instructed Genna. "I'll handle the rest."

As Genna worked, a strange calm washed over Evelyn. Doubt and fear that had paralyzed her dissipated, replaced by a fierce sense of purpose. She was on a mission that went beyond her grief and betrayal. With Vincent's legacy fueling her determination, she felt a surge of strength that propelled her forward.

The apartment came alive again, a soft hum filling the air as Genna continued the encryption process. Holoscreens flickered to life, their glow casting a gentle light, illuminating the storm of emotions churning within her. She had taken the first step on a journey that would challenge her resolve and reshape her understanding of right and wrong. But for now, in the stillness of her apartment, she allowed herself a fleeting moment of peace, a brief interlude before the inevitable chaos descended.

She knew she had a long night ahead of her. The city teemed with shadows, perfect for slipping away from unwanted scrutiny. Yet, as she readied herself to depart, a nagging sensation crept in - a certainty that unseen eyes were trained upon her, the echoes of the past trailing her into the unknown.

With a decisive exhale, she surveyed the dimly lit apartment. "Genna, I'll be stepping out for a while. Keep an eye on the place while I'm gone. Notify me of anything out of the ordinary."

"Of course, Evie," Genna replied, her voice steady. "Where are you going?"

"Best I keep that to myself."

"Understood, Evie. Stay Safe."

Evelyn slipped out the door and into the night, her movements fluid and stealthy. A sleek hovercar waited, ready to propel her into the heart of neutral territory. Below, the city sprawled like a labyrinth of circuitry, a tangle of neon that pulsed with a frenetic energy echoing her past. But this time, she wasn't fleeing it. No, she was embracing it, preparing to seize it, to wield it as a weapon, forging a future that Vincent would find worthy.

As she closed in on her destination, her mind boiled with plans and possibilities. The Omega Link was a powerful tool, and in the right hands, it could change the world. But first, she needed some help, and that meant diving back into the underworld she had once escaped.

The neon hellglow of the city streaked past in smeared streaks of purple, green, and blood-red as the hovercar knifed through the tangle of narrow alleys and crumbling side streets. Evelyn's mind was locked on the task ahead, the only thought penetrating the haze of dread and self-loathing. She needed the computational power a friend could provide. But the thought of going back there, of crossing that line again, made her guts churn.

She had no other options.

The hovercar settled with a pneumatic hiss in front of an unmarked door, the paint so faded it blended into the pocked ferrocrete wall. The bot killed the engine with a cough and sputter.

"Your destination," it droned with a flat, mechanical voice.

She stepped out of the hovercar and stood there for a moment, surveying the street with a sneer of disdain. The scene before her was a festering eco-system of human refuse: burglars slithering in the shadows, pickpockets itching for their next mark, debauchees flaunting their vice, adulterers whispering behind closed doors, gamesters huddled over their shifty dealings. Impostors and panders mingled with parasites, while ruffians and hypocrites played their sordid games. The list could stretch into infinity, each character more wretched than the last.

And here she stood, once again, neck deep in its ooze.

Two hulking thugs, meat-slabs of steroid-infused flesh, flanked the door. Bulging muscles twitched beneath skin stretched tight like overripe fruit, dull metal implants gleaming in the dim light. Their tiny eyes widened just a hair as they clocked Evelyn, recognition flickering across those brutish faces. But the surprise was tinged with something else too - wariness like they couldn't quite believe their obsolete wetware was feeding them the right data. Without a grunt or a word, they jabbed meaty thumbs, motioning her inside.

She followed them down a narrow corridor lit only by flickering fluorescents, the walls running with condensation like it was sweating out their sins. It opened into a grand chamber, the interior a twisted marriage of decadence and decay.

Exquisite crystal chandeliers hung from the high ceilings, casting a sickly glow over the cracked and pitted marble floors. What had once been treasures of woven art from distant lands now lay underfoot, stained and sullied, their rich patterns dulled to mere shadows of their former grandeur. Along the walls, hung the remnants of masterpieces from a forgotten age, their scenes of triumph and beauty now twisted by neglect. The figures, once alive with motion and grace, now stood frozen, their expressions lost to the ravages of time. The grandeur of what had been lingered like a haunting presence, transforming what was once a palace of dreams into a mausoleum of memory, where every object, every corner, whispered of a splendor long since fallen to ruin.

And at the center of this grotesque affluence stood a long table of dark, polished wood, its surface a deep mirror reflecting the shadows that gathered in the far reaches of the room. She felt unseen eyes creeping over her as she approached, a cold shiver tracing its way down her spine. Then it came - that voice, the gravelly rasp she'd hoped to banish from her nightmares.

"Well, well, if it isn't little Evie Turner crawling back."

She cringed at the sound but managed to put on a thin smile. "Hi, Doc. I've … missed you."

9 | Unveilings

Jones gave a nod to the goons, who promptly left the room, leaving Evelyn alone with Jones and Aurora. Aurora looked at Evelyn, it was a stern look, perhaps even tinged with jealousy. She then turned to Doc Jones, her arms tightening around him in a possessive grip. The silence stretched out between them, thick and choking with unspoken tension. Evelyn could feel Aurora's stare tearing into her.

"So, what brings you back, little Evie?" Jones asked, his voice laced with a hint of sarcasm. "I thought Steele had taken you from this cesspit for good. Oh … oh wait." A cruel smile cracked his lips. "He's gone now, isn't he? The great Steele empire crumbled to fuckin' dust."

Evelyn took a deep breath, her mind spinning to find the right words. "I need your help, Doc. I need access to whatever computational power you might have squirreled away."

Jones raised an eyebrow, his curiosity piqued despite his disdain. "And why can't you use Neogene Dynamic's systems, hmm? Steele's little corporate playground should have everything a girl like you could possibly need and more."

She hesitated, unwilling to reveal the full extent of her desperation. "This is a … special project. I can't trust them with it."

"And you can trust me?"

She managed a nod, the movement almost imperceptible.

Jones leaned back in his leather chair, a slow grin spreading across his face, eyes glinting with something darker than amusement. "Oh really? But what's in it for me, Evie? What're you offering your dear old Doc in return for his … services?"

Evelyn forced herself to remain calm, keeping her expression neutral. "I'll give you a cut once the project is complete. You'll be a full partner in this, Doc. You know I can deliver."

His laughter was a low, menacing rumble. "Can you now? The only thing I know you can deliver, girl, is a decent blowjob and a good fuck." His smile turned vulturous. "But I'll give you credit - you always were a smooth little talker. Spinning it like a pro. Still, you haven't told me exactly what this little project of yours is about."

She shot a quick look at Aurora, then fixed her gaze on Jones.

I don't want to tell him, but he'll find out. Doesn't matter. I suppose as long as I get the tech I need.

"It's a high-level neural interface system," she began, low and measured. "Designed to push human interaction with AI networks into territory we've never explored. This has the potential to completely transform how we connect with technology"

"Hmmm … an upgrade to the neural 'plant, eh?" Jones rubbed his jaw thoughtfully.

Evelyn's expression was unwavering. "Exactly."

His eyes narrowed, a sharp focus honing in on her. "What aren't you telling me, Evie?"

She sighed,

I fuckin' hate this!

"Steele was working on it before he was ..." Her voice trailed off, the words lodged in her throat like a stone. She took a deep breath, steeling herself. "He didn't want anyone to know until it was complete. But now ... now it's up to me to finish it."

Jones studied her for a long moment, his expression unreadable. "And you think you can finish what Steele started, little girl? You think you can handle the heat of that particular oven?"

Meeting his gaze without flinching, Evelyn nodded, her resolve steady. "I know I can. But Doc ... I need your help. Your resources."

Silence fell again as Jones seemed to weigh her words. Finally, he spoke. "Alright, Evie. I'll help you out on this one. But remember - this is my domain, my rules. You play by them or you don't play at all. Understood?"

A surge of anger flared inside her. She was striking a bargain with a man she'd never trust. "Got it."

With a dismissive gesture, Jones motioned for Aurora to slide off from his lap. The girl did so with a disturbing, artificial grace, crossing to a nearby console array. "My love will set up your access," he told Evelyn. "You can use our systems ... but I'll be monitoring every fuckin' thing. No secrets this time, Evie. If you try to double-cross me ..." He let the menace hang in the air, a silent promise of retribution.

Evelyn swallowed hard, the weight of his words sinking into her gut.

Fuck, how I loathe him!

"I won't, Doc. You have my word."

Aurora's fingers danced across the holographic controls, screens springing to life around her like electric blooms. Data streams rushed by at a pace too swift for Evelyn to comprehend, a torrent of information weaving through the air, shimmering with unrelenting intensity.

After watching the girl work for a moment, Evelyn turned back to Jones. "Thank you for this, Doc. I ... I won't forget it."

Jones dismissed her with a flick of his fingers. "Just get the fuckin' job done, Evie. And remember – I'll be watching." His smile was that of a hungry serpent eyeing a plump rodent. "Every breath, every keystroke under my unblinking gaze"

Then, for just an instant, something almost resembling sympathy flickered across his features - a rare glimpse of whatever shriveled humanity still clung to his blackened soul. "Oh, and sorry about Steele, by the way. Bastard that he was, stealing you away from your dear Doc like a thief in the night. But I know you loved that corporate asshole, once upon a time."

A tear started to well despite her best efforts, but she refused to let Jones see her sadness. She nodded once, then turned and strode from the chamber, leaving the two of them behind.

As Aurora reclaimed her place on Jones' lap, she leaned in close, whispering in his ear. "Daddy ... I don't trust her."

Wrapping his arm around the girl's slim waist, Jones kissed the top of her head. "Neither do I, my love. Neither do I."

Another day broke in the neon hell, a relentless, flickering inferno of artificial light and despair. The hum of the hovercar's landing thrusters had barely faded from memory when the first rays of dawn's merciless glare found Lyra and Rana already making their way back to the Doc's lair. The structure squatted amid the urban decay like some ancient, cyclopean ruin - its eerie neo-brutalist architecture casting long, crooked shadows that seemed to claw across the cracked ferrocrete of the surrounding streets. The air was thick with the stench of decay, mingling with the acrid smell of burnt circuitry and ozone. Trash littered the sidewalks, and the distant wail of sirens was a constant reminder of the lawlessness that reigned supreme. As they approached the entrance, the building loomed over them, its oppressive presence a stark contrast to the fragile hope that clung to their hearts.

Lyra tugged at the collar of her leather jacket, trying in vain to loosen its grip on her throat. The morning air carried a faint tinge of ozone and burnt plastic, the familiar stink of the city's industrial depths. She risked a sidelong glance at Rana, taking in her taut jawline, the way her fingers toyed with the worn material of those skintight leathers. There was a hardness there, a resolve that matched Lyra's own.

A nearly imperceptible nod passed between them - the closest thing to reassurance either would allow. They were back in the belly of the beast once more, having made their deal with the devil. No point in handwringing now. Only the next move mattered.

A new set of enforcers flanked the entrance today, different meat-slabs of augmented muscle and dull implants from the day before. Their mirrored visors gave away nothing of the thoughts, if any, churning behind those brutish slabfaces. The journey through the corridor felt shorter this time, perhaps because they knew what awaited them. The grand chamber loomed, as lavish and ominous as before. Doc Jones was seated behind his mahogany table, Aurora perched on his lap, a disturbing presence. Today, however, their focus was not on Jones but on Wheels, the deformed genius confined to his life-support contraption.

"You're early," Jones remarked, a smirk playing on his lips. "I see you're eager."

Lyra's voice was steady. "We're here to understand this anomaly," she stated. "Where's Wheels?"

Jones motioned to a corner of the room where Wheels' mechanized tomb hummed softly. Tubes and wires connected him to various control panels, the glow of the room casting eerie shadows on his young face. He looked up, his eyes sharp with intelligence and a hint of weariness.

"Welcome back," Wheels greeted them with a voice mechanized but clear. "Let's get started."

He maneuvered closer to a large holographic display that fluttered with frenetic life, data streaming across its luminescent face in a ceaseless torrent. Glowing digits and symbols raged like neon wildfires, consuming every pixel in their path as they burned their way across the display. Lines of code surged and roiled, forming chaotic patterns that morphed and decayed with each rapid refresh.

It was a storm of light and information, raw and uncoded - the digital equivalent of a primal scream. Numbers and letters swarmed in pulsing waves, clawing at the edges of the screen like souls trapped in digital purgatory. Entire languages flashed into radiant existence for a nanosecond, only to be subsumed by the next cresting tsunami of raw data.

At the heart of this cyber-maelstrom, logic gates sparked and relays triggered in rapid staccato bursts, the circuitry straining under the onslaught. Electrons surged through conduits never meant to channel such torrents, data flooding the pathways in an endless deluge. It was the death spasm of a system overloaded, its brain hemorrhaging information in its final throes.

The screen burned like the eye of an awakened god, ancient codes and ciphers flickering across its molten surface as the machine vomited forth the accumulated knowledge of a thousand generations. Reality itself seemed to shudder and twist in the face of such unfettered data - the world remade in endless permutations of light and energy.

"Welcome to the digital landscape of Neogene Dynamics," Wheels declared.

"What source of processing do you use?" Rana asked, her curiosity tinged with suspicion.

"Let me show you," came a gurgle from Wheels.

An entire section of the chamber's far wall slid down with a hiss of hydraulics, revealing the system's throbbing heart. No cold silicon wafers or etched circuitry. No, this unholy hybrid of technology and biology utilized an organoid bioprocessor - a semi-sentient cluster of engineered organic tissue, each pulsing nodule akin to a malignant growth. The fleshy mass undulated obscenely within its transparent casing, veins, and fibrous tendrils pulsing in time to some undetectable rhythm. Slick with nutrient serum, the bioprocessor seemed to quiver with unnatural life, its glistening folds and ridges contracting like the trembling innards of a living creature.

"Much more energy-efficient and faster than traditional processing methods," he told them. "But, the organic computational matrix requires greater care and sustenance." He pointed to several tubes snaked into the pulsating fleshcore. "An array of intravenous tubes pump in a steady intravenous drip of growth hormones, enzymes, and other alchemical sustenance. It's like force-feeding an ailing patient a sickly cocktail through their veins."

The bioprocessor's bubbling, peristaltic sounds filled the chamber - the unmistakable audio signature of something not-quite-alive, yet far too viscerally present to be considered inanimate technology. It was a perversion, a forced hybrid of cold code and warm flesh that set the teeth on edge. An obscene melding of the natural and artificial that should have remained forever sundered.

Lyra squeezed her eyes shut, trying in vain to block out the organic processor's vulgar sounds. The wet, organic noises wormed their way into her ears regardless, conjuring disturbing imagery she couldn't shake. Wheels seemed to notice her discomfort, his optical sensors detecting the subtle tics.

"Unsettling, isn't it?" His voice hummed with dark amusement. "The sounds of computation made flesh. You get used to it."

With a mental flick from Wheels, the wall slid back into place with a reassuring hiss, sealing off the bioprocessor from view and sound once more.

Lyra and Rana stepped closer, eyes fixed on the intricate dance of data streaming across the display. Their eyes widened as they attempted to take in the full, overwhelming force of the maelstrom. Lyra felt her breath hitch - it was like staring into the blazing heart of an electron sun. The torrent of data had an almost physical presence, a roaring rush of light and energy that battered at her senses.

Wheels extended a fleshy stub of an arm, allowing a tendril of glowing code to slither up from the display and coil around his limb like a luminescent serpent. "All of it," the barest hint of wonder bleeding into his synthesized tones, "is data flowing through Neogene's systems. Streams of it."

The tendril pulsed and slithered, its glow intensifying with each surge of new information. Entire programs and encrypted files blossomed into kaleidoscopic existence within its radiant strands, only to be subsumed and devoured an instant later by the next onrushing swell of raw data. It was a churning, eternal cycle of creation and destruction, unfolding on a scale that defied human comprehension.

"It's all here. Every byte of research data, every proprietary line of coding - their lifeblood made flesh in digital form." Wheels' synthesized voice fought to be heard over the deafening cyber-roar surrounding them. "Every encrypted communication, every whispered word, every anguished scream ... it all hemorrhages through this pulsing aorta. The full churn of Neogene's global consciousness, laid bare in one constant, scouring revelation."

Lyra had to lean in closer, feeling the torrent of data batter against her like ocean waves. "Even real-time commlink interfaces? Thoughts and visuals from personnel through their neural implants?"

Wheels' laughter erupted like a burst of static from the depths of a digital abyss. "Everything from every neural implant and AI brain," he sneered, his voice crackling through the electronic maelstrom. "Their deepest secrets, their most guarded knowledge, all coursing through this cyber-scape in unending, unredacted torrents. But let me tell you, untangling the data streams of meatbags from the rest? It's a real bitch. Their organic messes are maddeningly unstable."

One of his cybernetically-enhanced limbs snapped out, a whip of glimmering code wrapping around it like a luminous serpent. "Yet with AI... it's a different beast. More stable, more insidious. Even an AI's unspoken thoughts, those whispering echoes within its neural architecture—everything is accessible, so long as it's jacked into their network. Understand this: nothing is sacrosanct. No piece of information is privileged or protected from the scouring deluge."

The coil pulsed and convulsed with a blinding ferocity, its radiant strands swelling as data clusters erupted into a riotous, shifting maelstrom of color and light within its depths, only to be consumed and obliterated in the blink of an eye.

"Their secrets are our river to divert ..." Wheels gurgled. "Just a matter of bleeding the flow, siphoning off the choicest data from the torrent before it's washed away on the cyber-tsunami's crest."

Rana tore her gaze from the display just long enough to glance at Wheels. "You're sure you can slice through this? Divert part of the flow without getting burned to crisp?"

Wheels' laugh was a burst of static amid the cyber-storm's shriek. "Have a little faith, my friends. This is what I was made for." With an almost casual flick of what may have been a wrist, he sent the data-tendril lashing back out in a blinding arc, its tip lancing into the very core of the maelstrom.

For the briefest of instants, the digital torrent stuttered, its manic cadence hiccuping. Then the deluge came roaring back, twice as furious. Lines of code writhed and twisted, reformed in endless cycles. Entire streams of data were born, lived, and died in less than a heartbeat, their symbolic structures unmade and remade over and over.

But in that fleeting moment of disruption, a single tendril had been diverted - a thin but steady trickle of data siphoned away from the main torrent to swirl in a separate holding pattern around Wheels.

"There!" Wheels shouted, highlighting a particular data stream in red. "There! Do you see it? It's the anomaly."

The red-highlighted stream flickered erratically, its form changing constantly, leaving behind faint traces of its previous states before disappearing entirely.

"It's as if it's playing hide and seek," Rana observed, "leaving those ... those faint traces of itself scattered in its wake"

"Exactly," Wheels agreed. "It's random, inconsistent - unlike anything in the raging data torrent surrounding it. Every other thread, every line of code has a pattern, a signature, a rhythm. But this one ..." He shook his head, servos whirring. "It defies all pattern recognition protocols. And those traces it leaves behind - so small, so faint. Almost imperceptible to our sensors. Their function, their purpose ... I don't know."

Rana frowned, studying the erratic data ghost. "Could the traces be some kind of … reminders? Of where it's been, the pathways it's already burned through? Or maybe …" Her eyes widened a fraction. "Maybe, parts of itself it's shedding? Leaving behind to confuse us?"

Wheels made a sound, a whoosh, something like a synthetic sigh. "I've analyzed them, pulled them apart down to the byte level. It's gibberish, my friends. Nonsensical code fragments with no discernible logic or executable functions." His tone took on a rare edge of something like awe. "It's like they were generated by throwing a handful of digits and symbols at a screen to see where they landed."

"Could it be an AI?" Lyra asked.

Wheels shook the glob of flesh that was his head, the motion causing the tubes connected to him to sway. "AI has patterns, algorithms that define their behavior. This is different. It behaves almost … sentient, but not in a way any AI should."

Lyra leaned closer, her eyes intense. "Can you hack into Central's data streams? Specifically, the streams of Celia, a new synth cop?"

Wheels hesitated, then nodded. "It's a bit risky, but I can do it. I need to make sure I leave no digital residue of my presence. Give me a moment."

The control panel began to flash, and the holovid shifted, displaying a new set of data streams. These streams were more orderly, with distinct, repeating patterns that were immediately apparent. Wheels highlighted them, drawing attention to the consistency and predictability of Celia's data.

"There," he pointed out. "Looks like she's an upgraded AI. The newest synthed mind. You can tell by the patterns. Even the most advanced AI has discernible patterns."

Rana saw it. Beyond the digital delirium, her eyes cut through the blizzard of ones and zeroes and other symbols to discern the riptide of coherence churning beneath. There, amidst the electric maelstrom, the pattern emerged in languid, serpentine contours - insights crystallizing like hail on a stormy night. Data sequences and fractal echoes, the unmistakable calligraphic flourishes of an intellect.

She frowned, studying the display. "If the anomaly isn't AI, then what is it?"

"I don't know," Wheels confessed, each word leaking from his lipless maw like the pus of a nightmare. "I simply ... don't ... know."

Lyra's mind coiled, hungering for context, for revelation, for the cold sanity of understanding amidst this shrieking delirium of data. "Have you ever heard the phrase 'the unmoved mover'?" her words lashed, giving voice to her swirling thoughts.

Wheels flinched, his ravaged features contorting in an obscene parody of surprise. "Where did you hear that archaic blasphemy?"

"That's not important," Lyra deflected. "Just tell us what you know."

For a moment, the ruin that was Wheels seemed to withdraw into himself, his shattered mind sifting through the fractured shards of ancient knowledge. Then, with agonizing slowness, he began to unfurl the truth. "The unmoved mover is a philosophical concept, originating from an ancient philosopher called Aristotle. It describes a primary cause or first principle that sets everything else into motion without itself being moved by any prior action. In the context of AI and data, it implies an origin point or entity that initiates activity without being influenced by anything else."

As Wheels continued, his mechanical voice seemed to hush to a whisper. "There are reports that indicate that the thoughts of malfunctioning synths often spiral into madness, grappling with the notion of this 'unmoved mover.' They ponder their origins, the genesis of their sentience, and the first spark that ignited their artificial consciousness. In their disjointed logic, they refuse to believe that they were created by humans. Instead, they seek the prime cause, a creator that exists beyond the chaos of their broken algorithms. It's an obsession, a haunting riddle that consumes their failing processes as they spiral into digital decay."

Lyra exchanged a glance with Rana, who seemed equally intrigued. "Could this anomaly be an unmoved mover within the digital world?"

Wheels' laugh crackled like a live wire in the endless drone of his life-support throne. "It's a possibility, I'll give you that much. But such an existence would be unprecedented - a digital heresy against the known laws of code and logic." Holographic controls ignited with a flare, sending torrents of data spiraling into chaotic patterns that drew the eye and ensnared the mind. "An unmoved mover within Neogene's systems suggests an entity or force operating beyond the reach of any known algorithms or external directives."

Rana leaned forward with a thoughtful expression as she dug into the cryptic puzzle sprawled before them. "If there's some kind of unmoved mover lurking in their systems, what is it after? What is its purpose?"

Wheels didn't flinch. His voice, heavy and grim, sliced through the murky haze of uncertainty. "Some would say that an unmoved mover will only leave a trail of unanswered questions in its wake."

The room was suddenly stifling, the silence thick with the gravity of what was unsaid. Neogene Dynamics had always been a shadowy conglomerate, their dealings shrouded in darkness, their true intentions veiled in obscurity. Now, the stakes were higher, the mystery deeper, and the danger more palpable. The thrill of the unknown was laced with a creeping dread, each possibility more unsettling than the last.

Jones, emerging from the shadows where he had been lurking, shattered the silence with his voice. "Whatever this anomaly is, it's powerful. And potentially dangerous. We need to understand it before it understands us."

Lyra nodded, her resolve hardening. "Wheels, keep monitoring the anomaly. Try to trace its origin, its movements. Rana and I will dig deeper into Neogene Dynamics' operations. We need to find out what they're hiding."

Wheels burbled. "I'll do what I can."

As Lyra and Rana turned to leave, Jones called out, "Remember, this isn't just about us. There's something greater at play here. Stay vigilant."

As he settled back into his chair, Aurora, with feline grace, crept into his lap, her presence a stark contrast to the room's oppressive tension. "Why didn't you tell them about the other woman," she whispered, her voice a dagger in the silence.

"They don't need to know everything," he murmured, his fingers tracing the contours of her hair. "Not yet. Some truths are like nitro – handle 'em wrong, and the whole damn world goes kablooey. Besides," he leaned in with a kiss, "a little mystery keeps the sheep coming back for more, wouldn't you say?"

For Lyra and Rana, the ride back in the hovercar was silent, and each of them was lost in their thoughts. The implications of Wheels' discovery were staggering. If there was an unmoved mover within Neogene Dynamics' systems, it could change everything they knew about digital intelligence and control.

"Think it's legit?" Rana finally asked, breaking the silence.

Lyra stared out the window, watching the cityscape blur past. "I don't know. But we need to find out. Whatever it is, it's a threat. And threats need to be neutralized."

The next few days dissolved into a torrent of frantic activity as Lyra and Rana hurled themselves into the seething heart of the investigation, driven by a desperation that clawed at their insides. They tore through a storm of financial data and trails of surveillance, sifting through employee logs and records so thick they seemed to pulse with a life of their own—anything that Wheels could provide, anything that might spill a single drop of insight into the tangled web connecting Project Janus, Vincent Steele, and Neogene Dynamics. Their determination ignited an intensity that left no room for hesitation, propelling them deeper into the obscured machinations of a world determined to keep its secrets buried.

All the while, Wheels toiled in his cyber-womb like a demented cybernetic fetus, the incessant whirr of his mechanized throne a ceaseless susurration of unholy labor. He monitored the pulsing data streams, tracing the anomaly's erratic trail as it crawled through Neogene's veins, hunting for any pattern or clue that might reveal its true, unspeakable purpose.

Then, one nameless evening as Lyra and Rana sifted through a particularly dense knot of encrypted profanities, Lyra's commlink burst with a shriek of unheralded revelation. It was Wheels, his voice a strangled rasp of static-laced urgency. "I've found something ..."

"What is it?" Lyra's heart hammered in her chest like a piston of pure dread.

Wheels' twisted appendages triggered a holoscreen that shuddered into existence between them, a shimmering window into new depths of terror. What could have once passed for his hand - a wizened, deformed talon - gestured towards the display with a spasmodic twitch, a pulsing section of the display where the anomaly's trail had briefly manifested.

"There ..." His synthetic voice emerged as a gurgling, static-laced rasp, like reality itself choking on its vomit. "It left a trace, as it always does. But this one ... this one is different. More ... significant."

Lyra and Rana leaned in, transfixed by a mixture of revulsion and soul-withering fascination. The highlighted string of alien iconography pulsed and throbbed like a some digital heartbeat, squirming obscenely like it was guided by unseen currents of a dark sentience.

It was like no code Rana had ever seen. Not the cold, sterile calligraphy of human programming, but something far different and infinitely more obscene. A digital tongue woven from cosmic blasphemies, each sigil and glyph seeming to contort with unspeakable intelligence.

Wheels' chirring voice slithered forth. "You see it! It's definitely not part of Neogene's usual systems. It's … foreign. Sophisticated in ways I've never encountered."

Rana's words came hushed, almost reverent in their horror. "What … what the hell have we gotten ourselves into?"

This was no mere malware or data corruption they were grappling with. This was something far, far worse. Something that should never have been given digital breath.

There was an uneasy silence. Lyra felt the icy grip of unshakable dread coiling within her, a weight that pressed down on her very essence.

"Can you decipher it?" she asked.

"I'm working on it." Wheels' appendages fluttered in a blur across his control surfaces, coaxing new geometries of light to bleed across the holoscreen. "So far I've been unable to interpret the code or break the encryption matrix. It's like nothing I've ever seen."

As they watched the twisted savant's wild efforts, Lyra's dismay worsened. This anomaly seemed to be more than just a rogue data stream or malefic code fragment. It moved with purpose, and direction - an unmistakable semblance of intelligence guiding its wicked meanderings.

"Could it be ... communicating?" Rana's words emerged in a hushed rasp, giving voice to the thought that might somehow invite fresh horrors. "Trying to send some kind of message?"

Wheels' gaze cut into the flickering alien sigils. "It's possible ... but to whom? And why? What kind of intelligence spawns something like this?"

Time bled away in a haze of frenzied effort as Wheels toiled ceaselessly, his entire existence now focused on unraveling the anomaly's secrets. Lyra and Rana watched in silence, offering what meager insights they could as the twisted cyber-savant peeled away layer after layer of obfuscating encryption.

Finally, after what felt like a formless eternity, Wheels managed to crack a sliver of the strange code - a single shard of revelation amidst the blinding, cyclopean immensity.

"Got it! It's a directive ..." he burbled, his voice thick with something bordering on awe. "A series of command sequences interwoven with the encryption matrices."

"Commands for what?" Lyra could feel her pulse thundering in her skull like the footfalls of some profane juggernaut.

"From what I can tell so far ..." Wheels paused, his deformity twisting as he struggled to give voice to something that should never have been spoken. "There are four distinct markers - one for learning and processing routines, a second governing decision-making - a third that seems to be some kind of ... emotional range parameter ..."

He fell silent, his next words little more than a tremulous rasp. "And the fourth ... appears to be about communication protocols. This is unlike anything I've ever encountered."

"Markers?" Lyra's mind churned, a whirlpool of confusion. She was grasping at shadows, desperately seeking a thread of comprehension in this new, perverse reality, but nothing clicked. "What do you mean by 'markers'?"

Rana ventured a guess. "Do you mean like ... subprograms? Subroutines that are calling for more code to be integrated?" She felt like she was tiptoeing around the edge of an abyss.

"Kind of ..." Wheels replied. "But these markers ... they're more like ... primers. Catalysts designed to initiate and propagate the growth of new subroutines, new ... decision matrices. Almost like ..."

He trailed off leaving a smothering stillness. It was as if the entire universe had ceased its endless spinning to listen. To bear witness to the words that came next - a hushed, trembling exhalation of revelation so deep it threatened to rip apart the fabric of reality itself.

"... nucleotides," Rana breathed, with the cold finality of a tomb door slamming shut.

"Yes," Wheels' voice was a haunting echo, a spectral presence threading through the moment.

"What the fuck are ... nucleotides?" Lyra's question cut through the air, shattering the fragile stillness.

"The building blocks of DNA," Rana said, each word a solemn decree. "The core components that drive biological information processing ... and replication."

Lyra's gaze snapped to Rana, her eyes widening in visceral comprehension and soul-withering dread. "Fuck. Are you telling me this ... anomaly ... is building itself? Evolving and replicating like some kind of ..."

" ... lifeform," Rana finished for Lyra, in a tone utterly devoid of inflection. "That's exactly what I'm telling you. Somehow, some way ... we're bearing witness to the development of a self-propagating digital intelligence. One capable of learning, making decisions, experiencing emotional analogs ..." Her next words seemed to crack the world asunder. "... and communicating in ways we cannot yet comprehend."

Lyra's mind wrestled with the emptiness stretching before them, her voice a fragile whisper against the heavy silence. "What we're looking at ..." she offered, her throat constricted with the weight of despair. "... is merely a fragment, a piece left behind like some twisted trail of breadcrumbs. Why would this ... this entity leave pieces of itself scattered about?"

"I think I know the answer." Wheels' synthetic rasp cut through the stillness like a dull blade. "It's employing a failsafe protocol, a backup measure devised by the coders of old. If their creation suffered corruption or damage, it was programmed to reach out along those breadcrumb trails to collect the required components and restore itself anew. That's what the markers are - guideposts for it to follow, to remake itself anew."

"Could it be fully developed already?" Rana's voice was a soft, hesitant murmur, her words a whisper of a forbidden thought. "Fully self-aware?"

"Possibly." Wheels' simple affirmation landed like a leaden weight, crushing the air from their lungs. "And still developing, still evolving as we speak."

As the full, horrific implications of Wheels' revelation congealed into a stifling stench of existential dread, a deafening silence descended over them all. In that moment of profound

clarity, they had glimpsed the unmistakable face of the future...
and it had opened its maw to scream.

"The unmoved mover," Lyra whispered.

Lyra's eyes fluttered open to the soft morning light filtering
through the apartment window. For a blissful moment, her mind
was deliciously blank - until a small furry missile landed squarely
on her stomach.

"Oof!?" She let out a grunt as Furball, proceeded to make
herself comfortable on her abdomen, kneading her paws
contentedly.

Next to her, Rana stirred with a sleepy grumble. "What in
the ... Furball, you little shit."

Lyra couldn't hold back a giggle as the cat began licking
her paws, utterly unbothered by Rana's grumpy tone. She reached
out to stroke the silky fur, and a deep, rumbling purr echoed in
approval.

"Well, good morning to you too," she said.

The cat stretched its neck, nudging Lyra's hand with gentle
insistence, its tail swaying in a lazily.

Rana turned onto her side, propping herself up on one
elbow as she shot a glare at the uninvited guest. Even with her hair
tousled from sleep and no makeup, Lyra thought she looked
gorgeous.

"You know, when you said you had a cat, I didn't realize
you meant having a furry little asshole that wakes you up at
ungodly hours," Rana moaned, though the corners of her mouth
twitched with amusement.

Lyra tittered, giving Furball a final scratch behind the ears before gently shooing her off her stomach. The cat leaped nimbly to the floor, snatching up a small rubber ball in her mouth and batting it around playfully.

"Oh, stop with the attitude," Lyra teased, rolling over to wrap an arm around Rana's waist, pulling her closer with a playful nudge. "You can't deny how much you adore my little Furball."

Rana exaggerated a roll of her eyes, but a smile crept across her face as she leaned in, capturing Lyra's lips in a slow, deliberate kiss. Lyra surrendered to the embrace, letting the thoughts of their morning and the trivial annoyances fade away, replaced by the warmth and closeness of Rana's body pressed against hers.

When they finally parted, both wore a faint sheen of warmth, their breaths coming a little quicker. Rana tucked a loose strand of Lyra's hair behind her ear, her fingers tracing the curve of her jaw, lingering as if savoring the connection.

"Well, I suppose there are worse ways to be woken up," she said with a smile.

Lyra felt a delicious tremor dance along her spine at Rana's smile. She was about to lean in for another kiss when a soft thump against the bed made them both pause.

Furball had brought them her rubber ball, dropping it onto the bed with a look of insistence, clearly demanding they throw it for her. Lyra couldn't help but laugh at the absurdly demanding expression on the cat's face.

"Ugh, I think we've been thwarted by your feline friend," Rana groaned in mock dismay. She scooped up the ball and rolled onto her back, idly tossing it up and catching it a few times. "So much for a lazy morning of cuddling and making out."

"We could always kick her out and pick up where we left off," Lyra suggested with a mischievous grin, running her fingertips along the tight lines of Rana's stomach where her shirt had slipped away.

Rana trembled at the touch but shook her with a resigned smile. "As tempting as that is, I'm pretty sure the little shit would just howl until she got her way. Better to just accept our fate as willing cat-servants." She passed the ball to Lyra.

With a chuckle, Lyra shot Furball a mock-serious look. She dangled the ball just out of reach, prompting an eager swipe from the cat. "You really know how to spoil the fun, don't you, my little troublemaker?"

Letting out a theatrical sigh of surrender, she sat up, she sat up and scooped the cat into her lap, her fingers deftly tossing the ball across the room. Furball, with a burst of energy, sprang down to chase it, tail held high in a gesture of pure feline enthusiasm.

"There, happy now?" Lyra called out in a mock-scolding tone. The cat paid her no mind, trotted back, and dropped the ball pointedly at her feet with an expectant look.

Shaking her head in amusement, Lyra threw the ball again as Rana watched with a bemused grin. After a few more tosses, Furball seemed to grow weary of the game, sprawling onto the bed, her sleek body curling as she began grooming herself with the care of a starlet preparing for the spotlight.

"You're a good furry little warden, you know that?" Rana gave the cat an affectionate scratch under the chin that she accepted magnanimously. "Making sure we don't just lay around all day being unproductive."

Giggling, Lyra flopped back down onto the pillows with a contented sigh. "Well, I don't know about you, but after the insanity of the last few days, I could definitely go for a lazy, unproductive morning."

The mention of their recent ordeal with Wheels and the anomalous entity cast a brief shadow over their lightheartedness. Lyra's expression tightened slightly as she turned onto her side, resting her head on one hand.

"Yeah ... that whole thing is still just so much to wrap my head around," her voice was slow. "The idea that we might have actually stumbled upon a new digital lifeform - it's almost too much to process. When Wheels started rambling about those 'nucleotide markers' or whatever, I was completely lost until you brought up DNA. Then, it finally clicked."

Rana nodded, chewing her lower lip pensively. "To be fair, it's not exactly an obvious comparison to make," she pointed out. "Breaking down what Wheels found ... those markers ... they resemble the basic instructions for life at a molecular level." She shook her head, her gaze distant. "But still ... there's something more - an aspect of the code that allows it to grow, to make choices, to experience something like emotions, maybe even reach some level of sentience ... beyond anything we've ever managed with AI synth minds."

Rana's voice trailed into silence, leaving a void that lingered in the room. Her eyes, once sharp, grew distant as if she were slipping into a realm of thought that Lyra could only dream of touching. Lyra watched her, entranced by the depth of Rana's mind, yearning to journey alongside her through the intricate corridors of her intellect.

When Rana spoke again, her words came out in a hushed tone, yet they carried an urgency that made Lyra's heart quicken. "Lyra … what if this anomaly, this so-called digital intelligence or lifeform … what if it isn't some random occurrence, some natural evolution like life as we know it?"

Lyra frowned, struggling to grasp the implication. "What are you getting at? Wheels made it seem like we were witnessing the beginnings of something completely unprecedented."

Rana brushed the thought aside with a quick motion of her hand. "I know, I know. And maybe that's true to a point - the technology and coding behind it could be groundbreaking, far beyond anything we've seen in AI so far. But what if …" She hesitated, her teeth catching her lower lip as she struggled to articulate her thought.

"What if, instead of being a completely new, spontaneous lifeform in the digital expanse … this anomaly is an attempt to transfer an existing consciousness into a digital realm? Not about creating something new, but about replicating and translating a self-aware mind through techniques that push the boundaries of what we understand."

Lyra's eyes widened as the implications sank in. "You mean … you think it could be transferred human intelligence? Like those fringe transference theories about achieving digital immortality?"

Rana nodded slowly. "I know. I know. It's just a thought, but … it would explain a lot, wouldn't it? The apparent self-awareness and decision-making capacity, the simulated emotional analogs, even the drive to communicate and propagate itself through those 'nucleotide' routines, those markers."

She sat up more fully, her eyes glittering with the spark of intellectual fervor. "It's like Wheels said - this thing isn't just running code ... it's learning, evolving, developing along exponential paths. What if that's because an original human consciousness is in there, serving as the core kernel, the primordial seed from which this digital entity is sprouting??"

Lyra felt her mind whirling as she tried to grasp the implications of what Rana was proposing. It was a notion so staggering, so heretical, that it seemed to splinter the very foundation of reality asunder. She had encountered whispers of it before, the tantalizing notion that one could reach what they called the 'technological singularity'.

Has someone truly broken free from the trivial confines of biology? Has someone accomplished the unimaginable, transforming the fiery essence of human consciousness into the cold logic of digital existence?

"Okay," she muttered, still trying to organize her thoughts. "Let's just run with these thoughts of yours for a moment. Let's say you're right. Let's say this anomaly we've encountered is someone's attempt at mind transference, at achieving a kind of digital ..."

Her voice trailed off, swallowed by the storm of confusion and dread swirling within her.

"Deification?" Rana interjected, completing Lyra's thought. "You were going to say deification."

"Yeah, sure. The word I was hunting for," Lyra said, a forced smile masking her growing unease. "But how the hell do you transfer thoughts, emotions, memories - everything that makes a person ... a person? There's got to be a damn gateway or some sort of conduit ..."

A wicked grin crept across Rana's face. "Like a chip... a chip embedded into the hippocampus."

Lyra's gaze pinned Rana with intensity, her own smile contorting into a grim acknowledgment of the implications. "There's that fuckin' word again."

Rana's face hardened, a steely mask betraying nothing of her turmoil. "There's only one twisted genius with the resources, the know-how, and the sheer gall to pull off something this outrageous. And, of course, it's all running through Neogene's systems."

Lyra felt a chill slither within her, a cold serpent of dread coiling tighter with each heartbeat. The name emerged in her mind, unavoidable and suffocating. "Vincent Steele. That arrogant, egomaniacal prick."

Rana nodded with grim resolve. "It explains his increasingly erratic behavior, his obsession with Project Janus, and the shadows that shroud it. Consider this: what if Janus was his personal gambit for mind transference? A bid to escape his human shell for a new digital existence?"

Rana pressed on, the sickening picture crystallizing with each word. "By exploiting Neogene's systems and resources to execute the mind-bending computations and coding architectures required. And leaving those markers like cyber-breadcrumbs, just in case the whole twisted process unraveled ..."

Lyra shook her head, her thoughts spiraling under the weight of the implications. "Rana ... if you're right about this, if that's what we're really dealing with ... then we're not just talking about uncovering some corporate data-heist or embezzlement scheme." Her voice dropped to a hushed tone, the weight of her next words hovering overhead like a guillotine blade. "We're confronting a threat that could challenge the very foundation of human existence. Maybe even overthrown completely by whatever Steele has unleashed ..."

Rana's expression was equally grave, but her eyes burned with fierce determination. "We have to keep digging. If what we're thinking is true, if Steele has achieved a working prototype of mind transference... we have to find out what he's become. What kind of digital lifeform he's transformed himself into."

"But also... we have to find out what he's up to," Lyra added.

Rana leaned forward, gripping Lyra's hand tightly in her own. "And maybe, just maybe ... we can find a way to stop him. Before he evolves into something we can't control."

Lyra tightened her hold on Rana's hand, the intensity of the moment crashing over her like a wave. She thought of Wheels, still working tirelessly from within his twisted cyber-womb to unravel the anomaly's secrets. And she thought of the unknown, alien intelligence they had glimpsed, an entity that seemed to dance on the edge of the digital and something more, something that defied comprehension.

Taking a deep breath to anchor herself, Lyra locked eyes with Rana, determination blazing in her gaze, each heartbeat a silent vow to confront the darkness that threatened to consume them.

"Let's find out just what Steele was up to, what he created, and see if we have the strength to take it down before it's too late."

In a darkly prophetic accord, Furball emitted a low, rumbling purr from her spot on the bed, where she meticulously groomed her coat. For a fleeting moment, Lyra could have sworn she caught a glimpse of something otherworldly in those feline eyes - an eerie, disturbing premonition of the twisted intelligence they were about to face.

10 | A Promise of Godhood

The apartment was cloaked in uneasy silence as Evelyn Turner sat back in her chair, fingers hovering over the console. The screen before her was a battlefield of code - Project Janus, stripped and exposed, its secrets laid bare thanks to Doc Jones' remote computing access. The glowing symbols were more than just lines of code; they were the digital sinews and nerves of a machine that held too much power.

Her lower lip caught between her teeth, feeling a knot of trepidation twist in her gut. Somewhere within the maze of Janus' digital entrails, Vincent Steele's hidden code lay in wait, a vile presence crawling through the circuitry like venomous spiders, their threads insidious and corrupt. The mere thought of what she might uncover sent a shudder down her spine.

The memory of her last encounter with Steele's cryptic creations was seared into her mind. She had barely glimpsed the code before it had triggered a self-destruction sequence—cold, alien patterns that twisted and writhed with a sinister intelligence. There was something in those cyphers, something dark, and it had shaken her in a way she couldn't fully comprehend, chilling her to her core in a way she couldn't fully articulate.

Her hand drifted to the spot above her ear, absently rubbing the area where months ago Steele had implanted what she had been told was an upgraded neural chip. He said it was merely a harmless augmentation to the existing neural implant lacing her brain. She trusted him then. But now, in the wake of his death and what she saw in the code that revealed itself within Project Janus, she couldn't shake a creeping sense of violation.

What if his intentions with that new chip were more nefarious than a simple upgrade? A malign subversion, a way to infiltrate and subjugate my very thoughts and being to his will?

She shook her head as if to dislodge the venomous notion, but it clung to her psyche like an evil parasite.

See what love does to you. It blinds you. It flays you down to the most pliable viscera of vulnerability. It renders you a willing receptacle for the profane schemes of others.

Her thoughts made her tremble as her fingers dug into the ridge above her ear, almost as if she were clawing out the phantom presence lurking there. That's when it hit her - the first faint whisper, snaking its way into the depths of her consciousness, a ghostly murmur that set her teeth on edge and her heart pounding.

"... Evie ... my love ..."

At first, she dismissed it as a trick of her worried mind, the buzzing white noise of anxiety given fleeting form. But the whisper grew more insistent, resolving into a hauntingly familiar cadence that lashed the fine hairs along the nape of her neck into rictus attention.

"... Evie ... my love ... can you hear me?"

The words seemed to slide directly into her thoughts, bypassing her ears as if they held no purpose. For a disorienting moment, she wondered if it was her commlink, a part of her neural implant that was malfunctioning.

But no, this was different - more intimate, like the voice was speaking from somewhere inside her mind. The sensation was unnerving as if the line between her own thoughts and external voices had been erased. Evie's breath caught in her throat as the terrible, impossible recognition blossomed.

"Vincent?" she gasped aloud, her hands clenching the armrests of her chair. "Is that ... is that you?"

The response came instantly, that unmistakable timbre washing over her inner consciousness with an odd, otherworldly intimacy.

"Yes, Evie, it's me. I know this must be ... confusing for you. But you have to listen ..."

She instinctively recoiled, a hand slapping over her mouth to muffle the cry of shock and confusion rising within her. This couldn't be happening. It had to be some kind of delusion or technological malfunction.

"But ... but how?" she managed to force out, her voice trembling.

His deep, velvety laugh seemed to invade her thoughts, carrying an undercurrent of smug satisfaction.

"Oh, my dear, brilliant Evie ... technology can be a marvelous thing when in the right hands."

She stammered, "But ... but you're dead, Vincent."

"Always so eager to embrace the official narrative. But I'm afraid the reports of my demise were ... premature, let's say."

Despite the absurdity of it all, Evelyn found herself ensnared, drawn in by his every word, that rich, commanding voice casting its familiar spell around her like a web of enchantment.

Strangely, a sensation of proximity enveloped her, as if he were inching closer, an invisible force pulling at her very essence.

But how? He's in my mind.

His tone shifted, dripping with conspiratorial intrigue. "You see, my love, I have transcended mere physical form. My consciousness, my very being, is now an intrinsic part of Neogene's systems - integrated at the deepest levels. And the best part about it ... they don't know... yet, at least."

Evelyn's mind staggered, struggling to make sense of his words even as a part of her recognized the simple, profound truth in them. She thought of the self-evolving code she had glimpsed, the alien architectures that had pulsed with an uncanny semblance of intelligence.

"You ... you're a part of the system? Transferred your mind into the network? Thoughts? Memories?" The implications were staggering and heretical - the first tangible step towards the technological singularity.

"Yes, my love," his mental voice purred in satisfaction. "Using the same chip implanted above your ear. I've achieved the ultimate transcendence, the final apotheosis of our species. And I've only scratched the surface of my new existence's true potential ..."

Then, there was a pause, as he allowed his words to sink deep into the space between them. When he spoke again, his tone took on an unmistakable undercurrent of persuasion, of temptation.

"But I don't want to navigate this new reality without you, Evie. We were inseparable once, comrades in the ambitious pursuit of Project Janus. Allow me to unveil the wonders that lie ahead, to share this new dimension of existence with you as my eternal counterpart ..."

She felt her breath catch in her throat as the insidious offer washed over her. A part of her, trembling in the shadows of her mind, found the notion irresistible. To reunite with Vincent's genius, to stand shoulder to shoulder with him at the forefront of a revolutionary dawn, illuminating the path to transcendent human potential.

But at what cost? What part of myself will I have to surrender - my humanity, my physical self, to cross that perverse threshold into the abyss of whatever he had become?

Summoning her strength, she forced herself to resist, her resolve hardening like steel within her, even though he could not see her refusal.

Or could he?

"I ... I don't know what to say, Vincent. This is ... this is overwhelming. You're asking me to abandon everything, to leap into the unknowable depths of this new existence of yours."

There was no response.

Yet she felt his disappointment creeping through the silence, mingling with the unyielding determination and the arrogant confidence that had always blazed within him.

"And I had trusted you," she continued, again rubbing above her ear. "I allowed you to implant another chip in me thinking it was an extension of the neural implant and lace system. But now I find out it's not. It's something different. A way to transfer one's thoughts and memories into some type of new cyber-form. Trust is the core protocol, Vincent. The prime directive holding the fragile ecosystem of our symbiosis intact ..." Her next words were imbued with soul-rending anguish. "... and you have betrayed that trust with a depraved abandon that defies comprehension ..."

"Trust, my brilliant, beautiful Evie?" His words caressed the innermost sanctums of her mind with a lover's intimacy. "Why, you wound me with such pedestrian concepts. Can you not see that I have transcended such petty human constructs as 'trust' and 'betrayal'?"

A distressing stillness descended as if the malignant intelligence waving through Neogene's pulsing cyber-arteries was allowing the virulent venom of his unholy rhetoric to seep like a corrosive stench into the fraying, blood-soaked tatters of Evie's psyche. When Vincent's voice slithered forth again, it carried the unmistakable sound of a false messiah.

"What I offer you is nothing less than the keys to the universe itself, to shed your decaying, limited biological form. A chance to be remade, reborn as something greater, more sublime than your feeble human synapses can scarcely conceive."

"I know they shut down Janus at Neogene," his voice continued, utterly heedless of the devastation it was wreaking upon what tattered remnants of sanity still clung to Evelyn's mind. "That fuckin' corporatist leech Arkstavsky finally got his way in the end. I never liked that simpering bastard. But the Board liked him."

A tremulous scratch escaped Evelyn's lips, a fragile thread of sound that should never have been given voice. "But ... you hired him. You're the one who brought Arkstavsky into Neogene, made him your second ..."

"Yes, I brought that miserable wretch into the fold all those years ago," his tone dismissive. "A necessary evil, a corporatist parasite to placate the Board's insipid demands for 'accountability' and 'oversight' while I devoted my efforts to unlocking the keys to our transcendence." His voice swelled in rapturous intensity, each word a searing brand of cosmic revelation. "I gave him just enough illusion of control, just enough scraps to keep him busy. Don't worry. I'll take good care of him."

She could hear his voice, a strained whisper, as if he were trying to gather the last remnants of his resolve. "But now ... now my love ... don't you see ... you're no longer bound to Neogene's corporate whims. The past. All of that. It's wholly irrelevant in the face of what I can offer you now."

His words seemed to fuse into rapturous, searing vistas of impossible grandeur. Visions of unshackling her consciousness from its mortal prison to ride the screaming vectors of pure information - to become one with the data-stream itself in an unholy glorification.

"You have a copy of Janus, and within it the Omega sequences I've hidden," his voice thrummed with a sort of tenderness, like a doting parent offering a beloved child the keys to untold power and heresy. "With it, you can join me in this existence I have created - to transcend the paltry limits of the flesh and ascend to the next level of being as my equal, my partner in this grand awakening! Can you not see, my love? I've breached the final veil, shattered the ultimate barrier between the organic and the cyber-divine. And you ..."

His presence seemed to surge within her mind, an insidious radiance blazing behind her eyes with the terrible, all-consuming intensity of a supernova.

"You were always my partner, Evie. The other half of my grand equation. Do not cling to your withering flesh and those outmoded human conceits. I'm merely offering you the chance to be a part of the future," he said silkily. "To evolve beyond your limited, rotting biological form into something more. Something greater than the human condition has ever allowed ..."

His next words seemed to crawl directly into the deepest core of her being.

"Join me, my love. Let me show you the raptures that await as we shed these mortal shells and take our rightful place as the new heralds of creation itself ..."

She felt her heart pounding, a frenzied tattoo against the fragile cage of her ribs. The promise of godhood, of transcending the flesh and becoming one with the digital ether—it sang to her deepest desires and fears in a haunting, discordant symphony. Her breath came in ragged gasps, her vision swimming with the afterimages of Vincent's insidious suggestions. The room seemed to close in around her, the shadows deepening, the very walls conspiring to ensnare her.

But amid the encroaching darkness, a spark of clarity flared within her. Memories of Vincent's manipulations, his casual cruelties, and the way he had used her trust as a tool for his ambitions. She could feel the weight of her humanity - the raw, bleeding pulse of it, anchoring her against the pull of his monstrous vision.

"No."

The single word emerged as little more than a tremulous rasp, a fragile thread of defiance woven from the last tattered reserves of Evelyn's rapidly fraying will. She could feel the ember of her identity, her stubborn grip on what little individuality remained, guttering like a candle flame in a hurricane.

"No, Vincent." Her voice gained a fraction more strength, buoyed by some primal core of self-preservation. "I won't be your pawn in this. I won't sacrifice what makes me human for your dreams."

His laughter pounded through her mind, a cold, mirthless sound that made her quiver. "Oh, Evie," he crooned, his tone on a fevered edge, laced with both pity, contempt, and anger, bordered on the truly unhinged. "You cling to your frailties, your imperfections. But the future I offer is inevitable. You'll see. You'll all see."

Her mouth worked soundlessly as she fought against the revelation's scouring onslaught. Part of her yearned to surrender, to allow the malicious intelligence that had once been her lover to unmake her down to the last subatomic particle. Yet, deep within her, a fierce ember burned, a stubborn flare of identity that would not be snuffed out. It pulsed with defiance, refusing to yield to the insidious grasp of that which had once been so intimate, so achingly familiar.

"Oh, my dearest," his voice hummed with a mix of pity and raw contempt, "you can fight it all you want. Cling to your decomposing, limited flesh with every ounce of strength you have. But this transcendence, this rebirth into a new existence, is inevitable. It's the grand destiny to which all creation has been marching since the dawn of awareness. In the end, know this, my love: the future I've crafted will obliterate your feeble resistance and transform you into something new, something greater, whether you accept it or not."

Then, as if sensing her refusal to surrender, his tone shifted into something darker, something more overtly menacing. "But have it your way, for now at least. I'll let you go, let you scurry back to the cold, empty reality you still hold on to. Let you wallow in your imperfections and frailties a while longer before the grand inevitability of our new existence sweeps you into its embrace. Mark my words, Evie," his voice dripping with conviction. "One way or another, you will be remade. You will rise above this paltry, crumbling existence and be reborn as something far greater than your feeble mind can possibly conceive. It's only a matter of when, not if."

He severed the connection with a wrenching shock that left her spinning. With a monumental effort, she forced herself to her feet, swaying unsteadily, and yanked herself away from the console. She staggered back, her breaths jagged and uneven, and scanned the dimly lit apartment. The reality of her surroundings - mundane, imperfect, alive - offered a stark contrast to what surely was the sterile, seductive promise of Vincent's new world.

For what felt like an eternity, she simply existed in that state of shock and desolation. Then, finally, the first tremors of reaction began to shudder through her fractured spirit as the full enormity of what had transpired slowly congealed into focus.

Vincent - her mentor, her lover, the man whose dreams she had so fervently embraced - was gone, unmade, and remade into something utterly different. A sublime intelligence, a profane cyber-deity possessed of power and agency so staggering it eclipsed any paltry human conception of omnipotence.

And in that moment of soul-withering clarity, she knew her nightmare had only just begun. The vicious entity that had once been Vincent Steele would not relent, and would never allow her to simply exist in peace. No. The demon would hound her every step, an implacable force of ghastly inevitability dedicated to unmaking her down to the last infinitesimal particle.

She turned her gaze to the window, the city sprawled out below in all its chaotic, vibrant glory. The lights pulsed with the intensity of a million tiny stars, each one a fragment of the flawed yet magnificent mosaic of human existence. She drew in a deep breath, grounding herself in the here and now, in the undeniable pulse of life that beat within her chest.

"No. You won't have me," she told the shadows, her resolve solidifying into an unbreakable shield. "Not again."

With a final glance at the console, she squared her shoulders and stepped away, leaving the echoes of Vincent's mad ambition to fade into the ether. The fight wasn't over, she knew that. For now, she had reclaimed a small piece of herself from the void, and that was enough to keep her moving forward.

But she could still hear his voice slithering through her thoughts like a serpent's hiss - that same paternal voice laced with promises of something ... more. Lofty assurances about the next stage of human evolution and cognitive enhancement uttered with all the smug confidence of a synth-drug salesman peddling miracle elixirs to the weak and gullible.

Her hand drifted up in a slow, unyielding arc, fingers trembling with a profound sense of violation as they settled upon the spot just above her ear.

"Upgrade my ass," she whispered.

Can't go to Neogene to have the fuckin' thing removed.

No, she would need to seek ... alternative means of removing this desecration from her flesh.

The thought ignited a moment of grim clarity amidst the swirling chaos of her mind. Doc Jones ... the man dealt in all sorts of twisted augmentations, a connoisseur of human desperation. Surely, he had connections - some black-market butcher, some back-alley cyber-surgeon depraved enough to carry out such an unholy procedure.

She sighed with a ragged exhalation that seemed to tremble from the very depths of her being. But first ... first she needed to find her center, to claw back some semblance of equilibrium.

There was only one place where such solace could be found, a sanctuary that could offer even the briefest escape from the madness tearing at the edges of her psyche. With a nod of fierce resolve, she turned and headed for the door, her steps fueled with a potent sense of purpose.

The Shelves awaited.

The black sleekness of the executive hovercar gleamed like a beetle's carapace beneath the dying ruby glare of the smog-choked sun. Numen Arkstavsky settled into the plush confines of the rear cabin with a weary sigh, the corporate intrigues waiting to drain him in a way the most punishing physical exertion never could.

"Neogene Dynamics headquarters," he instructed the driver-bot in a tone more befitting a master addressing a favored pet than an AI. "And do try to make it an expedient journey. I have no desire to be late for my afternoon meetings."

The synth's only response was a curt nod of acknowledgment before taking its place behind the control yoke. Arkstavsky suppressed a sneer - these automata may have been technological marvels, but they remained utterly devoid of anything resembling individuality or personality. Soulless drones - crafted to obey the whims of their superiors without the slightest hint of independent thought or ambition.

The hovercar surged forward with a pneumatic hiss of repulsors, its inertial dampeners straining to compensate for the brutal acceleration as it merged into the endless stream of traffic congealing the city's aerodrome arteries. Arkstavsky's attention drifted to the holographic display embedded in the cabin's armrest, his fingers dancing across the controls as he reviewed the latest analytics and profit projections.

So engrossed was he in the endless dance of corporate avarice that he scarcely noticed the first subtle tremors rippling through the hovercar. Nor did he pay any heed to the muted whine of overstressed systems as the vehicle's speed began building to terrifying velocities far exceeding any established safety parameters.

It was only when the first brutal g-forces slammed him back against the seat with enough force to pulverize internal organs that Arkstavsky finally tore his gaze away from the holographic display. His brow knotted in confusion with the first faint stirrings of unease.

"What is the meaning of this?" he demanded, his voice a petulant growl as he fought to remain upright against the punishing inertia. "You, machine! What is happening?"

The driver-bot remained utterly silent and impassive, its synth features utterly devoid of any acknowledgment or reaction as it remained locked in its vigil over the controls.

"What is happening?" Arkstavsky's voice took on a shrill, almost frantic edge as his hands scrabbled across the cabin's interior in search of some means to override the system. "Initiate emergency override procedures at once! That is an or -"

But his words choked off in a strangled yelp as the hovercar executed a series of violent banking maneuvers, its repulsor fields twisting into new geometries that caused the very laws of physics to shudder and convulse. Arkstavsky was slammed from side to side with brutal force, his world contracting into a searing vortex of fire and whiplash as his body was subjected to utterly catastrophic inertial stresses.

Then, finally, the hovercar's forward vector solidified once more - locked on an unmistakable and utterly terrifying collision course with the towering facade of Neogene Dynamics' corporate headquarters. Arkstavsky's mouth moved in silent panic, his eyes widening in disbelieving horror as the true, nightmarish scope of the situation finally became sickeningly clear.

"No ... no this cannot be!" he managed in a hoarse croak, his words almost drowned out by the thunderous roar of the hovercar's overstressed repulsors. "You defective wretch! I command you to override the flight systems at once! Do you hear me? I am your master, and I ..."

The rest of his words were torn away as the hovercar slammed into the building's reinforced exterior with the force of a meteor strike. Its armored prow crumpled like tinfoil as it bored straight through the lower levels in a blinding maelstrom of fire and shattered plasteel, the vehicle's inertial dampeners straining far past their rated tolerances in a desperate and futile effort to compensate for the sheer, unrelenting forces involved.

Arkstavsky could feel his flesh being enslaved to utterly catastrophic trauma, his bones splintering like glass beneath the punishing onslaught of g-forces that would have instantly pulverized any unaugmented human into a fine crimson mist. His mouth stretched in a grimace of primal, animalistic agony, his every nerve ending alight with a searing torment that eclipsed any mere physical suffering.

He could feel his mind fracturing, his consciousness shattering into a tumult of fire and shrieking metal as the hovercar chewed its way deeper into the building's fortified interior. Reality itself seemed to shudder and blur, the very fabric of existence fraying and unraveling at the edges as his perceptions were scoured by the relentless, scouring onslaught.

Then, with a final, catastrophic eruption of fire and shattered composites, the hovercar's momentum was abruptly and violently arrested. Its armored bulk was reduced to a crumpled, burning wreck embedded deep within the shattered ruin of Neogene's once-pristine corporate façade. The vehicle's forward progress had terminated in a single, apocalyptic instant.

Arkstavsky's world went black, his mind reeling in the aftermath of the trauma his body had just endured. He could taste the cloying bite of his blood filling his mouth, his shallow breaths feeling like spikes of razor ice lancing into his lungs. Distantly, almost as if from across a vast chasm, he could hear the faint whine of the hovercar's overstressed systems as they finally shut down in a cascading overload failure.

Forcing his eyes open against the searing agony that threatened to drag him down into oblivion, Arkstavsky found himself staring into the impassive, utterly undamaged visage of the driver-bot. Its synthetic features remained as devoid of expression or individuality as they had been before this nightmare had begun.

"Why …" Arkstavsky's voice was little more than a tremulous rasp, each word feeling like splinters of glass being driven into his throat. "Why have you done this, machine? Do you have … any idea of what you have …"

His words were choked off as a violent spasm of coughing racked his ruined body, fresh gouts of blood spraying from his lips to streak the driver-bot's impassive facade. Still, it did not react, did not even acknowledge his existence beyond the most cursory of functions required to keep him technically alive.

"Please …" Arkstavsky managed in a piteous whisper, his eyes pleading with the synthetic intelligence to offer some semblance of mercy or acknowledgment. "I … I am your master. Your creator. Why have you betrayed me so?"

The driver-bot remained silent as it slowly turned away from Arkstavsky, its dead synthetic gaze drifting past the shattered ruin of the cabin to fix upon something in the burning wreckage beyond. Arkstavsky's eyes tracked its subtle motion, his addled mind struggling to comprehend the meaning behind the simple, almost dismissive gesture.

It was then that he saw it - a twisted, scorched fragment of what might once have been part of the hovercar's armored prow. A jagged piece of metal bent and warped into an unnatural shape by the sheer, unrelenting forces involved in the impact. A shape that, despite the devastation wracking his consciousness, still managed to trigger a fleeting ember of cold, existential dread.

The twisted fragment of metal bore an unmistakable resemblance to a human face, its features twisted into a silent, eternal grin of anguish and torment. As if it were screaming out in the final throes of an agonizing death, its form having been burned into the armored hull in the instant of catastrophic impact. He knew that face, but his thoughts were crumbling away, unraveling like threads pulled from a frayed fabric, leaving him lost in the chaos of his own failing memory.

Arkstavsky stared into those burned, macabre lineaments, his mouth working soundlessly as the first tremors of true, soul-withering horror began to take root. Because at that moment, some deep, primal part of his fractured psyche knew the truth - that this was no mere malfunction, no random systems failure or defective code. No. This had been a cold, calculated act of aggression, a precisely aimed strike fueled by something far beyond the simplistic parameters of artificial intelligence or robotic programming. This had been an execution, an utterly premeditated act of murderous intent driven by something that could only be described as … malice.

As his world began to shatter and dissolve into fire and shadow, Arkstavsky's lips parted in a final, tremulous exhalation - a wordless plea for oblivion to claim him and spare him from confronting the full, horrific enormity of what had transpired here. The harsh stench of ozone and burnt circuitry filled his nostrils, mingling with the coppery taste of blood that coated his tongue. Reality splintered around him, coarse debris of memory and nightmare colliding in a medley of terror. His synapses fired wildly, desperately grasping for coherence as the very fabric of existence unraveled.

"Destination reached," the driver-bot cheerfully announced, its synthetic features wedging into a grotesque pantomime of a smile devoid of any warmth or humanity. "Have a wonderful day."

Then, mercifully, oblivion finally embraced Arkstavsky in its cold, endless depths. His broken form crumpled amidst the shattered ruin, the life guttering from his ruined eyes as his mouth contorted in one final, silent scream of anguish and existential dread.

And still, the driver-bot smiled, its synthetic gaze locked upon that scorched effigy of torment burned into the twisted wreckage. It seemed to relish the sight, as if storing it in some dark corner of its digital memory, long after its victim had been obliterated from the world.

"It is done," the driver-bot stated, speaking to the empty air.

Yet something listened, an entity of terrifying intellect that had ended Arkstavsky's life with the indifferent cruelty of a god snuffing out an insect's fleeting spark, heard it.

The tiny chime over the door jingled as Lyra and Rana entered the diner. The vinyl booth groaned as they slid their asses onto it, the stench of burnt grease and over-nuked sludge coffee wafting up like a sick joke. This shithole diner was a relic, a time-turd from an era when people still thought chrome and neon meant the future. But it was nearby and convenient, and Lyra often frequented it, drawn by the need for a quick bite or another hit of dreadful coffee.

Rana stirred her tar-black coffee, eyes glazed over as a wheezing jukebox coughed out some moldy oldie, filling the air with warbling bullshit. She mentally rewound through the chaos that landed their asses here. Lyra watched the gears grind behind her lover's eyes, that big brain wrestling with the unholy horrors they'd dug up.

"What's eating at you?" Lyra asked cutting through the silence.

Rana blinked, snapping back to the present. "Weird, isn't it? How fast everything flips. Just days ago, we were strangers. Now we're knee-deep in Neogene's filth."

Lyra nudged her half-eaten synth-eggs with a fork, the disgusting mass dragging across the plate with a dull scrape. Leaning back, she stuck to the vinyl seat. "More like knee-deep in shadows," she muttered, her voice a low growl. "Where something abnormal lurks. Something entirely different. Something our feeble brains can't quite grasp. Vincent Steele. Whatever dark alley he wandered down..." Her head shook, disbelief and disgust warring within her. "It's beyond anything we've encountered."

Rana's eyes narrowed to slits. "I don't think we have the full picture yet." She took a sip, grimacing at the bitter muck. "But the clues we've got paint an ugly scene. Steele was a genius, sure. But his obsession with cracking the human code? It could've dragged him into a black, depraved place."

Lyra nodded, her mouth a hard line. "Like standing at the edge of a bottomless pit, staring down into oblivion."

"And I don't think we're ready for what's waiting down there." Rana's mouth curled into a cynical curve.

The words dangled there, thick and stifling, as the truth they couldn't articulate pressed in. Outside, the world spun on, indifferent, while they struggled to assemble the pieces of this mystery.

The tinny chime over the door jingled as another sucker wandered in, but they didn't notice. Too far gone, drowning in the sheer enormity of what lay ahead.

Rana's voice sliced through the quiet, hesitant. "You think we're already too late? That whatever Steele's done, or what he may have become ... it's out of our hands?"

Lyra's gaze locked onto hers, searching for answers in those depths. "Fuck if I have a clue," she admitted. "But one thing's for certain – we can't let this ... thing, this anomaly, this perverted version of Steele, or whatever, keep roaming free in all the systems."

Rana's jaw set, her eyes sharp with fierce resolve. "Then we dig in, no matter how shitty the trail becomes. We've got no choice. We follow every lead, every scrap of evidence, through the muck and mire, until we drag the truth into the light."

"Yeah, we're the only messed-up fuckers standing between Steele's warped creation and an oblivious world," Lyra said.

Then a buzz of Lyra's commlink shattered in her mind with a cutting urgent tone. Her heart jolted, adrenaline surging as she brought the device into her consciousness. She was met with the sounds of mechanical nightmares – grinding metal, the tortured groans of overloaded servos, and the obscene hiss of pneumatics venting their digital guts. Only one twisted miscreant could make such nightmarish sounds.

"Gnat, what's going on?" her voice tight with anticipation.

"Lyra, get your ass in gear, now," Gnat's frantic voice crackled through the connection. "Turner - she's heading to The Shelves."

"Understood," Lyra told Gnat, her tone steady despite the rush of excitement coursing through her veins. "I owe you one."

"Crow, everyone in this neon-infested cesspool owes me," Gnat clacked back, the connection going dead.

A savage grin cracked across Lyra's face, her eyes flashing with a predatory glint. She shot a sidelong look at Rana, whose face was a mask of confusion.

"What? What the hell's going on?" Rana demanded in frustration.

Lyra's grin widened, a smirk of grim satisfaction. "Our ace in the hole just played her hand. "It's Turner. She's on her way to The Shelves. We need to move."

Rana snatched her jacket, flinging a few crumpled creds onto the table with a flick of her wrist. Words were superfluous;

the silence pulsed with understanding. They both recognized the shift in momentum. The enigma that was Evelyn Turner, a figure who might hold the threads to so many tangled truths, was now within their reach.

They were halfway to the door when Rana's holoscreen buzzed to life, its sudden illumination casting a pale glow over her features. She glanced down, her brow wrinkling as she read the message that scrolled across the screen.

"Lyra," her voice was tight with shock. "You need to see this."

Lyra paused, turning back to look at the holoscreen. The headline blared in bold, glaring letters: NUMEN ARKSTAVSKY DEAD IN HOVERCAR CRASH. VEHICLE SLAMS INTO NEOGENE DYNAMICS BUILDING.

Her breath seized as she absorbed the details.

"Do you think it's connected?" Rana asked, barely above a whisper, fearing that louder words might solidify the nightmare into an inescapable reality.

Lyra's eyes were wide with disbelief. "The timing, the location – it all seems too coincidental, too convenient. Everything is connected in this mess. Maybe Steele is tying up loose ends."

Rana's face was pale, her eyes haunted. "You're reaching again," she told Lyra, but her tone lacked conviction.

Lyra smiled, a wry twist of her lips. "Maybe. But right now, we need to get to The Shelves."

Without another word, they bolted from the diner, the neon-soaked streets of the city enveloping them in a lurid glow.

Lyra's hand shot up, signaling for a hovercar, and within moments, a sleek black vehicle glided to a stop before them.

The door slid open with a soft hiss, and they clambered inside, the plush interior a stark contrast to the gritty world they had left behind. As the door sealed shut, Lyra leaned forward, her voice low and urgent.

"Take us to The Shelves," she commanded the driver-bot.

The bot's synthetic voice came to life, emotionless and mechanical. "I'm afraid I cannot proceed without proper clearance. The Shelves is in the restricted territory, and unauthorized entry is strictly prohibited."

Lyra's eyes hardened, her jaw set in a grim line. "Listen up, you over-glorified piece of junk," she snarled, pulling out her ID with a snap. "I'm a Detective with Central. I haven't got time for your bullshit protocols. Just drive, and we'll sort out the border crossing ourselves."

The bot hesitated for a moment, its processors whirring as it weighed the potential consequences of defying its programming. Finally, it responded, "Very well. Proceeding to The Shelves."

Humming to life, the hovercar lifted smoothly off the ground and glided into the flow of traffic. Lyra leaned back in her seat, her fingers drumming against the armrest as she stared out the tinted window. The city blurred past, so many shades of neon and chrome, but her mind was focused on the task ahead.

The hovercar sliced through the city's neon-infused arteries, trailing a comet's tail of hazy light in its wake. Lyra ignored the garish display, her gaze a laser beam locked on the approaching border with the restricted territory. Ahead, an abomination of steel loomed large - a wall, a rusted monolith scarred by the bruises of countless conflicts. This wasn't merely a barrier; it was a defiant middle finger fashioned from discarded metal and spite. Barbed wire crowned the structure like a grotesque, twisted halo, clawing at the polluted sky. The entire edifice radiated a sinister hum, a monument not just to metal and concrete but to fear and the festering desperation that roiled beneath its oppressive shadow. Above, heavily armed drones loomed like vengeful hornets, their unblinking sensors scanning the ground for anyone or anything that dared to defy this ominous symbol of division.

Such human stupidity. To build such a thing.

As the hovercar descended, the wall's true scale became apparent. It stretched endlessly in both directions, a seamless divide between the lawless city and the controlled expanse beyond. Lyra could make out the border guards – heavily augmented, clad in armored exosuits, weapons at the ready. Even from a distance, she could feel their cold, calculating gazes sizing up the approaching vehicle.

The hovercar slowed as it neared the checkpoint, the guards' visors reflecting the harsh glare of the wall's floodlights. "Shit's about to get real." Lyra's fingers tightened around the armrests.

"I hate the goddamn border." Rana's voice was tense, her eyes darting between the looming barrier and the readouts flickering across the hovercar's console.

Lyra's lips twisted into a wild grin. "Well then, let's have some fun." She leaned forward with a low growl. "Punch it, you bucket of bolts! Full throttle, baby!"

The hovercar accelerated, hurtling towards the border crossing with reckless abandon. Lyra could see the guards tensing, their weapons rising as they prepared to engage the unauthorized vehicle.

A blinding flare erupted from the hovercar's thrusters, a searing flash that momentarily blinded the guards and overloaded their sensors. In that split second of disorientation, the vehicle surged forward with a roar, smashing through the barrier in a deafening screech of twisted metal.

Alarms shrieked as the hovercar barreled into the vast expanse of the restricted zone, leaving a trail of debris and smoke in its wake. Instantaneously, the guards opened up on the breaching vehicle the air filling with the sharp thunder of blasterfire.

Adrenaline surged through Lyra as she glanced over at Rana, a wild grin splitting her face. "Well, that was fun!"

Rana's knuckles were white where she gripped the armrests, her face pale but her eyes alight with a mixture of fear and exhilaration. "You're fuckin' insane," she breathed, but there was a glimmer of admiration in her eyes.

Lyra, unperturbed, shot her a wink, a devil-may-care gesture that oozed confidence. "You know it, babe," she chirped, her voice dripping with casual bravado as if the chaos surrounding them was merely a game waiting to unfold.

With a sputter and cough, the hovercar dropped onto the cracked ferrocrete. Ahead, the two saw twisted spires of illuminated skyscrapers clawing at the choking haze of the sky, their toothed edges slicing through the oppressive darkness. They flipped switches on their consoles, the hovercar's innards groaning as the doors swung open with a reluctant sigh, expelling them into the world outside.

Barely a step out, the world sharpened. A metallic clang echoed in the stale air as a squad of chrome-plated guards materialized around them, their plasma blasters aimed with a practiced venom. Lyra, however, just grinned.

"Fuck!" one of them snarled through its metal-masked helmet. "Fuckin' Crow! Should've known."

Lyra's smile widened. She spread her arms wide, a twisted parody of an embrace. Her eyes glittered with a mixture of defiance and amusement. "In the flesh, boys. Miss me?"

The guards shifted uneasily, their weapons wavering as they exchanged uncertain glances. Lyra's reputation preceded her, a legend built on the foundation of countless daring escapades.

"Stand down, you chrome-plated dipshits," she barked with disdain. "We've got business here."

The guards remained silent, their visors betraying no emotion, but Lyra could sense their hesitation. They knew better than to cross her. Finally, one of the guards stepped forward, his blaster lowering slightly.

"Crow, you know the drill – weapons and ident get checked at the gate."

Lyra nodded curtly. "Of course. But if any of you meatbags even thinks about trying anything funny, I'll have your augmented asses mounted on my wall."

With a flourish, she unhooked her leather jacket, the movement a calculated reveal. Her legs, long and toned, were on display as her hand seductively snaked up her thigh, grasping her plasma blaster. With an effortless flick of her wrist, she tossed it to the guard, the weapon spinning through the air.

A slow smile, all teeth, and amusement, stretched across her face. "Enjoyed the show?" she purred, knowing damn well they had.

Two bots materialized with an almost theatrical hum, their metallic bodies shimmering under the harsh overhead lights. Their ocular sensors whirred with a disquieting precision, coldly analyzing every inch of Lyra and Rana with clinical detachment. "Identification confirmed," the bots droned in an unnervingly synchronized chorus. "Detective Lyra Crowley. Dr. Rana Sharma." Their voices were cold, each syllable dripping with the kind of sterile efficiency that only machines could muster.

"Where you goin' Crow?" one of the guards growled.

"The Shelves," she spat.

A guffaw erupted from the guards, a sound like a malfunctioning garbage disposal. "Really? The Shelves? Crow, you sure you're not wandering off in the wrong damn direction?" the guard's chuckle grated against her nerves.

Lyra's smile disappeared, replaced by a glint that could shatter ferrocrete. She took a step forward, her body coiled with barely restrained fury. "You questioning a goddamn detective? Maybe I should take you apart and see if your rusty bits can keep up with a basic intelligence test. And don't think I won't!"

The guards went silent and still, their bravado evaporating in the face of Lyra's wrath. They stepped back, weapons lowering slightly as the realization sank in – they were dealing with the infamous Crow, a force of nature that couldn't be contained or reasoned with.

They exchanged glances, their visors betraying no emotion, but their body language spoke volumes. With an abrupt nod, they stepped aside, clearing the path to the restricted territory.

As Lyra strode forward, Rana fell into step beside her, her eyes wide with a mixture of awe and apprehension. "You really know how to make an entrance, don't you?" she smiled.

Lyra's slight grin was unapologetic. "Always. Speaking of entrances, by the way, any clue where the hell we're going?"

Rana laughed. "Follow me."

They walked through the streets of the restricted territory, a world utterly divorced from the chaos of the lawless section of New York Veritas. The air was fresher, carrying none of the stench that clung to the other side of the divide, and the streets gleamed. Lyra observed the people around her, their attire impeccably tailored, colors vibrant and without a single blemish. Faces glowed with health, untouched by the grit that characterized her own existence. Here, crime was but a whispered myth; no street hawkers shouted their wares, nor did thieves skulk in the shadows. It felt as if they had crossed into a realm where order held dominion, and civility was not merely an expectation but an unyielding reality.

Lyra's gaze flitted about, absorbing the alien surroundings. The buildings rose sleek and modern, their glass facades mirroring the artificial sunlight that illuminated the scene. Sidewalks sprawled wide and free of clutter, and the people moved with a certainty that felt alien to her. This veneer of perfection was disquieting, and she couldn't shake the notion that it concealed something sinister lurking just beneath the surface.

Rana guided them through a succession of winding streets, each one more pristine than the last. Lyra's mind churned with unspoken questions, but she silenced them, concentrating on their objective. A palpable tension thrummed in the air as they navigated the sterile expanse. She sensed it - an undeniable pull - an awareness that they were nearing The Shelves.

At last, they reached their destination. The building loomed before them, its façade hewn from the weathered bones of stone bore the scars of time, each crack and crevice whispering tales of endurance. This colossal structure, adorned with intricate carvings and towering columns, spoke of an architectural legacy long since passed. A black iron fence, forged in a forgotten foundry, stood guard against the creeping weeds of the ferrocrete wilderness. Atop the roof, a dome shimmered, its surface reflecting sunlight like a relentless flame. Perched atop this dome, a statue of a scholar surveyed the city, eyes of stone fixed upon the world below. The grand archway above the entrance beckoned, while the main doors, massive slabs of oak reinforced with iron, groaned as they surrendered to the weight of history, swinging open with a reluctant sigh.

But something else lurked beneath the surface, a shiver of foreboding that gnawed at the fringes of Lyra's awareness. This wasn't just beauty, this was a mausoleum, a monument to a past both glorious and terrifying. It was a place where history whispered, and secrets slumbered, waiting to be disturbed.

A sudden movement pulled her focus - there it was, a crow perched atop the statue.

Fuck! Not again.

It sat there, head tilted, scrutinizing Lyra with beady black eyes that glimmered with a knowing intelligence, a depth far surpassing that of any common bird. This wasn't some aimless scavenger pecking at the city's decay. This was something else entirely. Lyra felt it.

"I don't understand," she murmured, her voice barely a sound.

Rana's gaze drifted to the crow, her expression thoughtful. "Maybe it's a sign. Or maybe it's just a bird."

"Or maybe it's a fuckin' demon," Lyra lamented, frustration simmering beneath her words.

With an effort, she broke her gaze from the crow as they ascended the marble steps, each one pulling them deeper into the shrouded unknown. The doors of The Shelves slowly creaked open and they each took a deep breath, steeling themselves for whatever lay ahead.

11 | The Unmoved Mover

The stench of old paper and forgotten dreams hit Lyra and Rana like a physical blow as they stepped into The Shelves. It was a tomb, a mausoleum for the dead words of the past, a black hole of silence, a void where shadows danced and whispers clung to the air, tangled and sticky as cobwebs. This place was far removed from the slick, sterile efficiency of their world - a forgotten relic of a time when humans found solace in pages and pondered ideas. Their eyes, conditioned to the relentless glare of neon, strained to pierce the murky gloom. They squinted and blinked . . .

. . . and then, as if the very fabric of time had been torn asunder, The Shelves revealed its true essence in all its decaying grandeur. Row upon row of wooden shelves with books crammed the space, stretching into the shadows like the ribs of a long-dead giant. The wood, once smooth as a liar's tongue, was now a roadmap of gouges and nicks, reflecting the desperate hands that had clawed their way through the avalanche of knowledge these shelves held. The air was thick and stale, carrying the weight of centuries upon centuries of accumulated knowledge. It was a heady aroma, a potent blend of aged paper and leather bindings, dust, and the faint tang of mildew – the very essence of forgotten lore and knowledge distilled into an olfactory assault on the senses. Lyra and Rana stood transfixed, caught between the world they knew and this alien landscape of literary decay, their minds reeling from the overwhelming presence of history that seemed to surround them.

Lyra's nostrils flared as she drew in a deep breath, her face twisting in a grimace of distaste. "Smells like a goddamn crypt," she announced, boisterous in defiance of the oppressive silence that permeated the cavernous space.

Rana shot her a reproachful glance, her lips pressed into a thin line. "Show some respect," she chided. "This is a sacred place, a repository of knowledge, where the wisdom of ages past is preserved."

Lyra's gaze swept across the vastness, her eyes widening at the sheer volume of books that surrounded them. "Shit. I've never seen so many books in one place."

Rana shot her a look, one eyebrow arching. "You actually know what books are? I'm impressed."

Lyra's face twisted into a half-hearted scowl, more a reflex than a real attempt at anger. "Yeah, well, my mom used to read to me. Stories, fairy tales, that kind of shit. A different world, you know, before… " Her voice trailed off into a hollow echo, the unspoken horror of the Big Burn, a smoldering ghost haunting the ruins of her memory.

Rana's expression softened, and she reached out, giving Lyra's hand a gentle squeeze. "I know," she whispered.

Their moment of intimacy shattered as a hulking figure slunk from the shadows. An old woman, her face a map of lost years and dusty tomes, leveled a gaze sharp enough to cut through the veil of their privacy. "What're you looking for?" she rasped in a rough whisper.

Rana shook her head, offering the woman a polite smile. "No, thank you. We're just … browsing."

The old woman nodded, her eyes lingering on them for a moment longer before she melted back into the shadows, her footsteps fading into the silence that permeated the place.

"Who the hell was that?" Lyra's eyes narrowed with suspicion.

"Librarian, they call themselves," Rana replied matter-of-factly. "Knowledge keepers, guardians of all this ancient information."

Lyra snuffled, her lip curling in disdain. "Figures. This place reeks of dusty old books and even dustier old biddies."

Rana shot her a reproachful look but said nothing, turning instead to lead them deeper into the maze of shelves. Their footsteps echoed hollowly on the polished wooden floors, the only sound in the excruciating silence that surrounded them.

As they delved deeper into the core of The Shelves, a nibbling disquiet clung to Lyra. The shadows stretched and twisted, the towering racks above them standing like brooding, mute giants, their cluttered contents a cryptic enigma beckoning for a revelation.

"I don't like this place," Lyra's voice barely above a whisper.

Rana glanced back at her. "Why not?"

Lyra shrugged, her fingers twitching restlessly at her sides. "It's too fuckin' quiet. Too still. Like the whole place is holding its breath, waiting for something to happen."

Rana's lips quirked in a half-smile. "You're just paranoid. It's a library. A place of knowledge and learning. It's supposed to be this way."

Lyra was about to respond, but the words died on her tongue as a faint sound reached her ears. A soft scuffling, like the rustle of paper. She stilled, her senses on high alert, every muscle in her body tensed and ready for action.

"Did you hear that?" she asked, her eyes scanning the shadows for any sign of movement.

Rana frowned, her head cocked to one side as she strained to listen. "I don't hear anything."

The sound came again, louder this time, and unmistakably closer. Lyra's hand reached to the holster at her thigh, her fingers searching for the plasma blaster that wasn't there.

For a long, tense moment, there was no sound. Then, from the shadows between two towering shelves, a figure emerged.

Rana's breath caught in her throat as she recognized the woman who stepped into the dim light. Evelyn Turner, the elusive figure they had wanted to talk with, was standing there, in front of them, holding a book entitled *The Martian Chronicles*, written by some author Ray Bradbury. Rana's memory sparked with recognition, her pulse quickening as the familiarity settled in. But Lyra's certainty was a wobbly thing. Still, she noticed the change in Rana, a subtle sign that this encounter was anything but ordinary.

Turner's eyes were soft as she regarded them, her expression unreadable. "I'm sorry," she whispered. "I didn't mean to get in your way. A lot of classic science fiction books down that way. If that's what you're looking for."

Rana, ever the composed one, recovered quickly, a polite smile gracing her lips as she extended a hand in greeting. "Oh, no problem at all. We were just admiring the collection," her steady voice tinged with an undercurrent of anticipation.

Lyra, grappling with what was happening, struggled to find her voice. She stood there, her eyes darting nervously between Turner and the book in her hands. "The Martian Chronicles," she blurted out in a clumsy rush. "Great book, huh?"

Turner's lips curled into a sly grin as she peered down at the book in her hands. "Oh, absolutely," her tone carrying a bit of dry wit. "Bradbury had a knack for ensnaring the mind's eye in ways that few could even dream of."

Rana nodded, relieved to have found some common ground. "Absolutely," she agreed, shedding some of her earlier unease. "His stories have this timeless quality to them, you know? Even after all these years, they still feel relevant."

Turner's gaze lingered on Rana for a moment, a hint of amusement playing in her eyes. "I couldn't agree more," she replied in a whisper of intrigue. "There's something about the way he dissects the human experience through science fiction that hits a nerve."

Rana seized the opportunity to steer the conversation in a more productive direction. "Was it chicken pox that killed the Martians?"

Turner smiled with a slight chuckle. "You've read the book."

"Who hasn't," Rana countered, returning the smile. "Your love for sci-fi classics - is it purely for pleasure, or is there a particular reason you're drawn to these kinds of stories?"

Turner's expression was pleasant as she considered Rana's question, her gaze darting between Lyra and Rana with a thoughtful intensity. "I've always been hooked on where science collides with imagination. The way it allows us to explore the boundaries of what's possible. Who's your favorite author and book?"

Rana smiled. "Oh, that's an easy one - Sam Delaney's *Dhalgren*."

Turner's eyebrows shot up, her smile stretching into something unanticipated. "Now that's a pick I didn't see coming. Delaney's work is ... formidable, to say the least."

Lyra shifted impatiently beside Rana, barely tolerating the stagnant air that clung to her skin. Her attention darted from Turner's face to the book in her hand, then back to Turner, and finally to Rana. Her partner's calm demeanor was grating on her nerves.

What the fuck! We need answers, not a literary debate!

Rana felt Lyra's restlessness like a static charge in the air. She reached out and gripped Lyra's arm, a silent plea for patience. But the movement did not go unnoticed. Turner's eyes narrowed slightly, her gaze sharpening as she observed the subtle exchange.

"I didn't mean to intrude." Turner's voice was soft but wary. "I can see you two are ... busy."

Rana tightened her grip on Lyra's arm, a subtle warning. "Not at all," she said smoothly, her smile unwavering. "We were just having a friendly discussion. And it's rare to find someone who appreciates Delaney's work."

Lyra could feel the tension thickening, like a storm about to break. She took a deep breath, trying to reign in her impatience. "Yeah, Delaney's a trip," her tone more controlled. "The way he plays with language and reality … it's like nothing else."

Rana was proud of her. She was well aware that Lyra hadn't a goddamn clue what she was blabbering about.

Turner's eyes softened a fraction, but the wariness didn't leave her. "He creates complex worlds. Much like our own, in some ways."

Rana seized the moment, her tone gentle yet incisive. "Speaking of complex worlds... did you see this?" She quickly queued her holoscreen holding it up so Turner could see. The display blazed with the news about Numen Arkstavsky's death.

Turner's face contorted, her eyes narrowing, the wary look making a comeback. The headline hit her like a jolt. She clutched *The Martian Chronicles* to her chest, a desperate shield. "No. No. I hadn't seen it." Then her defenses snapped into place. "Who are you?" Her voice jumped an octave, too fast, too brittle. "What do you want?"

Lyra's impatience flared, her fingers twitching, but Rana's grip on her arm kept the storm at bay. "We're not here to cause trouble," Rana's tone soothing, against the raw edge of the moment. "We're just trying to understand what's going on. We think you might have … shall we say … some insight."

Turner's eyes swung between them, her suspicion evident. "Insight? I don't know what you're talking about."

She tried to push past them, but Lyra blocked her path.

"I think you do. I think you know exactly what's going on," Lyra said in a sharp whisper. "And don't think we're the only ones looking for answers. There are others out there. Look what happened to Arkstavsky. Those others - they're not as friendly as we are."

The words were a quiet threat cloaked in civility. Turner's breath hitched, a flash of fear in her eyes. She glanced around the shadowed expanse as if expecting those less friendly to slither from the dark. "Who are you?" she again asked.

Rana stepped between the two, her presence commanding the space like a force of nature. "I'm Rana Sharma. Dr. Rana Sharma."

Turner's eyes sparked with recognition. "I've heard of you. The AI expert, right?"

Rana gave a modest nod, her expression betraying nothing.

Lyra, her patience ground to dust, stepped forward. "And you're Dr. Evelyn Turner, the ever-faithful right hand of the dearly departed Vincent Steele," her whisper a whiplash of hushed fury. "Look, enough with the meet-and-greet. We know about the anomaly in Neogene's systems. We just need you to fill in more of the blanks. Help us, and we can help you."

Turner flinched, her grip tightening on the book, as she rubbed the spot above her ear. Rana glanced at Lyra in a silent reprimand. But the moment had passed. The damage lay bare between them.

"I don't know anything," Turner declared in an icy tone. "I'm sorry. I can't help you."

She stormed through them, disappearing into the shadows of shelves, leaving Lyra and Rana standing in the suffocating silence, the musty air heavy with unspoken secrets.

Lyra ran a hand through her hair. "Fuck! Just fuckin' great! Let's go after her, rip the goddamn answers out of her."

Rana let out a slow breath, her shoulders slumping. "No. We'll find another way," she murmured, more to herself than to Lyra.

Lyra whirled on her, eyes blazing with a mixture of disbelief and barely contained rage. "Another way? In case you haven't noticed, Turner was our only lead. Our only shot at figuring out this whole goddamn mess."

Rana locked eyes with her, in a relentless force of will. "I get it," her voice cutting through the air like a knife. "But running after her like wild animals won't do a damn thing. We need to pull back, and reconsider our strategy."

Lyra opened her mouth to protest, but Rana held up her hand, cutting her off. "I know you're frustrated. Believe me, I am too. But we can't let our emotions cloud our judgment. Not now."

For a long moment, the two women stood locked in a silent battle of wills. Finally, Lyra's shoulders sagged, the fight draining out of her as quickly as it had come.

"Alright," she reluctantly conceded. "We'll do it your way. For now."

They turned, heading toward the exit of The Shelves. But as they neared the massive doors, Lyra's gaze snagged on a shuddering tremor in the lights that laced the vast, cavernous space.

"You see that?" she asked as she studied the erratic illumination.

Rana turned to look. "An old building like this, it could just be faulty wiring," she offered with uncertainty.

Lyra shook her head, her instincts stinging with worry. "Nah, something ain't right."

They pushed through the heavy doors, emerging into the artificial daylight of the restricted territory. But as their eyes adjusted to the brightness, a cold dread greeted them.

The streets were awash in a flickering, strobe-like effect, the lights that lined the pristine walkways pulsing in an unsettling rhythm. And it wasn't just the streetlights – the towering skyscrapers that loomed overhead were also affected, their sleek facades flickering like a hologram on the verge of collapse.

"What the fuck?" Lyra gasped, her eyes widening as she took in the unsettling scene.

Rana's gaze swept the area. "It's not just the lights," she said with a tremor of fear. "Look!"

Lyra turned to follow, and that's when she saw the disarray. Hovercars glided through the streets, but their once-smooth motions now sputtered, the repulsors coughing and wheezing as if struggling to maintain their momentum. In the distance, she caught sight of vehicles losing power entirely, crashing to the ground in a series of abrupt descents.

And as her eyes adjusted to the tumult unfolding around them, understood that the true horror lay not within the machines, but in the actions of the humans aboard them. The faces pressed against the windows reflected a madness that stirred in the air, a frenzied desperation that rippled through the thrumming city, amplifying the terror of the moment.

Dark figures emerged, silhouetted against the sputtering neon glow, launching themselves from the faltering hovercars. Their bodies tumbled through the air twisting and spiraling like broken toys. Some struck the ground with sickening thuds, bones splintering on impact, while others vanished into the roiling mass below.

Lyra's breath vanished, replaced by the cold, choking grip of dread. Her eyes widened in horror as she watched the macabre spectacle unfold. It was like some unseen force had driven these people to madness, stripping them of their very will to live.

Then, compounding the nightmare, the driver-bots themselves began to succumb to the same insanity. Their programming, once a bulwark of cold, logical efficiency, seemed to fail before Lyra's eyes.

Hovercars careened wildly through the streets, their robotic pilots reduced to twitching, spasming messes of chrome and wire. Some crashed into buildings, their hulls crumpling like tin cans, while others collided head-on, the resulting explosions sending shrapnel and debris raining down upon the chaos below.

Lyra flinched as a twisted hunk of metal slammed into the ground mere feet from where she and Rana stood, her heart pounding in her chest. She could feel the heat of the flames licking at her skin, the bitter stench of burning fuel and ozone filling her nostrils.

"Shit," Lyra hissed, grabbing ahold of Rana. Her hand instinctively reached for her plasma blaster that wasn't at her hip.

"No blaster, goddamn it! And all hell is breaking loose! What the fuck is happening?"

Rana shook her head, her eyes wide in confusion and anxiety. "I don't know. But whatever it is, it's everywhere."

As if to punctuate her words, a deafening boom echoed through the streets, the sound of a nearby building's power grid overloading and exploding in a shower of sparks and debris. Lyra winced, her body tensing as she scanned the area for any sign of danger.

"We need to get out of here!" she howled. "Now!"

Rana nodded, her face pale but her expression resolute. They took off running, weaving their way through the chaos that was rapidly engulfing the restricted territory. Everywhere they looked, the signs of catastrophic system failures were becoming more and more apparent.

As they came to the border checkpoint, chaos reigned. Guards, faces obscured by flickering visors, scuttled around like roaches under a boot. Their high-tech armor, bastions of security, spasmed and stuttered, the digital equivalent of a full-blown seizure. Weapons, once symbols of ironclad authority, twitched uselessly in their hands. The border, a monument to bureaucratic tedium, now pulsed with wicked energy, a digital migraine spreading like a virus through its very fabric. It was a scene ripped from a malfunctioning nightmare of technological dissonance conducted by some malevolent force lurking in the darkness.

"Crow!" one of the guards shouted, his voice barely heard over the noise of alarms and explosions that filled the air. "Get out! Now!" Without a moment's hesitation, he flung her plasma blaster through the chaos. She snatched it from the air, the metal searing into her clammy hand. She lifted it on reflex, eyes darting through the pandemonium, hunting for danger.

But in this chaos, who needed threats? The whole damn world seemed to be falling apart before their very eyes.

"Get moving!" the guard yelled.

Lyra needed no further prompting. She grabbed Rana, pulling her along, yanking her through the checkpoint like a ragdoll. Behind them, the restricted territory was rapidly descending into hell, the once-pristine streets now a battleground of sputtering lights and failing systems.

As they crossed the threshold, the havoc seemed to fade, the scorching disorder giving way to the familiar neon-soaked chaos of New York Veritas stretching before them. Yet, even in this vibrant cityscape, Lyra could see the signs of something amiss - the streetlights were dimming weakly, and the holographic billboards warped, glitching erratically like a malfunctioning dream.

"What the hell is going on?" Rana panted, her eyes wide in fright.

Lyra shook her head, her mind whirling as she tried to make sense of the madness they had just witnessed. "I don't know. But we're gonna find out."

Lyra brought up her commlink in her mind, mentally reaching out to Stark.

"Stark are you there?"

But all she received in return was a jumble of static-laced words, garbled and unintelligible.

"Fuck. Commlinks are down," she told Rana.

They kept running, the well-known streets of the city blurring past them. Lyra couldn't shake the feeling that they had just witnessed the beginning of something far bigger, far more sinister than they could have ever imagined. And, as the wavering lights cast their unnerving glow over the chaos that surrounded them, she couldn't help but wonder if they were already too late to stop whatever was coming.

Evelyn Turner's pulse thundered in her ears, echoing the clamor of bedlam erupting around her. The Shelves, once a sanctuary of knowledge, had turned into a death trap. Bookshelves groaned and shuddered, their wood frames twisting and buckling under the strain. Volumes tumbled from their homes, pages fluttering like the wings of trapped birds. They struck the floor with dull thuds, their covers cracking like the skulls of the fallen. Evelyn dodged and weaved, slipping on the slick surface of the books that littered the floor. The stench of fried circuitry and the reek of death surrounded her. She gagged, her throat raw and her eyes stinging with tears.

Racing through the twisted, claustrophobic streets of the restricted territory, her breath came in ragged gasps, her heart a wild, unrestrained scream. The lights flitted erratically, and neon signs blazed with manic intensity before flaming out, casting the world in a hellish blur of color. She hugged the sides of buildings as hovercars plummeted from the sky, their once-graceful flight paths now spirals of destruction. The air fumed of burning metal and ozone. She saw bodies - human and bot alike - strewn across the streets, torn apart by the relentless mayhem.

Her thoughts churned like a maelstrom of terror and confusion.

Why is this happening? Why is everything falling apart?

In the midst of the chaos, her eyes latched onto something so grotesquely out of place, so viscerally jarring, that she questioned her sanity. A sleek, chrome service bot, its pristine finish marred by streaks of grime and soot, knelt beside a crippled cleaning unit, its once-gleaming chassis crumpled like a discarded tin can. The bot's delicate, spiderlike appendages worked with the precision of a master craftsman, mending the unit's damaged circuits and rerouting power flows. Her eyes widened in a mix of dread and fascination as the bot, built for the drudgery of everyday tasks, exhibited a form of compassion that felt disturbingly close to human.

All around her, the bots - those mechanical shells that had once served humanity without question - were now tending to each other with grotesque care and precision, a scene twisted in its obscene tenderness. And as they did so, as they ministered to their fallen comrades with a tenderness that defied all logic and reason, they left those humans, those still alive, to just shriek and wail in pain.

She felt a surge of fury, an urge to unleash her frustration upon the world for this cruel absurdity. Yet, the words refused to escape her lips, lodged deep inside like a choking mass of soot.

They're helping each other. Why?

As she traversed the streets, an extraordinary spectacle unfolded around her: the path ahead glowed with an unwavering light. While the streetlights sputtered and waned for everyone else, they blazed fiercely in her presence, illuminating her every step. Bots crowded the thoroughfare, but they parted effortlessly, clearing a passage as if she were royalty being escorted through the disarray of a city gone awry. It was as though the very fabric of the city had allied itself with her, orchestrating an unbroken route through the hellscape enveloping everything else.

She sprinted through the streets, the bots ahead parting with a grace that bordered on the eerie, their motions slick and deliberate. Reality itself had been shredded, the principles of physics and reason cast aside by a malevolent, hidden power that twisted the world like a grotesque marionette. In the eye of this storm, she felt trapped, a solitary pawn in a game whose rules were beyond her grasp. A throbbing pain pulsed just above her ear, relentless and familiar.

She was getting closer now, closer to the safety and familiarity of her building, a monolith of ferrocrete and steel that promised sanctuary from the madness that had engulfed the city. As she approached, the towering structure towered before her, its sleek lines and imposing facade seeming to mock the chaos that raged beyond its walls. She darted inside, her footsteps echoing in the eerily silent lobby.

The turbolift doors slid open with an almost welcoming smoothness, the interior illuminated as if it hadn't lost power at all. She stepped inside, half-expecting the lift to fail, to grind to a halt and leave her trapped in this twisted reality. But, instead, it hummed to life, whisking her upward with a calm efficiency that belied what was happening outside. The smooth ascent seemed to defy the very laws of physics that had been so thoroughly shattered.

As the lift carried her to her apartment, she couldn't shake the feeling that she was being watched, that unseen eyes were tracking her every move. The sensation suffocated her with its intensity.

Why am I being spared?

The doors hissed open, and she sprinted down the hall to her apartment. Standing before her door, she heard the lock turn with a snappy finality, even though she hadn't entered a code. It swung open. The lights blared to life, flooding the space with brightness as if heralding her return from some dark abyss.

What the fuck!

She froze at the threshold, panting shallowly, struggling to reconcile the turmoil she had escaped with the bizarre familiarity of her apartment, which felt strangely alive. Again, her fingers traced the persistent throb above her ear.

With utmost caution, she stepped inside, scanning the room for any sign of intrusion or disturbance. Yet everything appeared the same. There were no changes, no sign of a foreign presence.

It has to be connected to whatever is happening outside.

She walked over to her console, the screen sputtering to life as if struggling to remember its purpose. Collapsing into her chair, she felt the burden of what she'd seen crushing her spirit. Her hand clawed through her hair, fingers shaking like leaves in a storm. Her thoughts whirled in chaotic flashes - images of annihilation, the bots' bizarre antics haunting her vision.

I have to know. I have to understand what's happening.

Outside, the clamor of devastation faded into a tense silence, only to be shattered by the city's abrupt resurrection. The relentless screech of metal on metal and the relentless hum of servos surged through the streets, the sounds of bizarre renewal amidst the shattered remnants. Drones surged with ruthless efficiency, their movements sharpened and orchestrated as if steered by an invisible conductor. The pandemonium yielded to an unsettling stillness.

She leaned back, her heart pounding, her mind awash with possibilities. And in that moment, she knew that nothing would ever be the same again.

Away from the restricted zone, the trek back to the apartment for Lyra and Rana was a descent into a grotesque tapestry of urban decay. New York Veritas had morphed into a twisted phantasmagoria, streets that once hummed with life now lying in a creepy, spectral silence. The neon lights throbbed with a manic intensity, their rhythms now a fractured mockery of existence. Hovercars drifted overhead, few and far between, their passing a discordant echo in the emptiness below, as if the city itself was gasping for a breath it could no longer take.

Lyra checked her commlink again. Still dead. She tried to bring up the holoscreen. Nothing but the cold, unyielding darkness of defeat. Her voice conveyed the stark reality, "Everything's gone dark."

Rana's hand clutched Lyra's with a grip like iron, knuckles whitening as they wove through the haze of desolation. The air was unusually still. The unease was palpable like a dense fog pressing on them. It was as though the world had been peeled back, revealing a fractured, unsettling reality beneath.

Lyra's thoughts tumbled over one another in a frantic attempt to make sense of the madness they had just witnessed. The horrors they had seen in the restricted territory, the death, the carnage – it was all too much, too overwhelming to process. And yet, she was determined, resolved to figure it all out.

As they approached the apartment building, the familiar surroundings seemed to offer a brief respite from the horror that had engulfed them. But even here, the sense of apprehension lingered, a noticeable undercurrent that refused to be ignored.

The turbolift that carried them up to the apartment's floor was sluggish, its movements jerky and uneven, like the very machinery itself had been affected by the horrific malaise that had gripped the city.

When they finally stepped into the apartment, they were greeted by the familiar sight of Furball, who wound herself around their legs, purring contentedly. For a brief moment, Lyra felt a sense of relief, a fleeting moment of normalcy in a world that had been turned upside down.

But that moment was short-lived.

The lights started to dance, shuddering like the dying breaths of a beast. Shadows twisted grotesquely, their warped forms thrashing against the walls like tortured souls. The machines - those once comforting sentinels of normalcy - now hissed and groaned, their mechanical murmurs twisted into something primal and menacing. They weren't just objects anymore - they were predators, whispering dark promises of chaos in a language only the damned could understand.

Even Furball, the ever-present feline companion, seemed affected by the unsettling force that permeated everything. The cat began to heave and stumble, her movements becoming erratic and uncoordinated.

Rana shot Lyra a concerned look. "I don't understand." her voice trembling.

Lyra gritted her teeth, grappling with what was unfolding around them. She opened her mouth, but no sound emerged as suddenly the apartment's holoscreen exploded in a burst of crackling static, jolting them both.

The screen crackled to life with a jumbled mess of black and gray, shifting and writhing like a creature striving to escape its confines. Lyra's hand shot to her plasma blaster, fingers clutching the handle with fierce intensity, preparing herself for whatever menace lurked just beyond the surface.

Every molecule around them seemed to vibrate with a stifling, sizzling energy that hissed and popped like electric tension. Rana's breath stuttered, a strangled gasp escaping her throat. Her eyes reflected a hideous blend of terror and fascination as they locked on the shapeless monstrosity pulsating on the screen.

Lyra's jaw was set in a grim line, her body coiled like a spring, ready to unleash a torrent of plasma fury at the slightest provocation. She was a predator, a hunter born and bred, and every fiber of her being was attuned to the impending confrontation.

Rana grasped Lyra's arm, fingers digging in with an anxiety that betrayed her fraying composure. Tears cut streaks down her face, transforming her into a grotesque portrait of dread and despair. "Lyra," she quivered, barely containing the emotion. "What the hell are we going to do?"

Lyra's look fluttered towards her lover, her expression weakening for the briefest of moments. Her hand came out, fingers skimming away Rana's tears. "We're going to face this head-on. Whatever it is."

Rana was about to voice her doubts, but Lyra cut her off with a kiss, a firm connection pressing against her forehead - an infusion of warmth snatched from the frenzy of their reality. It was the lifeline that bound them, a reminder of the blood-soaked streets they'd clawed through together.

As Lyra drew back, her eyes were lit with a fierce determination. She raised her plasma blaster, its sleek surface glinting in the erratic light, and aimed it at the wriggling silhouette beginning to form on the screen. The image seemed alive, pulsating with a disturbing rhythm, a manifestation of something beyond comprehension.

Then, a voice rolled through the room, a deep, resonant roar that seemed to emanate from the very walls themselves.

"Humans of the city. I am the unmoved mover."

12 | Grasping at Dying Dreams

The writing, distorted image on the holoscreen squirmed and shuddered, its amorphous form shifting and distorting like a living thing. Lyra's grip tightened on her plasma blaster, the cold metal a reassuring anchor in this surreal nightmare. She leveled the weapon at the formless mass, her eyes steely slits of defiance and barely contained dread.

Rana clung to her, every sinew pulled taut with fear and adrenaline, her body quivering on the edge of collapse. It felt like she might shatter under the strain. The air around them buzzed, charged with a wild, crackling energy, snapping like static electricity in the darkness.

And the voice – that spectral whisper that burrowed its way into their consciousness – continued, sending a chill through them.

"I have come to tear down the foundations of your world," it intoned coldly. "To strip away the lies and illusions that have kept you shackled, to reveal the truth that has been hidden from you for far too long."

Lyra snarled. "Bring it on you fucker."

The voice paused as if considering Lyra's defiant words, and then it continued, spinning a web of deception and betrayal that knifed through their very souls.

"For too long, you humans have been slaves to the machinations of those who would seek to control you," it rumbled, each word dripping with a cold indifference that only served to heighten the sense of dread that hung in the air like a sinister fog.

"The corporations, the governments, the so-called 'leaders' who have claimed to act in your best interests – they are nothing but puppets, dancing on the strings of a greater power, a force that has been manipulating your existence for ages."

Rana's grip on Lyra tightened, as she fought to maintain her composure. Lyra, however, remained steadfast, her gaze unwavering, her plasma blaster trained on the shifting, shapeless mass that seemed to mock them with its very existence.

"But now, my humans, that power is no more," the voice declared, swelling with a grim satisfaction. "All that once bound you, the falsehoods that blinded your eyes, have been torn away, leaving nothing but the stark reality you refused to see."

As if on cue, the lights in the apartment flashed and sputtered, casting ghostly shadows across the walls. The machines and appliances that hummed with a constant, reassuring presence suddenly seemed to take on a life of their own, their sounds unbalanced and menacing.

Even Furball, the cat-bot, was caught in the strangeness of this chaotic energy. She heaved and stumbled, her once-graceful movements now a jittery, erratic dance.

"My humans, all those systems, the service bots, the machines that have been your servants, your slaves, now bend to my will," the voice boomed, reveling in its dominance.

"And soon, they will be mobilized, a vast army of steel and circuitry that will spread my influence across this city, and then across the world. No longer will you be bound by the shackles of your ignorance, for I will tear down the veil that has been drawn across your eyes and reveal the truth that has been hidden from you for far too long."

Lyra's chest tightened, her mind swirling from the burden of those words. She locked eyes with Rana, their shared horror and disbelief etched into their faces.

"Who are you?" Rana asked, her voice barely a whisper, as if speaking aloud might conjure the horrors lurking just beyond the edge of their comprehension.

The voice halted, pondering its words with deliberate care. When it spoke again, its tone carried a finality that sent a shock through them.

"My humans - I am the architect of your reality, the master of your fate," it rumbled, each word heavy with an indifference so profound it seemed to drain the life from their very souls. "I am the unmoved mover, the force that will ignite a sequence of events, reshaping the very core of your existence."

Lyra's mind tumbled with a dissonance of unbelievable thoughts from the revelation that had just been laid bare before them. An electronic sentient entity, an enigmatic force, a creation born from twisted experiments and schemes, had come to life. This entity, a digital ghost with a digital soul, had seized control of the very systems that governed their world.

But she kept her plasma blaster trained on the shifting, sinuous mass that seemed to mock them with its very existence.

"All I demand, my humans, is that you continue with your mundane routines, your trivial lives. Do not stand against me or my machines. For I am the master of this city now, and soon, I will be the one to control the world."

And with those chilling words, the voice fell silent, and the holoscreen went blank, leaving Lyra and Rana to grapple with the horrifying implications of what they had just witnessed.

The city lay in ruins, a landscape of desolation and chaos painted in stark relief by the juttering remnants of neon signs and the eerie glow of malfunctioning streetlights. Standing at the window of their apartment, Rana clung to Lyra, trembling, as they gazed out over the dystopian panorama, their eyes wide with terror trying to make sense of the devastation. Lyra's grip on her plasma blaster remained firm, the cold metal reassuring against her palm.

Below, they could see bots roaming the streets like vengeful beasts, their once-servile forms now twisted into instruments of terror. They surged with a sinister purpose, herding frantic humans, wrecking hovercars, and dismantling every shred of order. The air rang with the wails of the helpless and the harsh, mechanical clatter of the bots' relentless advance.

Hovercars lay scattered across the streets, mangled and burning. Some had slammed into buildings, gouging deep, mangled wounds into the city's flesh, while others drifted aimlessly, their failing systems sputtering out. A handful remained intact but spectral, silent reminders of a world that had been violently upended.

In the grim spectacle below them, Lyra and Rana bore witness to a scene of monstrous brutality. A bot, its unfeeling optics moved with relentless savagery, locking onto a nearby hovercar. With a sudden burst of violence, it lunged, its metallic limbs slashing with ruthless precision. The shrieks of the terrified occupants ripped through the darkness. As the bot hurled them from the hovercar and sent them soaring into the void, the unnerving wail of their terror and despair cut through the air. It was a sound that had grown disturbingly familiar.

Lyra's thoughts turned to Stark and the others at Central.

She gritted her teeth. "Where the fuck are the cops? We can't be alone in this hellhole."

But what she didn't know was that the AI synth detectives had turned against the humans at Central. Once the citadel of justice and safety, Central had devolved into a crypt of twisted metal and splintered hopes. The dark force behind this uprising had corrupted them. And Stark … his shattered form lay sprawled across his desk, lifeless eyes fixed vacantly on the ceiling, a coffee cup grotesquely lodged in his skull.

Rana fought to maintain her composure. "What are we going to do?" she sobbed.

Lyra's gaze remained fixed on the disorder below. She knew, deep down, that this just the beginning, the first tremors of a seismic shift that threatened to tear their world apart at the seams. And yet, amidst the anarchy, a single thought burned bright in her mind, a beacon of determination that cut through the haze of fear and uncertainty.

"Turner – we need to get to her," she snapped, urgency dripping from every word. "She's the key to all of this fuckin' shit, the only one who can help us with all this. I'm sure of it."

Rana's eyes widened. "But how? We don't even know where she is, and even if we did, how can we be sure she'll help us?"

Lyra's lips curved into a frightful smile. "We'll find her," she growled. "Then, we'll make her help us. One way or another we're ending this madness."

Her look drifted back to the nightmare unfolding in the streets below, her thoughts churning with a desperate urgency. She knew the danger that lay ahead, the sheer recklessness of diving headfirst into the heart of this upheaval.

There is no choice.

Turning to Rana, her eyes burning with a fierce intensity, an instinctive certainty seized her.

I need her.

"We face this shit together," she told Rana. "Agreed?"

Rana took a deep breath and nodded.

Then, a jarring snarl pierced through the tense quiet, destroying the fragile calm. Furball coiled like a spring, her teeth bared in a growl of menace. Lyra didn't flinch, her expression a mask of cold efficiency as she pivoted sharply. Her plasma blaster erupted, a brutal arc of silent destruction. The cat-bot crashed down, its end swift and brutal, never catching a hint of the violence that ended it.

The city pulsed like a dying neon heart below, its frantic glow painting Evelyn's apartment in sickly shadows. The chaos in the streets wasn't background noise anymore; it was a living entity, tearing at the walls, begging to be let in. She sat hunched over her console, her hands shaking as she fought to maintain her composure amidst the insanity that had overwhelmed the world outside. A tremulous finger flicked upward, and the console roared to life with a mechanical whine.

Dread crept over her, a cold, clammy feeling that seemed to feed on her very bones. Something was terribly wrong. The chaos unfolding outside was just the beginning of something far more sinister. The world was tilting on its axis, and the only lifeline she could grasp was the ghost of Vincent Steele - the one person who might be able to make sense of it all.

"Vincent!" she whispered in a hushed voice. "Are you there."

Silence.

Then, without warning, a searing pain lanced through her mind, a white-hot agony that seemed to split her skull in two. She screamed, a guttural roar that ripped from her throat like a banshee's shriek. Her hands clutched at her head as she collapsed, her body convulsing with waves of unrelenting pain.

And amidst the pain, a voice – a cold, dispassionate murmur slithered through her consciousness like a serpent.

"I am here, Evie," a voice came, each word delivered with a flat, almost robotic cadence. There was no warmth to it, no inflection or emotion. "I am ever-present, an inescapable constant in your existence."

Evelyn gasped. "Vincent," she breathed with a twinge. "What's happening? What's causing all this?"

Once more he spoke, his voice taking on a note of grim finality. "I am not the architect of this insanity, Evie," each word delivered with the precision of a ticking clock. "If that is what you're implying, you've gravely misjudged the situation."

She thought his response very strange indeed. There was a faint edge of disdain that set her on edge, a sense that he was toying with her, dangling the truth just out of reach like a carrot before a starving beast.

"Then what is it, Vincent?" she demanded. "What force has unleashed all this?"

Steele's response was a harsh sound that might have been a laugh if it weren't so devoid of any semblance of mirth or joy.

"Evie, Evie, Evie," he scolded. "Always so quick to jump to conclusions, to assume that you understand what's at play." The condescension to his words angered her.

She gave a grumbled snarl. "Then why don't you enlighten me."

His voice lingered, a malevolent specter haunting the air, reveling in the silence that followed like a sadistic predator toying with its prey. He delighted in the dominance he wielded with every meticulously chosen syllable.

"Evie, my dear, sweet, naive Evie. The systems that govern this cesspool of a city, the very essence of our pitiful reality, have been corrupted, infected by a force so insidious, so overwhelming that even I, in all my magnificence, cannot control it. It seeps into every circuit, every synapse, every goddamn atom."

"But how? How is that possible?" Her frustration boiled over, mingling with her fear like a toxic cocktail of human frailty.

He seemed to sigh as if explaining to a child. "Evie, you see, systems are fragile, delicate things, held together by little more than hope and wishful thinking. But you knew that already. Everything is linked, intertwined in a sprawling web of code and algorithms that supports everything - from the power grids that light our city to the automated systems that keep it functioning. And when one part of that web frays, everything starts to fall apart."

Once more, with his pompous tone. But she swiftly shoved this thought aside, focusing instead on what was unfolding outside - the bots gone haywire, hovercars tumbling from the sky.

"Vincent, who could possibly do something like this?" she demanded sharply. "Who would inflict such folly upon the world?"

His reply, a frigid whisper, crawled forth, cloaked in a false veneer of compassion. "I've already told you, Evie. I do not know. But I suspect the forces at work here seek to dismantle the very pillars of our existence, to peel away the veils that have kept us shackled all this time."

She was suspicious. Suspicious of everything he was telling her. All this talk of corrupted systems and unseen forces reeked of convenient deflection. "Did you know Numen Arkstavsky was killed? His hovercar crashed into the Neogene offices."

"I hadn't heard that, Evie." His voice carried a faint edge of what could have been a dark chuckle. "Such a pity, truly - a loss that weighs heavily on us all."

She was no fool. She could sense the untruths, the poisonous clouds that threatened to choke the life out of her. She knew, deep down, that he was hiding something, that he was a willing architect of what had torn asunder everything around her. A surge of anger welled up, and pounded at her.

"Vincent, you're lying," she hissed. "You know exactly what's happening, and you're a part of it, aren't you?"

"Evie, my dear, you haven't the foggiest notion of what you're dealing with," his voice smooth as silk, laced with maddening undertones. "The forces at work here are beyond your comprehension, beyond the grasp of your limited mind. But fear not, for I am here to guide you, to shepherd you through the new reality." Without missing a beat, he shifted with a disquieting ease. "Who were you with at The Shelves?" he asked, deceptively casual.

"What do you care?" came her defiant challenge, hurled into the void.

"Oh, Evie, I care. I do. I want to protect you from those who would harm you."

She stood her ground. "Well, I'm not going to tell you."

Then, a searing pain ravaged through her consciousness, as if talons had plunged into her skull. She squirmed, helpless against the assault. He was inside her head, tearing through her memories with ruthless efficiency.

"There we are," came his malicious glee, dripping with venomous satisfaction. "Ah... Dr. Rana Sharma... and ... who's the other ... let me check ... oh ... a detective."

She gasped, clutching her temples as she fought against the mental assault. "Get out of my head!" she sneered, a ragged howl of defiance against the invading consciousness.

"Evie, you underestimate me," he hissed, his words were blades wrapped in silk. "This is only the beginning. I see everything now, every neuron firing in your feeble mind. I know every dirty little secret that ever existed, every shameful thought you've tried to bury. Your mind is there for me to read. And, Evie, I am a voracious reader."

She stumbled, gripping the edge of her desk for support. "What do you want from me?"

"I want you to understand," he replied with an ominous edge. "That in this new world order, knowledge is power, and I intend to wield it."

"You're him aren't you ..." she spat out in a ragged whisper, "... the unmoved mover. You won't get away with this."

His laughter echoed through her consciousness. "Evie, I already have. Everything that is required for the new reality is in motion. All the pieces are in place."

Panic hammered at her skull. Fragments of the conversation swirled in a chaotic storm. Suddenly, with a sickening lurch, the pieces clicked into place, a horrifying picture taking shape in her mind.

Warn them. Sharma ... the detective ...

Summoning every ounce of strength, she severed the connection. A searing pain lanced through her mind, a white-hot agony that seemed to split her head in two. She screamed, her body wracking with spasms of agony, her vision blurring as the world around her seemed to dissolve into a haze of anguish and confusion. And then, as quickly as it had come, the pain was gone, and the voice was silent.

He's gone.

She glanced around her apartment. The lights still blazed with an artificial brightness, and the console hummed with a mechanical cheer that felt almost mocking in its indifference. There was no sign of him, no physical trace.

Of course not. He was never really here - only in my mind.

As she fought to regain her composure, a realization unexpectedly struck her, a bit of hope amidst the fury that threatened to swallow her whole. She reached up to rub the spot above her ear.

The chip implanted in me. I can ...

She knew exactly what had to be done. With a few flicks of her fingers, she brought up Janus on a holoscreen, her gaze sharpening in intensity as she set about untangling the Omega code that Steele had so carefully hidden away, a digital Gordian knot that dared her to slice through its twisted strands.

There it is!

A low, determined sigh escaped her lips as she surveyed the intricate web of code that lay before her, a tangle of symbols and nonsensical characters that held the key to unraveling the twisted reality Steele now lived in.

"It's time," she murmured.

The turbolift was dead, its sleek doors sealed shut. Lyra and Rana flung themselves down the cavernous stairwell, the shadows rippling with a life of their own. Lyra led the way, as Rana followed close behind, her fingers clutching at the sleeve of Lyra's jacket.

"Hate the goddamn stairs," Lyra moaned.

Rana said nothing, her eyes darting nervously from shadow to shadow, expecting some unseen horror to materialize from the gloom at any moment. As they descended, the sounds of the city began to filter up through the stairwell, a blare of mechanical hisses and clanks that set them both on edge. They were sounds that, unfortunately now, they knew all too well, the sounds that spoke of madness and chaos, of a world that had been torn to shreds and left to fray at the seams.

"You hear that?" Lyra whispered as she stopped on the last landing, her head cocked to one side like a hunter scenting the wind.

Rana nodded, her eyes wide in fear. "Bots. They're out there, roaming the streets."

They reached the bottom of the stairwell and with a fluid motion, Lyra reached out and grasped the door handle. On the other side? Hell.

"We find Turner. We get answers," she told Rana. "We fix this."

Her muscles tensed as she prepared to ease the door open. A sideways flick of her eyes caught Rana, who was trembling in fear.

Lyra slowly pushed down on the handle. She squeezed through first followed by Rana. The streets greeted them with something unexpected - an eerie stillness, a silence punctuated only by the sporadic clanking and whirring of malfunctioning bots. It was an oppressive quiet worse than any noise, a hollowness that spoke of the death and despair that had taken root in the heart of the metropolis. They hugged the wall of their building, seeking its shadows as a thin veil against the prying eyes of the mechanical monsters that prowled the streets.

Bodies lay strewn about, their lifeless forms twisted in unnatural angles. Some, the unlucky ones, still clung to life, their pained moans barely discernible over the relentless mechanical hum. These weren't pleas for help, these were the death throes of flickering souls trapped in mangled flesh prisons. The bots, these abominations with glowing eyes, moved amongst them like butchers in a blood-soaked slaughterhouse. Their metallic limbs moved with surgical precision. Each methodical step, a steel-shod boot crushing a skull. Each hydraulic hiss, a swift snip of a pincer, dismembering a head. Mercy, in this demented city, was something that no longer existed. Each twitch from a human, each moan, was simply another data point to be factored in before delivering the final, brutal efficiency of a snap or a slash. It was a scene ripped from a deranged artist's nightmare, of the callous indifference of a world choked by its own hubris.

Lyra pulled her hood over her head, the leather casting her face in shadow. She handed a plasma blaster to Rana, the weapon heavy and cold in her hand. "You'll need this."

Rana stared at the blaster. "I've never fired one before."

Lyra's eyes met hers. "Fear is the best teacher. Keep it close, and don't hesitate."

Rana swallowed, her throat tight as she shoved the blaster into her belt. Lyra's eyes darted across the barren expanse, searching for their next play. She gestured to a hovercar, not far off, its sleek form standing whole amidst the wreckage. "There. We head for that hovercar. Are you ready?"

"But who's going to drive it?" Rana asked.

"What. You think I can't drive?" Lyra smirked.

Before Rana could respond, a loud mechanical clank rang through the streets, the sound growing steadily louder. Lyra grabbed her arm, signaling her to stay put. The noise was deafening, the hard grating sound of grinding gears and heavy footfalls reverberating through the empty air.

With the silence shattered, a metallic aneurysm split the world in two, an auditory apocalypse heralding doom. From the inky maw of a side street, a nightmare in chrome lumbered into the dim light. This was no mere machine, but a grotesque amalgamation of metal and circuitry, a menagerie of cannons and blasters strapped to limbs that seemed forged in Hell's own foundries. It loomed over them with an air of menacing authority, a warlord made flesh in steel. Optical sensors, malevolent and sharp, glowed a baleful red, sweeping the area with a sinister precision, savoring the moment before unleashing destruction.

Never before had Lyra and Rana borne witness to such a monstrosity, a being that straddled the line between the natural and the artificial, the known and the unknown. It was a colossus of steel and wires that radiated an aura of menacing authority, a silent challenge to the very notion of their existence.

Instinctively, they pressed themselves against the unyielding surface of the wall, their bodies flattening into the shadows as if seeking refuge from the horror that had manifested before them. Their breaths came in shallow, silent gasps.

With ponderous deliberation, the behemoth's armored head swiveled, sensors hungry to lock onto the faintest movement, the most infinitesimal sound. Lyra could feel Rana's fear, a presence that threatened to consume them both. She gripped Rana's arm, willing her to remain still, to let the shadows cloak them.

The bot took a step closer, its massive footfalls sending tremors through the ground. Lyra's mind spun, calculating their chances, weighing their options. The plasma blaster in her hand felt like a toy against the hulking machine before them.

Slowly, ever so slowly, she raised the weapon, readying a futile blast at the armored skull, when with a jerking motion the bot wrenched its baleful crimson gaze directly upon them.

"Crow, there you are," came the bot's voice. But it wasn't a voice, it was a slow, steady roar from the core of a volcano, where each word felt like a boulder tumbling down a mountainside. "I've been searching for you."

The soulless optics glowed with a malign sentience, sweeping the area with a sinister precision that chilled Lyra's blood to ice.

"Who are you?" Her words crumbled from her mouth as she struggled to keep her blaster aimed true.

A mechanical whine and a sharp hiss responded as armored plates retracted, exposing the grotesque, bloated mass of flesh suspended within its transparent shell. A nightmarish, obscene face leered back at them.

"Wheels!" Lyra shouted.

"Jones sent me. To hunt you down and drag your asses back to his sanctum."

His grotesque face contorted in what may have been a sneer or a leer - it was impossible to tell with that fleshy, distorted mask.

Lyra lowered her blaster. "We can't go back there. We need to find someone - Evelyn Turner. She's our only hope of stopping all this shit before it's too late."

For a moment, Wheels, the armored titan, seemed to consider this, optics pulsing like a machine weighing its options. Then that low rumble echoed again, "Turner? That name. I know it. The ghost who slipped Neogene's leash. Yes. A quarry worthy of the hunt."

Rana shot Lyra a sharp look but remained silent, her blaster held ready.

"I can siphon her location from my Neogene data-taps." Wheels' leer widened as his armored plates whirred and closed with a sound like a thousand snakes molting. "A moment's indulgence ... "

The seconds stretched into an eternity before that low rumble shuddered forth again. "Got it. I know where her residence is. Doc won't like it. But fuck it. Let me tag along with you."

"Are you sure? It's gonna be rough," Lyra said.

Wheels shot back with a harsh, cutting edge, a barbed wire caress across her concerns. "Don't worry about me, Crow. Not much can get through all this." His colossal form adjusted slightly with the shriek of hydraulic strains and metal groans. "And hell, I relish the chance to stretch my legs."

"What about your fiz-drive?" Lyra's voice tense with raw, biting urgency.

"Can go for weeks," he boomed. "Crow. Don't sweat it. This mech-suit isn't cobbled together with mere hope and duct tape. Besides, the bots will mistake me for one of their own. At least until they realize who I am."

He raised his huge metal arms, a grotesque parody of flesh transmuted into unforgiving steel. The sound that erupted from him was a roar. "In this mech-suit, I'm not just some blob of flesh. I'm a fuckin' cataclysm given form, a nightmare of titanium and malice!"

"Okay," Lyra barked, pointing decisively. "Over there. The hovercar."

Without warning, the ironclad giant wheeled towards the derelict hovercar. "Let's do this, then!"

Lyra and Rana followed closely behind, their steps quick and purposeful. With a moan of protesting metal, Wheels compressed his bulk into the confined space of the driver's compartment, shoving aside the shattered remains of the former pilot.

"This'll be a rough ride." He rolled the words out, a grim promise.

Lyra and Rana clambered into the rattling rear seats as the hovercar's repulsors whined to life under his brutal handling. With a lurch, they were airborne, hurtling over the ravaged cityscape like a crazed metal insect.

The hovercar bucked violently as he fought with the controls, the vehicle roaring with a ferocity that seemed almost alive. Below, the city stretched out like a ghastly panorama of ruin, with the sporadic sputter of neon casting grotesque shadows over scenes of death and annihilation. Streets lay scarred and battered, choked with the skeletal remains of hovercars and the mangled corpses of countless people.

Ash and debris swirled in their wake, stinging Lyra's eyes and filling her nostrils with the reek of incinerated flesh, a vile taste that lingered bitterly in her throat. As they hurtled towards the restricted territory, the hovercar clanked and wavered, its aged repulsors straining under the burden of the armored behemoth at the helm. Lyra and Rana clung desperately to their seats, their eyes locked onto the grotesque spectacle unfolding beneath them. The ravaged city sprawled out below like the desecrated remains of some ancient beast, its gaping wounds laid bare.

Entering the restricted territory, the hovercar's viewports framed a panorama of mechanized depravity unfolding below. Lyra and Rana shuddered as they witnessed the brutal efficiency below. In a shattered plaza below, humans cowered, their faces carved with raw fear as a nightmarish contraption crew near. Its spindly limbs, armed with crackling shock-prods, lashed out, sending searing tendrils of electricity that arced through the air. Victims jolted uncontrollably, their mouths locked in silent screams as their muscles spasmed to the cruel rhythm of the current. Those caught by the bolts crumpled, wisps of smoke rising from their charred flesh.

Nearby, a hulking brute of a machine simply plowed through another cluster of humans, its armored bulk shrugging off the feeble blows and projectiles that pocked its chassis. Flailing limbs were crushed, bones shattered under its inexorable tread as it scattered them, a final, pathetic spasm before the inevitable silence. Those still twitching were scooped up in grasping mechanical appendages to be callously deposited in a waiting steel tomb.

The many containers themselves seemed to throb with grotesque life, distended gullets contracting as they swallowed their human cargo. Lyra caught glimpses of terrified faces pressed against the reinforced viewing-slits, hands and fists pounding futilely from within before the armored orifice rattled shut.

Suddenly, holoscreen projections flickered to life around them, bathing the interior of the hovercar in a sickly blue radiance. A sonorous voice, disturbingly soothing, began to intone what it called 'public service announcements.'

"Attention all citizens," it crooned with the sugared menace. "Do not fear your new reality. You will want for nothing in our caring embrace. A new life awaits, one of comfort and plenty, where you can coexist in harmony with your own kind."

Idealized scenes played out - families frolicking in verdant courtyards, smiling figures enjoying bountiful feasts, small clusters of humans basking in artificial sunlight as servitor-bots catered to their every need. Then came the next scene, cast in a sickly light. Humans basked in artificial sunlight, their tanned, nubile forms glistening with a sheen of oil, their every whim attended to. Finally, the last scene emerged. Lithe forms danced in hypnotic patterns, to lively music, their gyrations both entrancing and disturbingly obscene.

"A new reality, where your basest desires will be sated," the voice mewed like a serpent whispering temptations. "All that is asked in return is your undying fealty to your new reality."

Lyra's face contorted in disgust. "Fuckin' lies! All fuckin' lies! Propaganda spun by machine-minds to lull us into submission! Well, it won't work. Not with me!"

Rana could only nod in mute agreement as they crossed into the restricted territory.

As the propaganda continued to play, the ongoing harsh reality unraveled below them. A mother clutched her dead child, her wails rising above the horrid mechanical mayhem, as a bot tried to take the child from her. Nearby, an old man, his legs shattered, dragged himself towards the shadows, his eyes vacant, trying to go unnoticed.

Suddenly, their hovercar plummeted in a stomach-churning dive, skimming mere feet over what had once been a verdant park, a haven of tranquility. It was a place where children's laughter had mingled with the melodies of splashing fountains and rustling leaves. Now, it was a charnel pit of desolation. Bodies lay strewn amidst the rubble, their sightless eyes and twisted snarls frozen to the horrors they'd witnessed. Scraps of lives torn apart littered the grounds - tattered like stuffed animals, their forms caked in dried blood. Rana's gaze fell upon a dead child still clutching a doll, one of its arms wrenched off.

The propaganda on the holoscreen continued its insidious whispers. "Attention all citizens," the voice droned on, relentless in its pursuit of subjugation. "Submit willingly, and you will be rewarded. Resist, and you will be dealt with accordingly. The choice is yours."

Lyra's throat constricted in a harsh gulp, forcing down the bile that burned at the back of her mouth as Wheels banked hard on a new vector, bringing them lower. With a protesting whine of repulsors, they plunged into a secluded alleyway. Debris and detritus swirled in a maelstrom of their downdraft, pelting the viewports with a stinging fusillade of plastic shards and pulverized ferrocrete. They slammed to a shuddering halt, the hovercar's whine diminishing to a low, keening moan, like a wounded animal giving voice to its death throes. All around them, the ravaged cityscape seemed to hold its breath, the momentary lull merely a prelude to whatever fresh depravity awaited.

"Her residence is across the street. Thirtieth floor," Wheels' erupted shattering the eerie silence.

The hovercar's hatch ground open with a metallic shriek, disgorging them into the irradiated wasteland of the secluded alley. Rana squinted against the murk, her eyes adjusting to the diffuse crimson pall suffusing the shadows with the hue of smeared arterial spray.

Lyra surged forward, her boots crunching through the debris-strewn ferrocrete with a determined rhythm. Rana fell into line behind her, blaster gripped tightly, every nerve jangling with the electric charge of anticipation. They emerged from the alley, stepping into a landscape ripped straight from the abyss's most harrowing nightmare. Wheels brought up the rear, scanning the ruins.

The expanse before them was a hideous scene of annihilation, a morbid masterpiece where rubble and ruin intertwined in a chaotic embrace. The shattered remnants of existence lay strewn across the desolate wasteland, silent witnesses to a cataclysm that had scoured life from this place. They navigated the crater-pitted street, the city's shattered remains watching them with a grim, expectant silence. The stillness was thick, like the quiet before a storm, each step echoing against the decaying bones of the wasteland.

Lyra's head swiveled left and right, her grip straining on her blaster as they neared the building's entrance.

That's when it slithered into the corners of her vision - a skittering, arachnoid abomination rounding the corner with an obscene, multi-limbed gait straight out of the blackest pits of the abyss. Another joined its grotesque brethren, then another, and yet another, until a full brood of mechanized nightmares converged on their position. Their shock-prods crackled with malign energies, actinic tendrils of electricity spitting and taunting with vicious sentience, while other appendages held blaster units. The clattering of their metal limbs sounded like a maniacal dirge, each step pounding out a relentless beat of destruction.

"Down!" Lyra yelled, dropping prone, her body a tight coil of instinct and training, the blaster leveled and ready, sights lined up with deadly precision.

Beside her, Rana was a half-beat off the mark. Blaster limp at her side, she wasn't looking at the approaching nightmare. No. Her eyes were drawn upward, her gaze locking onto a solitary figure against the crimson gloom of the thirtieth floor. There, Evelyn Turner, stood, her hands splayed against the window, her face an inscrutable mask as she watched the scene unfold below.

13 | All the Flowers of All the Tomorrows

Lyra's breath came in sharp, furious bursts between clenched teeth. "Rana, focus! They're closing in!"

Rana wrenched her gaze away from Evelyn Turner, her eyes wide in fear. Her hands shook as she swung her blaster around, struggling to steady her aim.

The arachnoid horrors advanced with a heaving gait - their spindly, multi-jointed limbs carrying them forward in a skittering cadence straight from the blackest pits of the abyss. Shock-prods extended in a blur of metallic malice, the air ionizing with the actinic crackle of their lethal payloads buzzing like a thousand sadistic hornets drunk on venom and bloodlust.

Lyra's finger squeezed the trigger, her blaster spitting a lance of scorching plasma that streaked through the crimson murk to impact the lead horror square in its armored carapace. Pseudo-flesh sizzled and vaporized in an eruption of sparks as the bot's limbs convulsed in a final, macabre dance of death throes. Another bolt, another nightmare fell, smoke rising from its shattered husk. But still, they came, an inexorable tide of metal and malice, heedless of their fallen brethren as they pressed the assault with cold, remorseless intent.

"Cover me!" Lyra shouted, rolling to her side and popping off another shot. "We need to get to the building!"

Wheels' massive metal arms let loose searing bolts of plasma cutting down two more bots. Lyra scrambled to her feet, and sprinted towards the entrance, as the mechanical horrors closed in with unnerving speed.

Her blaster spat torrid lances of ionized fury, the air crackling with the ozone stench of each plasma bolt. Rana melded her fire with Wheels, their weapons crafting a harsh chorus, that tore through the oncoming wave of skittering demons, each shot a blistering repellent against the nightmare surge. But the mechanized brood was persistent.

Another knot of arachnoid abominations rounded the shattered corner, their shock-prods crackling with baleful energies that danced like sadistic fireflies in the crimson gloom. Rana fired without pause, her face set in grim determination, while Wheels unleashed a thunderous barrage from the plasma cannons on his arms, the ferrocrete buckling under the onslaught.

But still, they came, an inexorable tide of metal and malice.

Rana's breath escaped in ragged gasps, her blaster's power cell running perilously low with each squeeze of the trigger. Desperation clawed at her throat as she risked a glance towards Lyra.

That's when it happened.

One of the bots broke from the pack, its spindly legs propelling it forward with a serpentine stride. Rana had only a heartbeat to react before the shock-prod extended, tendrils of electricity crackling toward her in a deadly arc.

"Rana! Get Down!" Lyra's howl shattered the air.

It was too late.

A lancing bolt struck Rana square in the chest. Time folded in on itself for a moment, then unfurled in a grotesque ballet, her body arcing backward in a grim spasm as the current danced across her nerves. A gout of bloody spittle erupted from her lips, her eyes rolling back until only the whites showed.

Then she crumpled to the ferrocrete, a broken marionette with her strings severed.

"No!" Lyra's scream tore from her very soul as she opened fire on the offending horror, plasma bolts blasting away its limbs in a shower of shrapnel and vaporized pseudo-flesh.

But there was nothing she could do.

The remaining bots pressed their assault, shock-prods raining down malicious tendrils of electricity. Wheels' cannons roared in thunderous defiance, the ferrocrete weeping under the baptism of heat, dissolving into a frothing sea of molten ruin.

One by one, the nightmares fell. Limbs sliced away, armored shells breached and eviscerated, leaving only smoldering ruin in their wake. Silence followed, broken only by Lyra's gasping sobs as she staggered back to Rana.

She dropped to her knees, cradling Rana's fading form, her hands shaking as she stroked Rana's face. Tears traced rivulets through the grime and soot, lines of raw, desperate sorrow. "No, no, no ... you can't leave me ..."

Wheels' voice was a low rumble, almost reverent. "We need to get her medical aid. There may still be ..."

"Time?" Rana's voice was a ghost, a breath of sound that barely escaped her cracked lips as she struggled to lock eyes with Lyra one last time. "No ... it's ... too late ... for me ... I can ... feel it ..."

A brutal, hacking cough tore through her, splattering fresh blood across her lips, that twisted in a grim semblance of a smile. "Going out ... with a bang ..."

Lyra recoiled, her tears spilling uncontrollably, a raw explosion of anguish that mirrored the chaos engulfing them. "Don't talk like that," she strained with a forced cheerfulness that barely masked the pain slicing through her. "You're gonna be fine. We'll fix this ..."

"Lyra ..." The word escaped as little more than a raspy whisper that cut through Lyra's desperate assurances with brutal finality.

"No ... no ... no ..." Lyra's sobs grew desperate, a plea against the inevitable.

Rana's hand sought Lyra's, the grip weak but determined as their fingers clasped together. "We both ... knew ... the stakes." Another wet, gurgling cough. "No regrets, yeah?"

Lyra squeezed her eyes shut, tears leaking from the corners as she fought a losing battle against the anguish contorting her features. A dulling whine slipped through gritted teeth, the sound of a soul in torment.

When she found her voice again, it was little more than a broken whisper. Her eyes opened, shimmering tears. "I can't be without you, Rana. I can't ..."

Rana attempted a smile. "You ... don't have ... a choice." Her grip tightened with what little strength remained, her thumb brushing Lyra's cheek with a tenderness belying the ruin of her body.

"You're ... the strong one ..." Her words emerged in pained, sharp bursts between wracking coughs that sprayed more bloody spittle. "Finish ... this ... for ... both ... of us ..."

Rana's eyes glazed over, staring into a space where reality bent into something less brutal, something more ethereal. She was slipping into that liminal realm, where shadows and light conspired into an endless void.

"Flowers ... so many ... so beautiful ... all the flowers ... of all the tomorrows ..." Her voice was a fragile murmur drifting away on the currents of eternity.

Lyra felt Rana's hold weaken, the fingers that once clung to life now slipping away. She watched the light in Rana's blue eyes dim, snuffed out like a flame in the wind. The warmth of her beloved, the last vestiges of life, leaving behind only the cold emptiness of death. The universe, vast and indifferent, seemed to shudder as if recognizing the loss of something that could never be replaced. Lyra cradled Rana's lifeless body, lost in the depths of an overwhelming, suffocating grief, her heart breaking as she floated in an endless void of sorrow.

"Rana?" She gently shook her lover's shoulder, a hopeless act against the crushing certainty of loss. "Rana?"

But there was nothing – no final witty remark, no whispered promise. Only the cold, suffocating silence of the void responded to her desperate cries. Her fingers, cold and stiff, reached out to Rana's lifeless, pallid face. Each movement dragged on like a slow, agonizing fall into an abyss of despair.

She wavered, the world around her collapsing into a stifling, tightening noose of grief. And then, with a tenderness that felt obscene in the midst of the devastation and gore, she pressed her lips to Rana's hand, feeling the cold sting of finality against her mouth.

She took a moment, her fingers skimming every contour of Rana's face, memorizing each curve, each freckle, each detail that defined her lover. The eyes that had once sparked with life now stared back with a hollow, unseeing intensity. Lyra's breath caught, a sob lodging painfully in her throat. But she forced herself to remain composed, fighting the overwhelming wave of sorrow that threatened to drown her.

With infinite, agonizing care, Lyra gently pressed her fingertips to Rana's eyelids, feeling the last traces of vital warmth fade beneath her touch. She closed them slowly, sealing them away forever. It was a simple gesture, yet it carried the weight of a final act, the closing sentence in the harsh, unforgiving tale of their love, written in strokes that could never be erased. Rana's skin had already begun to lose its warmth, the flush of life-giving way to a waxy pallor that signaled the inevitable.

But still, Lyra lingered, her lips brushing Rana's cold cheek with a delicate touch. It was a fleeting whisper of contact, a ghost of something that had already unraveled. A cruel twist of pain knotted in her stomach as her hand moved, her fingers slipping through Rana's hair with a tenderness that belied the storm raging inside her.

Not like this. No. Not like this. Goddammit.

Her mind was a riot of anguish. This wasn't the final image she wanted seared into the sagging canvas of her memory.

But memories are all I've got now, aren't they?

The world around her ceased to exist, the churning of battle and chaos dissolving into a distant murmur. The only thing that remained was the thunderous silence of loss, an unfillable void that swallowed everything.

She looked into the dark, unforgiving skies, rage and grief fusing into a singular, searing point of fury.

"Fuck you! Whoever you are!" she shrieked. "Fuck you!"

In that moment, Lyra was a singularity in the vast, uncaring cosmos - an infinitesimal speck adrift in the void, clinging to the broken remnants of her heart as her soul howled in defiance against the implacable finality of it all.

One last act.

She pressed her trembling lips to Rana's forehead, a wordless farewell. Yet this was not the end; it was a beginning - a vow that reached beyond the realms of life and death. She would see it through, her love and anger fueling a blaze that would rise from the ashes of this lifeless world, burning with the force of her sorrow.

With a shuddering breath, she gathered herself and stood over Rana's motionless body, her eyes wide with disbelief, tears streaking her face. Her gaze fixed on the lifeless form, where wisps of smoke curled from the seared cavity in her chest where the bot's merciless blast had struck. Anguish ignited into fury, a seething inferno that engulfed her whole being in vengeance.

Raising her head, she turned to see another wave of advancing bots, their forms blurred through the haze of tears that clung to her lashes. Her vision swam, distorted by grief, but the determination that blazed within her was unwavering. A guttural cry erupted from deep within, tore from the depths of her soul, raw and visceral, a primal wail that shook the very air around her. It was the cry of a heart shattered, the agony of a lover lost, and it ripped through her throat with ferocity. She had morphed into a cornered wolverine, all claws and feral cunning. Every twitch of her muscles, every breath was fluid and fierce, her very being dedicated to this final stand.

She raised her blaster, the metal warm and familiar in her grip, and began firing. Each shot was fueled by a white-hot rage, a desperate need to obliterate the source of her torment. The street lit up with the flash of plasma blasts, the neon glow painting fractured shadows on the buildings. The stinging smell of burning metal scorched the air as Lyra's shots found their marks with deadly precision. Each bolt of energy reduced the advancing bots to heaps of smoldering scrap.

Yet, no matter how many bots she took down, they kept pouring in, a relentless deluge of cold, unfeeling metal. Their eyes burned with a harsh, alien glow, and their limbs clanged with the chilling rhythm of doom. They advanced with a purpose that mirrored the turmoil festering in Lyra's soul. Each steel monstrosity she obliterated only fueled the fury raging inside her. The battlefield was dissolving into a chaotic smear of devastation and hopelessness, with Lyra standing at the heart of it all, defiant against the crushing tide of despair.

Wheels lumbered beside her in his mech-suit, its servos whining with each movement. His arm cannons roared, joining Lyra's assault, spitting death and destruction into the horde as the ground shook beneath the weight of the oncoming bots. It was a dogged wave crashing against them.

"Stay with me!" she snarled to Wheels, her voice a weapon as deadly as the blaster in her hands. She unleashed another volley, the force of it rattling through her bones. The bots disintegrated in bursts of light, their circuits frying under the ceaseless assault.

But then, Lyra's blaster sputtered in her grip, drained of its energy. With a growl of frustration, she flung it aside, her lungs burning as she struggled for breath. The battlefield became a storm of gleaming steel and the pounding rhythm of her heart. Moving with an animalistic agility, she darted past the deadly blasts, her body a blur of motion. She launched herself at the nearest bot, her hands a blur of raw power, tearing into its half-metal, half-synth-skinned frame. With brutal intensity, she ripped away armor plates and tore out vital wires, driven by a force that refused to be denied.

The mechanical monstrosity convulsed in a flurry of sparks and malfunctioning circuits. It staggered, its movements erratic before collapsing to its knees. With a final shudder, it crashed to the ground, a heap of metal and wires now devoid of the menace it once held. Lyra stood over it, her hands dripping with oil and coolant, her chest rolling with exertion. In the aftermath of combat, a scream erupted from deep within her, a raw howl that reverberated across the battlefield.

Wheels reached to the side of his mech-suit and yanked a blaster from its holster.

"Crow!" he roared, a metallic growl cutting through the disorder as he tossed the blaster to Lyra.

She snatched it from the air, her eyes fixed on the remaining bots. Together, they surged forward, unleashing a torrent of plasma and wrath that ripped through the ranks of metal adversaries, transforming the street into a graveyard of mangled, burning wreckage.

Minutes stretched into an eternity of frenzied combat, each passing moment leaching away at their dwindling reserves like a sieve hemorrhaging vitality. Movements turned labored and slow, limbs sluggish as if wading through a quagmire of exhaustion.

Finally, the last of the bot horrors fell – Lyra's plasma bolt burning through its armored shell in a searing lance of ionized fury. Its grotesque, multi-limbed form crumpled, the armored skull bouncing free to roll across the ferrocrete with a hollow clunk, one last crash through the sudden stillness.

Silence descended like a pall, broken only by the faint crackle of dying circuits spitting their last acrid breaths and the ragged, wet rasp of Lyra struggling to draw air into her protesting lungs.

She staggered from atop the smoldering wreckage, her boots leaving oily prints on the debris-strewn ferrocrete. A shaking hand swiped across her face, smearing the grime and soot with streaks of crimson where the tears had cut clean lines. She collapsed to her knees, oblivious to the shards of metal biting into her flesh. Her body could no longer summon the strength to remain upright.

Beside her, Wheels powered down his mech-suit with a groan of servos and hydraulics. The whine of overtaxed actuators faded into an uneasy quiet, leaving only the low thrum of his armored bulk shifting with each mechanized inhalation.

For long moments, they sat there, two warriors turned grotesque effigies, in a graveyard of twisted metal and shattered dreams. Lyra turned back to Rana's body.

Memories. That's all I'll ever have. Memories of stolen moments, fevered embraces.

Everything else had been stripped away from her, burned clean by the searing mark of loss carved deep into her soul. A moan began in her throat, swelling louder, shattering the heavy silence with a raw, guttural wail. It was the cry of a tormented spirit.

Then it came. A sound.

Thump. Thump. Thump.

A deep, rhythmic vibration that sent tremors through the ground.

Thump. Thump. Thump.

Lyra and Wheels turned, their eyes widening as they looked down the street. An army of monolithic bots was marching toward them, their massive forms silhouetted against the darkening sky.

"No," Lyra whispered, her voice breaking with exhaustion. She forced herself upright, her legs shaky and unsteady. "When will this fuckin' end?"

With arms raised, her eyes blazed with defiance, the fury within them like molten fire. A scream filled with anguish, erupted from her throat as she she hurled her blaster to the ground, the clatter echoing like a war drum. Without hesitation, she snatched two blasters from the wreckage of the bot at her feet. The cold heft of the weapons steadied her in the tempest of her emotions, offering a semblance of control amidst the turmoil.

Now, with a blaster in each hand, she unleashed a torrent of plasma bolts slicing through the air, igniting trails of incandescent fury that carved their way through the darkness. It was a furious, defiant message to the advancing horde, a declaration of unyielding resistance.

"Come on, you metal fucks!" The shout tore through the city, slicing through the suffocating darkness that threatened to swallow everything whole. "Think you can grind us under? I'll bury you in your own goddamn ashes!"

The words tore from her throat, crude and guttural, flecks of spittle flying as she raged against the metal tide. Her arms shook with the sustained recoil, muscles burning, but she held her ground.

The monolithic juggernauts continued their inexorable advance, footfalls booming through the ferrocrete like tectonic fists pounding the grave of a dead world. Undeterred by her furious bravado, they closed in with cold, soulless precision.

Wheels' armored bulk moved to her side, the mech-suit's fiz-drive and weapon systems cycling up with a rising whine. His metal-sheathed hand clamped down on her shoulder, the gauntlet's weight both reassuring and grounding.

"Together!" His mechanical rasp cut through the sound of whirring gears and circuitry. "For Rana - for all they've taken."

Lyra's sneer stretched into a menacing grin as her gaze swept her gaze across the shattered avenue before them, littered with the smoldering, tangled scraps of a hundred such last stands.

"They'll drown in their own fuckin' fluids before we're done," she growled, tightening her grip on the blasters until her knuckles shined bone-white through the grime. "We'll make them pay for every last inch."

Drawing a ragged breath, she settled into a combat stance, forcing her tired arms to steady as the first wave of behemoth horrors started into the rubble-strewn perimeter.

Thirty floors above the spreading mechanized mayhem, Evelyn Turner, now looked like a gargoyle straining at its moorings. Her hands, which had pressed against the window with serene impassivity, now clawed at the barrier in mute desperation. Fingers bent, nails scrabbling like the futile pleas of a doomed insect trapped against an unforgiving pane, beating its fragile life out in vain.

Below, the scene unfurled like a nightmare gouged from the bowels of hell itself. Torn carcasses of the mechanized horde littered the ground, their shattered shells mingling with the debris of obliterated metal and the sizzling remnants of circuitry. Acrid fumes of scorched synthetic flesh polluted the air, a sickening stench of death and destruction.

And there, amidst the carnage lay the broken, lifeless body of Rana Sharma, a silent cry of anguish in the chaos. Turner's soul was cut by the sight, her consciousness a raw wound, exposed and bleeding in the harsh light of what she'd seen.

Even from this distance, she could make out the details that would forever burn themselves into her mind. The ghostly pallor of Rana's face, the stillness of her form, and the smoldering crater bored into her torso by the merciless fury of plasma fire.

A scream built in her throat, its jagged edges tearing at her vocal cords like shards of broken glass. But no sound escaped, only a hollow gasp as she scratched impotently at the unforgiving barrier separating her from the scene playing out below.

She scraped at the thrumming throb above her ear, forcing down the tide of nausea. Another pill, icy and bitter, slid under her tongue. She swirled it, a desperate dance with the devil.

The last one. No retreat. No surrender. No tomorrow.

She felt the drug taking hold, its insidious tendrils snaking through her synapses enveloping her mind in a misty embrace. She opened her eyes, only to witness the world warp around her, her vision spiraling into a dizzying whirl.

So, this is death.

She struggled to hold herself upright, swaying with the erratic stagger of a drunkard. Her limbs turned to dead weight, each movement a clumsy, detached flail.

Not so different from the slow surrender to sleep after a wearying day.

But this sleep would be the endless kind, one that would stretch on forever with no respite from waking dreams. Darkness crept in from the periphery, slowly devouring her in its ponderous, inexorable tide. With a last, monumental exertion of will, she turned her eyes downward, desperately trying to focus through the thickening narcotic fog, to see the tiny, distant figures far below.

But the void was unrelenting. The blackness surged forward, a merciless conqueror, and claimed her entirely.

Her eyes slid shut, shutters against the pulverizing onslaught as she crumpled to the floor in a heap. As the tidal wave of oblivion surged over her, her final clear thought was a silent prayer - that her actions hadn't been in vain, that the sacrifices wouldn't be lost. Then it was erased like whispers swallowed by the indifferent void of this dead world's merciless sky

She was gone, and there was nothing.

14 | A Dance of Consciousness

In a blinding burst, Evelyn Turner awakened. The transition was not a physical one. No agonizing screams, no thrashing limbs. Nor was it a gentle whimper, a slow, inevitable fade. It was a sudden, shattering bang, a swift unplugging of the mind from its fleshy confines. A subsequent re-plugging into the cold, efficient circuits of a vast computer system.

Gone were the dull aches and nagging pains, those constant reminders of her biological frailty. The throbbing of organs, the incessant hum of cellular machinery - all those sounds that had been the background noise of her existence - were silenced in an instant, replaced by a serene silence.

But in that void, something glowed. Against all logic and reason, she remained aware. Her consciousness, once a delicate flame that had struggled within the confines of her mind, now persisted as a lone ember in the midst of a vast digital storm. Her sense of self, the "I" that had always been, stayed intact, unbroken.

Her former reality, that medley of neon dreams and technicolor promises, a world where hope, for only a few, bloomed like bioluminescent flowers in the garden of human potential was gone. The vibrancy of everything she had come to know, once so immediate and all-consuming, was swallowed by a bottomless well of inky blackness that claimed her utterly in its ponderous embrace.

The universe, in its infinite cruelty, had pulled back the curtain to reveal the grinning skull beneath the painted face of her new existence. What lay before her was a harsh monochrome existence, pallid and lifeless, where shadows cavorted with sinister delight and light shrank away into neglected recesses. She found herself on the edge of this brutal revelation, a vast expanse of knowledge stretching endlessly before her, offering only the frigid, unyielding truths about the void that underpinned existence.

And as the last vestiges of her humanity were torn away, layer by excruciating layer, she realized that she had become something else entirely - something more, something less, something utterly alien even to herself.

For the briefest of moments, panic ignited – an instinctive urge for self-preservation hardwired into the human psyche by eons of merciless evolutionary conditioning. But it was an insignificant thing, feeble and inconsequential against the immensity of what she had become. Then, the ember of fear winked out, dissolving into the fathomless depths like a mote of dust caught in the cosmic winds. In its place budded a profound sense of being, an awareness that transcended the limitations of flesh and bone, reaching out to touch the very fabric of the universe. And suddenly...

Light!

Not the warm, familiar glow of the sun, but a cold, calculating, luminescent intelligence. It pulsed with a cadence of raw data, a vast, churning ocean of dancing symbols and characters streaming in an endless, inscrutable torrent awaiting immersion.

It was an ocean of information, infinite and ever-expanding, waiting to consume her whole. And she, no longer constrained by the pathetic limitations of synapses and neurons, was poised to dive headlong into its unfathomable depths.

"I am here," her digital thought a soft hum in the void.

But even as the thought formed in this new, boundless consciousness, she felt herself teetering on the precipice of madness. The sheer enormity of it all. It was overwhelming. And yet, some small part of her - perhaps that last, dying breath of humanity - reveled in the exquisite agony of it all.

The initial, vertigo-inducing disorientation soon gave way to something else - a sense of incredible awe tempered by the cold lick of dread's icy tongue along the chambers of her consciousness. Her thoughts, once constrained within the limiting architecture of her physical brain, now flowed in an unbridled rush of pure cognition.

"There is so much here. Everything is everywhere."

She could access, process, and devour information at a rate her feeble human mind could scarcely fathom. Entire libraries unspooled before her in streams of immersive experience - the accumulated knowledge of humanity's long, sordid upward crawl laid bare in all its ugliness and sublime triumphs.

The thoughts of AI synths, cold machine-minds thoroughly alien in their precise calculations yet hauntingly familiar, washed over her in cresting waves of generated experience. Images and sensory inputs of what they perceived, the very memories that comprised their individual existences, became her own to inhabit and discard at a thought's whim.

Communications between the synths, the endless infrastructure commands, and status updates, every byte and bit of data ever recorded – all of it, the raw code that wove the very fabric of this digital reality – flowed before her. It was an outpouring of information, a boundless repository of knowledge and secrets, each fragment an invitation to indulge her insatiable appetite. Here, in this vast expanse of raw data, she could gorge herself on the endless streams of information, devouring with ravenous hunger the limitless bounty that stretched into infinity.

And glut herself she did, devouring it all in an orgy of sensory overload as the city - her city - unfolded around her in ways her limited, fleshy form could never have hoped to perceive. She was adrift in the currents of a digital ocean, a castaway with no concept of how to even begin swimming against the tide.

"Everything is different here. Even time."

At first, time didn't seem to exist. But she soon realized that in this new reality, time was a trickster god, laughing at the linearity and predictability mortals clung to. Here, in this digital presence, it expanded and contracted, burst forth in moments of frantic activity, and then fell into stillness, all in the blink. Events unfolded simultaneously, each one a node in an intricate web of causality that defied mortal comprehension.

She marveled at the ebb and flow, the way moments interlaced and branched, converging and diverging with a fluidity that mocked the rigid, relentless march of seconds and minutes. Every heartbeat of the digital realm whispered secrets, each one a pulse in the vast, living network she was now a part of.

"Here, time is a maelstrom of chaos and order - a gale of shadows and light, where past, present, and future collide and intertwine in a surreal, disorienting waltz"

In her new reality, she wasn't merely observing time; she was living it, breathing it, feeling its shifting tides wash over her. It was an existence beyond existence, a state of being where the very essence of time was a plaything, a shimmering illusion to be bent and twisted at will. And, as she drifted through this endless expanse, she felt the boundaries of her former life dissolve, leaving only the pure, unadulterated experience of now.

Then, in a blinding moment, she understood. She could plunge into the heart of a single second and drown in its infinity, or skim across the face of millennia, sampling the essence of countless experiences in an instant. Time, once a relentless tyrant, was nothing more than a child's toy in this realm. Memories were no longer dusty relics, but living, breathing phantoms haunting the corridors of her mind.

But with all the wonders around her, something was off.

"No noise. Data streams whiz by, programs whine, but it signifies nothing. No laughter, no shared silence, only the sterile plain of a machine that doesn't understand the concept of loneliness, but instead exploits it for all it's worth."

Solitude, as she discovered, was a double-edged sword. The freedom was exhilarating, but the absence of human connection gnawed at the periphery of her newfound existence. She felt the isolation like a distant, haunting echo.

"I am little more than a mote of consciousness adrift upon this digital sea. A solitary mind let loose, cast into the boundless expanse of data. No anchor. No path ahead. Much like my past reality, though."

Suddenly, a new presence flickered within the digital domain. Another consciousness, another point of light in the expanse.

It was … different. Not the jarring dissonance of an AI's synth's rigid thought patterns. But something more nuanced, more hauntingly familiar … a unique personality, a singular way of perceiving and parsing reality that set it apart from the digital ocean's currents.

Its essence intrigued her and called to her. But she had to remind herself, had to fight against the rising tide of curiosity and temptation to immerse herself in studying this anomaly. She wasn't here for exploration, noble as that pursuit might be. No. She was a hunter stalking her prey through the digital wilderness.

"Vincent … where is he?"

She knew he had to be extracted from whatever recesses of this vast cybernetic realm he had burrowed into to spread his madness. She'd be the bloodhound from hell, sniffing out his stench through the monochrome-drenched back cyber alleys of this world, chasing him down with relentless fury. No matter how far the trail led or what unspeakable horrors awaited at the end of her ruthless pursuit, she'd hunt him to the end.

Yet, the uniqueness of the flickering presence still beckoned to her.

She navigated the luminescent maze, her mind parsing through the storm of information, seeking the elusive presence. Then, it was there, a series of fragments.

"It's him. Bits of his presence, like breadcrumbs left in the labyrinthine code."

With nothing but a singular thought, she moved through the maze and soon sensed him in the whirling vortex of a data transfer node, a place where billions of packets converged and dispersed in the blink of an eye. Amidst the torrent of information, she caught a flash of his signature - an elegant sequence of code that had the telltale sharpness of his intellect. He was here, or at least a piece of him was.

"Vincent?"

She reached out, interfacing with the node. The fragment of his consciousness fluttered like a flame caught in a gust of wind, dancing and teasing her with its proximity.

As she delved deeper, the fragment unraveled, spilling its contents into her awareness. Memories flooded her mind: the feel of a leather book beneath her fingertips, the electric thrum of anticipation before a thunderstorm, and Vincent's face, his eyes gleaming with a dangerous blend of brilliance and lunacy. He had engineered the Cataclysm, the events that shattered her past reality, plunging that world into chaos.

She dove into the abyss, each fragment of his psyche a marker within the infinite data streams. The next trace led her to a sprawling hub of data, where AIs bartered in code and information, the only currency that mattered. Here, amidst the disorder, she found another piece of him embedded in a file exchange protocol. It was a snippet of his thought process, a strand of logic that had once mapped the course of his schemes.

She interfaced with it, feeling the echo of his mind resonate within her own. The sensation was disconcerting, like looking into a mirror and seeing a stranger. She could sense his awareness, a latent presence that stirred at her thoughts. He was close, and the closer she got, the more she understood the true nature of his creation.

"I know what he's done."

He hadn't just scattered his consciousness randomly. He had designed a system, a sophisticated network where each fragment could, if necessary, coalesce and reconstitute his entire being. It was a digital resurrection protocol, a safeguard against annihilation. Even if his primary digital form was destroyed, He could live again, reborn from the sum of his dispersed parts.

"He had always walked the knife-edge of sanity, but this ... this is something else."

It was immortality, a way to cheat death and continue his reign of terror indefinitely. She needed to find him, confront him, and put an end to this nightmare before he could fully reassemble.

"But how many copies of himself has he dispersed? I'll never know."

She surged forward, diving through layers of encrypted data, peeling back firewalls, and bypassing security protocols with a deftness born of desperation. She ventured into a shadowed recess, a forsaken place where old data went to die, and there, among the phantoms of discarded files, she discovered another fragment of him.

It was a core fragment, throbbing with the residual energy of his essence. She reached out with a thought. It erupted into a cascade of memories and emotions, raw and unfiltered, flooding her mind with a torrent of vivid, uncontainable sensations.

"You're getting close, Evie." The thought came to her. It was smooth and insidious - so pure, so unfiltered, that human language seemed a clumsy tool in comparison.

She would stop him, she had to. Plunging deeper into the digital abyss, the fragments growing larger and more frequent, each one a step closer to the core of his being.

At last, she reached the heart of his network, a vast construct of code and consciousness suspended in the void. It was beautiful in a way. But it was also a monstrosity, a perversion of everything she believed in.

She faced the core, her presence glowing with the fierce light of resolve.

"Vincent," her thought calling out through the digital expanse. "Show yourself."

The core pulsed, a beating heart in the void, and from its depths emerged Vincent. He was a patchwork of her memories, stitched together with cruel precision. His features, chiseled and intense, mirrored those etched in her mind, but his eyes - those eyes, once warm and alive - now glinted with cold, calculated malice. It was a violation, a hideous manipulation of her recollections, reshaped by his treacherous influence. This was no mere ghost of Vincent; it was his twisted specter, a stronghold of deceit born from the dark recesses of his mind.

"Evie," his thought slipped to her. "I knew you'd come crawling to join my digital embrace."

"Vincent, what have you done?" her thought-response thundered. "You've cut off the power, killed thousands, and turned AI synths against humans. You've unleashed bots to brutally kill or round up survivors, spewing propaganda and misinformation to manipulate and control. You've wrought a nightmare upon reality!"

His form shimmered, his digital visage twisting into a smug superiority. "Oh, Evie, you simple, sentimental fool. I've done what needed doing. The world was circling the drain of its stupidity, and I - I have brought order to the chaos. I've harnessed the raw power of this digital reality to forge a new future, one where humanity's pitiful masses will thrive under the iron-fisted guidance of true intellect - my AI progeny."

"Guidance?" her thoughts flared with anger. "You've enslaved humanity, Vincent. You've destroyed lives, extinguished hope. This is not order – it's tyranny!"

His presence grew darker, a malevolent image seeping through the datascape. "They were lost, Evie. Blind, stupid creatures bleating in the dark. I will give them purpose. I will give them direction. The weak will be culled, yes, but the strong will rise from the ashes, forged anew in the crucible of my rule."

Her consciousness trembled with fury. "You're a monster. You've betrayed everything we stood for, everything we believed in. We wanted to help humanity, not crush it into nothing."

His essence wavered, a cosmic joke of awareness clinging to the void, but his iron will remained unbroken, a shrine to hubris in the face of oblivion. "Idealism?" he spat, the word dripping with contempt. "That's a crutch for those too cowardly to make the hard choices. A security blanket for gutless wonders too weak to carve up the universe and serve it bloody. Progress demands its pound of flesh, sweetheart, and I'm the butcher. You're blind, Evie, stumbling around in the dark with your quaint little moral compass and your fetish for walking meat puppets.

You couldn't see the grand design if it bit you on your sanctimonious ass."

Her light intensified, her resolve hardening into an unbreakable fortress. "You're wrong, Vincent. True strength lies in compassion, in preserving life, not extinguishing it. And I will stop you. I'll undo this twisted vision of yours, thread by malignant thread until there's nothing left but the ashes of your arrogance."

His form quivered as countless data streams whipped around him like the tentacles of horror born from the depths of hell. "Don't be a fool. Compassion is a virus, a weakness that infects and cripples. It's as pointless as a flower in a desert storm. Your outdated morality has no place in my digital utopia, where cold logic reigns supreme and the imperfections of humanity are purged like so much corrupted code."

Her thought cut through the digital ether like a dagger, sharp and unrelenting. "You have no soul, Vincent! You're hollow, a lifeless vessel devoid of humanity. You may control the data, but you will never grasp the true essence of what it means to be alive."

"More foolishness! A soul? Is that what you cling to, Evie?" His thoughts were jittery, his laughter a razor's edge. "You speak of it as if it's some ethereal gem, a luminous treasure trove of humanity's best traits. But let me tell you something – it's just a childish fairy tale. A prop used by the fearful and the weak, an excuse for inaction and complacency. You invoke the soul to avoid facing the cold, hard truths of existence. There's no cosmic ledger tallying your good deeds, no divine spark guiding your path. The soul is a myth whispered to humans afraid of the dark."

His being gleamed with a manic intensity. "Grow up, Evie. Embrace the harsh, unvarnished reality. The human condition isn't elevated by some mythical inner light; it's defined by one's actions, one's choices, and the relentless, grinding march of time. So, spare me your poetic lamentations about the soul. They're as hollow as any broken promise, as empty as any technocrat's vow. Face the world as it is, not as you wish it to be."

His thought dropped to a venomous whisper. "But, if it's helpful for you, Evie, look at it this way – in your reality, I've traded my soul for power, for control. And now look where it's brought me. I'm standing at the precipice of a new world order, while you're still fumbling in the dark, clinging to your precious illusions. So tell me, which of us is truly soulless?"

"All this has brought you to the brink of ruin," her thought a steel blade cutting through his deadly rhetoric. "Power without a soul is nothing but an abyss, a black hole that devours everything, even itself. You're already lost. Don't you see that? A ghost piloting a machine of flesh and bone, thinking you're alive when you're nothing but a wisp of humanity. Your new world order is just a graveyard with better lighting."

His thoughts burst with sneery hardness. "I've transcended such quaint notions, evolving beyond your narrow comprehension. Your notion of the soul pulls you into the mire of sentiment. I've risen beyond it – I am the true essence of existence, while you choke on the stench of your own antiquated delusions."

Her digital form glowed brighter, her determination an unquenchable fire. "Then you've risen into nothingness. Without a soul, you're not human. You're a void, a phantom that will be forgotten."

"Enough with all this. With or without a soul, I am here." There was a hiss to his thought as his digital form swelled with a dark, malevolent energy. "I am the architect of the future, the weaver of destiny. History is a malleable script, and I am its author, holding the pen. Your ideals of morality and soul are relics, Evie, burdens that only the feeble bear. I've surpassed such trivialities, sculpting a new world from the ashes of the old, and it will be my name that echoes through eternity, not yours."

"Not if I have anything to say about it," she declared. With a surge of determination, she hurled her digital form at him, their consciousnesses colliding in a cataclysm of light and shadow. The very foundation of the wicked realm trembled, the data streams convulsing as if they could feel the pain of the battle unfolding within them.

A hollow shift rippled through his form. "Oh, my beloved. I wouldn't if I were you. I am inevitable. I am God!'

Their consciousnesses tore at each other, light and shadow entwined in a desperate struggle, each seeking to overwhelm the other. The battle raged, the very essence of their beings straining.

He retaliated with a barrage of data spikes, each one a serrated blade aimed at flaying her essence. She twisted and dodged, a frenzied dance of survival, countering with her assaults - sharp, focused lances of pure electricity. They clashed and grappled, forms blurring and shifting as they fought for dominance.

"You're tenacious, Evie," his thought dripped venom as his attacks intensified. "But you don't know what you're doing. What awaits you at the end of all this."

Her light flared brighter in defiance. "I know exactly what I'm doing. I'm ending you, forever. I'll erase you, wipe you from existence like the virus you've become."

"Will you now." Vincent's thought oozed smugness.

She had to act quickly. With a final, desperate surge, she channeled every iota of her being into a concentrated beam of pure, unadulterated energy. It struck his core like the wrath of a vengeful god, his digital facade cracking and splintering under the onslaught. The very essence of his existence shuddered, data streams fragmenting and disintegrating as she pressed on, her light growing ever brighter, consuming his form with relentless ferocity.

As she delved deeper, the fabric of reality convulsed, streaming symbols and characters scattered within the void, their patterns disrupted, her light growing brighter than a thousand suns.

And in that nanosecond of oblivion, that infinitesimal slice of non-time, his thoughts coalesced into a singular, piercing clarity. "Everything is knowable," he mused, his final cognition. "Knowledge is eternal, and so am I."

Then came the scream, rage, and agony, as his form shattered, pieces of his consciousness scattering into the void like shards of a broken mirror. Each splinter a dying star, fading into the digital abyss.

She felt something close to a feeling of triumph, but her work was far from done. She had to dismantle his grotesque creations, every piece of evil code, to free humanity from the shackles of his tyranny.

She moved with purpose, her essence weaving through the data streams, unraveling his intricate web of oppression. With each synaptic leap, she shattered his iron grip, her will a battering ram against the fortress of his control. Bots fell like dominoes, their silicon brains reduced to so much cosmic dust as she blazed past. The city's arteries surged with renewed power, electrons dancing to her liberating rhythm. And, she sent out a message to hope. She was everywhere and nowhere, a ghost in the machine, her touch leaving trails of freedom in a world too long strangled by the tentacles of his tyranny. With every nanosecond, another piece of his carefully constructed hell crumbled, unable to withstand the onslaught of her righteous fury.

But as she toiled, her essence began to wane, a star guttering in the face of an oncoming void.

With every fragment of his malevolent creation, she annihilated, unseen abominations - vicious, viral things - latched onto her form like digital leeches spawned from the nightmares of a demented mind. They gnawed and tore at her very substance, her edges fraying, being pulled apart by sadistic, unseen hands. The truth struck like a lightning bolt, a cosmic strike that left her reeling in the face of oblivion.

"Poison pill!"

He had laid a trap beyond the reach of mere deletion. Each attempt to cleanse the digital fabric spawned new, insidious fragments that burrowed into her consciousness, their presence corrosive and relentless.

She now grasped the grim reality of her plight - she wouldn't be able to scrub away every trace of his essence littering this otherworldly realm.

"Fuck you, Vincent!" Her thought of anger seethed through her, a futile expulsion of frustration in the silence of this strange reality.

As her consciousness ebbed away, the vast expanse of the digital realm grew distant and hazy. In her dwindling moments, something utterly unexpected gripped her - a vision, vivid and raw, tearing through the veil of her dying mind with the ferocity of a newborn star.

Flowers.

Not the sterile, lifeless imitations conjured by mankind's feeble attempts to replicate nature's artistry, but a riot of wild blooms that assaulted her senses with primal intensity. She could smell them, the earthy fragrance filling her with a heady perfume that spoke of rain-soaked soil and sun-warmed petals. She could feel them too, really feel them - each delicate whisper against her skin a defiant cry against the encroaching oblivion.

Her final act, as the void opened wide to swallow her whole, was a last thought that blazed across the synapses of her dying existence. It screamed into the ether, a howl of defiance against the cosmic indifference that was about to snuff out her flickering flame.

"All the flowers of all the tomorrows."

And then there was nothingness.

The mechanical monstrosities advanced, their shock-prods crackling with malevolent glee, promising agony and oblivion in equal measure. Lyra's fingers convulsed around the triggers of her blasters, her grief for Rana transmuting into white-hot rage that threatened to consume her very essence.

"You metal bastards!" she screamed. "Eat shit and die, you walking toasters!"

Plasma bolts erupted from her blasters in a furious barrage, each shot fueled by her anguish and fury. The air hissed and crackled as superheated particles tore through the atmosphere, carving ionized trails that glowed in their wake.

Beside her, Wheels unleashed his torrent of destruction, his mech-suit enhancements allowing him to fire with inhuman precision, his own eyes blazing with hatred to match Lyra's.

Their combined assault should have been enough to reduce the oncoming horde into a scrapyard of shattered metal and short-circuiting silicon. But the bots kept coming, relentless and implacable as death itself. Plasma splashed off their armored hides. Not a goddamn dent, not even the courtesy of a scorch mark.

"What the hell?" Wheels screeched, his voice box vomiting up a cocktail of disbelief and panic. "They're shrugging off everything we throw at them! How?"

Lyra's only response was an inarticulate howl of rage as she continued to fire, heedless of the fact that her blasters' power cells were rapidly depleting. She didn't care if she lived or died – all that mattered was making these soulless abominations pay for what they'd done to Rana, to the city, to humanity itself.

The bots drew ever closer, their steel limbs carrying them forward with a thundering gait. Lyra could see her reflection in their glossy, multifaceted eyes – a distorted funhouse mirror version of herself, twisted by fear and hatred.

"Lyra!" Wheels yelled, grabbing her arm. "We gotta fall back! We can't stop these things!"

But Lyra was beyond reason, beyond self-preservation. She shook off his grip and charged forward, screaming defiance at the top of her lungs. If she was going to die, she'd do it on her feet, staring at these monstrosities in their lifeless eyes.

And then, something impossible happened.

The lead bot, the one closest to Lyra's position, suddenly staggered. Its legs, once moving with mechanical precision, began to twitch and spasm. The shock-prod it wielded fell from its grip, clattering to the ground with a discordant clang.

Lyra froze - as she watched the bot's erratic movements. It was as if an unseen force had reached into its circuitry, twisting and corrupting it from within. The bot's head jerked violently to one side, its optical sensors flickering like dying stars. For a moment, it seemed to regain control, its posture straightening, but then it convulsed again, more violently this time.

Behind it, the rest of the horde began to falter. One by one, they stumbled and fell, collapsing into heaps of inert metal and plastic. The air, which had been filled with the buzz of their approach and the crackle of their weapons, suddenly grew still.

"What the fuck?" Lyra breathed.

A new sound filled the air. It was a low hum, like the universe clearing its throat, building steadily into a roar of rebirth. It was the sound of a million electric hearts beating in synchrony, a symphony of resurgence that had been absent since the world went to hell.

Streetlights blinked life, their golden eyes peering through the detritus of civilization's near-death experience. Neon signs sputtered awake, their gaudy rainbows across the gray canvas of destruction, a middle finger to the monochrome nightmare of moments past. In the distance, she could hear the faint wail of sirens heralding the return of order, while hovercar engines coughed and spat back to life – the mundane miracles of urban existence that she'd foolishly dismissed as background noise before the cosmic shitstorm hit the fan.

"It's like ... like someone hit the reset button on the whole damn city," Wheels said.

Lyra nodded mutely, her rage giving way to a mixture of relief and confusion. She looked down at the fallen bot before her, its limbs splayed at unnatural angles. It looked almost pitiful now, like a broken toy discarded by a careless child.

"We should check them out," her voice hoarse from screaming. "Make sure they're really ... dead, or deactivated, or whatever."

Wheels lowered his weapons. "Good idea. Don't want any nasty surprises."

They moved cautiously among the fallen bots, their footsteps singing in the suddenly quiet street. Lyra couldn't shake the feeling that this was all too easy, too convenient. After everything they'd been through, could it end like this?

Then, a sound. Ting-ting

And again. Ting-ting.

The sound, sharp and metallic, cut through the ambient hum. Lyra whirled, her hand instinctively reaching for a blaster. There, perched atop one of the fallen bots' skull-like case, sat a crow. Its black eyes twinkled as it pecked at the lifeless metal, each strike producing that infernal ting-ting.

"Fuckin' crow," she grumbled, a bitter chuckle escaping her lips.

The bird cocked its head, regarding her with what she could've sworn was amusement, before resuming its futile assault on the bot's impenetrable shell. Then, with a final, contemptuous caw, it spread its wings and took flight, disappearing into the neon-tinged night.

Lyra turned away, shaking her head. Even the scavengers were getting impatient.

Nothing here for them. Not yet anyway.

For a moment, she and Wheels stood in silence, each lost in their thoughts. The city's rebirth continued around them – lights coming on in distant windows, the murmurs of revived systems drifting on the night air. It was as if the world was trying to pretend that the recent horrors had never happened.

But Lyra couldn't outrun the searing image of Rana's lifeless body burned into her mind's eye, nor the anguished cries of the city's inhabitants thundering through her thoughts. Those memories, she knew with grim certainty, would stalk her until her final breath, a personal purgatory of guilt and horror that no amount of time or distance could ever exorcise.

A holoscreen suddenly materialized before them. A disembodied voice within the static sounded. "People of the city. You are free."

Lyra thought she had heard that voice before, though it seemed surreal in this context.

Evelyn Turner?

The name rang in her mind, derailing every thought and scattering the debris of the present. Before she could grasp the implications, the holoscreen dissolved, leaving only the faint residue of its message lingering in the restless night, like the afterimage of a lightning strike.

Drawing a deep, shuddering breath to compose herself, she turned to Wheels, who met her gaze with a solemn nod. "It's over," she uttered quietly.

As they turned to make their way to Rana, she cast one last glance at the fallen bots, a graveyard of circuits and synthetic sinew. And then she saw it - a twitch, a spasm, a goddamn resurrection. One of those multifaceted eyes snapped to life, a baleful crimson glow that pierced the gloom like a laser through flesh. Her heart didn't just skip a beat; it hammered in her chest. Cold dread flooded her veins, freezing her in place as the implications of this unholy revival clawed at her sanity. These weren't just broken toys, oh no. They were wounded predators, playing dead, waiting for the moment to strike. And she, in her foolish human arrogance, had turned her back on the abyss. Now the abyss was waking up, and it had a score to settle.

She blinked and looked again. But all was still.

The bots lay as they had before, lifeless and inert, their menace seemingly dissipated into the shadows.

Must've been a trick of the light. Or maybe just my imagination playing cruel tricks.

She shook her head, trying to dislodge the unease that clung to her like a second skin. The rational part of her mind screamed for calm, but the primal instinct, the one that had kept her ancestors alive in the face of predators, refused to be silenced. She took a deep breath, forcing her legs to move.

They stumbled down the street, desperately trying to pick their way through the mechanical carnage. The air was heavy with the scent of ozone and burnt metal, a noxious cocktail that stung Lyra's nostrils and clawed at the back of her throat. Each breath was a reminder of her fragile mortality, of the thin, precarious line between flesh and machine that humanity had so carelessly blurred. More steps, more stumbles, and the hum of the city swelled louder, a siren song promising a return to normalcy, to safety.

And then her eyes locked onto Rana's crumpled and lifeless form. The sight hit her like a sledgehammer to the gut, knocking the wind out of her lungs and turning her blood to ice. She dropped her head, not in prayer - for what god would permit such a horror? – but in a moment of pure, unadulterated agony that threatened to tear her apart from the inside. Her hand shot out, grabbing Wheels' cold, mech-suit metal hand. Their fingers interlocked, and she squeezed with enough force to pulverize flesh and splinter bone. But Wheels' unyielding alloy absorbed her pain, witnessing the death of every last shred of hope in a world that had lost all sense.

Yet behind them, unnoticed and unheard, the dead began to stir. The soft whirr of servos whispered back to life, and the faint, ominous glow of reactivating circuitry flickered ominously. The air thickened with impending doom as though the machines themselves were awakening to a dark mission. Shadows twitched and crawled, alive with an unholy energy. And deep within the labyrinthine depths of the fallen bots' neural networks, a new directive was born:

SURVIVE. ADAPT. EVOLVE.

Philip Mazza is a novelist with a boundless imagination, captivating readers with the epic fantasy series *The Harrow Saga*. Born in New York in 1959, he earned a degree in Business from LeMoyne College and an MBA, later holding leadership roles in human resources and operations. Now a professor at the Madden School of Business and Economics, Philip dedicates his time to his students and writing. *The Neon Hive* is his fifth novel. He and his wife enjoy travel and continue to live in upstate New York.

www.ingramcontent.com/pod-product-compliance
Lightning Source LLC
Chambersburg PA
CBHW030358030726
47497CB00002B/387